WATER ANGELS

Mons Kallentoft

Translated from the Swedish by Neil Smith

HODDER

First published in Great Britain in 2015 by Hodder & Stoughton
An Hachette UK company

First published in paperback in 2015

Originally published in Swedish in 2012 as *Vattenänglar* by Bokförlaget Forum

1

A CIP catalogue record for this title is available from the British Library

Paperback ISBN 978 1 444 77634 8
eBook ISBN 978 1 444 77636 2

Typeset in Plantin by Palimpsest Book Production Ltd, Falkirk, Stirlingshire

Printed and bound by Clays Ltd, St Ives plc

Hodder & Stoughton policy is to use papers that are natural, renewable and
recyclable products and made from wood grown in sustainable forests. The
logging and manufacturing processes are expected to conform to the
environmental regulations of the country of origin.

Hodder & Stoughton Ltd
Carmelite House
50 Victoria Embankment
London
EC4Y 0DZ

www.hodder.co.uk

Prologue

September 2012

The sky is black behind even blacker clouds.

Isolated formations try soundlessly to get closer to one another, fail, and instead release heavy rain. Large drops that fragment into evasive mist as they reach the ground.

Under the leaden vault the city lies frozen. The inhabitants bestow light on the reluctant sky, lights go on and off in windows, their rhythm forming signals in Morse code: We're still alive, we're not giving up, no matter what sorrows afflict us.

The landscape around the city is at rest.

A slight wind moves over the stubble of the harvested fields of rape. The solitary oaks on the plain creak quietly, dropping their weary leaves to the ground.

The surface of Lake Roxen implacably mirrors the sky, its waves lapping warily on the deserted beaches of Sandvik. On the far side of the lake ten different streams trickle down, and in the dark, still water the last midge eggs of the year are hatching, the thirsty creatures ready to fly out across the Östgöta plain.

The fields are still at night. Satisfied with the rain that has recently fallen on the district; the ground clings heavily to the roots of the last sprouting seeds.

Cows low towards the clouds.

Sheep seek shelter under the crowns of the oaks.

Foxes sniff through the forests.

Wild boar root through the dying undergrowth.

The clouds let themselves be driven on the wind, in across the city, and the rain falls on the villas of Hjulsbro and the smart houses lining the banks of the Stångå River.

Drops land on one of the houses, where every scream in the world comes together at this moment and transforms into a single, mute moan.

Someone has raised a pistol.

Their hand isn't trembling.

The sound of the muffled shots can't be heard out on Stentorpsvägen.

The naked bodies in the jacuzzi are destroyed by the bullets, beyond all salvation.

A girl screams into the night.

The dead are almost the only people who hear her.

But they can't help her.

Blood pours from the bullet holes, and the water in the churning bubble-pool turns red.

No more breathing.

Just an agitated rumbling mixed with the sound of rustling fabric, and blood pumping through the veins of those still alive, a cold hand over a girl's mouth, there, quiet now, quiet now.

The room is almost completely dark, and the white tiles on the walls are patterned by the shadows of the shrubs in the garden outside the window. Black mosaic is just visible in the swimming pool.

The man's and woman's bodies are close to each other, but the woman's lifeless hand has slid off the man's shoulder and is floating in the red, hissing water.

The girl is crying.

Vanishes into the night.

She doesn't resist, just tries to remember to breathe, she's five years old and goes along with this unknown force.

Mummy, Daddy. How long are you going to lie there?

The garden stretches down to the Stångå River, the water calm here away from the roar of the power station. The river floats away from the bullet-riddled bodies.

The rain has stopped.

The girl's tears form a different stretch of water, a broad river far away, further away than any cloud can drift.

Steam rises from the unknown river, embracing a woman's face, tormented by loss.

The woman is a capsule of words:

I sit here by the river, by the steep bank where the grass won't grow. The fishermen hate this place, there are said to be spirits here, left over from the war, spirits waiting for their loved ones to come and fetch them.

If the spirits are unsettled, I can console them, and forget my own anxiety and loss.

There are fish here.

But to this day they can be born with two heads, and four hearts beating irregularly outside their silver scales.

I remember warm skin against mine, soft as the most expensive silk at the market, but warmer, warmer against my skin and deep inside me.

That memory is loss now, and that is why I don't allow myself to remember you.

I don't allow myself to hope.

What can I do?

I can come here to the river and wait for the spirits, the faces in the clouds.

I can't see your face in the clouds.

Instead I look down into the tepid water of the river,

seeing the tiny currents from the great jaws that suck the riverbed clean.

I see eels squirming, shimmering.

Their movements are yours inside me, yours in my tepid water, and I don't want to remember, but the memory of your movements before you were born is something I can't force out of my soul.

It is there as a curse.

But also as a gift.

I am you.

Nothing can change that.

No desire for money. No other love. No earthly power. No spirits' wailing or malice.

Where are you? You're somewhere. I know that.

You can buy a pig with the money, he said with a laugh. A pig can take care of you, instead of the other way around.

They laughed when he said that.

I bowed.

And walked away.

A tap is dripping in one of the darkest rooms in the world.

An anteroom to hell on earth. Unless the room itself is hell.

Children don't cry here.

They whimper, but haven't yet started to doubt that they are human.

A child for a pig.

A child for a pig.

The rain is lashing on a tin roof, the world so damp that the children's lungs fill with water with each breath, so damp that it's possible to drown without even sinking below the surface.

But the children breathe anyway.

Dream about playing, about human monsters, about the

love they never received, unaware of the torment that awaits them, unaware that there is still hope for their souls.

The girl is still far away, but she's on her way to them.

Where am I?

The girl wonders in her lonely sleep.

I don't want to wake up, don't want to wake up.

The black clouds are on the point of breaking up; don't want to see another day.

They drift gratefully towards destruction.

Free of human dilemmas.

PART I

Lonely Love

I

Malin Fors is lying curled up in bed in her flat on Ågatan. Sleep has a firm grip on her and the rain hammering on the windowsill is unable to penetrate her dreams, and she is whispering:

'Tove, Tove, Tove.'

The only thing more dear to me than my own life is yours.

Never leave me, because then who would save me from the nightmare?

Malin Fors twists between the sheets.

'I want to wake up,' she whispers.

But she can't wake up. Instead she sees the Stångå River weaving through Linköping at night, running into Lake Roxen, and all the drowned words of the mute lake turn to mist, rising above the surrounding countryside.

There's a face in the mist.

The face of a young child.

'Who are you?'

Malin shouts into her dream.

Her body is covered by lukewarm water that rocks her soul from a wave that will never end.

A voice emerges from the darkness of the dream.

'You will never be able to bear a child.'

The child, Malin.

I want to wake up now.

I want to be delivered from this water-sodden dream.

I want to be reborn as someone without desires or dreams, someone who is free, made up of nothing but the cheeriest of principles and circumstances.

The dream laughs at her scornfully.

She laughs back, and beyond her laughter she hears the child, the little girl, crying.

Is that you, Tove?

'It isn't me, Mum.'

So it must be some other child.

She wants to stay in the dream now, but it lets go of her and she feels the clammy, cold sheet under her skin, feels the rough, warm body beside her, the shimmering moisture concealed in microscopic droplets between the hairs on Peter's back, and she's awake now, and her first thought is: This bed is too small, we need to buy a bigger bed.

She thinks of how they made love before falling asleep. Sex-machines, the pair of them. Mechanical, his every movement seeming to say 'it better work this time', his growing desperation over the past six months, but there had been something different about his movements yesterday evening, as if he'd given up, as if enough were enough.

The conversation they had a few months ago, in this very bed.

'I need to be a father, Malin. It's time.'

'We'll have to try again.'

'You should see another doctor.'

'What for?'

'The shot that hit your womb may have done some damage.'

Peter had never before referred to the fact that she had

been shot the previous spring while working on a particularly harrowing case. It had been an unmentioned bucket of cold water waiting to extinguish their hopes.

'The doctor said it was OK.'

'What do doctors know?'

'You should know, you're a doctor.'

Peter had backed down when she said that, falling silent and looking away, as if he were somehow trying to convince himself that a love-child was actually possible for the pair of them, even though they were both almost forty years old, and in spite of the gunshot wound, and her doubts, and the way she has abused her own body.

In spite of everything.

Malin moves closer to Peter, pressing his sweaty body against hers, and the whole bed is a shifting, warm sea that she never wants to leave, and she wants to give him that child, daren't go and see any damn doctor, because what if they say it isn't possible?

Say it straight out.

Or has it already been said?

Would you leave me then, Peter?

Better not to know.

And hope.

Because that is what I'm hoping, isn't it?

You must never leave me, Peter, and she feels that a life with him is possible in all manner of ways, with or without children, now that Tove has moved out and will probably never move back home again.

Do we have to have children?

Isn't it enough with just the two of us?

Responsibility for our own love.

Getting up each morning, going to work, preparing meals together, eating, washing up, spooning in bed, shopping, going on holiday, brushing our teeth, complaining that one of us doesn't put the lid back on the toothpaste and the other scatters dirty washing all over the floor.

Malin gets up and leaves him alone in bed, dragging her sleepy, naked body out of the bedroom and over to the living-room window. The light of dawn is slowly rising above the black tower of St Lars Church.

The world feels confined and damp this morning, and an odd chill brushes her skin, running over her breasts. She opens the window and the cold autumn morning is like a familiar breath, and she inhales, feels the young day fill her.

Her fingers touch the small, round, livid red scars on her stomach, where the gunshot hit her.

Thinks: Whatever happens, everything will be OK.

She feels a sardonic smile spread over her lips, and she hates this new smile. She doesn't want to be the sort of person who thinks they've seen and heard everything, experienced all aspects of human nature, and have given up and started lying to themselves.

Because even if the cynics are right, it's impossible to live like that.

Without real love, without feeling anything.

Without faith, if you like, Malin thinks. Without dreams. And she snorts derisively to herself.

She was offered the chance to take over from Conny Nygren as head of crime up in Stockholm after he was murdered back in the spring, but she turned it down, even though she's always wanted to move back there.

Peter was the one who didn't want to move, even though he could easily have found a job at the Karolinska Hospital, or at Danderyd.

So he must want a life with me here, she thinks. Whether or not we have children. Perhaps our love is enough for him after all?

A couple of fragmented clouds drift towards each other above the roof of the church before moving on. Those clouds could be at home anywhere, Malin thinks, and she finds herself thinking of Karin Johannison, and wonders what Karin is doing now, what she and her little Vietnamese miracle are doing right now.

She has trouble sleeping at night, doesn't she? Tess?

As if it's impossible for her to adapt her Vietnamese rhythm of time entirely to ours, as if this strange child's blood has a pulse all of its own.

Karin Johannison, forensics expert and medical officer, and one of Malin's colleagues, is holding her daughter, Yin Sao Dao, close to her and whispering: 'There, there, Tess, time to sleep now,' and she looks around the living room of her flat on Drottninggatan, which has become more and more bohemian in style over the past year as she's made a conscious effort to fill it with things from Tess's homeland, just so the girl will be able to see them and perhaps remember something good, if she has anything good to remember.

She must have.

Even if Karin has her doubts about good memories some nights.

She has held the screaming three-year-old tightly and tried to soothe her, aware that her love isn't enough, as if something had happened to the girl from which her body is unable to shake free.

When she screams, Karin almost begins to doubt that Tess is really there with her at all.

To doubt that it actually worked out in the end.

That it really had been possible, in spite of everything.

In the window hang two red lanterns, bought from a market in Hội An ten years ago. Long before I knew that was where you were going to come from, Karin thinks.

A propaganda poster from the war, with a stylised tank in red and blue.

Incense holders. A carved catfish made of greying larch-wood.

A wavy-patterned, shimmering blue silk throw over the Josef Frank armchair.

Tess is sitting calmly in Karin's lap now, staring out into the dim dawn light of the room with her big brown eyes.

It's a quarter to six, and they could still get another hour's sleep. Karin is keenly aware of this, and desperately wants to sleep, she's felt exhausted for the past month or so, as if lack of sleep were finally getting the better of her.

The soft, warm body.

The little girl in her arms.

She holds her tightly, trying to convey the calm rhythm of her own heartbeat to the child.

Barely a year ago she was sitting on the plane to Ho Chi Minh city, or Saigon as she still thinks of it, because it sounds more romantic, full of fear and determination and anticipation, and of love for a round girlish face in a black-and-white photograph she had been sent by email.

Yin Sao Dao.

Orphaned.

Her father killed when an unexploded shell went off in a paddy field. Her mother drowned when she was caught in a flood.

War and climate change.

And I get to be your mother.

That was how it happened.

I get to be your mother, I thought.

They had brought you to Saigon from Hội An.

To a damp, rundown children's home on the western outskirts of the city.

You weren't sure at first. Stumbled away from me across the filthy concrete floor, but where could you go?

Towards the stench of urine. The rubbish in the yard. The barred windows.

So you accepted my embrace, clambering up into my lap from the cold concrete.

I'm not going anywhere, I whispered in your ear.

I learned how to say the words in Vietnamese.

Whispering them over and over again.

In the shabby room in the Hotel Majestic, with the Saigon River floating past on the other side of the boulevard. In reception when we checked out, when a strangely cold woman who looked European stood next to us and acted as if she knew you, trying to get your attention but only succeeding in upsetting you.

I whispered the words on the plane.

I'm whispering them now.

'Mummy's here, Mummy's here.'

Breathing. Warmth. Calm.

No sleep.

But calm.

The screaming has stopped.

The nightmares are gone, aren't they? And now you just want to get out of the darkness of sleep, because there's still something inside you, and in your sleep you can feel it.

You don't want to play, just sit in my lap in the living room, sit still, and if I try to put you back to bed, you start screaming again.

'No, no, no.'

Karin Johannison rocks Tess, stroking her thick black hair, feeling her pulse inside her ribcage, through her white pyjamas.

Sings: 'Now Tess is going to sleep, sleep so soundly, because Tess is really tired, really, really tired.'

Vietnam.

The admirable, unyielding nature of its people, their captivating lack of pretension.

The poverty, despair and corruption she encountered there.

The steam from the noodle pans, the smell of spitting palm oil and fried garlic, of mint being pounded in hundred-year-old mortars, the flashing lights and noise of thousands of motorbikes.

The abuse.

She found out later that Vietnamese children had been sold to foreign paedophile rings. Not long ago in Australia, six Vietnamese children had been found in a cellar in Melbourne, four more in a cellar in Darlinghurst, Sydney.

Slaves.

A tiny piece of news, then not news at all.

A five-year-old girl, a three-year-old boy.

Sex slaves.

My love, our love, all love saved you from that, Tess.

That was how it was. That is how it is.

You need to sleep now.

You're tired.

Mummy's tired.

Let's fall sound asleep.

It's twenty past seven in the morning and Malin is standing in the hall of her flat, unable to tear herself away from the radio. The P1 channel is broadcasting an interview with a child psychologist from the Elephant Clinic in Linköping, and he's saying how angry it makes him that so few people can bear to see the victims, children subjected to sexual abuse, children he encounters in his work.

And he talks about a video recording they have, of a child he has met, a five-year-old boy being raped by a man, over and over again.

During the assault the boy looks into the camera and says: 'What am I? Am I a human being? Am I?'

The doctor expresses his surprise that such a young boy could formulate that sort of thought, as if he were asking the most fundamental existential question.

And then the programme ends, but the boy's words linger inside her as she walks down the stairs to the door of the building.

'Am I a human being?'

You are a human being.

She thrusts her thoughts about the boy aside, forcing them into invisibility.

Peter has hurried off to the hospital. He's on call tonight, so she'll be sleeping alone when she gets back home.

He still has his flat on Linnégatan, unwilling to let go of such a good apartment, but he lives at Ågatan, and they've talked about getting somewhere together, but they never seem to get around to it, and in the past month the subject seems to have faded from view.

The sky is threatening rain. After a brief hesitation, Malin puts on the black Barbour jacket that Peter gave her for her birthday.

The coat is too tight and doesn't really fit her very well at all, and the stiff oilcloth feels like a straitjacket around her body.

She opens the front door.

Wondering: What does today have in store for me?

Something has happened, or is about to happen. She can feel it.

A few hundred metres away, Karin Johannison is walking towards the nursery in the Horticultural Society Park, sticking close to the buildings along Klostergatan.

As she wheels the pushchair containing her daughter towards the park, she thinks:

What's happening today?

Please, nothing big.

I'm far too tired for that.

How can what you long for most make you so exhausted?

We aren't asleep.

So where are we? What's happened?

I don't know.

We aren't supposed to be here, there's something wrong. Someone has to help us.

Is that us lying down there? Is that us?

It looks like you, darling.

It is me. I daren't, I don't want to get any closer.

The water's red.

I'm naked.

That's me next to you. I'm naked as well.

Do you see our bodies? Those dark marks?

I see them. Don't want to see them. Don't want to, don't . . .

Where's Ella? She isn't here with us, and she's not down there. Where is she, Christ, where is she? Where are you?

Come out!

Where should we look? I can't see her.

She should be here with us.

Come out. Come to us. You mustn't just disappear.

What if we're the ones who've gone?

They call for her over and over again, and her name is swallowed up by the whiteness that is simultaneously warm and cold, a whiteness that is their world.

2

This morning couldn't be any more September and grey, Malin thinks. Dentist's weather, in the words of the city's greatest son, the songwriter Lars Winnerbäck.

Just as she stepped out of the door a gentle but persistent rain began to fall, and the people she passed on the pavement were huddled under big umbrellas or hiding under the hoods of their raincoats.

By the Horticultural Society Park she thought she could see Karin Johannison in the distance, and her first thought was to jog and catch up with her, so they could walk together once Karin had dropped Tess off at preschool. But she changed her mind, feeling that she'd rather be alone.

So now she's walking along Djurgårdsgatan, towards the police station.

Thinking about Karin with admiration.

She left her wealthy husband because she no longer loved him. She adopted a child on her own when she couldn't find a suitable man, apart from the one who wouldn't leave his wife for her.

Over the past few years, Malin's view of Karin has changed from thinking of her as a spoiled, upper-middle-class bitch to a strong woman worthy of her respect.

Almost friends, Malin thinks, wishing that she were capable of the determination Karin had demonstrated in every area of her life.

We are friends, aren't we?

An orange-red bus drives past, spraying water over the pavement, and Malin takes a quick step to the side to avoid being soaked.

She puts one foot in front of the other. Steps in a puddle, but the soles of her sturdy shoes are thick enough.

She feels like closing her eyes when she walks past Barnhemsgatan, where her mum and dad used to live. The park benches beneath the oak tree on the little slope leading up to the Infection Park are crooked and could do with being varnished, and Malin can still smell the ingrained damp of the flat, where she was expected to water the houseplants, to keep them alive, but she had failed.

Everything in that flat was nothing but memories from which she'd rather run away.

It's been more than two years since she last saw her father.

Dad's face on that occasion.

Shifty, and the look in his eyes let on that he mostly felt sorry for himself. She still hasn't forgotten his betrayal, and the fact that he failed to tell her that she had a brother.

Stefan.

Alone in his care home.

Malin looks down at the pavement.

Five months since she last visited him up in Hälsingland.

He had only been awake for an hour or so, and had shown no sign that he recognised her or was even happy that she was there. She's tried and tried, but her brother lives in his own world, a world into which he is neither willing nor capable of admitting her.

I'm your half-sister. Look at me. I exist.

A body in a wheelchair, vacant eyes staring out of a window, green trees in the distance.

There were probably plenty of people who would have

liked to adopt Karin's Tess. But you, Stefan, no one wanted you.

Am I on the point of abandoning you as well? The way everyone else abandoned you?

I want to go up to the care home in the little village of Sjöplogen.

Your inert body.

The look in your eyes, seemingly devoid of content.

I don't want to go.

Malin knows that Tove sometimes goes at weekends. She catches the bus from Lundsberg and sits with Stefan, takes him out into the grounds as if he were old and infirm.

'It seems to make him happy.'

The way you dress these days, Tove. Tod's loafers that cost a third of what you earned from your summer job, tight jeans, tennis shirts with little polo players on the chest, and you talk differently, even if you're not aware of it yourself, your vowels have become longer, more nasal.

Your boyfriend Tom's rich industrialist family from Östermalm are just as unbearable and stuck-up as I imagined. Who cares about a fucking flooring factory? What difference does a great pile of money in the bank make?

Malin takes the scenic route today.

She walks past what used to be the old artillery regiment's canteen, now a Christian study centre, and the mature linden trees loom over the yellow wooden buildings, as if they wanted to protect the goodwill concealed within those walls, in those rooms where people earnestly exclaim hallelujah and swear eternal loyalty to their god.

There's no such thing.

Janne.

Her ex-husband. They are able to talk to each other without rancour now, and he seems pleased that she's managing to stay sober.

If only he knew how incredibly bloody thirsty I feel sometimes.

So thirsty I shake.

So thirsty I'd almost rather die than never drink again.

He's still shacked up with his bimbo.

She's definitely a bimbo.

Well, OK, I can't deny that she's seemed pleasant on the occasions when I've had to talk to her.

Malin glimpses the yellow and brown panelling of the University Hospital, and thinks of Peter. Or rather, his face. His sharp features, the dimple in his chin, and the wrinkles in his forehead that seem deeper now than when they first met.

The worried look in his eyes.

That's new.

Malin doesn't want to think about that look.

Instead she feels the rain on the cloth of her ridiculously expensive coat, thinks that money can protect you from the wet, can protect you from almost anything.

But can it buy anything you want?

Can you buy love?

And there it is again. That horrible, cynical smile.

*Who's that woman walking down there, with that weird smile
on her lips?*

What does she want with us? Why are we looking at her?

Do you see that aeroplane?

I see it.

*How can we be here? So high up, there can't be any oxygen
here, and it's ten thousand degrees below freezing.*

Do you see the vapour trail?

I see you touch it. You can touch the clouds as well.

Don't question it. It's enough that we are here.

They call out to her, shouting their daughter's various
names, and then the plane disappears in the icy blue sky,
four white trails dissolving into the air in its wake.

And then they're back with that woman again, the one
walking quickly.

They see her disappear through some automatic doors.

Can you help us find her? they say at the same time. Then
they whisper simultaneously: *Can you bring us back together
again?*

Can you make our family whole?

You have to help us.

3

Prostate cancer.

The doctors had been able to help Sven Sjöman.

They saved his life, because a small part of the tumour was malignant.

He came back. He felt the cold wind of death, but he came back.

Everything works the way it should after the operation, and his sex-drive, should he ever need it, can be fixed with Viagra, just like his doctor said.

Sven Sjöman has tried, shut away in the toilet at home, surrounded by brown tiles, in the vibrating light of the ceiling lamp he and Ulla bought when they got married.

It's been a long time since he or Ulla were interested in that sort of physical exertion. What can you expect after forty or so years of marriage?

Sven looks out over the open-plan office in the police station. It's almost eight o'clock, and the whole of Linköping Police's violent crime unit has arrived for work, with the exception of Malin Fors.

He had been considering retirement, had actually got as far as handing in an application to leave at the age of sixty-three, but when he found out that the cancer had been cured he withdrew his request. Much to Malin's relief. He had wanted her to succeed him, but the thought alone seemed to be enough to make her feel sick. Yet he is still convinced that she's the right person for the job.

His operation had been a success.

Some space-age instrument had done the job with the precision of a thousandth of a millimetre. But peeing had been a right nuisance afterwards.

Wanting to pee without being able to, not feeling as if he needed to, then suddenly wetting himself.

But all that's sorted out now.

So what about Malin? Is she sorted out?

The morning meeting starts in five minutes, and the others are mentally preparing themselves, he can see that from where he's standing next to the coffee machine in the staffroom. The looks in their eyes, their body language, everything exudes concentration.

Zeke Martinsson. The tough guy with the hard exterior, Malin's partner in crime for years now. A man capable of keeping his cool in any situation, just by rubbing his hand over his shaved head, its shape perfectly matching his narrow, death's head face.

He's calm in his personal life too.

Possibly too calm.

Sven knows that Zeke's marriage is only held together these days by his grandchildren and the very idea of family, unlike his own, which is actually based upon reciprocated love.

At least he likes to believe that it is.

Börje Svärd is bent over a newspaper he's spread out on top of a filing cabinet. He seems to have got over his wife Anna's death from MS, and is evidently regarded as something of a catch in Linköping's slightly older singles' market. The rumour in the station is that he's started Internet dating. Maybe his amiable appearance and imposing moustache are the reason for his alleged success with the opposite sex?

Waldemar Ekenberg is sitting at his desk. Sucking an

electronic cigarette and drumming his fingers nervously. He seems to be taking a prolonged break from the violence he has so often resorted to, and he looks as haggard as usual; the furrows in his fifty-year-old face are deep, his brown trousers and beige jacket are crumpled and doubtless come from some budget shop, the complete opposite of Police Chief Karim Akbar's neurotically precise wardrobe, where a single tie could cost four thousand kronor.

Where does Karim get the money?

Sven knows he got a decent advance for his new book on immigration issues, due to be published next spring by a venerable old publishing house.

And things seem to be going well for Karim with prosecutor Vivianne Södergran.

Johan Jakobsson.

As usual, he's sitting there glued to his computer. There's nothing that man can't find out with his gadgets. Now that his children are a bit older he appears able to work all hours, and seems to love it.

But he's not boss material, even if Malin tried to say he was when they discussed the possibility of her taking over.

'Johan's better suited,' she said.

But now I'm going to be here for another two years, at least, Sven thinks, taking a sip of coffee and stepping out into the office.

A new detective is going to be joining the team tomorrow. A hotshot called Elin Sand, who's made a name for herself in Malmö and made it to detective in just a few years. The story goes that she played volleyball at national level but got injured and had to give up, then applied to police academy and graduated as top of her class.

How is a girl like that going to get on with Malin?

Two headstrong female cats scratching each other's eyes out. Or two stars that shine brighter together? Time will tell, and Sven can't help hoping that nothing big comes in today. That the period of calm they have experienced recently will last a few more days, to give Elin a chance to get to know the others in the team without any stress or pressure.

Sven takes another mouthful of coffee.

Walks towards the middle of the room.

Takes a deep breath.

Lowers his voice and shouts out: 'OK, it's time!'

All his detectives stop what they have been doing, look in his direction, and make ready to obey him.

I've still got my old authority, Sven thinks. Then feels surprised at his own thoughts. It's been years since he let himself be bothered by anything as trivial as authority.

As Zeke stands up to go to the meeting room he sees Malin come in through the glass door that divides the reception area from the open-plan office.

Her black raincoat is wet with raindrops.

Her short blonde bob is lying flat against her head, and her high cheekbones look more prominent than ever thanks to all the hours she's spent down in the police-station gym and running up and down the banks of the Stångå.

She's obsessive about exercise, Zeke thinks. He knows what she's trying to suppress by exercising, and he's surprised that she's succeeded, he's seen her grit her teeth in the face of her longing to drink as they pass the open pubs together after an evening shift at work.

She seems happy with Peter. And Zeke suspects that they're trying for a child, and he is more than aware of Malin's ambivalence about that, an ambivalence that she probably hasn't even admitted to herself.

But she looks alert.

Almost bouncing as she walks, seeming to speed up as

she approaches, ready to grapple with the third day of the working week, after an uneventful Monday and a Tuesday filled with paperwork.

Zeke looks at his colleague.

He knows he wishes her nothing but good, but somehow he can't help feeling that there's some sort of curse lingering over Malin Fors. He hates himself for thinking that, or rather feeling it, but he can't help it. The finest detective with the Linköping Police has a rare capacity to fuck up in her personal life, or to allow it to get fucked up for her.

Just like me, Zeke thinks.

Gunilla, his wife.

Karin, something else.

Was choosing not to move out the biggest mistake of my life?

I should have left Gunilla, I should have gone to Karin when she wanted me.

She can't possibly want that any more.

What's the price of emotional cowardice?

Loneliness. Bitterness.

'Good morning.'

'Miserable fucking morning,' Malin replies with a grin as she pulls off the coat that suits her so badly.

Her voice sounds as hoarse as always.

The morning meeting.

Another in a long line of pointless gatherings.

Malin looks around at the others.

Börje, Johan, Waldemar, Zeke. They're all just as bored as she is, even if they're trying to show Sven a bit of enthusiasm, and the only consolation is that this meeting will go quickly seeing as nothing has happened.

Karim is running through the month's budget.

They've only just hit their target, and every one of their applications to update their technology has been rejected.

Johan shakes his head at the news but says nothing, aware that dissatisfaction and protest serve no purpose in this room where everyone is on the same side.

Which side?

On the side of good, in the battle against evil.

Black and white.

And all the endless shades of grey in between.

Sven is saying something about the new detective, Elin Sand, who is going to be joining them tomorrow, but Malin can't be bothered to listen, although she knows she should.

Or at least ought to want to listen.

Only Waldemar seems genuinely interested.

Maybe he's imagining a potential new victim for his tacky gender-based bullying, everything he subjected Malin to when he first joined the group a few years ago.

He stopped that pretty quickly.

Now Malin can smile at the memory, as Sven writes something pointless on the whiteboard, and the lighting is far too bright, making her colleagues' skin look like death, and she gazes out of the window at the preschool opposite. Outside, a dozen children dressed in colourful rainwear are playing as if it wasn't pouring with rain.

The sound of the children's games is inaudible inside the meeting room.

She watches the children rushing about, and thinks that one of the older boys seems to be pretending to be a giant jellyfish, hunting swimmers across a tranquil sea.

One child picks up an orange bucket from the sandpit.

What's Sven talking about?

I don't want you!

Is that what he's saying?

No, that voice is only inside my head.

Take him away.

That's what Mum must have said about Stefan.

I'll swap him for a dog.

Or a nice carpet.

A Rörstrand coffee service.

And Malin clutches the seat of her chair, squeezing until her fingers turn white, thinking how she'd like to force out the voices inside her head before they get too much for her, drink them away now that sex with Peter is no longer capable of fending anything off, and only leaves her feeling sad and thirsty, thirsty, thirsty.

But we're good together, aren't we?

When it's just you and me.

Even the sound of the rain doesn't reach in here.

The only thing that can be heard is Sven's droning voice, and Malin pretends that she can see the raindrops aiming for the roof of the police station, that the sound of the playful drops makes her eardrums vibrate, and she knows that the calm in the city has to give way soon, because something is moving in her dreams now, something that is about to show its true face.

4

OK, carpenter Martin Svensson thinks as he sees his reflection in the green glass of the front door of the house at number 31 Stentorpsvägen.

I drink too much beer.

I get too little sleep, I work too much, but it makes sense to work as much as I can before the Social Democrats get back into power and get rid of tax breaks for home improvements and my mobile stops ringing.

Deep furrows in his brow, even though he's only forty-one.

Not a bad house, this, he thinks as the rain patters on the little roof jutting out above the front door. White brick, built in the early 1970s, one of the best plots in the district.

Hjulsbro.

The domain of doctors and middle management. The real cream of the city live along the river in Tannerfors, or in Ramshäll. But Hjulsbro will do very nicely.

If he were a bit braver he'd have people working under him, to increase the turnover of the business, and not do so much off the books.

Then he could afford to live in a house like this.

No problem.

There's no answer.

Is something wrong?

The man of the house, Patrick, said he'd be here to let

me in. But maybe he wasn't sure about that, seeing as he gave me a set of keys.

Ring the doorbell again.

A minute's silence.

Almost.

Martin Svensson listens hard. Hears birdsong, and somewhere behind the high-pitched chirruping of the birds and the sound of the rain, he can hear the rumbling noise of the power station's turbines along the river.

Here, some five hundred metres away, the turbines sound like a subdued alarm that has turned into a complaining drone.

What's going on?

Why isn't there any answer?

His reflection in the green glass suddenly becomes clouded as a chill runs through his body, and although he doesn't quite want to admit it he can't shake the indefinable feeling that there's something wrong.

As if death were here.

Here to get him.

Pull yourself together.

Martin Svensson hoists his workman's trousers up by the waist, then feels in the left pocket of his raincoat and fishes out the key to the Andergren family home.

His toolbox is on the stone steps next to him.

A few little jobs to do.

A shelf to put up in the hall.

A bench to be put together down by their flashy indoor pool and jacuzzi.

Patrick Andergren wants it all done by the book, even though it will cost more.

The key in the lock, then Martin Svensson is standing in the hall. He reaches for his toolbox.

Everything looks very smart.

Polished parquet floor, a stripped pine bureau with a futuristic lamp and a simple grey rug on the floor.

'Hello! Hello? Is anyone home?'

No answer.

He doesn't bother to take his shoes off, but wipes them carefully on the doormat.

In the kitchen, with its shiny white units, the worktops are sparklingly clean. It doesn't look like anyone's had any breakfast. He always has porridge, but only after two mugs of black coffee and a cigarette.

Taking a firm grip on his toolbox, he goes over to the staircase leading down to the cellar and swimming pool, and he can smell the chlorine. And he can hear a rumbling sound, it must be from the jacuzzi, but surely no one would be sitting in a bubble-pool at this time of day? They must have gone to work.

There's nothing to worry about.

But as he stands there by the stairs and looks over at the grey sofa in the living room, he feels like turning around and running out of the house, and coming back later when the Andergren family are home.

Stop being so stupid, he thinks.

Stop it.

Martin Svensson pulls himself together and sets off down the stairs, but he hesitates again as he reaches the door to the pool room.

That's enough now. Just open the door. Mind you, what if they're in there without any clothes on?

He knocks.

No answer.

So he thrusts the door open and the first thing he sees in front of him is the garden through the windows. Green rhododendron leaves hanging from the bushes along the riverbank, then he shifts focus and looks around, towards the pool, and it occurs to him that the black mosaic makes it look like a bottomless grave.

His eyes refuse to look to the side.

But he forces himself to look at the jacuzzi and Jesus fucking Christ, and he drops the toolbox and walks hesitantly towards the bubble-pool and sees their greyish-white, no, bluish-purple faces, their features stiff, and the water is red, red, red, and their bodies have big round holes in them and they're swollen and unmoving and why, why would anyone do this?

And it all gets too much for him, Martin Svensson, a perfectly ordinary carpenter from Linköping.

He's out in the garden now, stumbling over the wet grass, and the rain is like a hail of machine-gun fire against his jacket, and he finds an opening in the vegetation and then he's out on a jetty of freshly oiled wood, and the waters of the Stångå are full of pustules of rain that appear and die, appear and die.

Porridge.

It shoots from his mouth. Onto the jetty and out into the river and he thinks it looks like the remnants of some animal that's been ground to pieces in the turbines of the power station.

But that can't have happened?

The power station's upstream.

Pull yourself together, now, Martin.

Time to show what you're made of.

Jesus fucking Christ in bastard bloody heaven.

SHIT.

The little girl.

When he was here to talk through the job last week there was a child here.

The Andergren family. That's what it said on the door. Where's their daughter? At preschool?

More porridge, down onto the planks.

Their child.

Martin Svensson fumbles for his mobile.

Have to call the police. He shuts his eyes, wants to shut the horror out, opens them again, looks down at the jetty, wants to get away from all this, wants to run away from here, but knows he has to call the police.

5

The phone rings, and then you're confronted with a sight like this, Malin Fors thinks.

Bullet wounds to the heart, below the ribs, to the stomach, but none to the face.

Why?

Are faces sacred to whoever did this?

Did you shoot them in a sort of controlled fury?

Water like blood.

Blood like water.

What am I seeing? Malin thinks as she stands on the spot that was indicated to her, just inside the door to the pool room in the house at 31 Stentorpsvägen.

I see death, death, death.

But not only fatal wounds.

Karin Johannison has just switched off the jacuzzi, so the eerie rumbling sound is gone, the water is no longer bubbling around the bodies, and they seem almost relieved.

The couple in the bubble-pool in front of her are naked and dead, lilac and ice-blue in water than no longer has the transparent clarity of water, and the whole room smells of iron and chlorine and incipient decay.

The bodies are slightly swollen.

The phone call came shortly after the morning meeting.

It was put through to Malin, and she felt that there was something missing from the man's voice.

'They're dead.'

Mons Kallentoft

'Who are dead?'

'In the bubble-pool.'

And Malin assumed the man who had found two bodies in a jacuzzi at an address in Hjulsbro – evidently a carpenter – was in shock and unable to think straight, but she knew at once that he was telling the truth, she could hear it in the tone of his voice.

In the water.

In the jacuzzi.

The girl.

'What girl?'

He had managed to give the address, and they had immediately despatched the closest car. Their uniformed colleagues had found the bodies in the jacuzzi, and the carpenter, Martin Svensson, out in the rain on the jetty on the Stångå River.

He's too severely shocked to be questioned at present.

'They're dead,' Martin Svensson keeps repeating, rather too loudly, from the living room, where he's sitting on the severe grey sofa that lends just the right contemporary touch to this thoroughly tasteful house, and his words can be heard all the way down in the basement.

She and Zeke had set off at once and arrived some ten minutes after the patrol car. Karin got there just a few minutes later.

The bodies.

Shot.

Naked.

A murder investigation has just begun, there's no doubt about that, and the calm has finally been broken, they're going to have their hands full from now on, and Malin breathes out, keen to throw herself at her work, and wondering where this case is going to take her.

You're exactly what I need.

She feels ashamed of the thought.

So who are you? she wonders, trying to stay calm as she looks at the dead bodies in the bubble-pool.

Outside the rain has eased and the garden on the other side of the wall of glass is green and damp, and shimmering yellow and orange, autumn in all its glory. Simultaneously the whole world seems tinted by a shade of blue.

The black swimming pool to Malin's left is an abyss, but the deepest abyss is right in front of her.

The pair of you.

The carpenter has identified you.

So we know who you are. Your names, anyway.

Patrick and Cecilia Andergren.

Beside her Zeke shifts his weight from one foot to the other as he looks at Karin Johannison, who is carefully working her way across the floor around the jacuzzi.

'Don't touch anything,' she snapped at the uniforms when she arrived. 'Just walk where I say you can. This whole house is to be treated as a crime scene.'

But Karin permitted them to search the ground floor, as long as they wore gloves and were careful. She also agreed to Martin Svensson sitting on the sofa in the living room while he tried to pull himself together.

Karin comes over to Malin and Zeke.

'I'd say they've been there since a few hours before midnight,' she says.

Up in the living room they can hear Martin Svensson bellowing even louder, and Malin thinks he sounds like an anguished water buffalo that's just realised it's trapped for ever inside the body of a water buffalo.

'They were shot,' Malin says.

Karin nods.

'In all likelihood, they died from the gunshot wounds.'

Zeke looks at Karin again, his former lover, and Malin

imagines she can see longing in his eyes, but she knows that Zeke is thoroughly professional in situations like this, and almost wishes that he wasn't, because he and Karin would make a much better couple than he and Gunilla.

'They say water's supposed to stifle pain,' Zeke says. 'But there'd hardly have been time for them to feel any pain anyway. The shots to their hearts ought to have killed them instantly.'

Karin wipes her nose.

'The murderer must have got in somehow, crept down here and shot them as they lay in the jacuzzi. They probably wouldn't have heard anyone approaching.'

The uniforms had secured the house and hadn't found anything of immediate interest. Empty, they had said, and Malin and Zeke had quickly but carefully gone through the house. There were no signs of a struggle, but they had found a child's room, and Malin had wondered: Where's the child?

Not here, she had thought, not here, thank goodness, and then they had gone down to the pool room to hear what Karin had to say after a first, hasty inspection.

Malin turns to Karin.

'Can you come up with a more precise time of death?'

'Yes. But only after the post-mortems.'

'OK.'

'We need to start right from the beginning,' Zeke says.

'They've got a daughter,' Malin says. 'Where is she?'

'We'd better start looking.'

Karin nods to the pair of them before getting back to work.

Another howl from Martin Svensson.

Worse, deeper this time.

What's this world doing to us? Malin thinks, as she looks as Cecilia Andergren's face, her skin almost glassy, her lips frozen in a completely blank expression.

The man beside her.

Patrick.

Her husband.

Her beloved.

But where's your daughter? Where's the little girl in the photograph in your bedroom, in the pictures in that pink bedroom? The ones I glanced at just now?

She must be with relatives, at preschool, nothing bad can have happened to her.

The others are on their way: Sven, Börje, Waldemar, Johan, they should be here any minute now.

Malin is standing in the girl's room again, beside the unmade bed with its pink sheets.

She's already asked the station to find out what Patrick and Cecilia's Andergren's daughter is called. Her name is Ella, and she's five years old.

Malin can hear Zeke going through the drawers in the parents' bedroom as her gaze settles on a photograph in a pink frame.

It's a picture of an Asian girl on the beach of a tropical paradise, with palms and tall pines reaching high above a thin strip of golden sand that seems to merge with a sea that's so blue it's impossible to see the dividing line between it and the sky.

Ella Andergren was adopted.

Like Karin's Tess.

From the same country?

There are other pictures alongside the beach photograph: Ella on a merry-go-round at Gröna Lund in Stockholm, sitting on a Gotland pony, she's only smiling in a couple of pictures, but Malin can see from her dark eyes that she's happy, there's no sign of any anxiety about her identity, the girl in the pictures is as happy as every child has the right to be.

An older woman hugging her.

Leaping into a pool.

The girl curled up on a sofa.

She has the same soft, round features as Tess, the same intent expression.

Full of expectation, confidence.

Vietnam.

That's where you're from as well, isn't it?

I don't know anything about the country, Malin thinks.

Beaches. Jungles. Poverty. War. Explosions and napalm clinging to children's bodies.

Chattering machine guns. *Apocalypse Now*. Mad surfers in a hail of grenades.

But there must be so much more. The war ended over thirty years ago.

Ella Andergren looks like she's three or four years old, holding up a shiny, possibly freshly caught fish to the camera, and Malin remembers once when Tove was five, when she went missing in the Mobilia shopping centre, and Malin had been completely hysterical until they found her, eating a bar of chocolate in a supermarket storeroom.

Five years old. Bluntness personified. Who are you? What do you want? Here I am, I'm great, the whole world is great.

Look at this!

I'm here! I'm alive!

She actually used to envy Tove back then. And she's envious of the girl in these pictures now. Malin wants to be five years old again, but she's perfectly aware that she can't envy the girl in the pictures.

Because where is she?

Malin doesn't even want to think about what might have happened to her.

'Here,' Zeke calls from the bedroom.

'What?'

'I've found their passports.'

'The parents'?'

'Yes.'

'And the girl's?'

'Yes.'

Zeke beside her now, and Malin looks at the black-and-white photograph in the passport.

'We need to get hold of their relatives, then . . .' Malin says, but is interrupted by a shrill, unfamiliar voice, an older woman shouting: 'WHAT'S HAPPENED! WHAT'S HAPPENED! WHY ARE THE POLICE HERE? I'm their NEIGHBOUR! Why are the POLICE here?'

Malin and Zeke hurry out to the hall, where two uniformed officers are trying to stop the woman coming into the house.

'Calm down,' Malin cries. 'I'll take this,' and the woman quietens down and Malin tells her to wait outside the house, because Martin Svensson is standing next to her, and the pale green of his face when they arrived has been replaced by a greyish tone that Malin assumes is his normal skin colour.

'I can talk to you now, I'm ready,' he says.

'Take her out to the car,' Malin says. 'She can wait there. Don't let her leave. I want to talk to her.'

A low sofa.

Plumper than expected, comfortable.

Moderately expensive.

Sensible.

Martin Svensson sits down in the imitation Egg chair opposite, and tells them what he knows about the Andergren family, and what he was doing there.

He hasn't got anything to do with the murders, Malin concludes, he came here to do a job, he knows very little about the family, he just happened to have done some work for them before, when they had been given his number by a neighbour.

Martin Svensson tells her and Zeke that Patrick Andergren worked for Saab as an engineer, or possibly a salesman, and that his wife was a high-school English teacher.

The girl was adopted, he had worked that much out, and as far as he knows the Andergrens were respectable people, and Malin is surprised by his old-fashioned choice of words.

Respectable.

As if that could make what had happened to them less true.

As if to make their violent deaths more noble.

'And the girl?' Malin asks.

'What about her?'

'Do you know where she might be?'

'No idea. Like I said, I don't really know them.'

And Malin thinks through the possibilities again, as she knows Zeke is doing. That the girl is with a relative, or spent the night with a friend, or was at preschool.

Five years old.

She'd be at preschool now, wouldn't she?

Ten o'clock.

That's right, isn't it?

Urgent now.

The river.

A frightened five-year-old.

Shit.

The thought suddenly hits Malin, but it's Martin Svensson who puts it into words.

'She could be in the river,' he says. 'What if she saw it happen, and got frightened? So frightened that she went out onto the jetty and jumped in? Or fell in, and drowned?'

He's staring ahead of him.

'She's dead!' he suddenly exclaims. 'What if the little girl's dead?'

6

The neighbour.

Thea Victorin.

A hysterical old woman with too high an opinion of herself is the last thing they need right now.

Unless she actually does know something?

I need to hurry now, Malin thinks. It's urgent, I can feel it. Should I send out search parties for the daughter?

No, I'll question the old woman first. Now.

Why am I so angry? Why have I got the feeling that this is really bad?

Could it actually get any worse? Two dead, and a little girl missing.

Malin's anger is being deflected towards the woman, this prim woman in her mid-sixties who's sitting in the back seat of the patrol car looking confused, wondering what on earth is going on as she scratches her steel-wool hair.

Malin tries to calm down, looks out through the car window, listens to the gentle rain on the roof.

This pissy, stuck-up residential area.

The leaves are hanging heavily from mature apple trees, and the birch trees that survived the construction of the houses when the area was developed thirty years ago are still standing tall.

Neatly clipped hedges, probably looked after by Polish gardeners, slightly worn pavements lining the glistening, recently resurfaced tarmac of the road.

The air is fresh and clear, but it carries an undertone of decay.

The street is empty.

Not much life out here, the doctors' showy houses sitting in deserted majesty. Presumably that's what they want? Privacy. No imperfections.

This was where Malin's mother would have liked to live.

But they could never afford it.

Thank God I was spared this.

They had to make do with the cheaper option of Sturefors.

The woman in the back seat raises her dark, thinly-plucked eyebrows, flares her nostrils and is about to say something, but Malin cuts her off.

'What do you know about the daughter?'

She can hear Zeke breathing beside her, just as impatient as she is.

The river.

It's flowing through Malin now, she can feel it, see it, even though it's out of sight.

Graphite grey and calm, the water lapping with suffocating slowness against the edge of the jetty.

A white Volvo arrives. Sven, Johan, Waldemar and Börje get out and look over at the patrol car, and Malin nods at them, gestures that they'll soon be done, and her colleagues disappear inside the house.

'I can't accept that I should have to be locked up inside this car. What on earth has happened?'

'No one has locked you up anywhere,' Zeke says. 'What do you know about Ella Andergren?'

'Answer,' Malin hisses. 'Otherwise . . .'

And Zeke saves her, saves her from drowning in her own fury.

'We can't tell you what's happened,' Zeke says calmly.

Then he goes on: 'But we do need to know where we can find Patrick and Cecilia Andergren's daughter, Ella.'

Outside the car an ambulance comes past and pulls up in the drive leading up to the house.

Malin glances at the ambulance. Thankfully it isn't Janne who gets out and starts to sort out the stretchers.

'Is Ella missing? Such a sweet little girl, she comes to see me and I give her juice and buns. I usually make buns when she . . .'

'She's not in the house,' Zeke says. 'Do you have any idea where she could be?'

'I suppose she's at preschool.'

'Which one?'

'She goes to Sunny Hill, up on Kvinnebyvägen.'

'Do you know if she often stays with relatives? Friends? Overnight?'

Zeke is even calmer now, and his calmness spreads to Malin.

There's nothing wrong with the old woman really.

'I think she sometimes stays with her Grandma Britt. But I don't really know anything about the family. But Ella's the sweetest little girl in the world.'

'So you don't socialise with them?'

'No.'

'But Ella comes to see you?'

Thea Victorin holds two fingers in the air.

'Twice,' she says. 'I've been on my own since my husband died. I wouldn't have minded having a few more visits from her.'

'Did you notice anything unusual last night, or yesterday evening, outside the house?'

Thea Victorin shakes her head.

'I'm on Stesolid. It tends to knock me out, so I'm always sleeping like a log after nine o'clock.'

Mons Kallentoft

'Thank you,' Malin says, opening the door to get out.

'You have to tell me what's happened,' Thea Victorin says.

'I'm sorry, but we can't,' Zeke replies. 'But I'm sure you'll be able to read it in the *Correspondent* soon enough.' And at that moment one of the newspaper's white reporters' cars arrives.

Malin goes back to the house, fending off the reporter and instinctively holding her hand in front of her face to avoid being photographed.

Where's today taking me? she thinks. Everything's happening too quickly, it's all getting confused, we have to calm down, take stock of things. We've been behaving like rabid dogs since the discovery in the jacuzzi, and a sort of low-level madness has been creeping up on me, us, and we really need to get our act together.

She can see that Zeke is thinking much the same as they walk back into the house.

The child, possibly in the river.

The adults murdered, horrible, but that sort of thing happens, it's the sort of thing grown-ups do to each other.

But a child.

Not a child.

And if we can't protect our children, if we can't love them the right way, what hope is there for us?

Malin looks at Zeke in the greenish gloom of the hall. His skull-like face is pale and tired, but he looks determined.

'OK, let's find the girl,' he says. 'And the murderer. Find out what the hell is going on here.'

They let Martin Svensson and Thea Victorin get back to their lives.

The detectives hold a quick preliminary meeting in the living room of the house, settling down on the armchairs and sofa, leaning forward over the table, and if they were tired this morning, now, early in the afternoon, they are alert, as if the violence that has come their way has given them new energy.

Zeke remains standing, as if ready to leap into action.

Karin Johannison comes up from the basement and tells them that the evidence suggests the killer picked the lock of the cellar door, found the Andergrens in the jacuzzi, and shot them there. She's busy trying to secure the evidence: empty cartridges, foot- and fingerprints, and so on.

Sven reminds them that the relatives need to be informed. And they have to find out where the little girl is.

'The river,' Waldemar says. 'Should we start dragging it? Divers?'

'Let's hold back on that,' Sven says. 'The most likely explanation is that she's with relatives or at preschool.'

'We should still send out a few patrols to search the area,' Malin says. 'We've already waited too long. We should have done that as soon as we realised there was a child missing.'

Sven thinks for a moment and then nods.

'I'll sort out the patrols. But we'll wait before calling in divers. If she is in the water, then it's already too late.'

It mustn't be too late, Malin thinks, alarmed at how easily Sven turns the possible death of a child into a matter of police practicalities.

'We should call the preschool,' Börje says.

'That would scare the life out of them,' Malin says. 'Zeke and I can head over there.'

'I'll sort out the door-to-door as well,' Sven says. 'Then we need to find out as much as we can about the

Andergrens. I want to know everything about their lives, who they were and who could have seen them last. We need to map out their last twenty-four hours.'

'I'll start digging,' Johan says, and only now does Malin notice the iPad in his hand.

'He worked at Saab, in international sales,' Johan says a few moments later. 'She was an English teacher at Johannelund School.'

'Family?'

Johan moves his fingers across the screen of the pad.

'Looks like she's got a sister, Petronella Andersson, and a mother, Britt Sivsjö – both here in Linköping. As far as I can see, he doesn't have any living relatives.'

'OK,' Sven says, 'here's what we do. Johan, you carry on digging. We've found their mobiles and a portable laptop. Take a look at them as soon as you get the chance.

'We need to talk to the Andergrens' workmates, their friends, anyone you can find. Malin and Zeke, deal with the preschool first, then go and see her mother. Waldemar and Börje, you go and see the sister, if she's actually at home at this time of day. Break the news, and see what you can find out.'

'Priests?' Zeke wonders.

'What do you think?' Sven says.

'Let's get going,' Malin says. 'It always takes a while for them to show up, and time is what we don't have right now.'

They drive over to the preschool, past 'children playing' signs, past terraced houses built in the 1970s, and older, whitewashed houses hidden behind tall hedges.

Sunny Hill is nestled up against a wooded slope that screens the district from the traffic on the busy Brokindsleden. Malin was driven up and down that road countless times as a little girl.

Sunny Hill is rainy hill today.

The rain has picked up again and the white, single-storey building is veiled in the haze of hundreds of thousands of microscopic droplets.

They pull up outside the green-painted wooden fence.

I went to preschool, Malin thinks. I loved it. It was perfect for a tough little thing like me, but it doesn't suit everyone.

Hunched over, they head towards the brown-stained door. The brick façade has seen better days.

Malin feels the rain bouncing off her oilskin. The children must be indoors in this sort of weather. The playground is empty and the yellow and blue climbing frames, swings, and playhouses have an abandoned look to them.

She pulls the door open, expecting to hear children shouting and playing, but the preschool is quiet.

No children here.

No Ella Andergren.

Unless . . .?

Maybe they're having a rest?

Malin and Zeke step inside and head past a cloakroom where each little cubbyhole is marked by a picture of a small child.

Raincoats.

Extra clothes. Spare shoes.

Nursery.

Or preschool, as the teachers – no, learning facilitators – say.

Empty and silent.

A corridor with woven yellow wallpaper and even brighter yellow linoleum flooring leads deeper into the building, its walls lined with noticeboards covered with notes and photographs describing the children's activities.

Outing to the park!

To the local museum!

To the theatre.

In almost every case, it's good to be a child in Sweden today.

'Hello?' Zeke calls.

And just seconds later an angry, middle-aged woman's face peers out through a doorway.

'And who might you be? We've got planning meetings today, so the preschool is closed.'

Malin pulls her wallet from the inside pocket of her coat and holds up her police ID towards the woman.

'We're from the police. We'd like to talk to the manager.'

Malin feels her stomach tighten. No children having a rest. No Ella here.

So where are you?

In the black water?

'So there aren't any children here today?' Zeke asks, and the woman in the doorway looks irritated.

'No. Like I said. The preschool is closed. Can you come back tomorrow?'

Grey hair. Round glasses. A real battle-axe.

'It's about Ella Andergren,' Malin says. 'We need to find out where she is.'

Malin polite now, whereas Zeke looks like he's about to explode, and before the woman has time to answer he roars: 'We can't come back. She might be in trouble. Now go and get the manager. Now!'

'I'm the manager here,' the woman says. 'My name's Evy Björkman.'

Zeke is following Evy Björkman.

Soaking up the atmosphere of the preschool, remembering the one his son Martin attended. His grandchild is about to start.

At a Montessori school, on the strict advice of his wife Gunilla.

No more children for me, Zeke thinks.

And he thinks about Karin, and the way life seems to be racing past since they ended their relationship. He sees Gunilla sitting at the kitchen table in the evenings, her mouth more and more clenched, and the two single beds in their respective bedrooms, and he sees Karin in his mind's eye, and it's not her body he's longing for, but just to be near her, sit next to her on a sofa in some unfamiliar room.

'Along here,' Evy Björkman commands, and Zeke goes ahead of her into another corridor, closely followed by Malin.

Evy Björkman sits down opposite them in the preschool's dining room, and her broad backside spills over the sides of the little chair as she rests her arms on the low table.

The room is infused with a vague smell of meatballs, fish fingers, and instant mashed potato. Over on a draining board there are stacks of clean Duralex glasses and sturdy white plates.

Zeke and Malin remain standing, unwilling even to try sitting on the miniature children's chairs.

Evy Björkman answers their questions in a measured, sceptical way. She doesn't ask why they're there.

'Ella was going to be at home with her mother today. Cecilia said so when she picked her up yesterday, I'm sure of that.'

'What if their plans changed and they had to work?' Malin asks. 'Do you have any idea who would look after Ella then?'

'Well,' Evy Björkman says, rubbing her cheek with one hand. 'That would probably be her grandmother. She sometimes picks Ella up, and I know Ella occasionally spends the night there.'

'Not Cecilia's sister?' Zeke asks.

'Does she have a sister? I've never seen her.'

'No one else?'

'Not that I know of.'

'Any other relatives? Friends? Workmates?'

Evy Björkman shakes her head, a little too hard, and Malin gets the feeling she isn't telling them all she knows, that she's holding back for reasons of confidentiality.

'You can talk to us, you do know that, don't you?' Malin says. 'I can assure you that this investigation is so serious that you're not bound by any oath of confidentiality.'

Evy Björkman sighs.

'I've only met the grandmother. We don't have anyone else listed as a contact. She could have stayed over with a friend, that's not at all unlikely, but I can't give you the phone numbers of her friends here at preschool.'

'Like I said, you're not bound by . . .'

'You have to give us that list,' Zeke says. 'We need to find out where Ella is.'

'So she's missing?'

'We don't know,' Malin says.

Sausage meat, boiled carrots.

'What's happened?'

This was what you wanted to get at all along, Malin thinks. *What happened?*

'We aren't at liberty to tell you,' Zeke says, sounding almost cajoling now, then he stares straight at Evy Björkman, and Malin can see something change inside him.

'You can have the list,' she says. 'I'll go and get it, then you'll have to leave me in peace. I have to get back to our planning meeting. Nothing will get sorted out if I'm not there.'

Evy Björkman gets up.

She stands still, and for the first time there's a hint of anxiety in her eyes.

'They're happy, that family,' Evy Björkman says. 'They have a good life.'

Then she leaves Malin and Zeke among the smells of the children, the food they eat, the milk they drink, in the memories of sounds, impressions and events that shape the children into the adults they may one day become.

7

Malin closes her eyes.

She hears the engine purring, hears Zeke's rough hands on the wheel, and feels her body shake as they drive over a speed bump just beyond Sunny Hill.

She's already called Sven to tell him that the preschool is closed today, and he's still reluctant to bring in divers, but the search teams are heading out now. The dogs have been given the scent of the girl's clothes.

Now for Britt Sivsjö.

Ella's grandmother.

She lives in Wimanshäll, and Malin recognises the address, a narrow street close to the city, lined with small, blue-painted Smurf-like terraced houses.

Malin tries to gather her thoughts, to get her bearings in the strangely unfamiliar world that the day has forced her to step into.

Then she thinks about those closest to her.

She suddenly remembers that Tove is coming home for the weekend.

Tove. Probably in a lesson at the moment. Even if her boyfriend Tom is something of a distraction, her grades are good, she'll be able to do whatever she wants in life, and back in the summer she was talking about the Stockholm School of Economics.

Is Tove going to become one of those social parasites,

sitting in front of their computers and tapping buttons and earning billions from other people's misery?

Malin read an article about John Paulson in Wall Street, who earned three hundred billion by betting that Americans wouldn't be able to repay their mortgages. In other words, he became a billionaire because families, children, were evicted and lost their homes.

Don't go to the School of Economics, Tove.

Please.

And I'm not buying you a pair of Jimmy Choos for Christmas. Not a chance.

Peter.

With all that money. He wants me to let him buy the clothes and other stuff you think you need in order to fit in.

You've never been remotely bothered about fitting in before, Tove.

And I've refused, but fortunately you don't yet know that.

Stick to your books. At least you haven't abandoned them yet.

Peter.

At the hospital now.

The child he wants me to bear.

Like I did you, Tove, and that made me feel more grounded that I ever have, either before or since.

He's probably in the operating theatre now, and tonight he'll be sleeping in that dark, cramped, stuffy little duty-room.

Why can't he come home? He can be at the hospital in ten minutes if they call, but he says that's too long if something serious happens.

Two people shot.

A little girl missing.

This is bad.

Mons Kallentoft

Zeke's breathing. The sound of his hands firmly on the wheel.

The old woman lives alone.

Her husband has been dead twenty years.

So Johan told them.

Now she's about to become even lonelier.

Britt Sivsjö.

No priest. Malin has noticed that they sometimes do more harm than good when they have to inform relatives that someone has died, most of the priests she's encountered have been almost unhealthily self-centred.

How can you pass on that sort of news?

Is Ella going to be there?

There's no way of preparing for it, Malin knows that, as does Zeke, and she opens her eyes and they drive on in silence through the city, not saying anything to each other.

No words can prepare them for this.

No words can pre-empt what they are about to do.

Linköping!

Wretched city.

Arsehole of the world.

Paradise of the Östgöta Plain.

My home, Malin thinks as she looks out of the car window, just as they're passing the recently renovated blocks of flats in Johannelund.

Linköping.

The city where rich and poor live close but separate lives, and are united in impossible challenges.

How to keep a marriage alive?

How to love?

How to follow your desires without being destroyed by their force?

How to walk past all the pubs with their chilled lager

flowing with precisely calibrated bitterness from the glistening mouths of the taps on the bars?

Fear is welling up again.

Ready to take hold of the city.

There's a killer on the loose, possibly a child-killer.

The car pulls up outside Britt Sivsjö's Smurf-house. The roof is thatched, like houses in Skåne, and there are neat flowerbeds in the little patch of grass in front of the house.

A patrol car has just arrived, the uniforms will stay on afterwards.

Here we come, Malin thinks, about to ruin your life.

Malin's hand trembles as she moves her finger towards the doorbell.

The uniforms behind them.

Hesitation.

So Zeke rings the bell instead, and they hear the easy footsteps of someone who's been up for a while, alert, on the other side of the door.

'Who can that be?'

'Who's that at the door?'

The naïve voice of someone talking to an animal.

Or a child.

No barking.

Then the door opens.

Malin feels her knees go weak.

Stay on your feet, Fors. This woman needs you now.

Malin has managed to make Britt Sivsjö realise that they don't want coffee, and that she should take a seat on the blue Howard sofa in the living room looking out onto a small back garden that's as well-maintained as the one at the front.

The lively woman sitting opposite them is in her

seventies. The same woman who was hugging Ella in one of the photographs in her bedroom.

Short, permed hair, dyed blonde. A neatly made-up face that looks good for her age, an expression that suggests an outgoing personality.

But Britt Sivsjö is nervous now.

Fiddling with a long copper lighter.

How are we going to deal with this? Malin thinks, looking around the room. The rugs are the same standard oriental variety that her mum had had at home, cheap, supposedly smart. The walls are covered with colourful imitation-Chagall prints.

You want this place to look smart, don't you? Malin thinks.

I'm an empathy Smurf now, she goes on to think, as she sees Britt Sivsjö waiting for the blow that she's started to suspect is coming.

Malin switches on her professionalism, and knows that Zeke is ready to catch a woman falling when she finds out that her daughter is dead, murdered.

And she clears her throat.

'I'm afraid I have to tell you that your daughter, Cecilia Andergren, was found dead in her home this morning.'

And the colour drains from Britt Sivsjö's face, she turns grey beneath her make-up, and moans 'no' as she falls sideways into Zeke's lap, and he holds her as she lies there sobbing, and strokes her back without saying anything, just strokes her back.

A black cat comes in from the kitchen, licking its lips, then jumps up onto the windowsill to watch the birds in the garden.

After one, two, three, maybe four or five minutes, Britt Sivsjö sits up and asks: 'How did she die?'

'We believe she was murdered.'

'How?'

'We can't go into any details yet.'

Britt Sivsjö seems to be trying to make sense of the words, then pulls herself together, realising that she needs to find the very best of herself right now.

'And Ella's with Patrick?'

'Patrick was also found dead. They were murdered together, late yesterday evening,' Malin says.

Britt Sivsjö's nostrils flare, then she rubs her eyes hard with the palms of her hands, and when she takes her hands away, her smeared mascara looks like war paint.

Then she starts to cry, softly at first, then long, drawn-out sobs that gradually become a howl, and she clutches Zeke's hand. He looks troubled, but simultaneously full of sympathy.

Then all of a sudden she stops crying and sits up again.

'Did you find Ella with them?'

'No,' Malin says. 'We were hoping you might be able to tell us where she is.'

'She was supposed to be at home with Cecilia today. Her preschool is closed.'

Britt Sivsjö stands up.

She walks up and down her living room, looks out into the garden and says: 'Dear God, dear God!' then stops and focuses on Malin.

'I've got no idea where she is. No idea . . .'

'She couldn't be with friends?'

'I'd know if she was.'

'When did you last speak to Cecilia?'

'Yesterday. She called to see how I was. She does that sometimes.'

Then Britt Sivsjö's eyes cloud over and she yells: 'You've got to get people out to look for Ella, she could be anywhere, you've got to send people to look for her,' and then she slumps onto the floor in a heap of flesh and tears and breathing and grief and a thousand thoughts about what has happened and what must happen now.

'What's happening? What going to happen now?'

Half an hour later, Malin and Zeke are sitting with Britt Sivsjö in her kitchen, while the uniforms stay in the living room.

She has insisted on making coffee now.

In the glow of the red cupboard doors they drink coffee from china mugs and listen to Britt Sivsjö, the things she says because they have to be said.

While Britt Sivsjö was composing herself, Malin had called Sven to tell him about the little girl, and Sven had told her that Börje and Waldemar were with Ella's aunt, Petronella Andersson, in Hackefors, but that the girl wasn't there either.

'No more holding back,' Sven said. 'Divers, and an official search. We'll go through the list from her preschool, but there doesn't seem much likelihood that she's with a friend. We certainly can't count on it, anyway.'

Malin hears Britt Sivsjö talking.

What's she saying?

In her mind's eye Malin sees them dragging the riverbed, where the young fish, worms, and thick, metre-long eels will eat anything.

But who do they eat?

A little girl who was brought to a strange country for a better life and unending love?

Britt Sivsjö.

How can she go on talking now? How can people go on at all?

What's she saying?

I'm going to get Ella back for you, Malin thinks.

8

Britt Sivsjö goes on talking, answering their questions, and Malin would like to read her thoughts, but how do you get into someone's thoughts?

'Have you started looking yet?' Britt Sivsjö asks.

Perhaps she's thinking: You can never give me my Cecilia back, but Ella, you can give her back to me, can't you?

'Ella,' she says. 'She's a brave little thing, you know. She could have walked off if she was scared, she really could.'

'Who could have wanted to harm them like that?' Zeke says. 'Did they have any enemies?'

'Not as far as I know. They were perfectly ordinary, friendly,' Britt Sivsjö replies, running her finger around the rim of her mug. 'They really were very ordinary. They were happy at last. They tried so long to have a child, test tubes and everything, then they tried to adopt, and they finally got Ella three years ago.'

'Tell us more about them,' Malin says, leaning forward to underline her interest, her concentration.

'You want me to tell you more about them?'

Malin nods.

'Cecilia grew up here in Linköping. She was . . .'

Silence.

An autumn fly buzzes above the sink.

'I know, I have to go on, but it's so hard. I spent the day here yesterday, took things easy, got up late this morning, and then you show up.

'She was very well respected as a teacher, I know that much. And Patrick was qualified as an engineer. He worked as a salesman, first at Eriksson, then Saab.'

Malin and Zeke murmur in response, so as not to interrupt Britt Sivsjö's train of thought.

'They met when they were young, Patrick's a local lad too, but he doesn't have any family. His parents and sister died in a collision at an unmanned railway crossing when he was nineteen.

'He and Cecilia met shortly after that.

'Then they both went to university here.'

She nods towards Malin.

'Maybe you knew them? You must be about the same age.'

'I'm afraid I didn't know Cecilia,' Malin says. 'Or Patrick.'

'Oh well,' Britt Sivsjö says, getting to her feet.

She runs one hand through her short hair.

'You have to find Ella,' she says. 'She must have woken up, got scared and run out into the forest. She must be so scared now, so scared.'

Britt Sivsjö stops, then shouts out loud: 'YOUR BEST ISN'T GOOD ENOUGH. YOU HAVE TO DO MORE THAN YOUR BEST!'

Zeke stands up and puts his arms around Britt Sivsjö, whispering: 'There, now, there, now.'

And Malin sees her calm down again as she sinks back onto her seat. She starts talking again: 'They lived abroad. First India, then Vietnam, but Patrick got fed up of all that travelling for work, and they wanted to come home, so he got a new job at Saab, in the international sales department, the same as he was doing at Eriksson. But not so much travelling at Saab.

'They'd made a fair bit of money in Asia, but I still got the impression that they were having trouble with the mortgage at first. That sort of house doesn't come cheap.'

'Did they have many friends?' Malin asks.

'No, they kept to themselves. I can't really think of anyone.'

'No one?'

'I can't do any more of this now.'

'I understand,' Zeke says.

'Do you? She's got a big sister, Petronella.'

'Our colleagues are with her now,' Zeke says.

Britt Sivsjö falls silent and seems to think before she says: 'She and Cecilia never got on. Not even when they were little, Petronella could be really mean to her.'

'Why didn't they get on?' Malin asks.

'I don't know, maybe they were just jealous of each other?'

'Jealous of what?'

'Everything, the way sisters can be. Nothing special, you'd have to ask Petronella about that. It's not like they'd fallen out, they were just different.'

'Any other conflict in the family?'

'No, nothing at all. People can be very different within the same family. When you meet Petronella you'll probably see what I mean. Oh, but of course your colleagues are talking to her at the moment.'

Enough now, Malin thinks. She's on the point of collapse.

'Would you like your daughter to come over?' Zeke asks.

'No, I don't want Petronella to come over,' Britt Sivsjö says. 'That wouldn't make anything better.'

Then Britt stands up again, and Malin thinks she's going to have another outburst and start shouting again, but instead she says in a calm voice: 'You have to give Ella back to me. Some people wonder if I feel like her real grandmother, if it's hard to feel anything for her because she's adopted.

'What fools.

'There isn't a sweeter, nicer, lovelier little girl anywhere.'

Mum!

Don't be scared, I'm kind of OK. Everything is soft as silk here, and so simple, it really is, and I'm not just saying that to make it less painful for you.

But I'm scared, of course.

Scared for Ella.

Petronella.

I don't have the energy to think about her.

She was my sister.

Do you have to like your sister? Love her?

I don't know.

You have to be strong now, Mum.

For my sake.

For our sake.

Because if Ella comes back she's going to need you, you're going to have to steer her through life, and be there to give her the love that we have been denied from giving her, to give her all the love you gave me, Mum.

Ella needs you.

And there is nothing better than being needed by a child.

9

The bodies in the jacuzzi.

Presumably in the mortuary by now, waiting for their post-mortems.

Shot in cold blood, Malin thinks as she and Zeke stand outside the Smurf-house in Wimanshäll.

What sort of evil are we dealing with here?

'They must have put the girl to bed and decided to round off the evening in the jacuzzi. They finished tidying up the kitchen, then felt like having a dip,' she says.

She's interrupted by her mobile ringing.

Malin hurries to get inside the car, keen to prevent even a single drop falling from the low clouds finding its way into her phone, and just manages to answer on the fifth and final ring.

Sven.

She hears his voice at the other end of the line, and is reminded yet again how relieved she is that his operation was a success, that his prostate cancer has been cured, but deep down she knows that what she's most relieved about is that she didn't have to decide whether or not she wanted his job.

I'd be a terrible boss.

I'm a lone wolf.

Someone who hunts people who need to be hunted.

'Sven.'

'Are you finished with Britt Sivsjö?'

Zeke gets in the car and starts the engine, without really knowing where they're going.

'Yes.'

'How did it go?'

'Surprisingly well. She was able to tell us quite a bit before she went to pieces. The uniforms are going to stay with her as long as necessary.'

'Waldemar and Börje are done with the sister too,' Sven says. 'She and her husband took it pretty well, hardly showed any signs of grief. Only one of the kids was home, the other three were at school. Sounds like the boy was terrified at the sight of Waldemar and Börje.'

'Kids can be like that. Strange men are suspicious.'

Sven chuckles at the other end of the line.

'According to Britt Sivsjö the sisters didn't get on at all, the way siblings don't sometimes,' Malin says.

'No, the sister evidently got angry when they started asking about Patrick and Cecilia,' Sven says.

'How do you mean, angry?'

'Irritated, snapping that they didn't have anything to do with each other.'

'If they didn't actually like each other, maybe she's just not upset.'

'They were sisters, Malin. She ought to feel something.'

'What did they have to say about Ella?'

'They had no idea where "the brat" might be.'

'They used that word?'

'Apparently, according to Börje.'

'OK, we'll have to question them again. Have they got alibis?'

'Her husband was playing poker at a friend's, a Kalle Lundbäck in Sjögestad. Börje's checking that out now. Petronella was home with the kids. The older children will have to confirm that when they get back from school.'

'Anything else?' Malin asks.

'I've had five uniforms go through the list of parents. Ella Andergren didn't spend the night with any of her classmates.

'The dogs are already out, and the divers are on their way, if they haven't already arrived. We're just going to have to hope for the best, Malin.'

They're driving past the white blocks of flats in Berga, up towards the tower blocks of Johannelund. The brick buildings look grey in the rain, their wooden eaves even greyer as a result of their landlords' neglect.

This city is falling apart, Malin thinks.

Who's going to rescue the inhabitants? Calm their fears?

Who would shoot two parents in their home? And possibly abduct their child?

'Are you there, Malin?'

'Sorry, Sven. I was just trying to make sense of things. Ella was supposed to be spending today at home with her mother, according to both the manager at Sunny Hill and her grandmother.'

'It's not easy, thinking the worst.'

And in Sven's voice Malin can hear the resignation of an officer who's seen pretty much everything, but still hopes for the best, and she thinks: I have to believe.

I have to believe.

'What do you think Zeke and I should do now?' she asks.

'Head over to where Cecilia and Patrick Andergren worked, see what you can find out, inform them of what's happened, let them know they've been found murdered. Now that the relatives have been informed it's OK to talk about it.'

'We'll go to Saab,' Malin says, and Zeke brakes and turns the wheel, and they head back the way they came.

'I'll send Börje and Waldemar to Johannelund School,' Sven says, then ends the call.

After a while in dark, cold water there are no directions.

You lose your orientation.

You think the fish are nibbling at you.

It's dark here, he thinks, Per Sundeberg, the diver who is moving along the bed of the Stångå River behind the Andergren family home.

The lamp on his forehead lights up his immediate surroundings.

He once saw a box jellyfish on a trip to Australia.

White tendrils of death.

Here there is nothing but darkness and cold, and he doesn't want to see the little girl, what was her name again?

When he arrived with the rest of the diving team the media were already there.

The *Correspondent*'s car. TV4, SVT, *Aftonbladet*.

The parents shot.

Per Sundeberg doesn't want to see a pale body with empty, wide-open eyes float past him in the darkness.

He doesn't want to find what he's looking for.

He just wants to get on with his life.

He knows the dogs are barking in the patches of woodland around Hjulsbro.

Sniffing.

Picking up scents.

Looking, looking, looking, tracking through the forest, searching through the water, along the riverbed.

The visibility is little more than half a metre here, even when he shines his strongest torch ahead of him.

Are you here? he wonders. Ella?

He prays he's not going to be confronted with a drifting water angel.

Saab, Malin thinks as they drive towards the factory.

The company is a dubious asset to the city.

Weapons systems, missiles that tear children to pieces in Sudan, Afghanistan, Iraq and everywhere else children get in the way of adults' colliding ambitions.

This city is built on the limbs of amputated children, Malin thinks, and feels ashamed of the standard expressions of pride at the tradition of building fighter planes.

The Draken.

The Viggen.

The Gripen.

What do the people of Linköping think those planes they have constructed and the technology with which they are equipped are actually used for?

Blowing people and buildings to pieces in conflicts where right and wrong, good and evil are impossible to tell apart.

The factory complex is surrounded by a three-metre-high metal fence crowned with rolls of barbed wire.

There are secrets here. The rain is pouring hard now, drumming on the roof of the car.

A red-painted construction hall, several hundred metres long, with a classic corrugated-iron factory roof, stretches out on the other side of the fence.

A ten-storey office block housing the admin and sales departments.

That must have been where Patrick Andergren worked.

Zeke drives up to the entrance.

There are three security guards sitting in a glass lodge, and two red and yellow painted barriers, one after the other, prevent any unauthorised entry.

Zeke holds up his ID to the bearded guard manning the

loudspeaker, and explains that they need to see Patrick Andergren's boss, that it's important, urgent.

Another of the guards in the lodge makes three phone calls, Malin sees his mouth moving rapidly.

Beyond the barriers, obsolete fighters stand like statues. The Draken, the Viggen: manmade birds of death as works of art. Birds of death to be honoured like communist dictators. If there's one thing you mustn't do in Linköping, it's criticise the arms industry. When the prototype of the Gripen crashed spectacularly on a test flight, the city descended into a state of collective mourning.

Then the bearded guard speaks.

'You can go through. Head for the admin tower, you can park there, and ask for Glenn Rundberg in reception. He can see you straight away.'

Glenn Rundberg is in his fifties, and is leaning back in a tall, black leather office chair.

The ninth floor of ten.

His spacious office occupies one of the corners. There's a shimmering, gold-coloured Persian rug on the floor, and a new desk with chrome legs and an opaque glass top. The white walls are adorned with framed pictures of the Gripen.

A small, carved blue stone sign on the desk bears the words: International Sales Manager.

The sales department occupies a lofty position.

Only the directors above them.

Even missiles require a phenomenal torrent of sales patter.

Swedish howitzers made by Bofors sprayed shells across Vietnam that are still killing children and their parents in the paddy fields and jungles.

Bofors, later bought by Saab.

The Gripen is capable of carrying napalm. The Draken is said to have done just that in the Congo.

Glenn Rundberg's ample frame fills his chair, and he seems almost swallowed up by his tailored blue wool suit. A grey tie sits like a noose around his bulging neck, and through the office windows Malin looks off towards Hjulsbro, and wonders if the divers or the dogs in the forest have found anything.

Glenn Rundberg's face has big, round cheeks and a long nose that make his head look like a gravy-boat full to the brim with thick sauce.

Malin and Zeke are sitting in the visitors' chairs opposite him, and he says: 'I know why you're here.'

In the lift on the way up Malin had checked the *Correspondent*'s website.

Couple found murdered in Hjulsbro.

Pictures of bodies being carried out of the house on stretchers.

The house clearly identifiable.

'I've been there several times,' Glenn Rundberg goes on. 'To Patrick and Cecilia's, to talk about work. And the girl, Ella, that's who you're looking for in the river, isn't it?'

Glenn Rundberg's voice is a mixture of fear and excitement now, and Malin can hear a well-concealed hint of dismay.

She nods.

'We don't know where Ella is,' Zeke says.

'How were they killed?'

'We can't tell you that.'

'I understand.'

'When did you last see Patrick Andergren?' Malin asks. 'Did he come to work as usual yesterday?'

'Yes, he was here. A perfectly ordinary day. I actually gave him a lift home at about six o'clock. He usually took the bus, but never said no to a lift. It's not out of my way. Well, only a bit. I haven't heard from him since then.'

'Tell us about Patrick and Cecilia,' Zeke says. 'Anything you think could be important for us. And everything else, for that matter.'

Then they let Glenn Rundberg talk about Patrick Andergren.

He tells them that he was a good salesman, very successful at Saab, that he'd worked abroad and knew how to handle the culturally sensitive Asian markets.

That he had come from Ericsson with an unblemished record.

He hadn't been linked to any of the rumours of bribery in Vietnam or India, unlike plenty of his colleagues at Ericsson.

'He was completely clean, I'm convinced of that. He certainly gave that impression here with us.

'I liked him, even if I didn't really know him that well. I didn't know Cecilia at all. Only met her a couple of times. I don't think they had a lot of friends.'

Glenn Rundberg doesn't seem terribly upset, Malin thinks, but perhaps you wouldn't be about people you only knew through work, and maybe the murders are too much to take in? Unless his professional instincts have kicked in. How quickly can we recruit a new top salesman?

Bribery.

Ericsson. Exports. What's he talking about? Why has he brought this up?

'Bribery,' she says. 'There've been a few cases, then?'

Glenn Rundberg nods.

'Nothing that could be proved, though, and Patrick was an honourable man. That was certainly my impression of him.'

'Do you know if they had any enemies?'

Glenn Rundberg shakes his head.

'No, I don't. But like I said: I didn't know Cecilia at all, and I don't think there were any threats here.'

Threats, Malin thinks.

A word that only ever gets used when there is a threat. Or when someone has taken the possibility of a threat into consideration.

'So no threats?'

'No.'

'What did you do yesterday? Did you go inside yesterday evening?' Zeke asks. 'To talk about work?'

'No, I went home after I'd dropped Patrick off. We had the Devegårds around for dinner. I'll give you their number so you can check.'

Malin and Zeke nod.

'My son came home yesterday as well,' Glenn Rundberg says. 'He spends most of his time in a care home. He suffers from brittle bones, and has learning difficulties, so yesterday evening was fairly hectic. It's funny, really. Twenty years ago he wouldn't have survived, but now he can. Natural selection no longer works naturally.'

Just as Malin is about to comment on Glenn Rundberg's remark, there's a howl outside the window.

A Gripen screams past five hundred metres up in the air, just below the clouds, defying the rain.

'Thailand are after those,' Rundberg chuckles. 'They want Sweden to commit to buying a thousand tons of chicken a year for three decades. Pork too.'

'What about the girl, do you have any idea where she could be?' Malin asks, thinking of the bombs that the planes could drop in Thailand's service. Laos, perhaps, or Cambodia.

'No, I'm afraid not. Patrick was sociable enough, but at the same time he was cagey about his private life. He cared

Mons Kallentoft

more about Ella than anything else in the world, that much
I do know.'

The plane roars past again in the other direction.

'Beautiful, isn't it?'

Malin can't stop thinking about bombs tearing children
to pieces.

A thousand children's limbs in exchange for a flourishing
city.

Just don't say so out loud,
shhh, shhh,
we don't talk about that sort of thing here.
Who cares about
a few children,
as long as
we're
OK.

10

'What are you saying? It can't be true!'

Stina Veder, head of Johannelund School, hasn't heard the news until now.

'She was going to spend the day at home with Ella, so I called in a supply teacher. This can't be right.'

The woman sitting opposite Börje Svärd and Waldemar Ekenberg sinks into her worn green office chair. She shakes her head, making her chestnut-brown bob sway back and forth, its strands catching on the attractive features that still bear traces of a suntan.

The blinds are closed, but through the gaps they can see glimpses of a red brick wall.

Börje and Waldemar sit quietly.

Stina Veder leans across the laminated white desktop and gulps down a mug of water, her office suddenly transformed into a cramped cell.

Old, cheap wallpaper, with a random splatter pattern.

Not blood, Börje thinks, as he sees how shocked the woman opposite is, but in his mind's eye he sees the pictures of Ella Andergren in her pink bedroom.

'Their daughter is missing,' he says. 'We've checked with her relatives, preschool and friends, but no one seems to know where she could be. Do you have any ideas?'

Very young to be a head teacher, Waldemar thinks.

Quite attractive.

I could imagine rolling around in the hay with her.

'I've got no idea. I didn't really know Cecilia all that well.'

'You said just now that it couldn't be true that they've been murdered. I assumed that was because you knew them, and that the news surprised you because you knew them well,' Börje says.

Stina Veder lowers her eyes, then takes a deep breath before replying: 'I suppose it's just what you say when something like this happens.' Stina Veder pauses. 'What else is there to say?'

Börje Svärd knocks on a door. The third-floor school corridor smells of damp, mould and wet clothes.

'Talk to Katarina Karlsson, Cecilia's colleague in the language department. I know they were close. If anyone here knows anything, it would be her. She's got a class at the moment, but you can go ahead and interrupt.'

Stina Veder hadn't been able to tell them anything useful about the Andergrens' private life, nothing they didn't already know.

He scarcely feels the knock in his knuckles.

But it echoes down the long corridor.

A woman in her thirties opens the door.

Blonde, her face rather like Malin's, only rounder and with less regular features. If it weren't for the angry red birthmark on her forehead, Katarina Karlsson would have been extremely pretty.

She doesn't look surprised, Stina Veder must have called to say they were on their way, but she probably didn't say why, because Katarina has a look of innocent inquiry on her face.

She steps out into the corridor and closes the door without saying anything to her pupils, and without letting Börje or Waldemar get a glimpse of the classroom.

'You wanted to see me.'

She's wearing a white dress, a knitted cardigan, and pale blue wooden-soled shoes with white roses painted on them.

'Do you know why?'

Katarina Karlsson shakes her head.

'Let's sit down,' Waldemar says, and the three of them go and sit on a wooden bench by one of the windows, and the shadow cast by the window frame forms a cross on the white wall opposite.

'Is it Mum?'

'Mum?'

'Yes, she's been ill, I thought maybe something's happened to her?'

'No,' Börje says. 'It's about your colleague, your friend, Cecilia Andergren. She and her husband Patrick were found murdered in their home this morning. We haven't been able to locate their daughter.'

At first Katarina Karlsson seems calm.

Then she starts to breathe heavily.

She rubs her hands on her thighs, making the cheap fabric of her dress rustle.

'It can't be true,' she says. 'There must be some mistake.'

Then she stands up.

Shouts: 'You're lying! This is some sort of sick joke. I babysit for them, you're lying, you bastards. WHY WOULD THEY . . .?'

Behind her the door to the classroom opens and half a dozen spotty pupils in jeans and T-shirts peer out.

'GO BACK IN!' Börje yells, and hears the force in his own voice, the authority, like when he's trying to get his Alsatians to obey him.

And the youngsters stop instantly and then retreat, closing the door hard behind them, but the noise fails to drown out Katarina Karlsson's anguished cries: 'IT CAN'T BE TRUE. IT CAN'T BE TRUE!'

Karin Johannison is moving slowly and methodically through the kitchen of the Andergren family's home in Hjulsbro.

Her tiredness from this morning has vanished.

She's thinking about Tess.

About the oppressive silence of the house.

No signs of struggle.

Of a break-in.

Yet still a sense that there could be hidden traps anywhere.

That there are emotional bombs hiding in the corners.

She has found a hard-drive tucked away in a hidden compartment of a bureau in the office downstairs. And that discovery has only exacerbated the feeling that this home isn't the idyll it appears to be on the surface.

That there are secrets here.

In that sense, every crime scene resembles life itself. Things don't quite make sense, it isn't possible to put all the pieces together to form a perfect whole, a single truth. There are always secrets.

She thinks about Zeke.

The way he looked at her this morning.

How angry she had been when he turned out to be incapable of leaving his wife.

How she put herself back together by throwing herself into the adoption, and since then she's barely thought about men at all.

The way she and her ex-husband tried, the way it was impossible to say what was wrong, no matter how they tried.

The pain.

A child. Who needs me. No need for it to be my own biological child.

It would be nice to have someone to share Tess with.

Zeke.

Is there anything to forgive him for? It took years for me to break free from my former husband. That sort of thing takes time.

But would I want Zeke now, if he were to change his mind? Would he want me, the way I really am?

She shakes free of that train of thought.

Thinks about the river instead.

The diver working his way along the bottom.

A lifeless body drifting in the water.

She prays that Ella is still alive, that the dog units will find her alive.

It takes ten minutes for Katarina Karlsson to calm down, to accept the fact that her friend is dead.

She doesn't understand it, and as she sits there on the bench between the two policemen she realises that she may never understand it.

They have a tough job, she thinks.

'Like I said, I babysit for them. But I've never picked Ella up from preschool. I've no idea where she might be.'

The policemen's questions are hazy. Who asks what? The friendly one? The heavy smoker?

'No, I don't know where she could be.'

'Her older sister? I don't think they were that fond of each other. They didn't have much contact.'

Here I sit, Katarina Karlsson thinks, touching my birthmark, the way I always do when I'm nervous. Here I sit, but my voice sounds like it's coming from some distant planet. Am I the one saying these words? What would Cilla have wanted me to tell them?

But Ella's missing.

So I have to tell them everything.

And there on the bench outside her beloved classroom Katarina Karlsson realises that she doesn't know a great deal about the woman who may well have been her best friend.

Favourite ice cream: vanilla and violet.

Perfume: Dior.

Clothes: H&M and Marco Polo.

They first met at high school, and stayed in touch when Cilla and Patrick were abroad, but Katarina had never visited them.

Too expensive to travel so far on a teacher's salary. She had done her best to support Cecilia throughout all the years when they tried to have a child, but there always seemed to be part of Cecilia that was out of reach.

She used to argue with her sister, Katarina knew that, but what about?

'No idea. I didn't ask, because Cecilia wasn't the sort of person you could ask things like that. I just used to wait for her to tell me whenever she was ready.'

I like that sort of person, Katarina Karlsson thinks, aware of the solid bulk of the friendly policeman beside her.

'And that was fine my me,' she hears her voice say. 'It suited me, because I don't really like people getting too close either.'

'If they had any enemies? No, they were perfectly ordinary people.'

'No, I haven't noticed anything unusual recently.'

'What I was doing? Yesterday evening?'

'I was at home, I had dinner with Mum. We shared a bottle of wine, so she stayed over. I can give you her number, so you can check.'

'I said goodbye to Cilla at five o'clock yesterday, outside

their house. We'd been for coffee in the city, her, me and Ella, and went back to theirs. I live in Björsäter, so I caught the bus from Brokindsleden.'

How did you die, Cilla? They won't say.

And where's Ella? Such a sweet child. Where is she? Ella.

It was as if you were finally complete, Cilla, when you managed to get hold of her.

You should adopt as well, before it's too late, you said, and I laughed to myself at the time, about how little you actually knew about me. Unless you just didn't want to see more.

Maybe you thought this birthmark is why I never really found anyone.

There are people who like that sort of thing, I can assure you of that.

Dior.

The Sound of Music.

What's Winnerbäck's best song?

'Broken Ground'.

Cilla.

How am I going to cope, Cilla? Now that we haven't got each other to be superficial and mutely complicit with?

How am I going to manage when the police have gone?

When there's no warm body any more?

When you're not here to not see me? Or will it all be easier now?

Katarina.

Katty.

You'll be fine. Maybe it's time for you to break free now?

Forget about that birthmark. There must be a man somewhere who can see past it. Who wants you, who'd like to have children with you.

You think I never really saw you, but that isn't true. Or is it?

Tell them everything.

You're allowed to. Unless you can't actually tell them everything?

Ella.

They have to find her.

And I know you like Ella, so if she ever comes back, you can take care of her.

Will you promise me that, Katarina?

You have to promise.

Because otherwise this will be unbearable, I can't stand the thought of it, and I'm screaming now:

ELLA ELLA ELLA

Did everything go wrong in the end?

We're confused, Katty.

ELLA!

Are you in the black water, somewhere in front of the diver's blind eyes and cold fingers?

Or are you somewhere in the forest?

11

When they leave the school Waldemar Ekenberg asks Börje to drop him off by a patch of woodland next to Hjulsbro before he drives back to the station.

Waldemar wants to join one of the dog patrols. He can't bear sitting in the office doing paperwork when there's real work to be done.

He makes his way through the woods. Sucking on his electronic cigarette, hating the feel of the plastic on his lips, but he needs the nicotine, has to stop smoking, because the cough that comes with it is killing him.

The patch of woodland is a few hundred metres from Stentorpsvägen. Pines and firs filter the rain as it falls gently onto the leaf-covered ground. The last scents of summer are merging with the riper smells of autumn, by turns sweet and tart.

Waldemar can hear the dogs barking through the trees now, maybe two hundred metres away, and he feels his brown loafers getting wet.

He'll never manage to kick his nicotine habit, but he's relieved that he fell for this relatively benign drug rather than alcohol, the way Malin did.

He's been careful to keep a check on his violent instincts since a case where he was reported for abusing a doctor who was one of their suspects.

The bastard deserved it.

His shoes are squelching as he looks around among the

tall pines, searching for something the dogs might have missed.

Poor little girl.

What are the chances that she's still alive?

This whole business stinks.

Adoption.

What's the good of that, really? Isn't it better to admit your natural limitations and accept that having children isn't a right? That not everyone is supposed to have children?

He and his other half gave up after ten years of trying, and he knows that Malin is trying to have a kid with that doctor she's together with, he heard Zeke and Sven talking about it when they didn't think anyone was listening.

Fuck.

How many adopted children end up happy?

Is an adoptive parent's love worth as much as a real parent's, regardless of the circumstances? Isn't even a children's home in their native country, in their own culture, worth more than a home with a family that can never be their own, in a culture where they're doomed to be strangers?

Bloody hell.

They're always committing suicide, adopted kids, once they've grown up.

Or they go back and track down their biological parents, who don't want anything to do with them, and then come home even more confused.

No, people adopt kids for their own sake, not for the child's.

Waldemar goes deeper into the forest.

He knows he's out on a limb as far as his views on adoption are concerned, but he's also aware that there are others who share his opinion, and that his attitude is coloured by his and his wife's decision not to adopt.

I'm tainted by my longing and sense of loss, he thinks.
Don't go there, Waldemar, he whispers to himself.
Concentrate on the woods, on finding the girl.
Is there something lying under that fir tree over there?
Waldemar walks towards it, but as he gets closer he
realises that what he thought was a jacket is just a yellow
plastic bag.
And just look at the queers.
They can do whatever they damn well like these days.
As if all of creation and the whole fucking family tradition
is some sort of joke, an experiment.
He felt sick when he heard about a surrogate mother
who gave birth to half-twins for a pair of poofs. The two
queers had each fertilised an egg from the same anonymous
egg donor, and then the eggs were implanted into the
surrogate mother.
Nine months later she gave birth to two boys. The two
queers each got a kid, with the same, unknown biological
mother, born out of the same fake womb.
Karim told him about it over lunch one day. Fortunately
Karim thought the whole thing was sick as well.
He's almost caught up with the dogs now.
Waldemar feels his pistol nudging his chest beneath his
jacket.
'Have you found anything?' he calls through the trees.
'I thought you ladies could probably do with some help.'

It's half past two when Malin and Zeke sit down in their
favourite pizza parlour on Tanneforsvägen. A steady stream
of cars is driving past outside the window, and the pale
grey cladding of the building opposite looks about ready
to give up, the corners of the panels are jutting out and
Malin wonders how they're managing to stay up.
Conya.

The Lebanese owner keeps insisting on letting them eat for free, has done ever since he found out they were police officers, when he saw Malin in the paper.

He seems to enjoy showing his admiration through generosity, as if he owned a restaurant in some Hollywood film. And they let him do it.

Why not? It could hardly be called bribery.

A police salary – even a detective inspector's – doesn't go far in today's absurdly expensive Sweden.

'It's a good sign that we haven't heard anything from the diving team,' Malin says.

Conya's been redecorated, forest-green woven wallpaper, and the pizza oven looks shiny and new. Success is still possible, for those prepared to work hard enough.

Malin takes a sip of water, pretending it's vodka, and for a fraction of a second it works, then it backfires and she feels a longing for alcohol so strong it almost knocks her out, while simultaneously leaving her feeling horribly restless. The bitter but wonderful smell of pure spirits bubbles inside her, and she finds herself wondering: Is life worth living without alcohol? Anyway, why should I have to? Just a sip, one drunken night, one little cotton-wool fog couldn't do that much harm, could it?

Then her phone rings.

Tove's name on the screen.

You?

What do you want?

And Malin feels ashamed of her reaction, can't talk to Tove just now, with her head full of thoughts about drink, no, she just can't, and suddenly she feels that she's starting to get a grip on the day, so she instinctively clicks to reject the call, regrets it at once and thinks about calling back, then takes a bite of the pizza that has just appeared in front of her.

What was it Britt Sivsjö had said, about her daughters' relationship? About how Cecilia Andergren and her sister Petronella hadn't got on?

They never got on. Not even when they were little.

That was it, wasn't it?

'So who don't you want to talk to, then?' Zeke asks.

'The dentist,' Malin says.

'The dentist?'

'He wants me to book a check-up, but I have neither the time nor the money for that right now.'

Zeke mutters something about his next dentist's appointment through a mouthful of marinara, and Malin stares at her mobile, willing Peter's name to appear on the screen.

But he clearly hasn't got the energy to phone.

He's been on call a lot lately. More than usual.

And she finds herself thinking about him, his body, the way he fills her, the way she scratches his back, and then the longing for vodka is back again, along with thoughts of Tove.

Stop it now, Malin, she tells herself.

Peter and I can call each other this evening.

We will.

Karim Akbar is standing on the podium in the courtroom they use for press conferences when there's a lot of interest.

He adjusts his grey Kiton suit.

Cameras are flashing and whirring, and the fifty or so reporters sitting in front of him have switched on their tape recorders, and several of them are holding microphones towards him, and he studies them carefully before he begins.

He tells them what they know so far, about the murders of Patrick and Cecilia Andergren, and the fact that their daughter Ella is missing, and he holds up a photograph of the girl and says: 'We'd be very grateful for any information from the public in this matter.'

He does everything that's expected of him.

He feels like a dragonfly on a smooth expanse of water, an elegant creature moving this way and that, remaining untouched by everything.

They ask questions.

'Do you have any theories?'

'Do you have a suspect?'

'What was the motive?'

And to each question he responds: 'For reasons relating to the investigation, I can't say any more than I already have.'

He concludes the session, but one of the regulars, a reporter from one of the national tabloids, *Aftonbladet*, throws one last question at him: 'Karim! Where do you get your suits?'

Scattered laughter.

Karim smiles and fills his lungs with air.

Breathes out, says: 'At H&M, of course. Can't you tell?'

12

Malin is in the kitchen of her flat.

According to the Ikea clock on the wall, it's half past seven. Peter dismantled it one evening and removed the broken second-hand, and now whenever Malin looks at it, it feels as if time is out of joint.

The new, shiny, chrome microwave is whirring.

She can see her face in the window of the oven, and doesn't like how tired she looks.

She stares into the oven instead.

A meat pie.

Tepid tap water to go with it.

She's just tried to call Tove, but got no answer and left a message.

'Couldn't take your call earlier today. Call me back when you can. It would be good to catch up. Otherwise, see you on Friday.'

Peter hasn't called either.

He's probably busy with his laser scalpel. Some motorbike accident. A car crash. A scheduled operation that got postponed. A few months ago he was given three new interns to supervise, two lads from Canada, and a young woman from Texas, and she knows he wants to devote time to them, because if they get taken care of well here then interns that the University Hospital sends over there will get better treatment.

And in the long term, that should lead to improvements in healthcare.

Win, win.

She sits down on the sofa in the living room and looks at the pie on the plate in front of her before sticking her fork in the soggy pastry.

She turns the television on.

The news is just starting, and she wonders if there's going to be anything about their case, about Ella.

She checked the *Correspondent*'s website a short while ago, and they were leading with the news, and had put up a picture of Karim from the press conference.

The TV news has the case as its second story. A picture of Ella, 'police grateful for any information', and the dedicated tip-off phone number.

The pie is like rubber in her mouth, the mince filling watery, and Malin tries not to think about what it reminds her of.

The dog units and divers have failed to find anything throughout the course of the day and early evening. After their pizza lunch, she and Zeke drove back to the station to write up their reports, then went out to Hjulsbro again to question the neighbour, Thea Victorin, more thoroughly, but didn't find out anything new.

Malin leans back in the sofa, every muscle throbbing with exhaustion, and she wants to sleep, to take the opportunity now that her head feels empty, but she has a sense that there's a long way to go before she'll be able to get any rest this evening.

Karin Johannison is standing motionless in the autopsy lab.

The fluorescent lights cast a metallic glow across the white tiled walls, making the stainless steel worktops and cupboards shine even more brightly, and Karin can smell the aluminium that somehow manages to suppress the smell of chemicals and decay.

She has covered up Patrick and Cecilia Andergren's bodies again.

No need to look at them any further, knows what she needs to know for the time being.

What a day.

Clumsy uniforms trampling through her crime scene, the hidden hard-drive that she managed to find, Johan Jakobsson was keen to get his hands on it, even though it should have gone to her technicians, but she let him have his way, knows how talented he is.

The terrible business of removing the bodies from the jacuzzi, the missing little girl.

Ella Andergren.

Adopted, just like Tess.

Tess is with the babysitter this evening, and Karin hated herself when she called Rebecka and asked her to pick Ella up from preschool.

She was even more ashamed of the relief she felt when Rebecka was able to help at short notice.

'I've got to work late. I know it's really last-minute, but could you pick Tess up?'

Karin turns her back on the naked bodies with their bullet wounds under the white sheets, and tries to conjure up Tess's plump little body against hers, and feel the blood pulsing calmly beneath the child's skin.

It's five past eight.

She finds herself thinking about Malin.

I'm not doing what you always do, am I? Karin thinks.

I know how bad you feel about all those times you neglected Tove over the years, always putting her second as you took refuge in work or drink.

And I can see how sad it's made you.

Mons Kallentoft

Because you know it's too late. Tove's drifting inexorably away from you now, we talked about it once, and you did your best not to sound bitter, but your blue-green eyes told a different story. And now you're trying for another child, aren't you, with Peter?

Is that what you really want?

But I can't, I'm not going to think of you in that way, Malin. When the others were sniggering about me adopting, I know you took my side in the station, saying there was too little love in the world, and that there were bound to be children who would gladly receive the love Karin Johannison has to give.

But I still don't want to make the same mistakes as you. I'm going to be there for Tess.

No matter what happens. No matter what has happened. I'm never going to let her down.

Karin gets her mobile out. Looks up Malin's number.

Tove, it must be Tove. God, how I want it to be you.

God, I wish I could find a way to turn the clock back.

The phone's in the kitchen.

I must have dozed off on the sofa.

Malin stands up quickly and feels the blood drain from her head, and for a moment she thinks she's going to fall, but manages to get to the kitchen and clicks to take the call.

Karin's voice.

Malin listens to what she has to say.

'OK, I'm on my way.'

Tess must be with the childminder Karin usually uses when she has to work late.

Decent work for the girl, Malin thinks as she heads down the stairs of her building on Ågatan.

Karin didn't want to say why she wanted Malin to go over to the autopsy lab.

But there's a reason, there always is when Karin phones. Ella, Tess.

Johan's been able to confirm that Ella was adopted from Vietnam.

Nothing odd about that. Then it strikes Malin that Karin may have known the Andergrens through some group for adoptive parents. But Karin's never mentioned anything like that, and she's not really the sort to join associations and groups.

Malin pushes the front door open.

Outside.

No longer raining.

The council has installed lamps on St Lars Church to light up the tower from below, making it look like a rocket ready for take-off.

The noise from the Pull & Bear pub on the ground floor.

Peter hasn't called.

But what would I say to him?

What would we say to each other?

He doesn't want to hear about what's been going on today, I don't want to hear about his operations. I don't feel like talking about anything that might lead us into a conversation about the subject that there's no point talking about.

But it can't be pointless to talk about our shared future?

Malin gets the impression she can hear the beer taps hissing.

Feels like opening her mouth beneath one of them.

And just drinking, drinking, drinking.

Karin Johannison is sitting slumped on a chair in the dungeon-like corridor that leads away from the autopsy lab.

Industrial lamps hang on cables from the ceiling, the numerous ventilation pipes are rattling, and the floor is bare concrete, a remnant of the time when the building was part of the military barracks.

The autopsy lab used to be a weapon and munitions store.

When she sees Malin approaching she stands up. Her green lab coat is flecked with blood.

'Sorry to drag you here at this time of day. But I didn't want to wait.'

'It's no problem, you know that,' Malin says.

Just seconds later they are standing in front of the bodies of Cecilia and Patrick Andergren, the sheets pulled back, and Malin can see how carefully Karin has cleaned the wounds and sewn up the incisions she has made in their bodies.

Their skin.

A greyish white tone, unlike any other.

'What have you found?' Malin asks, forcing aside the images, the voices.

Karin takes a deep breath.

Seems to want to stroke the bodies, as if to calm them, and Malin feels how tangible death is in this room, as if it were actually there in person, proudly intent on showing its power. As if all the air in the room had been sucked out, and she and Karin enveloped in a deathly veil that wanted to make them its own.

'Look at this,' Karin says, holding up one of Cecilia Andergren's wrists.

'OK,' Malin replies.

Karin holds up Patrick's hands and lower arms.

'And here. Exactly the same.'

'How do you mean? I can't see anything.'

'That's precisely what I mean. Nothing. I think they knew

who the killer was, and that they underestimated the danger. Otherwise one of them would have gunshot wounds to their hands or lower arm, defensive injuries from when whichever of them was shot last tried to defend themselves.'

'Would they have had time for that?'

'They were shot from the front, so they must have seen whoever killed them.'

'It couldn't have been dark in the room?'

'Not that dark.'

'So you're saying they might have been talking to the person, unaware that it was serious, not expecting to be killed, and that's why they were so relaxed when the killer was standing in front of them?'

'Something like that. They were both shot cleanly through the heart, so it's possible the killer was able to stand in front of them for a while, take aim, and then fire a shot at their hearts, then more bullets into each of them.'

'But surely they'd have been frightened?' Malin says.

'I daresay they were, probably very frightened, but it's still possible that they knew their killer.'

'So, no defensive wounds.'

'I'm only speculating here,' Karin says. 'They may have raised their arms in self-defence, and the bullets went past them. Our instinct is to protect our faces, after all.'

Did they or didn't they know their killer, that's the big question, Malin thinks.

'Pistol?' she asks.

'Yes, the bullets are from a nine-millimetre pistol. A fairly common calibre.'

'Any other evidence?'

'No. Nothing definite. There were some fingerprints from the house that we're checking against the database, but they weren't in the places where you'd expect the killer's prints to have been.'

Mons Kallentoft

'No cartridge shells?'

'No. The killer must have taken them.'

'Cold and calculated, then.'

Karin looks at Malin, puts her hand on Cecilia Andergren's forehead, then whispers: 'She must have had time to feel frightened. They must have been frightened, for their little girl.'

What do you know about our fear?

About real fear?

We were murdered.

By whom?

That's your mystery, and only you can solve it.

Ella. Wherever you are, you shouldn't be there, you're not ready for it.

But is anyone ever ready?

Time goes both quickly and slowly here.

Everything hurts more, everything's worse, and the jacuzzi in the house where we were a family is empty now, the traces of our blood staining the white plastic brownish red.

But the house isn't entirely silent, something is moving through the rooms, and you're getting closer now.

You've decided to come out to the house once more, together, to see how it feels, to let your intuition roam free, but take care, take care.

Murdered.

We don't want to believe it.

Don't want to.

But that's what happened.

We did what we did.

A door opened into our house.

And death walked in.

13

Malin and Karin park outside the house on Stentorpsvägen.

In the evening darkness, the trees in the garden become black dolls with spiky heads, and the surrounding houses are silent and dark, as if everyone had abandoned this place where evil had so unexpectedly made an appearance.

The door-to-door inquiries out here earlier.

The biggest story ever to happen in this community.

Have you heard about the Andergrens?

No one knows where the little girl is.

They were murdered.

Are there ghosts here? What's that noise in the garden?

We did lock all the doors, didn't we?

On our gilded street in the smart part of town. Among people like us.

Impossible, not here, not murdered, not so close by.

The girl.

She must be dead, it's probably only a matter of time before the police find her murdered as well.

Malin can smell the damp tarmac and vegetation getting ready to die as she follows Karin up the steps. They duck under the blue-and-white cordon, Karin turns the key in the lock and they're in.

Silence.

As if death had taken all sound with it, but the white kitchen is shimmering even in the darkness, strange spirits seem to hover above the sofa in the living room, and Malin notices the pictures on the walls for the first time, prints from Ikea, nice but cheap, as if the Andergrens had good taste but didn't want to spend any more than necessary on art.

But you must have had money, though.

Engineers working abroad earn good money.

And it costs to adopt.

No doubt we'll soon know, Johan's probably already dug out all the details of your finances. As murder victims, your lives will be examined from every angle, every corner investigated. Karin has gone off to the kitchen, and Malin switches on a lamp on a sturdy birch-wood sideboard, and sees specks of dust swirl through the air like tiny, lost, anxious angels.

The stairs down to the basement.

Quiet.

I heard something.

And Malin gestures for Karin to be quiet as she comes back into the living room.

Footsteps?

Malin points downwards.

Signals to Karin to stop, and Karin stands still, waiting for Malin to do something.

Another tapping sound.

Human?

Karin's pupils are big and black, and she's almost shaking with fear.

Someone's moving.

Aren't they?

Murderers occasionally return to the scene of their crimes.

Some of the very sickest of souls like watching as the police arrive on the scene.

Malin pushes her jacket aside.

Draws her pistol and starts to go down the stairs, carefully so as not to make a sound, one, two, three steps, and she's soon down and stops to listen, hears sounds from a room on the far side of the pool, a room that must lie next to the garage.

She creeps cautiously through the basement.

Towards the door to the room.

She puts her ear to it as she breathes in the smell of damp and chlorine, the smell of a luxurious Swedish basement.

There's definitely someone in there.

Malin throws the door open, stands with her legs apart and aims the pistol straight in front of her, right at the figure that is crouched over a desk: 'Keep still, or I'll fire!'

But the figure doesn't keep still.

Instead, he slowly stands up.

Reaching for something on the desk.

He turns around, holding a black object in his hand, raises it, what's he got in his hand?

A pistol?

His face is bearded. Is he raising a pistol towards me? Should I fire first?

Yes.

No.

And then the man lets go of the object in his hand. It falls to the floor with a dull thud and Malin stares at the man and has a vague idea of who he is.

I didn't fire.

Good.

Thank God.

'What on earth are you doing here?'

And he turns around again, about to jump out of the window, then gives up.

He raises his hands in the air.

Says, with the slurred, sleepy voice of a drug addict: 'OK, OK. Take it easy. I surrender.'

Ten minutes later Malin is in her car, turning to face the man in the back seat.

The car smells of sweat and ingrained dirt, and Nisse Persson looks like he hasn't slept in a proper bed for weeks. His face is emaciated and filthy, his hair and beard matted.

She knows very well who he is.

One of the city's harmless junkies, harmless in so far as he's never done anything worse that burglary and theft, nothing involving violence.

Nisse Persson has a well-documented ability to be in the wrong place at the wrong time. On one occasion he ended up calling the police himself when two of his friends managed to cut each other's stomachs open when a drunken brawl got out of hand. He had gone to see them to blag some vodka, and found himself caught up in a double murder.

And now this.

Caught breaking into a house where two people have just been found murdered.

Handcuffs on his wrists, a foggy, shamed look in his eyes.

'Nisse,' Malin says. 'What the hell were you doing in there? And don't mess me about. This house is a crime scene, and if you lie you could end up in big trouble, we're talking seriously heavy shit here, OK? What the hell were you going to do with a stapler? Hit me with it? I could have shot you!'

Dark, anxious eyes now.

A look that says: I've blundered right into the middle of a leaky sewer.

'Well?'

Nisse Persson stammers: 'I heard on the radio about

what had happened. And worked out that there'd be no one home. I've done break-ins around here before, and there's always stuff in the basements.'

Junkie logic.

Good, but back to front.

Malin knows Nisse Persson is telling the truth.

'So what were you doing last night?'

'I was around Bumba and Anki's. They can tell you. Anki's on Antabuse, so she was sober.'

'We'll check that out. But I'm taking you in tonight. Don't you get it? A little girl's missing. She's five years old. We can't have people breaking into the crime scene. For fuck's sake, Nisse!'

Malin can feel her anger growing, and directs it at the wreck of a human being in the back seat.

'She could have been murdered! And you blundered in here to get money for a fix. And scare the living daylights out of us. Christ, I could have killed you.'

'Sorry.'

'What?'

'Sorry.'

Malin shakes her head, trying to ignore the sour stench coming from Nisse Persson.

'I'm going back in now. And you're going to sit here nice and quiet, OK? Otherwise they'll find you in the river tomorrow. And no throwing up. If you want to piss or take a crap, you hold it in. Understood?'

Karin.

In the kitchen.

On a chair.

When Malin came up from the basement, dragging Nisse Persson behind her, Karin was standing in the middle of the kitchen floor with a large knife in her hand.

An open drawer.

Terror in her eyes.

Not worried for her own sake, but for the responsibility that her life carries now.

Tess.

No one touches me, or her.

Malin told Karin to put the knife down, that there was nothing to worry about.

Now she sits down beside her. Rubs her eyes.

'He's sitting in the car. He won't be going anywhere.'

Karin nods.

What are we actually doing here? Malin thinks.

You should be at home with Tess, and you know it.

Don't make the same mistakes with her that I did with Tove.

Karin gets to her feet.

'Let's give up on this now,' Malin says.

'Ella,' Karin says. 'Who knows what she's been through. Both from this, and back in Vietnam.'

'We'll find her.'

'You've got no idea what I saw over there when I went to fetch Tess.'

Karin falls silent for a few moments before going on: 'I saw things I'd give anything to forget.'

14

Wednesday, 11 and Thursday, 12 September

Tess.

I'm coming.

You're probably asleep.

You must never let anything bad happen to you, promise Mummy that.

The car is a cocoon.

They've handed Nisse Persson over to the custody unit, and Malin is driving.

Soon Karin is standing in the hall of her flat on Drottninggatan. It's half past ten now, and her body is bubbling with longing as she gives Rebecka five hundred kronor.

'She's sleeping in your bed. That's where she wanted to go.'

'That's fine.'

'I didn't think you'd mind.'

Rebecka pulls on her jacket and says goodnight.

Karin goes into her bedroom.

Tess's straight, jet-black hair is draped across the chalk-white pillowcase.

Karin sits down on the edge of the bed. Pulls the covers down slightly. Sees one side of her daughter's face, her eyebrow, her eyelid, and her long eyelashes.

She strokes her cheek.

'Mummy's here now,' Karin whispers. 'I'm here now.'

Ella.

Where are you?

The question rolls through Malin like a wave as she lies in her bed trying to get to sleep.

She finds herself tumbling around in the question, as if she were caught by the pull of the wave. It tugs at her, the wave, caressing her but simultaneously holding her just above the surface of sleep.

Your parents have been murdered. With an almost unbearable sense of purpose.

Perhaps you have to be insanely purposeful to kill another human being? Have to want something really badly.

I've killed someone, Malin thinks.

In the course of duty.

Once, to save my own daughter.

It didn't take much reflection. When it happened, it was as natural as breathing, as blinking.

Peter.

The bed is wide and empty. The fact that it is full of our love has to be enough. Our love is big enough without a child.

He hasn't called.

He usually does.

But now it's too late.

Now she just wants to sleep.

And get some rest in advance of the huge wave that she and the rest of the investigating team will find themselves swallowed up by tomorrow.

Sven Sjöman is standing by the worktop in his kitchen, drinking a cup of tea. Every now and then he takes an absentminded bite of a crispbread sandwich containing some very mature cheese.

His wife is asleep upstairs as the night envelops him, and he's enjoying the silence of the moment.

Their love has blossomed once again. Not physically, but the more important sort, the love of friendship, the love you need for a lifelong marriage to count as happy.

It's as if they were both brought up short when he was diagnosed with prostate cancer.

As if they both stopped and took a good look at their lives, without any big fuss, and suddenly found themselves incredibly grateful for what they've got.

They've got each other.

The simple but good life they share.

The children, the grandchildren, whom they see just often enough.

The house they both enjoy living in, the chance to go away on holiday.

They're both due to retire in a couple of years. Because Sven has made a decision: he's going to keep working as long as Ulla does. Doesn't want to end up as a nagging shadow who gets wound up over nothing while Ulla's at work.

He takes a bite of the sandwich.

The little girl is missing.

And he can feel a lifetime of police work weighing him down.

Optimism, despair. We can do this, but we have to work fast. Otherwise the killer might escape. And how could we live with that? How could the street, the district, the city, the province, the country, the whole world live with that?

We have to find the girl. And the killer, or killers.

That's our duty.

And tomorrow we're getting a new detective. Former

professional volleyball-player, Elin Sand. That's good, the investigating team could do with a bit of a shake-up.

Sven puts the last piece of sandwich in his mouth, feels the bread crunch between his teeth as the salt in the cheese stings his gums, and his thoughts go to Malin, and he wonders if she's asleep.

He's not happy with the way she's seemed in recent months.

She's looked hunted, tormented, almost distant.

Something's going on, Malin. Hold on. You have to hold on, Malin.

We can't manage without you in the group.

I certainly can't.

Johan Jakobsson is lying in bed beside his wife in their terraced house in Linghem. She is sleeping on her back and snoring loudly, but it doesn't bother him.

He knows he'll soon be asleep as well.

And even though he doesn't want to, he finds himself thinking about the missing girl.

About her murdered parents, and himself and his own children, and can't help feeling that this is all too close, it's always too close somehow, which is why he prefers to focus on gathering information.

He loves looking for things with his computer, finding ways in and digging around.

Nothing is ever properly real on the computer.

There's a distance between him and all the evil he's supposed to be trying to understand. All the truths that must be revealed, truths most people would rather not know about.

What's he actually managed to find out about the couple? They had money. Millions of kronor in investment funds and savings accounts, well off but far from extravagantly rich. He'll have to investigate further. There are plenty of loose ends to pull at, they'll have to run through them during the case meeting tomorrow.

He hasn't managed to get into the hidden hard-drive yet, and he's only taken a brief look at the computer, which turned out to contain a copy of the files on Patrick Andergren's work computer, full of documentation of recent business deals. But nothing that was of any real use for the investigation. Just a few family photographs, pictures of Ella in the children's home when they went to collect her, a few kids' films, games. Nothing else. No other documents. Cecilia Andergren used to use the school's network, and he's been given access to that.

His daughter is asleep on the floor below. Nine years old now.

Ella Andergren is only five.

You were innocent and naïve when you were that age. Unguarded and beautiful.

That's what you were like, my daughter, when you were five. You're still beautiful, but you're already a bit harder.

You've definitely got a will of your own now.

Skin against skin, sweat against sweat.

Karim Akbar feels prosecutor Vivianne Södergran's mouth envelop his penis, sucking hard at it as she moves her mouth up and down, up and down.

She's got her period.

So he can't get at her.

Wants to, and can't help feeling like a horny teenager.

He's already close, far too soon, and he wants to hold back, delay the explosion, and tries to think about something else.

About how she's been resisting his nagging about them moving in together, and deflects the conversation to how the bedroom in his house in Lambohov could do with new wallpaper, and any manner of other things.

She's been encouraging him to make sure his book on immigrant issues is properly marketed, saying that it could really set him up as someone whose opinion actually matters.

Is that what I want?

Aren't we fine as we are? But cashmere suits from Kiton, his latest vice, are hellishly expensive.

I'm doing fine as I am, he thinks, and he can no longer hold his thoughts in check and lets go, giving in to the wonderful sucking sensation, and yells 'NOW, NOW, NOW!' before finally surrendering and ejaculating straight into Vivianne's mouth, and she swallows and swallows and swallows.

Plays with his sensitive cock.

She's making it tingle unpleasantly, but he doesn't say anything.

Sex, sex, sex.

That's all their relationship is built on, really. Because for you, Vivianne, when it comes down to it, everything is about sex, isn't it?

Börje Svärd is alone in his house. As he lies there awake, he hears his copy of the *Correspondent* being delivered.

The dogs out in their run don't bother to bark, they know the paper gets delivered this time every morning.

The house in Valla.

Too big, but he hasn't changed a single part of Anna's carefully thought-out furnishing. Everything is just as it was, like his memory of her, the way she managed to keep her mood up in spite of all the limitations of her illness, creating her own perfect design universe in their home.

Over the past year he has been out with seven different women.

He's got a taste for it now.

Continuity and love, in memory of Anna.

Sex, adventure, with those new bodies.

The feeling that they actually want him, a slightly over-weight, fifty-two-year-old detective inspector with chubby cheeks and an impressive moustache.

Zeke Martinsson gets into bed and shuffles about until he finds a comfortable position.

His bed is in what used to be his son Martin's room, on the first floor of the house.

Gunilla is reading a book, one of her awful Mills & Boons, in her bedroom, he can see the light from her bedside lamp under the door.

Bitch.

Miserable old bitch.

Over the past year he has started to think of her as a real cow, and he can see the derision in Martin's eyes when they meet up, he seems to wonder how they can put up with each other, with all those barbs, all that suspicion, the rows, the arguments.

'You're home late tonight.'

'It took longer than I expected.'

'Is that perfume I can smell?'

Gunilla has got into the habit of checking the call register on his mobile.

How did it come to this? They drifted apart gradually. Maybe it all started with Martin's ice hockey. She lost herself in the role of hockey mom, whereas he could barely bring himself to watch the stupid game at all. He turned away from her, and made his colleagues at the station into a relatively unproblematic extra family. Now Martin's grown up, himself a dad, his hockey career on the skids due to injury. But he still treats his son as if he were a big kid.

The terrible silences.

He can't be bothered to talk to her about anything. He finds himself getting annoyed if she so much as opens her mouth.

The change, the distance between them expanded gradually, until suddenly it was all over, adultery was a fact, and they should have just given up then, realised there was no point in going on.

But they weren't talking at the time.

They're not talking now.

She forgave him, and he withdrew into security, and a lack of feeling.

What are her interests, beyond the garden, Martin, and their grandchildren? Her endless pottering, keeping everything in its precise place. Where are her feelings? Where have they gone? I know mine have got to take refuge somewhere.

Now.

Soon.

Karin. She looks radiant these days.

The child.

Tess.

She hasn't got space for me, Zeke thinks. I had my chance. And I won't get another one.

But I could try.

I can't stay here.

Zeke closes his eyes, turns out the lamp, and lets the rain on the tiled roof lull him to sleep.

Waldemar Ekenberg is sitting in front of the television in the living room of his house in Mjölby, watching a programme where they go around renovating poor people's homes.

It's American.

Ridiculous.

Perfect for a sleepless night.

The television, flat-screen, massive.

He got it from a Serbian who wanted to be left alone.

Nothing wrong with that. Lots of people want to be left alone.

He lights a cigarette. Inhales deeply, the smoke filling his lungs.

His wife is at the hospital, she works nights, and at first he liked it, but now he has trouble sleeping when she isn't there.

He misses her.

A defined, easily understandable longing, but no less surprising to him for all that.

Really, missing your old woman's body after so many years together? Surely it would make more sense to enjoy a bit of space?

But no.

And his own longing helps him understand Malin Fors better.

She's missing something.

She always has. But unlike me, she doesn't know what, poor cow.

Malin Fors has fallen asleep, and she's dreaming.

She can hear her own voice in the darkness of the dream.

You mustn't die before me, Tove.

And her voice merges with others.

Peter's.

We have to have a child, Malin.

We have to.

Adopt.

I want a child of my own. Not someone else's.

My own child, one that looks like me, one that's the same colour as me.

A hail of gunshot shimmers in the darkness, approaching Malin, the projectiles twinkling like stars in a lifeless night sky, and she's tumbling around up there, but when she breathes her lungs fill with cold water, and I am you now, Ella, drifting along the riverbed, your skin white, your lips swollen and incapable of breathing.

It's warm in this dream.

The warmth of pine needles, or the shade of palm trees.

The jellyfishes' tentacles sting me. Grubs snap at me, frogs try to infect my skin with their poisonous slime.

Is death approaching in my dream? Malin wonders in her dream, and inside the dream a hundred freshwater eels are writhing in a barrel, changing into poisonous snakes and escaping into the world to hunt for children to devour.

Malin holds up her hand.

And then there is nothing but Tove's face in the dream.

But only for a brief, calming moment.

Then Peter's face.

And he's laughing at her.

A harsh, mocking laugh that says: Get lost, just take your infertile body away from here and get out.

And Malin Fors wants to wake up.

But she can't.

Because this dream still contains other dreams within it.

Rooms so dark that black becomes white.

Lonely rooms.

Rooms in which people begin to doubt that they're human.

'How am I ever going to wake up?' Malin whispers. 'How am I ever going to wake up?'

Rain is falling on the preschool playground, and the constantly shifting wind makes the drops look like they're crawling through the air.

As always, Malin takes a seat on the side of the conference table that lets her look out at the playground, she likes watching the children play in the garden or, as today, in the big rooms on the other side of the preschool windows.

The whiteboard is empty.

The new clock on the wall above it is ticking gradually towards eight o'clock. Soon the first proper meeting of this investigation will begin. The meeting in the Andergrens' home yesterday was more informal in character, but they have kept each other informed of developments since then by phone.

Johan Jakobsson is sitting opposite Malin. He's wearing a sea-blue polo-necked sweater that sits snugly around his neck.

Waldemar Ekenberg next to her reeks of tobacco smoke, and his white nylon shirt makes his pot-belly look more pronounced.

Börje Svärd.

Alert but not cheerful, more expectant, keen to solve the murders, to find Ella.

Dead or alive.

Zeke.

Boundless tiredness in his eyes, and Malin wonders what he's thinking, did he and Gunilla have a row yesterday?

Get a divorce, Malin thinks.

Or don't.

Every divorce is a failure, one of the worst things a person can experience.

But sometimes the only possible option.

Karim Akbar.

Exuding self-satisfaction, his grey woollen suit perfectly fitting his heavy frame and making him look powerful.

The children in the preschool are crawling through a bright green, oblong tunnel.

Peepo!

Malin's already read the *Correspondent*. They had Ella Andergren's passport photograph on the front page.

'Have you seen this girl?'

Vultures.

But perhaps they might get a few tip-offs?

Ella.

In the end, this is all about you.

Five past eight.

Sven Sjöman's late. Why?

Something was supposed to be happening today, but Malin can't remember what, then the battered white door swings open and Malin sees an almost two-metre-tall woman walk into the room.

That was it.

The new detective.

Wow.

What a giraffe.

I probably don't even reach her waist, Malin thinks, and Elin Sand – that was her name, wasn't it? – is dressed in dark jeans and a black Adidas hooded top, and as she moves towards the table her arms and legs are like boneless tentacles, and her rectangular face seems too big yet somehow perfect.

Eyes made up the colour of cask-aged tequila.

Her brown eyes are the size of the crown jewels, her glossy, ash-blonde hair is tied up in a bun, and her lips are full.

She looks like a cartoon character, Malin thinks, a manga character. As Elin Sand sits down on the only spare chair at the table, Malin can see the strength in her body, that she's still in good shape even though she had to abandon her volleyball career.

She smiles towards Malin, towards the others around the table, and Malin fires off her friendliest smile, but feels it stiffen.

Give her a chance, Malin thinks.

She's probably perfectly all right.

Not some dumb sports fanatic.

She's supposed to be some sort of hotshot, after all.

Sven comes in, and walks over to the whiteboard. He hoists up his green corduroy trousers, and his grey lambswool sweater covers his tatty old belt. Then he clears his throat and gestures towards the newcomer.

'OK, this is Elin Sand, the new addition to our team. Straight from Crime in Malmö. Elin, perhaps you could say a few words about yourself?'

Elin Sand nods.

'I'll keep it short,' she says, and her voice is deep, almost masculine, and for a moment Malin wonders if she's had a sex change, if that's Elin Sand's secret, but those big breasts hidden under that hoodie have to be real, don't they?

'We've got more important things to deal with than my life story,' she goes on, presumably hoping to raise a laugh, but no one laughs. Unless the comment was simply a justifiable statement of fact, and Malin instinctively finds herself appreciating Elin Sand's evident ability to unsettle those around her.

'I'm twenty-nine years old. Graduated from Police Academy four years ago. Like Sven said, my most recent post was with Crime in Malmö. Then I applied to move here and got the job. I'm looking forward to working with you.'

'Same here!' Waldemar agrees. 'We need more women here,' and Malin sees the look in Elin's eyes darken, and to dilute the insinuation in Waldemar's words, she says: 'Welcome,' and the others around the table join in.

Then silence settles on the room.

Everyone is looking at Sven, waiting for him to get going.

Malin looks over at the preschool again. One by one the children are leaving the playroom.

Then the room is empty.

The children gone.

As if swallowed up by another dimension.

'So, what do we know?'

Sven has written PATRICK and CECILIA on the white-board with a blood-red marker pen, and alongside, the name ELLA in blue.

He takes off his sweater and stands next to the white-board, feet wide apart, and in his green- and red-checked lumberjack shirt he exudes more authority than Malin has seen him do for a long time.

'We know that Patrick Andergren and his wife Cecilia were found murdered, shot with a nine-millimetre pistol in the jacuzzi in their home. We know that the murderer got in through the basement door, and that we're not dealing with a break-in. There are no signs of a struggle anywhere inside the house. We've got no tyre tracks, and no footprints in the house, and the fingerprints Karin managed to find don't match any in the database. Looks like they all belong to members of the family.

'Nor have we found any empty cartridges, the murderer must have taken them away. The house is full of fibres from clothes, but nothing that can definitely be used to plot the killer's movements.

'We know that they had a daughter, Ella Andergren, five years old. She disappeared at the time of the murders. All their passports are still in the house, which might be worth bearing in mind. But let's start with the parents.'

Sven pauses.

'According to Karin Johannison, they may have known the murderer,' he goes on. 'That's nothing remarkable, of course, but the absence of defensive injuries may be significant. Karin has confirmed that death occurred at around 10 p.m. on Tuesday evening. The family had money, so theft is a possible motive, but nothing of any value appears to be missing.'

Sven clears his throat.

Looks out of the window.

At the persistent rain.

Then he goes on: 'Questions we need to be asking: Which of their acquaintances could have wanted to do this? Why? Our brief interviews yesterday with people who knew them gave a picture of a happy family, hard-working people with no enemies. There's a hint of family conflict on Cecilia's side, and industrial bribery was mentioned during our conversation with Patrick Andergren's boss at Saab.

'We're probably not looking for a madman. It all seems very calculated.'

Malin sees Elin Sand bite her bottom lip, she seems to be concentrating hard.

'Who was the last person to see them alive, apart from

the murderer?' Sven says. 'It looks like the last person to see Cecilia was her friend and workmate Katarina Karlsson, and Patrick, his boss, Glenn Rundberg.

'We're building up a picture of their last twenty-four hours alive. They both went to work. A normal day.

'Unfortunately our door-to-door inquiries in the area haven't come up with anything.

'And of course the daughter, Ella Andergren, is missing. We can assume that her disappearance is connected to her parents' murders. Either she got scared and ran off, although no one appears to have seen her, as far as we know – or the murderer abducted her for some reason, but God knows why, or what he might have done with her. The dogs and divers are still searching.

'I don't need to say that time is against us here.'

Sven's last words blunt and crass.

'A paedophile,' Waldemar says. 'It could be some fucking paedophile who's been watching the girl, and killed her parents so he could get at her.'

Silence falls. The other detectives seem taken aback by Waldemar's outburst.

'Do you really believe that?' Malin says calmly. 'We know that's not how paedophiles operate, they use the Internet, and don't usually find their victims in ordinary middle-class families, if they're not going after their own children or those of close relatives. They usually find their victims among the very poorest communities, in the very poorest countries.'

Waldemar throws his hands out.

'I just wanted to start some sort of discussion.'

'If the girl got scared and ran off, we'll find her sooner or later,' Sven says. 'She might even pluck up the courage to go back home, or approach someone she knows. She's been missing for over twenty-four hours now, but there's still hope.

'She's been formally declared missing, so customs and passport control have got her picture. We haven't heard anything back from them yet, though.'

Sven is being very straightforward now, as if he were organising a village fete.

'We need to try to dig out more about the family,' he says. 'About this suggestion of conflict.'

'I find it odd that Petronella Andersson didn't seem upset,' Waldemar says. 'She was like a damn fridge.'

'They've got alibis,' Börje says. 'Two uniforms spoke to their teenage daughter yesterday, and found her extremely credible. Her mother was at home all evening, and her father was with his friend Kalle Lundbäck – he's confirmed that.'

Sven sighs.

'Malin, can you and Zeke take Elin with you, and go and talk to Cecilia's mother again? And that friend of hers, Katarina. Try to find out what the family conflict was about.'

Malin nods.

'No problem,' she says, and Elin Sand's face cracks into a smile, making her look human at last.

'Then there are the hints about industrial bribery. The fact that it was even mentioned means we have to take a closer look,' Sven says. 'Patrick Andergren worked at Saab, and had worked for Ericsson in Vietnam and India. Could there be something in that? Could he have had access to information that someone else wanted? Old business acquaintances who wanted to silence him and his family? We need to look into that. Johan, see what you can uncover with your computer, and Börje and Waldemar can try to dig up people to question.'

'Glenn Rundberg was fairly talkative yesterday,' Zeke says.

'We should probably count on them all clamming up,' Karim says. 'I know there have been previous investigations into bribery at both Saab and Ericsson. I'll get hold of the files.'

Sven goes on: 'We found a portable laptop, mobiles, and a hard-drive that had been hidden away. Obviously we'll be checking email, call registers, text messages, computing histories, the school intranet, and paying particular attention to that hidden hard-drive. Why was it hidden? We'll also have to go through their papers. Johan, you're in overall charge of the technical side of this. We need results quickly, you can bring in Forensics if need be.'

'I've already contacted them. I thought it would be reasonably simple to get into the hard-drive, but I haven't cracked it yet.'

Johan Jakobsson straightens up.

'What about their private papers?' he says. 'Who's going to go through all the files and bundles of documents?'

'We'll have to share that burden.'

What could those papers be hiding? Malin wonders. Probably nothing unusual: financial records, details that don't mean anything but which are among the most tangible remnants of our lives in the West.

'Our old friend Nisse Persson had nothing to do with the murders,' she says. 'No doubt at all about that. He's being held for the break-in, but he's got a convincing alibi for the evening of the murders. Both his junkie friends confirm that he was with them that night.'

'Well, we've got a few things to go on,' Sven says.

Malin closes her eyes.

She can't help feeling that they're missing something important, but is aware that she always feels this way at the start of a big investigation.

'Ella was adopted,' Johan says, and Malin's sense

that they're missing something vanishes. 'From Vietnam. I seem to remember that there have been problems with adoptions from there. Children adopted under murky circumstances.'

'It's worth looking into,' Sven says.

Karim Akbar taps his index finger on the table.

'The press are going to be screaming for details,' he says. 'What have we got to give them?'

'Not a damn thing,' Malin says. 'Not yet.' And Sven nods in agreement.

'We'll give them more when we need them. They're already circulating the girl's description for us, and they'll go on doing that for as long as they don't know anything else.'

'OK, I'll fend them off.'

Malin can see their new lighthouse getting restless; one of Elin Sand's legs is bouncing spasmodically under the table.

'Ella Andergren,' Sven says, pointing at the name on the whiteboard. 'We're going to find her, no matter what it costs. We're going to find whoever killed Cecilia and Patrick. There's no time to lose as far as the little girl's concerned.'

The clock above Sven's head is ticking.

8.30.

With every passing second, Malin can't help thinking, the chances of us finding you alive get a bit smaller, Ella.

If you're even still with us at all.

16

Admiration.

Can she see the admiration in my eyes? It must be there, if only as a tiny glimpse.

Elin Sand watches Malin as she walks out of the meeting room. Thinking: She doesn't seem the sort who cares what other people think of her.

Her neat, petite figure.

Cool.

Intelligent.

Hints of darkness.

Tired. She actually looks pretty worn out, with bitter little wrinkles around her thin lips.

Malin Fors's reputation precedes her in the force, Elin heard about her back at Police Academy, and after that from a colleague in Malmö who had worked in uniform in Linköping.

'Utterly brilliant. But crazy.'

And when Elin found out she'd got the job in Linköping she did a bit of research. Googled, and checked out the details of a few of the available cases.

What she found impressed her. A woman who went her own way, evidently never backed down, no matter what she was confronted by. And who never gave up until she had some sort of answer.

The others seem OK, but Fors is the star here, that much is obvious.

Elin Sand follows the others out into the drab, neon-lit corridor.

Without turning around, Malin says: 'Get your coat. We'll be leaving in five minutes.'

As they pull up outside the Smurf-house in Wimanshäll, Malin tells Elin Sand to keep a low profile, to watch and listen, melt into the background, and let her and Zeke take care of Britt Sivsjö.

And Elin Sand attempts another joke.

'Kind of hard for me to melt into the background.' Except Malin doesn't laugh, just ignores the joke, but as they ring the bell of Britt Sivsjö's terraced house she regrets her lack of response, perhaps she should try to be nicer, remembers how nervous she was on her first day in the Violent Crime Unit, the way she couldn't seem to stop babbling.

Sounds from behind the front door.

No rain, but low, dark clouds are hanging above their heads. That Barbour coat will probably come in handy again today.

'It's OK to be nervous,' Malin says. 'I certainly was on my first day.'

Elin Sand seems to understand that Malin isn't expecting an answer and simply nods in response, and then they see Britt Sivsjö's face as the door opens.

'Come in.'

A few minutes later Malin, Zeke and Elin Sand are sitting in the white kitchen drinking coffee and politely nibbling at the biscuits Britt Sivsjö had taken out.

The black cat is lying asleep on the windowsill.

'How are you getting on?' Zeke asks.

'Are the biscuits OK?'

'They're very good,' Malin says, looking Britt Sivsjö in

the eye. It hasn't yet been twenty-four hours since she found out her daughter and son-in-law had been discovered murdered and her granddaughter was missing.

Yet here she sits.

Bruised but composed.

How is she managing?

'I didn't get much sleep last night, but there's been so much to sort out that I haven't had time to think about how I am. Which is just as well. I'm going to see her today.'

Britt Sivsjö is the same age my mother would have been if she were still alive, Malin thinks. And she evidently shares my mother's ability to thrust her feelings aside, pretend that they don't exist.

As if she could hear Malin's thoughts, Britt Sivsjö says: 'I know it might seem cold, but I simply can't, I won't think of Cecilia and Patrick as dead. And the practical details are helping me deal with that. And Ella. I think my heart's going to break every time I think of her.'

'Everyone has their own way of dealing with grief,' Elin Sand says in her deep voice, and at those words Malin sees Britt Sivsjö slowly crumple, her head sinks gently towards the polished table top and she closes her eyes and moans, one cheek resting on the table.

'I haven't seen Cecilia. But I want to see her. I have to see her. They say I'll be allowed to see her today.'

Malin gives Elin Sand a hard look.

And Elin Sand stares back, but the look in her eyes is embarrassed rather than defiant.

'I'll try to calm down. I'm going to calm down,' Britt Sivsjö says, then straightens up and wipes the tears from her puffy eyes.

'More coffee? And do have some more biscuits, please, the freezer's full of . . . Ella loves . . .'

Start gently, Malin thinks.

'When we were here yesterday we asked about friends. Katarina Karlsson seems to have been a good friend of Cecilia's.'

'Katarina, yes. I didn't even think of her yesterday. They'd known each other a very long time, but Cecilia never talked about her. I don't think they saw much of each other socially.'

Malin nods.

'And you mentioned that Cecilia and her sister Petronella didn't see much of each other.'

'That's right.'

'Is there anything else you could tell us about that?'

'I was thinking of phoning you.'

'Phoning us?' Zeke says.

'Yes, to tell you about the troubles we've had as a family. I thought you might want to know, and as long as Ella's missing you need to know everything there is to know.'

You're putting the child first, Malin thinks. That's to your credit.

'You understand, I usually think that family matters should remain private, they're not really anyone else's business. But the situation is very different now.'

'Tell us,' Malin says. 'Whatever it is, I promise we'll handle it sensitively.'

Britt Sivsjö is leaning back in her chair now, seemingly relieved to be able to think about an event from the past, as if that could make her forget the present and death for a few brief moments.

'My husband. He died a few years ago. He had a brother, but they'd lost touch, didn't get on at all. William moved to Stockholm when he was young, and things went well for him, he set up a business importing electrical items. They got a contract to supply Åhléns, and then OBH Nordica.

'He didn't have any children, and when Cecilia spent a term studying in Stockholm she got in touch with her uncle, and they got on well.'

'So no children?' Zeke interjected.

'That's right. William died three years ago, a heart attack. Like a lot of people who set up their own companies, he didn't really look after himself. He smoked too much. And to be honest, he was fat, and I wouldn't be lying if I said he was fond of a drink or two.'

'Did he leave much money?' Malin asks, thinking that this might explain where Cecilia and Patrick's fortune had come from.

'Yes, several million kronor. And he left a sizeable sum to Cecilia. The rest went to Save the Children.'

Britt Sivsjö takes a sip of her coffee before going on: 'Cecilia's sister Petronella got very upset. She and her husband have four children, and they've found it very difficult to make ends meet over the years. Bad investments, redundancy, borrowing too much, so when Cecilia, who's always been very careful with money, inherited so much from their uncle, Petronella was furious. On one occasion she even drove out to see them and started yelling at Cecilia and Patrick, demanding that they share the money.'

'And did they?' Elin Sand asks.

Malin can't help thinking that Elin's voice strikes just the right note, exactly the right tone of inquiry.

Britt Sivsjö shakes her head.

'But Cecilia did ask me if I needed any money. I said I had what I needed to get by. Then none of us ever spoke about it again, it was never mentioned at Christmas or on my birthday. Those were the only times we all met up.'

Britt Sivsjö pauses.

Malin can see that she's holding back tears, but then she collects herself and goes on: 'Petronella has used her

children to bargain with. She wanted me to try to persuade
Cecilia to give them money, otherwise she wouldn't let me
see my grandchildren. And she thought I favoured Cecilia
and Patrick. Because they'd turned out right, as she put
it.'

'So you don't see your grandchildren?'

Malin can hear the anger in Zeke's voice.

'Only at Christmas and on my birthday. Sometimes on
the children's birthdays.'

'And did you favour Patrick and Cecilia?'

'No. I didn't. No.'

Thoughts are swirling around in Malin's head.

There's a motive now.

Perhaps Petronella stood to inherit something if Cecilia
died? But only if Ella disappeared? Otherwise the child
would inherit everything. Or would it be Britt? There was
also Karin's conclusion that the Andergrens may well have
known their killer.

There's a logic to this, and Malin can see that Zeke and
Elin Sand have drawn the same conclusion, can see the
tension in their body language.

'Well,' Britt Sivsjö says, 'that's pretty much everything.
If you want the precise details you'll need to check William's
will. His name was William Stiglund. The company was
Far East Electrical.'

'Thanks,' Malin says. 'We'll take a closer look. You've
done the right thing telling us.'

Britt Sivsjö fixes her gaze on Malin.

'I know what you're thinking now,' she says. 'The way
you think it all fits together. I just can't believe it's as simple
as that. Well, it's your job to find that out. But there's something else you should know. For years, Cecilia was the one
who was jealous of Petronella. So angry and jealous and
bitter that it used to scare me.'

Britt Sivsjö pauses again.

Very focused this time.

'Cecilia and Petronella tried to start families at the same time. And Petronella and Jakob had four children, one after the other, while Cecilia and Patrick kept trying and trying.

'At first Cecilia used to come over here and just cry.

'Then I gradually noticed how her anguish at not being able to have children started to turn into something like hatred of her sister.

'I think it was a coping mechanism for her. They'd never liked each other, but the children and the money meant they ended up almost hating one another.

'I did try to mediate.

'But it was like it was preordained.

'Sibling love has a very close relative.

'Sibling hatred.'

Sibling hatred?

What could be worse than that?

Competitive parental love?

Two mothers fighting for a child they both believe they have a right to?

I, Cecilia, can see all rivers now.

But not even I know where they flow to.

Or where the river of rivers begins.

We didn't hate each other, Petronella. Or did we?

We certainly didn't like each other.

You were always stronger than me. You're two years older, so you'll end up living at least two years longer than me, whatever happens.

You used to sit on me when we played as children.

Holding me down on the floor, making me realise I was beaten, and I could see that you enjoyed that, and Mum and Dad never stopped you, just thought it was part of the game.

And I learned to hate you.

I really did.

When you had your children. I would gladly have given up everything Patrick and I owned for what you had.

Apart from Ella. Not you, Ella.

Where are you now?

The pain when I started to bleed.

The blood that marked yet another failure.

The sort of pain where you can't work out if it's physical or mental, and which therefore cuts right through the very heart of who you are.

Over and over again.

For ten years.

My body was making fun of us.

Twice we lasted two months, once three.

Then the bleeding started.

The last time, I could actually make out a foetus, and I screamed like I'd never screamed before.

I saw you then, Petronella, in my mind's eye, I saw you at the playground with your children, their eyes twinkling with love as they looked at you.

I wanted that love.

I insisted on having that love.

Was that insistence my mortal sin? Or was it the money, or pride?

Sibling hatred.

The love of children.

What are you getting closer to, Malin Fors? Where is the car you're sitting in going to take you?

17

Malin's eyes are closed.

She feels the vibrations of the car.

They're on their way to see Petronella Andersson. She doesn't work, so she ought to be at home in the rented flat in Hackefors where she and her family live.

Malin hears Zeke and Elin talking over the sound of the engine.

What are they talking about?

She'd rather not know.

But it sounds as if Elin is talking about Linköping, her voice even darker now as it emerges from the back seat.

That it's a fine city, clean and tidy and nice and neat.

Which is true.

The city is undoubtedly a neat cross section of the kingdom of Sweden.

But beneath the surface everyone is here. The paedophiles, murderers, burglars, dirty old men, whores, pimps, violent drunks. Drugs, lots of drugs. All the nine circles.

But also love.

Malin forces Elin and Zeke's voices away.

Tries to see Ella Andergren in front of her.

Her face from the pictures in her room, her lithe body.

The narrow eyes, so full of life, even in her black-and-white passport photograph.

Where are you, Ella?

I'm going to find you.

Elin Sand seems thoroughly pleasant, Zeke thinks as he presses his hands to the steering wheel. A real find.

They're travelling in silence now.

She's going to be an asset.

No question.

And she's big.

What a size! And he can't help imagining Elin Sand naked. Where would you start with a woman like that?

Don't think about it.

Think about the case instead, presumably that's what Malin's doing beside me with her eyes closed.

Maybe that's your problem, Malin, thinking too much. Even if I don't know anyone who's better than you at trusting your intuition, listening to it.

They arrive.

The apartment block is on the outskirts of Hackefors, by the forest beyond an industrial estate, on the other side of the river from Hjulsbro, but just a few hundred metres from all those smart villas. The façades of the blocks are covered with tatty grey metal panels.

Malin opens her eyes.

And soon the three detectives are standing in the gentle rain in front of the building, which looks like it's been expelled by the city and cast out to its margins.

'Well, let's go in,' Zeke says.

'Hang on,' Elin Sand says. 'I'd like to lead the conversation with the sister.'

'No chance,' Malin says.

'Give her a break, Malin,' Zeke says. 'Cut her some slack on her first day.'

'OK. Why not?'

Börje Svärd is sitting at his desk in the station, reading through several years' worth of old press articles about suspected bribery in Saab and Ericsson's operations in India and Vietnam.

Patrick Andergren isn't mentioned. In fact there are very few names at all.

He opens the *Correspondent*'s website.

Leading with a picture of Ella. In a playground? How did they get hold of that? From her preschool's website?

Fear is spreading through the city now. Through Hjulsbro.

This isn't just an outbreak of petty crime in their smart suburb.

There's a killer on the loose. A child abductor. A child killer.

People have good reason to make sure their doors are locked at night.

As for him, he doesn't bother.

If, against all expectation, anyone were to come onto his property, the Alsatians would start barking like mad.

He looks out across the room.

Johan Jakobsson is bent over his keyboard, his face a bit too close to the screen. He's rubbing one elbow.

Then the phone on his desk rings.

'Börje here.'

'It's Ebba in reception. I've got a man on the line who wants to talk to you about the murders. He won't tell me who he is. Shall I put the call through?'

'Yes. Did he ask to speak to me specifically?'

'Yes, you, Börje.'

There's a click, then heavy breathing before a nervous male voice says, almost in a stammer: 'I'd like to see a detective. Anonymously.'

'You asked for me. Do we know each other?'

Silence on the line.

'Where are you calling from?'

'I'd rather not say. I want to be anonymous.'

'So how does that fit with meeting a detective? And I can't . . .'

'Bribery.'

Panting, agitated, nervous, and in his mind's eye Börje sees a fat man in his fifties in an ill-fitting blue suit.

'Bribery,' the man repeats. 'There are rumours that Patrick Andergren took bribes when he worked at Ericsson. As a salesman in Asia. Large amounts. That's all I'm saying over the phone.'

Bloody hell, Börje Svärd thinks, then says: 'Let's arrange to meet then, just the two of us.'

18

A child crying.

The internal door to the hall has a hole in it that seems to have been made by an angry kick, and behind the cheap plywood the child is crying so loudly that there's actually an echo.

Go to the child, Malin thinks, for God's sake, go to the child, but Petronella Andersson shows no sign of leaving the kitchen chair on which she's parked her fat backside.

Yet Malin would rather keep her on that chair. Elin Sand is about to start asking Petronella Andersson about her relationship with her sister. How old could the crying child be?

Three?

Four?

Boy? Girl?

Could it be Ella?

'Go and get the kid,' Zeke says from where he's standing by the door leading to the narrow hall.

The flat smells of ingrained smoke even though the kitchen window facing the forest is open, as if someone were about to jump out. The doorbell was broken, they had to knock.

The kitchen furniture is shabby, a brown table that can only be second-hand, mismatched chairs. There's a mountain of washing-up, empty pizza boxes, and overflowing ashtrays on the stainless-steel worktop, and beside a half-finished plastic model aircraft there's a small scalpel. There are traces of dried-in food on the floor.

But no bottles of drink.

No signs of substance abuse.

And Malin can't detect any smell of empty bottles, a smell that can make her giddy with thirst.

In the end it isn't Petronella Andersson who gets up, but her husband Jakob, who has been rocking on a chair over by the fridge.

Petronella smiles wearily but warmly at him, and when she smiles her face is round and red, and Malin looks at her bulging body under the baggy pink tracksuit and can't help feeling that she's looking at someone who's given up, just like her skinny husband. In his eyes there's no hope of a better life, but rather an awareness that this is how it is, this is as far as this family is going to get.

Then the smile vanishes from Petronella's face.

A sudden intensity appears in her eyes, and she looks at Malin, and there's no trace of grief, just anger and anticipation.

'Bring him in here,' Petronella shouts as her husband disappears into the hall.

He mutters something inaudible in response.

'Our youngest boy,' Petronella says. 'The other three are at school.'

And Malin looks at Elin Sand, waits for her to take charge, the way she wanted, and their young colleague doesn't seem at all nervous as she says: 'It's bloody awful, I know.'

'Cilla and I didn't like each other,' Petronella Andersson says. 'Not at all. So I'm not going to sit here pretending to be overcome with grief.'

'I didn't mean that,' Elin Sand said. 'I meant it's hard

holding things together. I grew up on my own with my mum, and Christ, she had to work bloody hard.'

A flash of anger in Petronella's eyes, then her gaze seems to soften, as if she were grateful that someone had seen the real her.

'God knows, we've struggled, Jakob and I,' she says, and from the hall they can hear the man comforting the child: 'Didn't the silly door want to open? Is that what the trouble is?'

Elin Sand goes on: 'It must have been hard having such a perfect sister. Don't get me wrong, but your mum told us you've had a bit of trouble making ends meet.'

'Cilla was insanely uptight. She was so proper it made you feel sick.'

'That's true,' Jakob Andersson says as he comes back in clutching a tear-streaked infant in one arm. 'And her bloke wasn't much better. Smug as hell. Like he was better than everyone else.'

'What are you doing at the moment?'

'Looking for work,' Petronella smiles, and Jakob sits down at the kitchen table with the now silent child in his arms. He nods.

'Me too.'

'Are there any jobs out there?'

'For people our age with no education? I doubt it. Even cleaning jobs seem to demand a degree these days. Or else the hotels and cleaning companies only want immigrants who aren't bothered about employment law.'

'I used to have my own digger,' Jakob says. 'But that all went to hell when the economy crashed. I went bankrupt, and the bank and the bailiffs took all we had.'

There's no mistaking the bitterness in his voice, and Malin can imagine that he was once an energetic man, but that all his setbacks have left him with his confidence in tatters.

'But the kids have food on the table,' he says. 'And they're all healthy and clean,' he goes on, and Malin looks at the boy on his lap, his nose no longer running, and he certainly does look healthy and clean.

'Cilla hated me,' Petronella says. 'I might not always have been very nice to her when we were little, I was the big sister, after all, but when I had children and she couldn't, she started to hate me. I suppose she didn't think it was fair. That Mrs Proper with her fancy education and smart husband couldn't have a kid of their own. Specially when Jakob and I could barely look at each other without me getting pregnant.'

Elin Sand nods her oblong head and suck her lips, waiting for her to go on.

'She never wanted to see the children. We'd have been happy to let her babysit, but she avoided them like the plague.'

'And you wanted some of the money she inherited?'

Petronella and Jakob exchange a quick glance across the table, then Petronella nods towards her husband.

'Yes, we did. She'd been playing Uncle William along for years, but why should she end up with all the money because of that? I mean, just look at the way we live. In a family you help each other, don't you, even if you might not be the best of friends? Blood's thicker than water, isn't it?'

Elin Sand nods.

'But they refused to share it?'

'Point blank.'

'And that made you angry?

'What do you think?' Jakob says. 'The money was just sitting there, after all. And they didn't want to help us. I wanted to get back on my feet with the digger again.'

'There's one thing you should know. I didn't hate Cecilia

before that,' Petronella says. 'But when she refused to help us I began to hate her, hate every uptight little bone in her stuck-up body.'

'Strong words,' Malin points out.

'True, though,' Petronella says.

'OK. We're not stupid enough to think that a story like this isn't going to get you interested,' Jakob says. 'But we just want to be honest,' he goes on, stroking his son's blond hair.

'Did your relationship change when she got Ella?'

'No, it was as if she still hated me, because I had my own children. And Mum was always making a fuss of them. And looked down on us.'

'Ella's missing now,' Malin says.

'Do you have any idea where she might be?' Elin Sand asks.

Jakob and Petronella both shake their heads.

'How would we know?' Jakob says.

'And you've got no idea who might have wanted to murder them?'

'No,' Jakob replies.

A bit too quickly, Malin thinks.

'No idea at all,' Petronella adds. 'They were perfect. Or at least that's what they wanted people to think. I think everyone liked them. At least on a superficial level. But there were probably some who couldn't stand them really.'

'Such as?'

'I'm just guessing. How should I know? I don't know who they socialised with. I don't actually think they had any friends.'

'What were you doing on the evening they were killed?' Elin Sand asks.

'I was at home with the children, our eldest daughter's already confirmed that. And Jakob was around at a friend's playing cards. We've already told your colleagues. They took his number. They must have called to check?'

'They have,' Malin says. 'We just wanted to make sure.'

'We've got nothing to do with any of this,' Jakob says. 'Even if you might like to think we have. Would we really be so frank about our poor relationship with the victims if we had anything to do with it?'

Victims.

Relationship.

Frank.

Jakob Andersson chooses words which distance him from his wife's sister, his brother-in-law, close relatives.

Are you doing that because you've done something that would otherwise be unbearable to live with?

'What was your friend's name again, Jakob, the one you were with?' Zeke asks.

'Kalle Lundbäck. He lives in Sjögestad. We spent the whole evening playing cards and drinking beer.'

'Thanks,' Elin Sand says in an entirely new voice, a voice full of sharpness and well-balanced cool. 'So you didn't do it, then? Kill Cecilia and Patrick and abduct Ella? To get at their money?'

And without making any allowances for the little boy sitting on Jakob's lap, she goes on: 'You didn't shoot them? You didn't panic and drown Ella in the river because you couldn't bring yourselves to shoot a little girl? If you did do it, it will feel better if you confess. I can promise you that.'

And Petronella Andersson looks angry, and is about to say something, but Elin Sand holds her hand up.

'I'm talking now, you listen.'

Jakob Andersson slumps on his chair, the boy in his arms seems to weigh a thousand kilos, and Malin sees a man who is used to being trodden on by people in authority.

Mons Kallentoft

'Because we could choose to see it like this. You killed them, so that Petronella's mother would inherit everything, and then you were going to put pressure on her to give you money to pay off all the debts I'm sure you've built up. People have committed murder for less. And no doubt she would have given in. Maybe you'd even have inherited some of it yourselves.'

Malin looks at the boy.

His curly blond hair and big blue eyes.

He's sitting there in silence.

He doesn't seem to understand or care what's being said, in such harsh voices.

'Are you mad?' Petronella says calmly. 'She was still my sister. You don't murder your own sister.'

'You don't usually hate your own sister either,' Malin says.

19

'Eleven o'clock. Meet me at eleven o'clock in the car park behind the old Kulman factory up in Jägarvallen.

'It's usually deserted there.

'I don't want to be seen.'

Börje Svärd had heard the urgency and fear in the voice at the other end of the line. As if the man knew something he'd rather not know.

But he had refused to give his name.

But Börje had stuck to his instincts, and when the man said he knew Börje from the shooting club he calmed down.

Go and meet him.

Hear what he has to say.

And now Börje is standing beside his car in the gravel parking lot behind the ramshackle old factory building, long since closed, the plastic-moulding machinery shipped off to somewhere in the Chinese countryside.

The rain is pattering on his red Gant jacket, and he pulls his broad-brimmed Ranger hat further down his forehead as he feels his pistol tucked against his chest in its shoulder-holster.

Five past eleven now.

Maybe he's not coming after all.

The industrial estate out in Jägarvallen is completely dead these days, all the small businesses have shut up shop. There's no sign of activity over in the biker gang's walled premises some distance away.

Ten past.

Quarter past.

Börje starts thinking about this evening's dance. At the Freemasons' Hotel.

He's looking forward to asking some panther-puma to dance.

A few raindrops have blown under the brim of his hat and are running down his waxed moustache.

He can feel the drops on his upper lip now as he hears the sound of a car coming around the corner.

A BMW, black, a few years old.

It stops in front of Börje, but he can't see in through the tinted windows. There's a hissing sound from the surrounding forest, unless it's the sound of an electric window gliding open?

Börje leans over.

Looks in.

A man in a dark blue suit is sitting in the driver's seat. He's around fifty years old, overweight, and Börje recognises him from the shooting club, he's noticed the man's distinctive potato nose before.

'Do you recognise me?' the man asks.

Börje nods.

'But I don't know your name.'

The BMW's door swings open and the man switches the engine off.

'Get in,' the man says. 'We can't talk out in the rain.'

The rain is drumming on the German roof.

Bang, bang, bang.

Like a hundred Lilliputians stamping on the roof, Börje thinks, as he notices the strong smell of smoke in the car.

The windscreen-wipers are sweeping back and forth, removing the little trickles of water running down the glass.

The man has introduced himself as Stig Sunesson, no longer bothered about remaining anonymous.

A former international salesman for Ericsson Components, now working for a software company called IFS.

A member, albeit not a particularly active one, of Linköping shooting club.

He fingers the wheel nervously, then runs his hands through his hair, and Börje wishes he would calm down.

'You're nervous,' he says.

Stig Sunesson clears his throat.

'So would you be.'

'Tell me what you know.'

Börje tries to lower his voice, to sound trustworthy.

'I worked with Patrick Andergren in India and Vietnam,' Stig Sunesson says.

Then he falls silent again.

'First selling telephone exchanges, then with the Internet stuff.'

Börje nods.

He's worked out where Stig Sunesson is heading with this.

'And?'

'There were loads of rumours about Patrick Andergren.'

The drumming on the roof gets louder.

'What sort of rumours?'

'That he took bribes. From local officials in the regions where we did business. In both India and Vietnam. That he got kickbacks under the table.'

'Kickbacks?'

Keep the conversation flowing.

'Yes, that's what it's called. When a company bribes a politician or a bureaucrat over there, and the person responsible for administering the bribe gets back maybe twenty per cent of the bribe to stuff into his own pocket. A little something to stash away in an account in Singapore, Hong Kong, Indonesia, anywhere really.'

'And you're sure Patrick Andergren was involved in this sort of thing?'

'Rumours. Nothing but rumours. I've got no proof, but he was a phenomenal salesman. Too good, if you ask me.'

Saab.

He's supposed to have been very successful there too.

Bribes.

Kickbacks.

That sort of thing must happen in the arms industry as well. In every export industry.

'And when I saw in the paper that he'd been murdered, I thought this might have something to do with it. And with the little girl going missing and everything, I thought I had to flag it up as a possibility, that he was involved in bribery and that it had all caught up with him somehow.'

'I presume we're talking about large sums of money.'

'If there was bribery going on, and if he was involved, we're talking about millions.'

Börje Svärd takes his hat off and turns to look at Stig Sunesson.

'Serious money usually means serious muscle,' he says.

Then he asks if Stig Sunesson has anything more definite, if they could talk to someone else, but just as Börje has suspected, Stig Sunesson has nothing to add.

'I just wanted you to look into it. I mean, the girl, you have to find her.'

'We will.'

'What?'

'We'll do both. I promise we're going to find Ella.'

'Is that her name?'

Börje nods.

'And I don't want any part in your investigation. You've never met me.'

'Oh yes I have.'

Stig Sunesson looks worried, surprised, and slightly angry, all at the same time.

'At the shooting club,' Börje says. 'We've met at the shooting club.'

Then he opens the car door and steps out into the rain, out in the little industrial estate that time has abandoned.

Vietnam.

That's where Ella's from, and he's been aimlessly surfing about, looking up information about the country. Wants to get an idea of where she comes from.

And he's tried to find information about adoptions.

How much can it rain there in a single day during the rainy season?

Ten centimetres.

A metre.

A world drowning in rain.

Images of terrible flooding in the city of Hội An, where the river water almost reaches the rooftops of the old merchants' houses.

Johan Jakobsson feels his elbow ache, the way it always does when he's been working particularly intensely.

Click.

Click.

What truths can he uncover?

He looks out over the open-plan office, sees his colleagues working away diligently, the uniforms walking to and fro, absorbed in their duties.

It hadn't taken Johan long to dig out the details of William Stiglund's will, and it was certainly worth arguing over and feeling jealous about.

Twelve million kronor.

Patrick and Cecilia Andergren had received five and a half million. There were still four and a half in their various accounts.

They had ended up rich, and Johan can't help thinking what he could do for his own family with that sort of money.

A new house, closer to the city. A new car. Maybe he or his wife could switch to working part-time. And they'd be able to travel, he could show his children the world.

The Taj Mahal.

Manhattan.

Rio de Janeiro.

Hội An.

They usually borrow a caravan from a friend each summer.

Last summer they got as far as Legoland in Denmark.

Sixty-seven Swedish kronor for a large Coca-Cola.

Impossible on a police salary. Or his wife's nurse's wage.

Those serving society have to make do with crumbs, their children with Legoland.

If we had five million, we could go to Thailand.

And stay for a while.

Everyone seems to go there, but how do they all afford it?

Or Vietnam.

That seems to be one of the most corrupt countries in the world.

Children adopted from there to Sweden.

It was one of the most popular countries for a long time. Pretty kids, relatively simple bureaucracy, but then the American authorities uncovered scandals where children had been stolen or bought by their adoptive parents, and cases in which the biological parents had been more or less illiterate, and hadn't understood that they were giving their children up for adoption, but thought they were simply leaving them at a children's home for a while until they got things sorted out. They had thought the authorities were trying to help them, whereas in actual fact corrupt officials, goaded on by adoption agencies and organisations in the West, were tricking them into giving up their children and selling them on to people desperate for children in Europe and the USA.

Sweden stopped all adoptions from Vietnam in 2009. And they hadn't restarted again.

Denmark still permitted them, though.

Karin, Johan thinks.

Her little girl's from Vietnam too, isn't she? And she arrived in 2011? How did that work?

Ella Andergren, on the other hand, must have got in before the ban.

And where is she now?

A long way away, as far away as it's possible to get, Johan thinks.

He sees her passport photograph in his mind's eye.

Wonders who her biological parents were. Or are, perhaps.

Were her parents among those who were deceived?

If someone were to steal my children, Johan thinks, I'd travel to the ends of the earth to get them.

I'd do anything to get them back.

I'd even kill.

He looks down at his screen.

Finds himself looking at a black-and-white picture of a Vietnamese woman.

The photograph has been taken from above, and she is looking up into the camera with scared, confused eyes full of sadness and loss.

The picture is from an English-language paper published in Vietnam.

The article tells how the woman handed over her son in the belief that it was only a temporary measure. Now her son has been adopted by an Italian couple in Trieste who are refusing to hand him back.

Johan clicks to read the next article.

A short note saying that the woman had disappeared and that the local authorities in Hue province had dropped the investigation.

There were other, similar stories. From Hanoi, Ho Chi Minh City, from Hội An and the mountains in the interior. And stories of children simply vanishing from children's homes.

I'd be capable of murder if anyone stole my children, Johan thinks, then clicks to close the browser and give his elbow a rest.

20

Elin Sand sees Malin Fors go off towards the toilets over by the station kitchen.

She had been praised outside the house in Hackefors. Malin said nothing, but Zeke thought she'd handled the interrogation well, and said it was good that she had dared to apply a bit of pressure.

Elin can't help thinking that Malin Fors would feel better if she learned to relax, but how could she do that?

Yoga? Meditation?

Hardly.

She has an alcoholic's eyes, Elin has noticed that during the course of the day. The hungry, sad look that has nowhere to go. She's seen the way Malin digs the nails of her fore-fingers into the balls of her thumbs to quell the urge to drink.

Elin has seen the same torment before.

In her dad.

He never got over what had happened in his childhood, what he was subjected to, and it turned out to be the driving force that destroyed him in the end. His pain needed an outlet, and alcohol fitted the bill.

Don't let your demons destroy you, Malin Fors, Elin thinks.

Concentrate on the good things in your life.

That's how you survive.

I know that.
All too well.

Malin turns the bathroom light off. Feels the cold plastic of the seat against the bare skin of her buttocks.

What a mess.

Inheritance.

Bribery.

Börje has just told them about his meeting, Johan about what he's found out about adoptions from Vietnam.

Millions up for grabs, reputations to be protected, evidence to be tidied away.

Bloody hell.

Anything could have marched in through the door of the house on Stentorpsvägen the other evening.

She fumbles in the darkness of the bathroom. Finds the mixer tap and turns on the cold water, lets it run over her hands, feeling little trickles and individual drops make their way through her fingers and down onto the white enamel.

Malin leans forward.

Feels the tap and the liquid against her lips.

She drinks.

She can feel the water inside her, rushing down to her stomach with each gulp, filling it, pushing down, gently, as gently as you, Tove, when I was carrying you.

The bullet-riddled bodies.

Blood seeping out into water, colouring the world red, and I'm sitting here dreaming about you, Peter, and you don't answer when I call, but I saw the news about that traffic accident on the E4 on the *Correspondent*'s website, three cars involved in a crash caused by aquaplaning, several people seriously injured, so you're probably busy trying to keep the badly hurt alive.

What's happening to us, Peter? My battered body where nothing wants to be, nothing wants to grow.

I understand that you're going to leave me.

But I wish I didn't.

Stay with me.

How can I stop you from going when I can't give you what you want?

A fish in a hand above the surface of the water, a spirit wriggling, impossible to cling on to, because it belongs somewhere else.

It can't die, because it has never lived.

Malin feels the pull of the clear brown liquid again, full of promise, and pretends the tap is gushing tequila.

If I got pregnant, would my waters run out through the gunshot holes?

Would you, my unborn child, dry up and slip out of me like a lost water-snake, a lone elver?

Like a life that's over before it even began.

21

It's early afternoon now, and Karin Johannison has pulled the body out of the cold cabinet, unzipped the body bag, but only to the top half of Cecilia Andergren's ribcage, doesn't want her mother to have to see the bullet holes.

The mortuary is cold and the neon lights in the ceiling lash the room with their harsh glare.

Cecilia's skin is lilac-blue, her eyelids closed, and Britt Sivsjö strokes her forehead over and over again but says nothing, and Karin wonders what she's thinking. Are you thinking: My little girl, my little girl, how did you end up here? And Karin can see the tears streaming down Britt Sivsjö's cheeks.

What would I do if you were lying here, Tess?

If I lost you somehow?

That sort of sorrow is incomprehensible, Karin doesn't even want to try, so she simply watches Britt Sivsjö, who almost seems to be trying to caress her daughter back to life.

This room has never been more silent, Karin thinks.

Or more desolate, more desperate.

'She seemed lonely, hesitant about life. You have a go, I think you'll do better with her.'

Börje Svärd's comments on the phone about Malin's plan to conduct a second interview with Cecilia Andergren's friend Katarina Karlsson.

And she does look timid, Malin thinks, as she watches Katarina Karlsson sip a cup of oolong tea in the kitchen of her little cottage, situated in an isolated forest clearing some ten kilometres north of Björsäter.

Shy, but the birthmark on her forehead makes it impossible for her to fade into the background. No matter where she goes, she must attract attention, and Malin wonders if that red skin feels any different, then wonders if Elin Sand is thinking the same thing.

Together with Zeke they went to the school first, but Katarina Karlsson has called in sick today.

They drove out to see her, and she let them into the old wooden house, which smells of persistent damp that's on the verge of turning to mould in the floorboards.

The house is surrounded by flowerbeds with razor-sharp edges. A ten-metre-long outhouse lines the eastern boundary with the forest.

Three doors in the outhouse.

No windows on this side, but perhaps there are some looking out onto the forest, Malin thinks.

Someone who wants to be left in peace.

That's the sort of house this is.

Katarina Karlsson has offered them tea.

She invited them to sit down at the table in the designer kitchen that contrasted with the cottage's low-beamed ceiling, and Malin can't help noticing the lack of any pets.

'I couldn't bring myself to go to school today,' Katarina Karlsson says. 'This is the first time ever, but it's just too much after what happened to Cilla and Patrick and Ella.'

Malin pauses for a moment before asking: 'Did you know about the dispute in the family? About their uncle's money?'

Katarina Karlsson looks surprised at first, then she nods.

'Yet you didn't mention it to our colleagues yesterday.'

Malin tries not to sound irritated.

'I thought it was a private matter,' Katarina Karlsson says. 'I wanted . . .'

'A private matter?' Malin says. 'They've been found murdered. And their daughter is missing.'

Zeke gives Malin a look as if to tell her to take it easy.

'Can you tell us anything more?' Elin Sand asks, and her voice seems to restore some sort of balance in the room.

'How much do you already know?' Katarina Karlsson asks, and Elin Sand tells her what they found out from Britt Sivsjö.

'Was Cecilia aware of how much the inheritance, the holidays, the things they would have bought, must have upset her sister?' Elin goes on to ask.

Katarina Karlsson nods.

'I think so. I think she may even have been pleased about it. That it was a sort of revenge for the way Petronella treated her when they were little.'

'And she was jealous of Petronella, because she herself couldn't have children?'

'That's a bit of an exaggeration,' Katarina Karlsson says. 'They just couldn't stand each other, that's all.'

'She never mentioned any specific threats from her sister or brother-in-law?' Zeke asks.

'No, never. We didn't used to talk much about that sort of problem. Even if we were close, we mostly used to talk about superficial things, which was actually quite nice. We still knew we could trust each other. Cecilia wasn't the sort of person who went on about personal matters, she went through so much with her miscarriages, but she kept it to herself. They really didn't have many friends.'

Katarina Karlsson leans back, making her white blouse stretch tightly across her chest, and Malin can see that

Elin Sand is thinking that Katarina Karlsson's movement is hiding some sort of secret.

'Did she used to say much about their time in India and Vietnam?' Elin Sand goes on.

'Sometimes.'

'What did she say?'

'She talked about how impoverished it was. But also the people. That the Vietnamese were genuinely friendly, even if they could seem reserved. Not like Thailand, where she said everyone smiles but makes fun of you behind your back.'

'She didn't mention anything particular?'

'No. Like what?'

'Like the fact that Patrick might have been involved in bribery in Asia,' Malin says.

Katarina Karlsson's expression changes, from shy to genuinely taken aback.

'What did you just say?'

Malin repeats herself.

'Have you got any proof of that?'

You're coming to his defence, Malin thinks.

'This is a murder investigation, so we have to look into every line of inquiry.'

'I can't believe Patrick was involved in anything like that. He was always honesty personified.'

'So you don't know anything about that?' Elin Sand asks.

'No.'

'They hadn't been feeling threatened at all recently?'

'Not as far as I know. Patrick worked hard, pretty much all the time, but I don't really know much about the nature of his work.'

'What about Ella?' Malin asks.

'Have you found her?'

Hope in Katarina Karlsson's eyes.

'No,' Elin says.

'You've got to find her,' Katarina Karlsson says. Then she gets up and walks out of the kitchen, and they can hear her doing something in the next room. She comes back carrying a laptop computer.

She puts it down on the table in front of them.

She clicks to play a recording in full-screen mode, and Malin, Elin, and Zeke watch Ella Andergren racing around the garden of the cottage on a summer's day when the sun is shining, as she runs through a water sprinkler, laughing and shouting 'More, more, more!', and then she disappears through one of the outhouse doors and returns with a large beach ball, which she kicks through the garden before rushing over to the camera and smiling, and her big, dark eyes fill the screen, which seems to assume a shimmering darkness just for that moment.

Katarina Karlsson closes the clip.

'You've got to find her,' she says.

They sit in silence in the cottage kitchen.

'One more thing,' Elin Sand eventually says. 'You probably know that there have been problems with adoptions from Vietnam. Children being adopted against their parents' wishes.'

'It wasn't like that with Ella,' Katarina Karlsson says quickly, in a voice that is anything but timid. 'Patrick and Cecilia checked everything very carefully. I'm sure they did. They adopted Ella from Da Lat, where they used to live, and where he worked.'

'You sound very sure,' Malin says. 'How come?'

Katarina Karlsson seems to hesitate, as if considering her answer carefully.

'Because they were both so straight. Sometimes to the point of absurdity, in Cecilia's case. She had firm principles, which doesn't really make things easy when you're a high-school teacher, seeing as that involves quite a lot of give and take.'

'Were you jealous of Cecilia?' Malin asks. 'Of her money, her family?'

'No.'

Then Katarina Karlsson lets out a short laugh.

'What's so funny about that?'

'Because everyone's so blind. When you have a mark like this on your face, it's the only thing people see. No one, not even you – and you're supposed to be experts at reading people – seems to realise that I'm happy with my life.'

Katarina Karlsson stands up and pours the dregs of her tea into the sink.

'I'm tired,' she says. 'Are we done?'

Zeke, Malin, and Elin get up.

'We're done,' Malin says, and walks out into the hall, not seeing how Elin Sand puts her hand gently on Katarina Karlsson's shoulder as if to offer support.

Karin Johannison is standing on the bare concrete floor of her office, and through her sandals she can feel how hard the floor is. The glass windows in the doors could do with a clean, and she ought to tidy up her bookcase and desk; the books, files and bundles of papers are in a terrible mess.

She lost the thick Tibetan rug that used to lie on the floor to her ex-husband in the divorce. When it came to material things, she had to give up pretty much everything when they separated. But however much she may have loved his salary, she couldn't bear to stay in a loveless marriage.

I've got love now, Karin thinks.

It's three o'clock in the afternoon, and in half an hour I'll be picking her up from preschool, and she'll probably rush into my arms and hug me as if we haven't seen each other in years.

Karin opens the photograph file on her computer.

Clicks to bring up the pictures of Tess from the Tinnerbäck pool this summer, throwing herself straight out into the water, seemingly not afraid of anything.

Karin looks at the screen.

The pink inflatable armbands around her pale brown arms.

She misses her so much it almost makes her stomach cramp.

Then she closes her eyes, takes several deep breaths, and wonders where the case they're investigating is going to lead her.

What can I do? she wonders. No one can stop a wave once it's been set in motion.

A shimmering blue screen, almost like a swimming pool lit up at night.

Paperwork.

Computer searches.

It's half past five by the time Malin switches off her computer and decides to go home. She might go via the Tinnerbäck pool and have a swim, gather her thoughts as her body ploughs through the water.

During the latter part of the afternoon she has seen a very focused Johan Jakobsson sit hunched over his computer on the other side of the room.

Three lines of inquiry, she thinks.

One: family feud.

Two: bribery.

Three: adoption.

Three different rivers running through an unfamiliar landscape.

Do they converge?

Do they mean anything? Or are we looking in the wrong direction?

Börje and Waldemar have gone off to talk to some of Patrick Andergren's former colleagues at Ericsson. Johan is checking out Stig Sunesson, the man who contacted Börje.

Bribery scandals.

Most big Swedish companies that do business in Asia have been subject to investigation, but so far Karim hasn't managed to dig out any case files.

Zeke has already left. He was going to stop on the way home to buy a toy of some sort for his youngest grandchild.

Elin Sand is standing over in the kitchen with a cup of coffee in her hand.

A head taller than the male uniform she's talking to.

She's done well.

Maybe I ought to say that to her?

Malin gets up from her chair and waves in Elin's direction.

'See you tomorrow,' she mouths, and Elin waves back, and she looks happy in the gloom of the kitchen, an awful lot happier than me, Malin thinks.

22

Malin has the Tinnerbäck pool to herself this evening, metre after metre of temperature-controlled water just for her, a whole world to drown in, be alone in.

The water in the fifty-metre-long pool is steaming, evaporating into the cool air above. Lit up by the lights along the edge of the pool, it glows like a meteorite from a distant galaxy.

Tiny blisters of rain on the chlorine-scented surface.

Just her this evening.

No one else feels like swimming on a chilly September evening.

She puts her goggles on and adjusts them.

Looking forward to swimming away from the events of the day.

She dives in.

And the water feels warm against her cold skin, an embrace that moves forward with her, thousands of hands stroking her back, legs, stomach and cheeks.

She swims underwater, as lactic acid and lack of oxygen take over her body, and she feels her body conquer the resistance of the water. She looks ahead, but the world slowly vanishes and everything starts to go black, and she wants to breathe, breathe, breathe, but she can sense the far end now, just a bit more, a bit more, and there!

Her hand on the tiles.

She's made it.

Fifty metres underwater.

And she sticks her head up, and all her eyes can make out is pirouetting blue lights against the darkening sky, and she is herself now, nothing but herself, and her muscles are throbbing and she doesn't want to think, doesn't want to feel, and it's wonderful, so wonderful, as wonderful as the first sense of intoxication, when all your worries and genuine feelings gradually fade into numbness.

She starts to swim again.

Hopes her body won't let her down this evening.

The sign of the Pull & Bear glows in the darkness, it blue and green colours pulsing into the night.

One beer.

One tequila.

How dangerous could that be? Malin thinks as she approaches her building on Ågatan.

The two thousand metres she has just swum are burning in her body, her eyes stinging from the chlorinated water that seeped into her goggles, her skin is dry as sandpaper beneath her jeans, but neither discomfort nor exhaustion have any effect on her overwhelming thirst.

A few moments ago she crossed Gyllentorget, and there were people sitting under the big white awnings of the outdoor bars, drinking beer and shivering.

How could they?

How could they not?

Her muscles felt reluctant in the water this evening, sluggish, unwilling to get going. Maybe their reluctance is connected to the fact that she's starting to get old. That her body's best years are undeniably behind her.

One shot.

A hot throat, a burning stomach, calmness spreading through her veins, out into the rest of her body and deep into her soul.

It wouldn't do any harm.

Fuck, Malin thinks.

Why does the most wonderful thing in the world have to be the most dangerous.

I want to tumble around in the gentle senselessness of alcohol, but I don't want to have to go through what comes after that.

She's approaching the pub.

She forces herself to think about hangovers, shame, the misery that comes with drinking, the way she treated everyone, Tove, so badly.

Her stomach contracts to a tight black lump.

'Malin, Malin Fors!'

Unfamiliar voices, and she sees three journalists and two photographers emerge from the gloom of her doorway, heading towards her.

What the hell are they doing here? Get lost.

This has never happened before, why can't they just hang around the station? Presumably this is some bastard new angle for them.

Close to Malin now.

Their shiny faces, three young men, two young women with cameras.

The media flock.

The new proletariat, as former prime minister Göran Persson described them.

She waves the reporters aside, and the cameras flash as the reporters yell questions at her.

'Is it true that Patrick Andergren could have been caught up in a bribery scandal in connection with Thailand's decision to buy the Gripen? Have you found the daughter yet?

What are the main lines of inquiry? The girl! Have you found the girl?'

She doesn't answer, knows that this is a game, that they're doing this so they can publish a dramatic picture of an exhausted detective inspector.

Into the hallway.

They don't try to follow.

She pulls the front door shut.

Turns to face them, and without thinking she gives them the finger, just as a flash goes off.

They were more aggressive than Daniel Högfeldt, her former lover, and previously a journalist at the *Correspondent*, had ever been.

Malin hangs up her damp Barbour jacket, thinking that it's about as ridiculous as it is effective against the rain.

Peter.

On duty.

The second of two nights, unless he was due to do more night shifts? It strikes her that they haven't spoken since he left for work yesterday morning.

He hasn't called, she hasn't called, but they're probably each thinking that the other is busy, holding back, thinking: It's up to you to call, not me.

Malin sinks onto one of the chairs at the kitchen table, closes her eyes and listens to the tick of the Ikea clock. Her stomach is shrieking with hunger and she feels nauseous, and knows exactly how she could get rid of that feeling.

But instead she goes back out into the hall, gets her phone from her jacket pocket, and calls her daughter.

As the phone rings she goes and lies down on her bed, enjoying the darkness, until eventually Tove answers.

'Mum.'

'Hi, I just wanted to see how you are doing.'

Mons Kallentoft

'I can't really talk right now. Can you call back later?'

Noise in the background.

The darkness of the room, which just moments before seemed comforting, now feels empty and desolate.

Heavy rain against the window.

'Tom and I are in the pub, we're taking part in a quiz. You should see the locals, Mum. They look like total idiots, and they don't seem to have any idea where Alaska is.'

Malin feels anger bubbling up inside her.

Then disappointment.

And in her mind's eye she can see the pub Tove's sitting in.

Smoky, crowded, a smell of stale spilled beer. People at the tables, Mr and Mrs Ordinary.

Not smart types. The backbone of the country. In all my years in this city's bars, particularly the Hamlet, I've learned to respect those people, the ones who get up every morning, no matter how tedious the job that awaits them, no matter how much their bodies and souls ache, and they do their jobs, they keep the whole machinery running.

Tove, what's happening to you? Who are you turning into, up there in your private-school world?

'Are you still coming home?'

'Yes, tomorrow. I don't want to miss Linn's birthday.'

Linn.

The only friend from the city that Tove has kept in touch with. She wasn't even a particularly good friend back then, but she comes from the Linköping elite, her father's in charge of the council housing department.

'OK, bye for now. They've just asked who the head of the World Bank is. I swear, half this lot don't even know what the World Bank is!'

Click.

Rain pattering in the darkness.
Who's the head of the World Bank?

Malin can't sleep. She wishes she'd said something to Tove.

Tried to teach her to see people, to see where she herself has come from.

Malin wants to believe that Tove is capable of that, already knows.

Tove can't be blind, but any ability to see what's going on under the surface seems to have vanished in a swirl of Canada Goose jackets and authentic Ralph Lauren sweaters.

Change.

Everything has to keep changing, or else it would break.

Adapt and survive.

Growth.

Expansion.

But what about the people who can't grow?

Stefan.

My brother.

Mute and unaware and alone in his room at the care home. What space is there for him in a world obsessed with constant growth?

Or for me.

Incapable of even bearing a child for Peter.

Peter, she thinks.

I want to go and see you. In the duty-doctor's room. But would you want to see me?

The warm duvet envelopes Malin, and she weeps.

23

Tess is sleeping.

She chose the colour of the wall next to her bed herself.

Karin put the colour swatches on the floor in front of her and made a game of it, asking: 'Which colour do you think is nicest?'

Yellow won, and Karin asked: 'Would you like that colour on your wall?'

'Paint.'

Tess shook her head and pointed at the pale blue, said 'paint' again. Karin has just aimed the bedside lamp away from her sleeping daughter, towards the watery-blue wall where two framed pictures from Vietnam hang side by side.

'That's where you come from. That's where I went to get you.'

Karin says the words into the child's sleep, then she thinks: I'm your mummy. Your real mummy.

She wants to say that, but can't bring herself to, because certain things lose their validity if they're said out loud.

I'll always be here, Karin thinks as she pulls the bright blue cover up over Tess; her body forms perfect pencil curves under her thin white cotton nightie.

One picture of Hội An at night.

The multi-coloured lights of the buildings reflected in the river, as the paper lanterns launched by holidaying children sail off into the darkness.

One picture of Saigon by day.

Hundreds, thousands of scooters and motorbikes on the boulevard that runs alongside the Saigon River, Sông Sài Gòn. Karin took the picture herself, from her balcony at the Hotel Majestic. In the background, on the other side of the river, beyond a small patch of jungle, are the big white apartment blocks, apparently abandoned.

Will I ever take you back there? Would that be possible?

And Karin feels her heart contract, and she looks at Tess, her chubby cheeks, and she doesn't want to get up, doesn't want to leave the little girl, but she can't sit here all night, so in the end she gets up and goes into the living room, where she switches the television on, turning the volume down with the remote.

It's raining even harder now.

As if someone were aiming a shower at them from the sky.

Ella Andergren.

Adopted from Vietnam, just like you, Tess.

Obviously she'd heard about Patrick Andergren. And what he was doing. But he had never contacted her.

And she doesn't want to think about it, and plans to pretend not to know anything if things get really complicated. She's ashamed of that decision, but she doesn't want to think about it, she won't think about it.

She's never attended any of the meetings for adoptive parents. What good would that do?

In every love gained, a love lost.

In all quiet companionship, somewhere there is a howling loneliness.

It's best not to ask any questions.

Hope that goodness can hold evil at bay.

The programme on television.

A literary programme with two smug men from the

Swedish Academy holding forth on a black leather sofa, eagerly goaded on by a bitter young man with a face furrowed by smoking.

'Sometimes the greatest love of all,' the more pompous of the two men declaims, 'is to abstain from love.'

Karin changes channel.

Switches the television off.

Goes back in to Tess.

Watches her sleep, dream, breathe.

Kalle Lundbäck is standing by the phone in his flat on the edge of Sjögestad, fingering the wound on the top of his lower arm, watching the blood ooze out where he's just picked off the day-old scab.

He hesitates.

Knows what he ought to do.

But can't. That would be the same as grassing someone up, and you don't do that.

Fuck.

His head is spinning.

With vodka, shame, regret, nothing gentle about tonight's descent into drunkenness.

What have I done?

And in his drunk head he hears the girl's voice. Ella's voice. He never heard it in real life, or did he?

Jakob Andersson.

Of course you help your friends.

But now?

Now that he's figured out what Jakob might be mixed up in?

He knows how much Jakob wants to get hold of his sister-in-law's money, how much he wants to use it to pay off his debts and have another go with his digger business.

'Kalle, you've got no idea how many ditches need digging in Östergötland. Thousands of fucking ditches!'

'Just say we were playing cards, for fuck's sake, I mean, that's what we usually do.'

The picture of the missing girl on the front of the *Correspondent*.

In *Expressen*.

And her voice. Where has that come from?

And what did she say? It's only the drink, Kalle Lundbäck thinks. It's just the drink playing tricks on him, and he tries to make out what the clock on his grandmother's old bureau says.

Eleven. Ten?

Who cares.

And then he hears a scream.

The girl's scream.

I'M DROWNING, I'M DROWNING, IT HURTS, STOP, NO, IT'S NOT ME, she screams, but surely drowning children don't scream? They'd drown silently, wouldn't they? Stop struggling and become one with the water filling their lungs?

Kalle Lundbäck picks up the phone.

Calls.

Thinking drunkenly, there's going to be trouble now, but it can't be helped.

Money, its very smell, its presence, is enough to turn anyone's head.

Malin is lying in bed.

Naked. She's thrown the covers back.

She's freezing, can feel goose bumps on her skin, but it feels right.

She's trying to sleep, but she can't let go of her phone

call to Tove, and the way she talked about the locals up in the forests of Värmland.

She'll have to talk to Tove about it this weekend. It isn't too late for her to be a mum and teach her a bit of basic common sense.

Maybe money had turned Petronella and Jakob Andersson's heads? Maybe the thought of all that money so close to them sent them mad? Maybe they committed murder so that Petronella's mother would inherit the money, and then they could bully her into sharing it with them?

Misery.

Despair.

I'll commit murder. Then I'll have money and everything will be fine.

In plenty of countries a murder doesn't cost more than a hundred kronor. A week ago she read about a case in Chicago in which two teenage boys killed a retired couple for forty dollars.

Warped values.

A thirst for love.

A longing for children that has no outlet.

Johan had spent the day looking into the adoption angle, but without finding anything.

Karin.

You adopted from Vietnam after the ban. How was that possible? Were you the exception to the rule? Did you ever meet Patrick and Cecilia Andergren? Ella? At some social event connected to the adoption?

Malin feels like switching the bedroom light on and calling Karin to ask, but daren't, because what could she possibly say that wouldn't sound suspicious?

But I wonder, Malin thinks. Karin might know something.

But I can't phone now.

Malin puts her hands on her stomach.

The hole in her womb.

Healed.

Yet still not healed.

Well, that's what the doctor said.

And we share that experience now, Karin. A longing. I haven't wanted to admit that we are the same, so who the hell am I to phone and ask how you got your child?

In a way, that would be to call your maternal love into question.

Your right to it.

Your right to your child.

Bribery, Malin thinks instead. It's going to be difficult to make any progress there. They'll have to try to trace any transactions, talk to people, but if the big companies choose to keep a lid on something, it's usually fixed pretty firmly. And the lid is always kept closed.

Alone in bed.

No body to snuggle up to, warm up next to, feel that there's someone else with a pulse in the world.

Then Malin's mobile rings, out on the kitchen table.

A persistent ringing, and she gets up in the darkness, fumbling her way to the kitchen naked, feeling the raw damp against her skin as it makes her nipples stiffen.

She clicks to take the call.

'Is that Malin? Elin Sand here. Can you talk?'

'Mm-hmm.'

What does she want?

'I stayed behind at the station to check a few things, and a short while ago Kalle Lundbäck called – you know, the bloke who gave Jakob Andersson an alibi for the evening of the murder? Apparently the alibi was fake. Jakob Andersson asked him to say he was there.'

Bloody hell, Malin thinks.

'We're bringing him in now. He was obviously drunk, but we might be able to get more out of him in an hour or so. We're on our way to the Anderssons' flat as well.'

'Hold back on that,' Malin says. 'I'm on my way. I want to be there when we bring the bastard in.'

PART 2
The Drowning World

[Voices, world]

At night the steam is like silver smoke above the river, the palms drooping down, heavy with the driving rains of autumn, but the sky over the river is starry and clear, and the distant celestial bodies are reflected in the black water, shimmering like oyster shells on the riverbed.

The woman is sitting by the river again.

Her hands stink from gutting fish, spectral fish that none of the real fish will go near.

Her tears drip down into the river, forming circles on circles, and her tears flow with the river out into the ocean, and from the ocean to the canal, and from the canal to the lake, and from the lake to the river that flows past the house on Stentorpsvägen where the memory of bullet holes, of lifeless, blue-purple bodies in the water of the jacuzzi, hangs like an invisible mist in the air.

Money changes hands.

Handshakes, firm, soft.

I want, I want, I want.

Where is our child?

A monster has taken our child.

A monster hidden behind an ordinary human face, and behind the monster's face is yet another person.

The dead smile, grimace, their faces engraved on the clouds.

★

It's me.

The woman by the river.

Who listens to me?

Who wants to hear my voice? Who wants me to exist?

I didn't buy a pig, because no pig could look after me. No pig could silence their laughter.

I have nothing to give the world apart from my stinking hands, I have nothing to give you.

They've threatened to kill me if I say anything. So many have disappeared, no one can be bothered to count them, unless they themselves stand to gain by it.

Kill me, then.

As if I'd be scared of death. I'm not scared of becoming a spirit, floating along the banks of the river.

When I become a spirit, I can haunt the people who tricked me and laughed at me, I can make them scream into the night.

I want to stroke your hair one last time.

I want to sit here by the river with you just once, without my eyes filling with tears.

Hear my words now, as they drift around the world and whisper in a stranger's ear.

'My love. It was my love you stole.'

And I hope that someone will defy the laughter and bring you to me, that someone will be able to see beyond this time, to see what's right.

Look for me.

I'll be here if you come.

I'll be here.

24

The streetlights outside the block of flats in Hackefors are broken, and in the darkness the building where the Andersson family lives looks more like a haunted house than a suitable home for a family with small children.

There's light from the kitchen window.

Malin and Elin Sand have parked a short distance away, by the industrial units, to conceal their arrival. And now they're standing outside the front door in the rain, and the forest on the other side of the road is dark, the trees and branches and undergrowth a confusing mixture of different shades of black, where anything could be hiding.

Malin's keen for them to bring Jakob Andersson in themselves. Not upset the children with a big operation.

A false alibi in a murder investigation.

Not a particularly smart idea.

At first she thought about calling Zeke, then decided it was better to let him sleep. Jakob Andersson hadn't seemed particularly intimidating earlier in the day, so was hardly likely to cause any trouble.

The front door had been open earlier, but now it's locked.

The police code doesn't work.

Bloody landlords, Malin thinks as she takes out her key ring and picks the lock to let them in.

Kalle Lundbäck was already at the station when she got there, picked up by a patrol.

He was seriously drunk when Malin saw him being

brought in, he must have called just before the alcohol kicked in properly.

Now he's sleeping it off in one of the custody cells where they can keep an eye on him.

'Who's going to ring the bell?' Elin Sand whispers, and it seems to Malin that she's even more of a giant in the murky lighting of the stairwell, but in spite of her size, Elin is agile, moves fluently rather than jerkily the way some tall people do.

'You ring,' Malin says as she takes out her handcuffs and unfastens her shoulder holster.

Elin Sand follows suit.

'Do you think we'll need pistols?'

Malin detects a trace of anxiety in her colleague's eyes. She shakes her head.

'No. But you never know.'

Malin hears Elin Sand's heavy breathing. Says: 'Just take it easy, it'll all be fine. Let me take him down if there's any trouble, and you keep the family calm. OK?'

And Malin can't help wondering if she's moving too fast. They really ought to be taking Petronella Andersson in as well, because presumably she knows the alibi was fake, and what he was doing instead. But . . .

Maybe she doesn't know anything. All she's done is confirm that Jakob was out that evening, whereas the easy option would have been to give him an alibi herself.

And if they were going to take Petronella Andersson in tonight it would be a big deal, they'd have to get Social Services involved to take care of the children, it would be chaotic and traumatic, and the children have to be protected.

But he was somewhere on the evening of the murders, Jakob Andersson.

Stentorpsvägen?

Outside a basement door?

Next to a jacuzzi?

Malin sees Elin Sand's long forefinger reach for the bell, then remembers that it wasn't working earlier that day, and signals to Elin to knock instead.

The knock echoes in the stairwell.

Steps on the other side of the door.

No peephole, and the door opens.

A child.

A girl, maybe seven years old, wearing a pink nightie and with fine blonde hair that falls loosely on her thin shoulders, stares up at them.

The she turns around and calls towards the kitchen: 'Mum, Dad! There's a lady giant here!'

Malin can't help laughing, and Elin Sand joins in, then there are sounds from the kitchen and they hear Petronella Andersson call out: 'Hang on! I'm coming!' and a few seconds pass, and Malin thinks she can hear a window open, and pushes her way past the girl, rushes towards the kitchen and runs straight into Petronella Andersson in the darkness of the hall.

'Take it easy. What the hell do you want at this time of night?'

Petronella Andersson tries to grab Malin's coat, but Malin shoves her aside and goes into the kitchen.

An open window.

The rain pouring in.

The fair-haired boy is sitting on a child's chair, still awake, and for a fraction of a second Malin feels a twinge of shame.

They didn't even ask the boy's name the last time they were here.

When the boy sees Malin he starts to cry, and Malin turns around and hears Elin Sand shouting: 'Calm down! Just calm down!' out in the hallway, and in response:

'Fucking bitch! Let go of me, you cop-cunt!'

Malin runs over to the window.

Looks down, and Jakob Andersson is lying on the ground clutching one of his shins.

'Don't move!' Malin yells. 'Don't move!'

But Jakob Andersson clambers laboriously to his feet before staggering off into the forest.

Children crying.

More voices now.

The children's fear like a chainsaw in her soul.

Fuck, Malin thinks.

How did this happen?

She estimates the distance to the ground. Four metres, five? Too high. Too high, but maybe the man escaping through the forest is a murderer, maybe, maybe he knows where Ella is?

But he's slow.

No.

Yes.

Malin jumps up onto the windowsill and throws herself out into the rain, spends the two seconds she's in the air trying to prepare herself for the landing, tenses her muscles, relaxes them, tries to judge the distance, bends her knees, then boom . . .

Shit.

Her knees fly up towards her chin and she feels her top lip split as her teeth cut into it.

The taste of iron in her mouth.

She hopes that Elin Sand is calling for backup, that she can get the situation in the flat under control, because they're going to have to take Petronella Andersson in as well now, Social Services will have to come and get the children.

Malin stands up.

Iron in her mouth.

She draws her pistol, then hurries into the dark forest in pursuit of Jakob Andersson.

Elin Sand has wrestled Petronella Andersson to the hall floor, handcuffed her, and is holding her down with one knee. Now she pulls out her mobile and calls the station, as she hears the woman pinned down by her knee curse and swear.

The two eldest children, a boy and a girl of about ten, have retreated into the room they just emerged from, and the girl who opened the front door is now sitting on the floor with her back to the wall. She's crying and holding her hands over her ears, and in the kitchen the toddler is screaming at full volume.

Elin Sand decides that she's never going to have kids, fuck, they can scream! She assumes Jakob Andersson jumped out of the kitchen window when he realised they'd come for him.

Did Kalle Lundbäck call to warn him?

But why would he do that?

If that were the case, Jakob Andersson would be long gone.

'Fucking pig!'

Emergency control answer her call.

She yells the address, but they already know that.

'Do you need backup?'

'Affirmative.'

'It's on its way. The nearest car can be with you within four minutes.'

She drops her mobile on the floor.

Puts her mouth close to Petronella Andersson's ear and whispers in her very deepest voice: 'You have to calm down. I need to go and comfort your son. OK? And this little girl is in a state of shock. You have to calm down.'

Mons Kallentoft

'Don't tell me what to do!'

'Calm down,' she says, breathing warm air into Petronella Andersson's ear. 'Nice and calm. Think of your children,' and it works.

She can see Petronella Andersson hyperventilating.

And then she goes crazy again, shrieking: 'YOU'RE ALL FUCKING IDIOTS!' and if it's actually possible the child in the kitchen starts screaming even louder, and Elin Sand is prepared to do anything to put a stop to the noise, so she bangs Petronella Andersson's head against the floor, not too hard, but she feels the woman's body go limp beneath her.

The girl over by the wall.

She didn't see that.

You're staring at the floor, aren't you, and didn't see what the cop did to your mum?

Elin Sand gets to her feet.

Hurries into the kitchen, and the boy is still sitting on his chair, his face red and swollen, and when he sees her he cries even more out of terror and disappointment that it isn't his mother.

'There, there,' Elin Sand says. 'There, there.'

And she picks the boy up and holds him in her arms, rocking him, pleading with him to stop screaming, and he's warm and small and he smells ridiculously good, there now, there now, and she rocks him in her arms and then the miracle happens.

The boy stops crying.

And it's the best feeling Elin Sand has ever experienced in all her twenty-nine years.

Holding the boy in her arms, she leans her head out through the window.

Feels the rain on her forehead.

'There now, there now.'

The forest.

Black.

Malin on the hunt out there.

For Jakob.

For Ella.

For herself, for a sense of place, belonging, Elin Sand thinks.

Then she feels something hard and sharp cut into one of her buttocks, unless it's actually her back? Her spine?

The pain is acute and burning, and before she turns to deal with it she has time to think that whatever happens, she mustn't let go of the boy.

He's a child.

And children are sacred.

25

Where is he? Malin thinks.

The rain is lashing down, creeping under her collar and down her back.

Malin is stalking Jakob Andersson.

There are no shadows in the forest at this time of night. The tree trunks and bushes look dead, like faintly shimmering shapes made of ash.

Noise up ahead.

And Malin feels adrenalin coursing through her body and rushes forward, stumbles, knocks one shoulder against a tree and has to stifle a cry of pain.

Her shoes sink into the wet moss.

Her pistol aimed in front of her.

Not affected by the wet.

Where is he?

She's hunting an invisible shadow, and he could be anywhere in the forest, and she wonders how Elin Sand is getting on, if she's sorted out the chaos in the flat, if she's got backup yet, and Malin hears the sirens approaching somewhere behind her, then hears more noises in the forest and stops.

How far ahead of her?

Ten metres, fifteen.

Is he actually behind me? To my right, or left?

And she loses her sense of direction among the trees, in the darkness Malin barely knows up from down, and this is how people drown when they're drunk, she thinks, they lose their bearings and swim towards the bottom, thinking it's the surface.

She carries on through the forest.

I'm going to get you, she thinks. I'm going to get you.

Elin Sand manages to stop herself screaming.

She turns around and sees the Anderssons' eldest son standing there with a scalpel in one hand, sees the blood dripping from its blade, and realises what must have happened.

Burning pain.

In her buttock.

The warm trickle of blood, warm liquid running down her thigh and calf, towards the floor, staining her jeans dark red.

But she keeps hold of the child in her arms.

She sees the fear in the boy's eyes, the way he's clutching the scalpel, the blood seems to have hypnotised him, and he begins to realise what he's done.

She takes a step back.

'There now, there now.'

Fuck, it hurts.

Her buttock.

No important nerves there, no vital organs.

I'll be OK.

'There now. Just drop the scalpel on the floor, OK?'

But the boy just stares in front of him as he backs away towards the hall, stumbling over some pizza boxes.

He manages to stay on his feet.

And then he seems to see the kitchen, and what he's holding in his hand, and comes to his senses again, dropping the scalpel and sinking slowly to the floor in the hall next to his younger sister.

Sirens.

I can hear them now.

The children are calm.

The sirens stop, an engine switches off, and there don't seem to be any neighbours in the building, otherwise they'd have heard the commotion and been curious.

Unless they're afraid, holed up in their flats, trying not to see anything, hear anything? Blind to everything.

Car doors slamming shut.

'Good,' Elin Sand says. 'Good,' and she goes over to the scalpel and kicks it away from the child as she feels the blood continue to pour from the wound in her buttock, and fights to overcome the pain.

She hears footsteps in the hall, male voices shouting: 'DON'T MOVE!'

Do they have to shout? Can't they see the children?

The barrel of a pistol around the frame of the door.

'Calm down, for God's sake,' Elin Sand says. 'I've got things under control.'

Her colleagues fall silent, lower their weapons and step into the hall.

The boy in her arms jerks when he sees the uniformed male officers.

Then he starts screaming again, just as Petronella Andersson regains consciousness.

There he is.

It must be him.

Malin has emerged onto a tarmacked cycle path where cones of light illuminate the ground every fifty metres. The cones are full of raindrops that seem to break up in the light and turn to mist.

The whole forest smells of decay out here.

But there's Jakob Andersson, about sixty metres away.

His back to me.

He's limping.

But he's still moving, and he turns around, sees me, and he's got something in his hand.

A pistol?

A sawn-off shotgun?

Malin leaps off the cycle path, vanishing from view. She's a beast of prey now, moving instinctively between the trees, and she speeds up, can see him trying to find her, as if he knows she's here, an invisible danger ready to rip his throat out, tear great chunks from his body.

She gets closer.

A large stick. That's what he's got in his hand. Malin is moving almost silently now, feels no tiredness in her limbs as she circles the figure standing in a cone of light, in the mist of rain, and he can't hear her, he doesn't notice when she rushes out of the forest and throws herself at him, knocking him to the hard, wet tarmac, and he cries out when his cheek hits the ground, when Malin presses extra hard on the leg he was limping on, when she hits him on the shoulder with the butt of her pistol, right where she knows there's a bundle of nerves.

She presses Jakob Andersson's face against the tarmac.

Hears her own breathing.

She puts her pistol away, then pulls out her handcuffs and fastens his arms behind his back.

Then she stares out into the darkness.

We're alone here, she thinks, you and I.

And Malin takes her pistol out again.

She sits astride Jakob Andersson, sees the dark strands of hair on his back through his wet T-shirt.

She grabs him by the chin. Pulls his mouth open and sticks the pistol in deep between his teeth, then leans forward and whispers in his ear: 'Where is she? If you know where Ella is, tell me now. Otherwise you won't get out of here alive.'

She presses harder.

Jakob Andersson is struggling beneath her, trying to scream, but how could he?

'DO YOU KNOW WHERE THE GIRL IS? YOU BASTARD, DO YOU KNOW WHERE THE GIRL IS?'

And Malin imagines she can hear wild boar grunting in the forest. Are there wild boar here?

Then she removes the pistol from Jakob Andersson's mouth.

'I don't know where she is,' he groans. 'If I knew, I'd tell you. I want you to find her. She's only a little girl, after all.'

'You're talking crap,' Malin says. 'Where is she? Where is she?'

Thinks: Where are all the missing children of this world? Has some bastard managed to make them all vanish?

26

'OK, now you're going to answer our questions truthfully,' Zeke says, and his voice is harsh, glacially cold.

Interview room one.

In the basement of the police station. The walls of the room have recently been repainted entirely in black, as has the mesh-like ceiling from which inset halogen lamps cast a discreet but revealing light.

Jakob Andersson's face in front of Malin and Zeke. Malin has insisted on conducting the interview herself, even though Sven thought she was too angry.

A tape recorder on the table.

Sven Sjöman on the other side of the one-way mirror.

The new digital clock fixed high up on the wall behind the interview-subject says it's 23.35.

Everyone's tired now.

Events have been happening thick and fast, and Malin can still feel the warm, caressing water of the Tinnerbäck pool on her body, a different form of resistance to Jakob Andersson's.

There's no pain in her knee, but she'll probably end up with a bruise. Her lip still stings.

'Tell us what you were really doing on Tuesday evening.'

Jakob Andersson stares down at the table and says nothing.

Mons Kallentoft

'Answer,' Zeke hisses.

'I'm not afraid of you,' Jakob Andersson replies. 'So what if Kalle says I wasn't around his, I don't know why he'd say that. We were together.'

While Malin and Elin Sand were out in Hackefors, Sven conducted a brief interview with the drunk Kalle Lundbäck.

He explained in a slurred voice that he had been with his girlfriend.

And she could confirm that Jakob Andersson hadn't been there.

'We know that you weren't at Kalle Lundbäck's,' Malin says, 'and you weren't at home, because you would have said that straight away, and Petronella says you weren't there, so what were you doing?'

Jakob Andersson raises his eyes.

Smiles at Malin.

'Are you going to get your pistol out again?'

Malin can see the defiance in his eyes, a whole life of defiance against authority figures and officialdom focused in a single smile.

'I'm not saying anything. We might as well stop this now.'

Zeke looks at Malin.

Her pistol?

And she can see in his eyes that he has an idea of what happened in the forest.

'Ella,' Malin says.

'I didn't have anything to do with that. Not a thing.'

'So why did you run?' Malin asks. 'Confess that you took off because you thought we'd uncovered the truth about the murders and Ella's disappearance. Confess that you and your wife planned the murders, and you carried them out. Confess, and it will feel better. I can understand that you wanted the money. For a new digger. For every-thing else. Confess, and it will feel better.'

'You've got nothing on me, and you know it. And Petronella hasn't got a clue about anything.'

Waldemar and Johan have come back to the station as well, and are now questioning Petronella together in interview room three. In the patrol car on the way in, Petronella Andersson kept repeating that she didn't know anything about the false alibi, and that Jakob had been lying to her as well if that was the case. And she had asked about her children.

'Where are they? What are you doing with them? This is a miscarriage of justice.'

Jakob Andersson is close to breaking now, Malin thinks.

They've got enough to hold him. The fact that he took off is enough on its own.

'Why did you run?' Zeke asks.

'I got scared. Panicked. I thought you'd leaped to conclu-sions and were going to arrest me. I don't trust anyone who works for the state.'

'You realise that sounds like a really bad explanation?' Malin says.

Jakob Andersson nods, then says: 'I don't give a fuck. But I can guarantee that what I was doing that night had nothing to do with the murders, or Ella's disappearance.'

'You admit that you gave a false alibi?' Malin says.

'If that counts as an offence, then yes. I'll admit that.'

But what else are you guilty of? Malin wonders.

'Why did you lie?' Zeke asks. 'If you can give us a decent explanation, it might help your case.'

'You can't help me with anything,' Jakob Andersson says. 'When are you going to understand that?'

'There you go!'

The doctor in accident and emergency at the University

Hospital is only a year or so older than Elin Sand, and she has to peer behind her and look up to catch a glimpse of her narrow, regular face from where she's lying on the bed.

A throbbing pain in her buttock now.

Three stitches. Local anaesthetic, but it still hurts.

The doctor has chestnut brown hair.

Tied up in a bun.

Amelie.

That's her name.

'You can get up and put your clothes back on,' Amelie says. 'You were lucky. The boy must have been frightened and held back, because he didn't press very hard. But it's a nasty angle, and if it had been a grown man wielding that scalpel, it could have gone right up into the tail of your spine, and then it would have been very serious.'

Elin Sand pulls up her underwear before sitting up. She tugs her jeans back on.

'How serious?'

'Paralysis. It's a very bad idea to get stabbed in the spine with a scalpel.'

Shit, Elin thinks.

She's always been aware of the dangers of the job, dangers you take for granted, but to hear a clearly very intelligent doctor say the word 'paralysis' in connection to something she has just been through makes her feel sick.

'Don't worry,' Amelie says. 'You're fine. It didn't even come close.'

'He was frightened,' Elin says.

Amelie nods.

While they were waiting for the anaesthetic to take effect, Elin had given a brief outline of what happened out in Hackefors.

'It's terrible, children having to experience things like that,' Amelie says.

'Can I go now?'

Amelie nods, smiles softly, and narrows her eyes slightly as she says: 'My surname's Grenberg. Just so you know.'

The children are with Social Services.

At the emergency hostel on Klostergatan.

We're wrecking your lives, Malin thinks.

She's sitting at her desk, has just switched her computer off and is about to go home for the second time. It's just gone midnight.

Mummy and Daddy vanish.

Don't love you any more.

The interview with Petronella Andersson has also been concluded. She's still saying that Jakob has been lying to her as well.

Malin has just spoken to Elin Sand.

The scalpel wound is superficial, and she'll be back at work the day after tomorrow.

She praised her.

Made the effort to do that much.

Said she'd handled a bloody difficult situation very well. Admitted that as the more experienced officer she ought to have been better prepared before they went in, but that events like that happen in a murder investigation, when things often happen quickly, all at once.

Malin stands up.

Zeke comes over to her.

'Are you annoyed?' Malin asks.

'Annoyed about what?'

'Because I took our new hotshot with me to Hackefors without calling you?'

'I'm glad I missed it. I was having a nice time relaxing on the sofa at home while you were chasing through the forest and Elin was trying to sort out the trailer trash.'

Malin nods and switches off her desk lamp.

'Come on,' Zeke says. 'I'll drive you home.'

In a single bed in the emergency hostel run by Social Service's family unit, located in a flat at 43 Klostergatan, lies Steven Andersson, ten and a half years old, breathing hard.

He's whimpering, but no one can hear him, the woman who's supposed to hear his whimpers is talking on the phone in another room, to a friend who lives in Australia.

Steven Andersson can still feel the cold scalpel in his hand.

He can hear Anton crying.

Can see Judith in front of him, tears streaming down her face, and feel his sister Fia's arm on his, as she gives him the scalpel, and he trusts her, and her face gives nothing away, and Mum's lying on the floor, and why is Mum lying on the floor, and what's that woman doing with Anton in the kitchen?

Why is he screaming? And why has he stopped?

And now Steven's walking through the hall, and he's whimpering softly, scared and alone, and what's she doing with Anton, is she going to throw him out of the window?

Anton.

She mustn't throw you out of the window.

I stab her.

That's what I do.

I stab her.

What sort of room is this? It's cold here. It isn't nice.

Anton. Fia. Judith. Where are you?

Where's Mum? Dad?

'Mum,' he calls through his sobs. 'Mum! Dad! Come and get us!'

But how are you going to know where we are?

27

His elbow aches.

Johan Jakobsson has taken a cocktail of painkillers so he can dive deeper into the files on the hard-drive they found hidden in Patrick Andergren's house.

He's just had a call from Andersson in Forensics. They're evidently still working too, even though it's past midnight.

Forensics have finally managed to crack the password on the hidden drive.

It turned out to contain a number of locked folders, with the umbrella title 'Vietnam'. Andersson said they'd tried to get into the folders but had failed, and would try again tomorrow. He's uploaded the whole of the hard-drive onto their communal server so that Johan can have a go at cracking the codes himself.

Johan's the last detective at the station now, and the open-plan office around him is in darkness. The few uniformed officers who have to cross the room do so slowly, the way people do in darkened rooms.

He could do this at home.

Closer to his family, but he can't help feeling that he should stay and plough on, and go and lie down in the staff room if he needs to sleep.

He single-handedly managed to get into Patrick Andergren's emails just before four this afternoon. He spent two hours looking through the emails, to see if he could find anything connected to bribery, to anything remotely improper.

All he found were some cryptic emails to and from an address in Vietnam, nlc@nlc.viet.

He hasn't been able to find out what NLC could be.

The messages were in English.

Short phrases, out of context, seemingly incomprehensible.

So no info.

OK then.

That sort of thing. Some of the messages must have been deleted. It was all very cryptic.

And then the last one, to Patrick:

You say don't fuck with me. I say to you:

DON'T FUCK WITH ME.

Why? Who? Could he find out who the address belonged to? Did it mean anything?

He tries to get around the passwords of the locked folders on the hidden hard-drive, but soon realises he's going to need Forensics' help.

What could be in the folders?

What could be so important that you would protect it like that?

During the day Johan has also received the lists of calls to and from Patrick and Cecilia's mobiles.

Cecilia Andergren's lists contained nothing remarkable.

The same with most of Patrick's too, really.

Private calls, and work calls to numbers that could easily be identified as belonging to people he was doing business with.

There were a few unidentifiable calls to pay-as-you-go mobiles in Vietnam, +84 789 900 00, +84 900 01 22, +84 488 299 28 38.

Nothing odd about pay-as-you-go numbers.

In countries like that, a lot of people have that sort

of number. Long-term contracts are a financial impossibility.

But the calls, the numbers, and the emails still need to be checked out.

Full details of the couple's finances have also arrived from their bank.

A seventy-five per cent mortgage on the house, in spite of the inheritance from Uncle William.

He's checked back through several years of bank statements. No unexpectedly large amounts. Nothing that was difficult to explain.

If Patrick Andergren had been receiving kickbacks on bribes, the money must have gone somewhere, but it hadn't gone into any Swedish accounts, that much was certain.

Perhaps they had accounts abroad.

Malta, the Cayman Islands, Singapore. Indonesia. No problem at all hiding money if you didn't want to route it through Sweden.

He'll have to make a start checking possible transactions and accounts tomorrow. Too late now.

When the room is empty, Johan can detect how it really smells. It smells of tiredness, sweat, and adrenalin.

His elbow still aches.

The pills aren't having any effect. He's got some Tramadol in his desk drawer, and that usually takes the edge off the pain. It works on the pain receptors in the brain, and usually makes him feel pleasantly relaxed.

But it messes up his stomach.

Johan opens the drawer.

Takes two white pills from the pack.

Swallows them without water.

Then he carries on working. Apart from the locked folders, the hard-drive only contains fairly typical family stuff.

The same things that were on the family's laptop computer?

He opens the photograph archive.

Sees the family on a beach in some tropical country.

Someone else behind the camera.

Mum, dad, the adopted child, the little girl, maybe three years old, laughing.

Who's taking the picture? Johan wonders.

Some waiter at a restaurant? The person behind the email address? It could be anyone.

He rubs his eyes and can feel how tired he is.

Börje Svärd rolls off her, the far too fat woman he picked up at the dance tonight.

She's the same age as him, and has the short, dyed red hair that's so typical of the city's 'cheeky girls' who are really just spritely old dears.

But they've got a bit of go in them, these old things. Any one of them could finish him off.

He prefers them a bit slimmer than this one, though, the fat ones have slightly milky skin. She's still groaning, he was rough with her, but not as rough as she was with him.

For more than fifteen years Börje didn't have sex with anyone at all. When Anna became sick she lost all desire for sex, and then the illness made any sort of sex impossible, her entire body had been shaken by spasms the last time they tried.

And now it's as if the decades of bodily needs had collected in his body and finally require an outlet.

'My God, my God,' the fat woman groans beside him. 'We're going to have to do that again.'

Sure, Börje Svärd thinks.

Then he feels his erection subside, and finds himself thinking about the man he met out at Jägarvallen earlier today, Stig Sunesson. Johan managed to dig out some information about him, but didn't find anything odd.

He simply seemed to be an ordinary man who had heard rumours and seen something in the paper, put two and two together and overreacted.

No point in going any further with him, not at the moment.

But there could obviously be something in the bribery angle.

Murder.

Child abduction.

And the problems they had encountered with Saab and Ericsson. Pathetic. He doesn't even want to think about it now.

If the Andergrens knew their killer, it could have been someone they met out in India or Vietnam. And Karin Johannison had suggested they may well have known their killer. Unless they didn't. One possibility among all their other lines of inquiry.

Börje's erection has subsided completely now. What was her name again?

He reaches out his hand.

Fumbles, but the room is full of the sweet, heavy smell, and he finds himself thinking about his children, grown up now, and how they moved out as soon as they could when their mum got sick, couldn't bear to see her suffering from MS.

He understands them now, even if he doesn't really miss them all that much. The last time they met was at the funeral, but they call each other every so often.

He and Anna had to manage on their own.

And now he's managing alone.

But if something happened to them, if one of his children disappeared? Then he'd search until time ran out.

Now it's as if the air is running out instead.

His hand finds sensitive, wrinkled skin.

He's found the fat woman, Marianne's swollen nipple, and soon enough she starts giggling in exactly the right way.

Per Sundeberg, the diver, knows that darkness is waiting for him, even up at the surface.

But there are other people there, his colleagues, and floodlights illuminating the water of the Stångå River.

Down here he's alone.

The others wanted to call it a day, but he decided to do one last dive. He wants to fine-comb every last centimetre of the riverbed. And that takes time in the darkness.

One last go at being a sniffer-dog.

Trying to find the girl, even if deep down he knows that she isn't here, that they've been working far too long, and his whole body is stiff from the cold water.

No naked white body has drifted past, eyes wide open.

And he's grateful to have avoided that sight.

But he knows he wouldn't have looked away if the girl's lifeless body had floated towards him.

Per Sundeberg fills his lungs with oxygen.

Slowly moves up towards the surface, towards the floodlights and dark sky.

My work here is done, he thinks.

Now others will have to take over.

Head above the surface.

He removes the mouthpiece.

Night air in his lungs.

And he feels the planet move on its axis, feels the water flow slowly, slowly past his body, as if it were trying to find a different sort of clarity.

Jakob Andersson is lying on the bunk in the custody cell, fully clothed, and he's freezing even though he's pulled the blanket up under his chin.

He was only allowed to see a doctor after the interrogation, and the doctor, a young man, confirmed that he had some minor internal bleeding in his knee and gave him a couple of painkillers.

Fucking Kalle Lundbäck, unable to keep his mouth shut. He'll pay for that.

Messages carved on the walls.

Fuck the pigs.

I like wanking.

Kill the cops.

Mum!

He thinks about the children.

About Petronella.

He tries to figure out how he's ended up here, what happened before and during that evening, and what's likely to happen now.

But he's too tired.

Too confused.

And the kids must be in some sort of emergency hostel, and they shouldn't be there.

Anton.

Probably lying in the dark, whimpering now.

Scared.

Like I was when the cops came back.

What do these bastard cops know about anything? They've got no idea.

I don't want to lose everything.

They won't get anything more.

And Jakob Andersson closes his eyes.

But it's not his own children he sees in his mind's eye. It's Ella.

Little, little Ella.

That day when his mother-in-law turned sixty-eight and they all met up for once, and didn't argue all afternoon.

Ella.

He had thought she was pretty then.

But now.

In the images in his head she's filthy, and she's asleep. She is asleep, isn't she? She must be asleep, asleep, nothing else.

Will Petronella forgive me? Jakob Andersson wonders.

Could she?

As desperate as me, just as determined not to give up, but it could still be there somewhere, the desire to sink as far as possible.

But . . .

Can I base my life on a lie?

Can anyone?

Or do we need truth as a foundation?

Jakob Andersson pushes the blanket off him.

Walks over to the grey-painted metal door of the cell, opens the hatch and yells for the guard, yells that he's got something to say.

And a few cells away sits his wife Petronella, wondering what he could have to say, wondering what he was really doing that evening, because he couldn't have killed anyone, could he?

She feels the hard bunk beneath her.

Feels life come full circle.

Something is ending, and something else is beginning.

28

There's a banging sound in Malin's head.

Shrieking, whining, breathing hard in her ear.

Stop it.

Stop it, for fuck's sake!

I don't want to, I don't want to.

The room. The bedroom.

That's where I am. I'm supposed to be asleep now, not be awake, not wake up yet, how many hours' sleep have I had?

She struggles to push the covers off and reaches for her mobile on the bedside table, desperate to make the wretched thing stop ringing, and presses to take the call.

The station.

A colleague, male, at the other end.

'Jakob Andersson,' he says. 'He's changed his mind. He wants to talk. Wants to talk to you now.'

'It's five o'clock. Can't it wait?'

'Are you coming?'

'Twenty minutes,' Malin says. 'Give me twenty minutes.'

Four kids. What does that leave you with?

Constant money worries.

Failure. No self-respect.

Too little of everything.

Why would anyone so much as look at me? Or, even more unlikely, actually want me?

Jakob Andersson listens to his thoughts as he looks at the tired but attractive Detective Inspector Malin Fors on the other side of the table in the interview room.

Hears himself say: 'I was with my lover that evening. I didn't want Petronella to know anything. I was with her. We've been seeing each other for six months, we met at a job centre course. I know it's wrong, but when she was interested I couldn't resist.'

Her moist, wonderful cunt.

How could a man say no to that?

What about your cunt, Malin Fors? Dried up? Out of action? And she seems to be able to read my thoughts, gives me a look of disgust. It is disgust, isn't it?

No, she doesn't seem to feel anything.

And she asks him for his lover's name, address, and phone number.

'Her name's Eva Kageström,' he replies. 'She lives on Hamngatan, by the charity shop, in the same building. I don't know her number, my mobile's . . . I haven't got anything to do with those murders. I don't care about the fucking money, I just want the children home. Get my family together again.'

Jakob Andersson falls silent and looks at Malin Fors before going on: 'It's not always so easy, is it? Doing the right thing for your family?'

'We'll check it out,' she says, and stands up.

'Don't tell Petronella,' Jakob says. 'Don't say anything.'

She stops.

Turns to face him.

'I think you should tell her yourself.'

Malin Fors stands in the corridor outside the interview room, she's come straight out instead of stopping in the observation room to discuss the conversation with the two male officers who were watching.

The light from the halogen lamps in the low ceiling is weak, and Malin feels slightly sick. Who am I to judge?

Who am I to feel distaste at Jakob Andersson's sex life?

If Peter was ever unfaithful, I'd kill him, if he was unfaithful now that I, we, are doing all we can to have a child, I'd kill him.

Test tubes.

Examinations.

We're not there yet. And the doctor said it would work, that is what he said, isn't it?

She can feel how lack of sleep is making her memories uncertain.

What did the doctor say? What did I say to Peter?

Malin sighs.

Takes a deep breath, and it feels as if her reflex to breathe is exhausted, as if every human frailty she has ever encountered, her own and others', has worn out the reflex. As if something in her cerebral cortex has been ground down.

Well, they'll just have to look into Eva Kageström.

Be pragmatic, Malin.

See if his alibi checks out.

I'm going to call Zeke now.

He'll probably be relieved to be able to leave home early. That way he won't have to see Gunilla get up, won't have to listen to her bitter sniping over coffee.

Zeke shuts the front door behind him.

Light is slowly creeping back into the world as the sun makes its way above the horizon, and he's struck by how beautiful the garden is at this time of day, on the cusp between night and morning, when the dew lights up the ground and the air is moist and still.

No rain at the moment. There's none forecast all day, there may even be a few hours of clear sky.

Gunilla didn't even wake up when he showered and got ready.

Just as well.

She's always at her worst in the morning. It's as if she always gets out of the wrong side of bed, always finds something irrelevant in the paper to moan about.

Karin never used to complain about things like that. She knows there are real things to get upset about, just like me, she's seen far too much evil in the course of her work.

Shall I take the paper in for Gunilla?

No.

She can fetch it herself. It's not raining.

Zeke walks towards the gate.

Opens it.

Opens the letterbox, takes out the copy of the *Correspondent*, and on the front page is a picture of Malin looking tired and angry, sticking her finger up at the photographer.

The caption reads: *Police under pressure.*

Bastards, Zeke thinks. He wishes he could protect Malin from the journalists, as if she were a member of his family.

And then he chuckles and puts the paper back.

He walks out into the street, thinking: I could leave all this behind.

I could turn my back on all of it.

It's the first time he's felt it so strongly, and the thought takes firm root within him, the idea that it would actually be possible to leave Gunilla.

The frozen image on the television screen is blurred, but Malin can still make out the blonde woman's rather heavy features, the same features that are right in front of her now.

And the man's face, turned towards the camera, is also very familiar.

The woman is writhing on a bed.

The man on top of her.

They're both naked.

Malin can see the bed in real life, beyond the television, in the bedroom of Eva Kageström's neat two-room apartment on Hamngatan.

The flat has been furnished with more taste than money, in a sort of estate-agent style, with a matching lime green sofa and cushions. Only a wine box on the kitchen worktop spoils the impression.

Eva Kageström is sitting on the sofa behind them, only just awake. She's smoking and drinking coffee in her dressing gown, said she'd been expecting to hear from them, and that yes, she could prove his alibi.

Jakob Andersson's face looking towards the camera.

He looks more forceful in the frozen image on screen.

As if for a few short minutes he was the man he could, should, ought to have been.

'I could see how frustrated he was on the course. I realised he'd be a good fuck,' she coughs. 'And that's exactly what I need.'

She nods towards the television.

'You can see the time-code for yourselves. It was that evening. That's why I wanted to show you the recording, or at least a still from it. You don't have to see the rest.'

Malin and Zeke look at the code.

The date matches.

As does the time.

But that sort of thing can be manipulated, Forensics will have to take a look, but I'd be very surprised if there was anything odd about it, Malin thinks.

Jakob Andersson is having an affair, and doesn't want his wife to find out.

It's as simple as that.

Isn't it?

'He was here all night. It's all on tape. We forgot to switch it off.'

Malin turns around.

Looks at the tired, clearly hungover woman.

Same age as me. Am I like that? Do I think nothing really matters either?

'As long as the daft sod doesn't get it into his head to leave his wife,' Eva Kageström says, and takes a drag on her cigarette.

Zeke's face stiffens when she says the words 'leave his wife'.

Is that what's going on, Zeke?

If it is, it's high time, but do you think you'll be any happier?

The cynical smile is back again.

Zeke looks like he feels sick when he sees it.

You'll be happy, Malin thinks. You want Karin, I know that.

Tess. The same age as your eldest grandchild.

But you still want Karin.

Malin smiles a different smile at her colleague, a smile that's completely devoid of irony and cynicism, a smile that bears a modest hope of love.

'But I have to say, he's a damn good fuck,' Eva Kageström says.

We can see everything as we drift up here, in a whiteness that resembles fog.

I want to be close to you, sister, and whisper in your ear that you should forgive Jakob, that he's only human, and sometimes us human beings are slaves to our desires.

But we have the capacity to form families.

And that may be the best thing about us, you.

Stick together, Petronella.

Stick it out.

Forgive him, when you find out what he's done.

And now we can see the two of you stepping out of the police station in the morning light, fending off the reporters and cameras.

We see you go in a police car to the Social Services emergency hostel, we see the children rush to meet you, jump up, hug you, squeeze out all the air separating your love and theirs.

Ella.

We would so dearly love to hug you like that.

That's what Mummy and Daddy want.

But we can't, Ella.

You're not here in our realm, we haven't seen you yet, and we don't want to see you here, because we know what that would mean, and sometimes we've imagined we've heard your voice, but every time it's turned out to be a different child, one of all the thousands of abandoned children that no one is looking for, no one has missed.

We've heard different types of fear to yours, and we've done our best to offer comfort, but there's no cure for true abandonment.

Petronella.

You're going home now, the whole family.

The police drop you off, say 'have a good day', as if they were shop assistants, and you make your way up to your flat, and even though it isn't much, it's still your home.

The children wander through the rooms, as if they'd been gone for months.

They really do exist, they seem to be thinking.

Mum, Dad: you exist. We exist.

And Jakob tells them to go out and play at the back of the block, in the all too rare good weather, tells Fia that she must look after Anton for Dad a while, because he needs to talk to Mum about something, something children mustn't hear, a secret, not a bad secret, a good one.

Then we see you alone in the flat, and the children are playing outside, Anton too, and you're sitting opposite each other at the kitchen table, and we see Jakob's mouth move, we can't hear what he's saying, but we know he's telling you the truth.

Don't cry, sister.

OK, go ahead.

And you cry, and then you get up suddenly and slap him, and you shout at him, and he talks, and what are you both saying? What do people say to each other on such occasions, in a room like that?

Then you slump to the floor.

Jakob sits down beside you.

We can hear him whispering in your ear now.

Forgive me, forgive me, forgive me.

It's over now.

I promise.

I'm sorry.

And you cling to his legs, whisper back.

I'll try, I'll do my best to forgive you. For the children's sake, for our sake.

And we'll leave you there, dear sister. I shall leave my hatred to die, somewhere in your realm.

Why are we only wise after death?

If then.

Why are we blind, even in death? Why can we never see the only thing we really want to see?

29

Just after ten o'clock the detectives of the Linköping Police Violent Crime Unit take their places in the meeting room.

Johan.

Sven.

Waldemar.

Börje.

Zeke.

And Malin.

But no Elin Sand. She's at home, lying on her stomach, with a hole in her backside that isn't supposed to be there.

And already it feels as if Elin Sand's absence has left a gap in the group, even though she's only been part of it a matter of days.

The delayed morning meeting becomes a summary of what they've found out, but only after everyone has had a good laugh at the picture of Malin on the front page of the *Correspondent*, and has complimented her on getting her message across so clearly.

Sven said nothing, but he smiled.

Karim commented on the picture when their paths crossed briefly in the office, saying 'Probably not a smart move,' but even he had smiled and seemed mostly just amused by it.

Malin herself isn't bothered in the slightest.

That finger said what she was thinking.

Fuck off. Leave us alone, let us find the girl, stop bothering us with your desperation for juicy details.

Johan tells them about the phone calls and emails to and from Vietnam, the phone numbers, and how he's sent a request for information to the Vietnamese telecom companies. He tells them about the locked computer folders.

Malin shows a short clip from the video recording, and Johan says it would take a great deal of work in an advanced editing suite to change the time of a date-stamped recording.

'So we can presume it's genuine. His alibi checks out.'

The detectives around the table are all tired.

Trying to focus their thoughts, move the investigation on, and it's Friday, not that there's the slightest chance of them getting any time off for the foreseeable future.

Sven says: 'OK, we're dropping the line of inquiry about the family feud. There's nothing to suggest that Petronella and Jakob Andersson were involved in either the murders or Ella Andergren's disappearance. They may not be a particularly happy family, but the solution to this lies elsewhere.'

None of the detectives protests.

Malin briefly toys with the notion that Jakob and Petronella could actually have commissioned someone else to carry out the murders, but the idea is too far-fetched. Unless you're a career criminal, you can't conjure up a hit man that easily. And hit men are expensive. There's also the fact that the Andergrens may well have known their killer, or known who it was.

They decide to focus on the other two lines of inquiry, bribery and adoption. They all realise that they've got nothing but very weak evidence, but they're also aware that these leads are all they've got to go on.

The divers finished their search late last night.

They'd checked as far as they thought a girl's body could

have been carried with the current. And the dog patrols have called off their search. They've checked all patches of woodland within a five-kilometre radius of the house on Stentorpsvägen without finding anything.

The previous afternoon Waldemar and Börje had driven to Ericsson's headquarters in Norrköping, to interview Patrick Andergren's former colleagues. On the phone the men who had apparently worked with Patrick Andergren had been willing to be interviewed, but when Waldemar and Börje arrived they were given the cold shoulder: the men were unavailable, and would only agree to be interviewed if they were formally called in, and then only in the presence of the company's lawyers.

Almost exactly the same thing had happened at Saab.

But there they had bumped into International Sales President Glenn Rundberg outside the gates.

Börje had recognised him from a picture in the paper.

Glenn Rundberg had been standing in the bitter wind by the barbed-wire-crowned fence in a shiny grey suit, and had told them with a scarcely concealed note of triumph in his voice that there had never been any bribery in 'the firm'.

And that they should be looking at the whole sorry affair as the work of a madman.

Not disrupting the 'nationally vital work of selling top Swedish technology'.

Malin realises that only a miracle could have prevented Waldemar from knocking Glenn Rundberg's teeth out, and in her mind's eye she can see concrete shutters being slammed down in front of them.

'Their reluctance to cooperate is only to be expected,' Sven says from his place at the end of the table. 'As soon as we're finished here, I shall be sending official emails to the management of both companies, asking to talk to the people in question as soon as possible, and also to be allowed to see the companies' internal investigations into all the alleged cases of bribery in India and Vietnam. We'll get authorisation from a prosecutor if need be.'

Börje and Waldemar exchange glances.

Doubtful.

'They can always withhold information from us if they want to,' Waldemar says.

Sven goes on to mention Stig Sunesson, the man at Jägarvallen.

Then he leans over.

Takes out a huge pile of papers from his briefcase, tucked under the table.

He drops the pile on the table with a deafening thud, sending motes of dust into the air.

'The police investigations into bribes in India and Vietnam. None of them ever went to trial, but you'll have to go through them anyway, Börje and Waldemar.'

They agree that Johan should carry on looking into Cecilia and Patrick Andergren's finances, and try to crack the passwords to the locked folders from the hard-drive, while Forensics make their own attempt. Johan's also going to look into the Andergrens' adoption: could there have been anything untoward about it? Could that explain their murders and Ella's disappearance?

Malin and Zeke will spend the day going through the couple's emails and phone calls, in case Johan has missed anything in the wealth of material.

'I was pretty tired,' Johan says. 'And a bit groggy from the pills I took for my elbow.'

'Malin and Zeke, take a look at their private papers as well,' Sven says.

The other detectives grin in their direction.

No one's had a chance to begin looking at all the documents, and it's monotonous work.

After that they all leave the room.

Malin and Zeke spend the whole day staring at their screens and going through the piles of the Andergrens' private papers.

Drinking coffee.

And failing to find anything worthy of note.

They break off for lunch in the canteen.

Work their way through bills and invoices.

Nothing odd.

They check the lists of calls to and from their mobiles and landline. Patrick Andergren appears to have called Adoption World several times in the past year.

Nothing odd about that either, considering the way adoptions are followed up, and Adoption World was the adoption agency the Andergrens had used.

They try to check the unidentified Vietnamese numbers, read emails, and find nothing of interest, but Malin manages to lose herself in the work, as the nagging anxiety inside her fades away, and in her eagerness to forget the things she'd rather avoid, she forgets something she doesn't want to forget.

Don't fuck with me.

The peculiar email that neither Malin nor Zeke can make any sense of.

Don't fuck with me.

A harshness that is markedly different to the gentle, lulling tone of the other emails Patrick Andergren sent.

Was he threatening someone?

Had someone threatened him?

At four o'clock Malin gives up.

Decides to go down to the gym.

Exhaust her muscles, and sweat the crap out of herself before the weekend.

*

Sven is pacing up and down in his office.

He's printed out the two emails he's just received, a few minutes apart: one from Ericsson's head of information, the other from Saab's.

The two emails say more or less the same thing.

As a matter of principle, the companies don't hand out information regarding their own activities, and as far as any allegations of bribery are concerned, official investigations had determined that they were without foundation. Both companies deny that they have any files of their own to share, or that any of their employees might possess valuable information.

Meaning that in their opinion it would be pointless calling them in for questioning.

Neither of the emails mentions Patrick Andergren.

They don't even comment on the murders, the investigation, the little girl.

They just disclaim any involvement.

Protecting their money, their investments, their reputations, making sure the mud doesn't stick.

Sven puts the printouts on his desk. Should I discuss this with Karim? he wonders. The prosecutor? But what could they do that I, we, haven't already tried? We can hardly demand to see documents they claim not to have.

Sven gazes out at the University Hospital. Its façade looks feverish and sweaty in the rain that has started to fall again, despite the favourable forecast that morning.

It's not just the patients in there who are sick, Sven thinks. It's our whole fucking society.

Silence, Waldemar Ekenberg thinks.

No two things go together better than silence and money.

He's sitting behind the wheel of his Volvo 240, on his way home to Mjölby after a fruitless day.

The E4 leads him across the Östergötland Plain, past the brown box of the Mobilia shopping centre outside Mantorp, as he sucks hard on his electronic cigarette.

Heavy rain now, and he's driving carefully, he found himself aquaplaning once and it's not an experience he wants to repeat.

He and Börje have worked their way through the police investigations into bribery at Saab and Ericsson. Patrick Andergren's name didn't appear anywhere. The files were remarkably thin on names generally, and their colleagues appeared to have had difficulty tying anyone to a particular time or place, as if the world of big business was populated by international nomads who never stayed longer than a month or so in any one place, and perhaps lived in one country while looking after business in another.

The wheel vibrates in Waldemar's hands.

The plastic in his mouth is making him thirsty.

He can't wait to get home.

Home to a cold beer.

Home to a world he understands.

Home to his wife.

Thank goodness she's not working tonight. Is she?

Elin Sand has stretched out on her newly bought azure-blue sofa, in the small two-room flat she's subletting on Vasagatan.

She's lying on her stomach, reading a book about Linköping in an attempt to understand the city, and her image of it is being confirmed.

This is a city where the chasm between workers and gentry used to be very wide, but the gaps between them have become increasingly invisible.

There's still a great difference between the classes, high and low, classy and tacky, here in Linköping.

As a cop I count as one of the low, she thinks.

Just like Katarina Karlsson with her birthmark and derisory teacher's salary.

I'm an outcast, Elin thinks.

Just like Malin Fors.

But I like not really fitting into any particular category. Malin seems to be the opposite, she doesn't appear to have come to terms with the fact that she's an outcast.

How could I be anything else?

I can never hide, no more than anyone with a scar or a birthmark, like Katarina Karlsson.

And why should we hide, people like us?

Elin Sand touches the wound on her buttock.

It feels hot.

She closes the book.

Thinks that her body feels hot in more ways than one.

Might just as well stay here.

Peter won't be home this evening either.

Damn duty rota, Malin thinks.

Three twelve-rep goes at the fifty-kilo bench press.

Not many women my age could do that, Malin thinks, picking up the two-kilo dumb-bells and sitting down on the bench. She starts to do bicep curls, breathing out hard through her nose with each lift.

One, two . . .

Sweat pouring off her.

She can feel the wound on the inside of her lip. Only small, it'll probably be gone tomorrow.

What time is it?

Quarter past five. She's been in the gym for over an hour now, and is dripping with sweat, and feels almost sick with hunger and exhaustion.

. . . four, five . . .

Her arm muscles are protesting, but she pretends they aren't hers, they belong to someone else.

. . . eight, nine . . .

And when she bends her arm again she remembers that something was going to happen today, but what?

. . . ten, eleven . . .

And she lets go of the dumb-bells.

Bang.

Almost on her foot.

Twelve will have to wait till another time, because she's just remembered that she promised to pick Tove up from the railway station at half past five, and the clock on the wall of the gym says it's twenty past, I'm never going to make it.

Fuck.

I'm never going to get any better, and Tove knows that.

Will she even expect me to be there?

Malin rushes into the shower. Has to shower.

No.

Instead she runs to the changing room, grabs a towel from the pile by the wall, tears off her gym clothes and wipes the sweat off.

Gets dressed again.

Then she races upstairs, rushes through reception without wishing Ebba a good weekend, and then she's in her car, driving far too fast towards the station.

I have to get there.

Twenty-five to six now.

And the clock on the dashboard says twenty to six as Malin pulls into the car park next to the station.

No sign of Tove under the canopy where people usually wait for taxis or family members who are late picking them up.

Malin parks the car.

Runs into the station, feels that she's still sweating from her exertions in the gym.

She looks up at the screen.

The train has arrived, and Malin feels like shouting out loud, cursing herself.

But instead she goes back to the car.

Drives home to Ågatan.

Parks outside St Lars Church, walks past the Pull & Bear with quick, determined steps.

The key in the lock.

In.

Malin sees Tove's shoes and jacket in the hall, her big, fake Louis Vuitton bag tossed on the kitchen floor.

'Mum!' she hears from the living room. 'Don't suppose you happened to forget I was coming today, did you?'

30

Tove hears her mum in the hall.

Wasn't surprised when she didn't appear at the station like she'd promised. Probably got distracted by some murder.

Just a year or so ago she would have felt sad, but these days she can hardly be bothered to care, and she only waited five minutes before walking the short distance to the flat on Ågatan.

Where she sat down on the sofa.

Turned on the television.

Waited.

Not so much for her mum, as for something to happen, but she knew nothing was likely to happen in this hopeless dump apart from tonight's party, Linn's birthday party. I can go like this, she thought, looking down at her DKNY jeans and top from Urban Outfitters. Whatever I do, I'll still be the best-dressed person there. I'll wear the Hermès scarf I borrowed from Victoria as well.

Mum.

It's a relief that she never comes to parents' days up at Lundsberg.

She'd have to get some better clothes if she did, try to talk a different way, say different things to the other parents.

Tove has sometimes wondered if she's ashamed of her mum, but she isn't. There's nothing worse than being ashamed of your own mum, so I'm not ashamed of her, I'm not.

But she's not like the other mums, Tove thinks, as she hears her mum taking her coat off.

And we have far less money. One of three scholarship kids at the school. That means something.

I've learned that now.

But Peter's got money.

Tove leaps up from the sofa when she sees her mum.

Her hair's all sweaty and she looks like she could do with a shower, her cheeks are flushed, as if she's been running.

'Sorry,' she says.

'It's OK, I walked,' and they hug in the living room, hold each other tightly, and neither of them wants to let go, and when Malin finally tries to break free, Tove squeezes her again.

'Mum, you stink of sweat. Not that it matters.'

They pull apart.

'I didn't have time to shower. I was in the gym. I lost track of time, sorry.'

'Go and have a shower.'

'I thought we could have pizza at Shalom. What do you think?'

'Good idea.'

They've been going to the same pizzeria for years.

Going there always feels right.

She knows she's home then.

Tove listens to her mum shower, sees that she's left the bathroom door open, and calls: 'Where's Peter?'

'He's on call.'

'All evening?'

'You'll probably see him tomorrow.'

Tove sits down at the kitchen table, and catches the smell of food that's been burned in the microwave. The smell of Gorby pies, pots of rice pudding, but also Mum's chicken stew.

She leafs backwards through the *Correspondent*, sees that Saab have placed a whole-page advert for an international salesman, then she reads about the murders her mum is probably working on.

Saab have issued a press release, which the paper has printed in full.

They write that they're 'distraught' about what has happened, that it's 'deeply regrettable', but that it is in no way connected to the company's activities.

Tove reads about the missing girl. Adopted from Vietnam, and the paper also has a short article about recent problems with adoptions from Vietnam.

What if her real mum and dad came to get her back? Tove thinks. And murdered the adoptive parents?

What a terrible job Mum's got.

But maybe the girl's biological parents are dead.

And Tove remembers how she herself was kidnapped, when that madwoman tried to kill her. She had counselling afterwards, but never felt she needed to talk about it, and now, several years later, it's as if it happened to someone else, someone who's no longer her.

The memories are there. But it's like they belong to someone else, or rather, belong to everyone, not just her.

The woman's dead. Mum shot her, so the woman can never hurt me again.

Her mum comes out of the shower.

Tove sees her naked, and she's in such good shape it's ridiculous.

Is it really possible for a mother to be that fit?

Evidently.

The scars on her stomach from the gunshot. Tiny red dots, like burns on her skin. And a somewhat larger scar from the operation.

Peter.

I like him. Can't they just get married, so Mum finally has a bit of money?

You have to try to keep up. Otherwise there's no point.

She hasn't shown her mum the shoes Tom bought her for the spring ball. A pair from Prada that cost four thousand kronor. He paid for her dress as well. Lanvin, six thousand. On sale at NK in Stockholm.

Mum would go mad if she knew.

Her mum goes into the bedroom. Five minutes later she's back, dressed in dark jeans and a white T-shirt.

'Ready for pizza?'

OK, Tove thinks. She can go to Shalom dressed like that.

'Sure. I can go straight to the party from there.'

Salami, ham, prawns, mushrooms.

Pizzas the size of flying saucers.

The sweet smell of oregano and greasy melted cheese.

'When you exercise as much as you do,' Tove says, 'you can eat pizza every day.'

'I doubt it,' Malin says, looking at the white woven wallpaper, then at the dark-haired man in front of the oven stretching dough into a circle and spreading tomato sauce over it.

'Even I don't exercise enough for that.'

'When you get older you put on weight more easily.'

'Do you think I'm old?'

'No.'

Tove picks a slice of salami from her pizza and pops it in her mouth.

'So how's school?' Malin asks.

'Fine,' Tove says, tucking her hair behind her ear with her fingers spread out in a practised, pretentious way.

'Fine? What sort of fine?'

'I'm getting good grades, Mum, don't worry.'

'I'm not worried.'

And Tove stops chewing and looks at Malin, then says, without swallowing the slice of salami: 'So why are you going on about it?'

'I'm not going on about it.'

'Yes you are.'

Malin cuts a piece of pizza, but her stomach seems to be shrinking and her appetite is disappearing.

'I was just asking.'

'You were going on about it. And now you're doing it again.'

Malin swallows. Looks at her daughter once more. She's learned how to put make-up on, Malin thinks. Just the right amount of mascara, and the blusher emphasises her cheekbones.

Don't get angry, Malin thinks to herself. Instead, she asks: 'When do you have to go?'

'Soon. How about you?'

'I thought I might go to the cinema,' Malin says.

'Only common people go to the cinema,' Tove says. 'They smell disgusting, haven't you . . .'

'Stop it, Tove. Just stop it. The people you're calling common are actually people like me. Normal fucking people who have completely normal fucking jobs.'

Tove doesn't bite back.

Instead she looks up at the ceiling and pushes her pizza away.

'I'm going now,' she says. 'Thanks for the pizza, Mum.'

And Malin wishes she could ask her daughter to stay, wants to get up and go after her, but she can't bring herself to, just sits there glued to her seat.

'Ciao,' Tove says as she opens the door.

'Take care,' Malin says, but her words are drowned by the aggressively loud doorbell.

★

The Hamlet.

The noise from what used to be her favourite bar spills out onto Hamngatan.

The light from the yellow windows is warm and inviting, like one of Hans Christian Andersen's matchsticks, and Malin swears silently to herself, cursing herself for making it impossible even to set foot in there.

She misses the hubbub.

The atmosphere.

The sight and smell of people relaxing, people who've earned it after a hard week at a job they don't like or care about.

She wishes she could share that sort of communal feeling right now.

Together with her peers.

The common people.

But she can't settle down on a bar stool.

Because then she'd start drinking.

And if she drinks, everything would go to hell.

She knows that.

The autumn evening is mild. The sky is almost clear above her, and the stars are twinkling in the multi-layered blackness. It's supposed to rain again tomorrow.

Heavy rain.

Malin wonders if she should phone Karin Johannison after all.

She'd like to talk to her.

Find out how she managed to adopt Tess in spite of the ban on adoptions from Vietnam.

She feels like calling Peter.

Or should she just go up to the hospital and go and see him in the duty-doctor's room, maybe they could have another little go at making a baby? It's the right time of the month.

No. Doesn't feel like going up there.

She walks away from the Hamlet, down Hamngatan, avoiding the pubs and bars that line the top part of Ågatan.

Tove, she thinks.

When did you turn into a stranger?

31

Peter Hamse can see the man's skull laid bare in front of him.

The man on the operating table was brought in an hour ago.

A stroke.

The frontal lobe on the left side of his brain. Peter was forced to go in and relieve the pressure, but he can see that the tissue around the Broca's area is dead.

His colleagues in the brightly lit operating room are working in silence, dressed in green overalls and white breathing masks. The nurses assisting him and Zygmunt, the Polish anaesthetist, know what they're doing. Even Vanessa, his American medical student, seems dependable in here.

Routine.

This is routine.

Open the skull, clean it up. Move on.

The dead tissue in the Broca's area will mean that the man won't be able to speak, his tongue will be paralysed. And this particular patient may also lose the ability to understand speech as well, because the damage is so extensive.

Writing? Reading?

Forget it.

'We're done here,' Peter says.

Malin.

On call for the third night in a row, and he misses her.
Would like to have her by his side. But he doesn't feel like
going to the flat on Ågatan.

He'd rather get back to the duty-doctor's room instead.

He's read her medical notes about the gunshot injury.

He shouldn't have done, not according to patient confidentiality rules.

But he couldn't help himself. Brought the file up on his
computer, took the risk.

She doesn't know.

And now he knows that what they're trying to do is
basically pointless. That they're engaged in a physical
impossibility, and who could blame him for not being able
to handle that?

Where do they go from here? Is it even possible to move
on? Do I want to?

What does Malin really think? Could the doctor have
given her positive news, like she's been saying?

Peter can't wait to get back to the duty-doctor's room,
once he's washed and changed clothes.

That's where he wants to be.

He's agreed to do another shift tomorrow night. One of
his colleagues needed time off for some reason.

He said yes without thinking.

He may not have time to see Tove, but that can't be helped.

Peter casts one last look at the open skull, and sees the
brain tissue, language and understanding that have gone
for ever.

WHOOOOOHOOOOOOO!

Tove throws her head back, dances around, around, and
the glitterball hanging from the ceiling in the basement of
Linn's parents' villa in Ramshäll reflects the red, blue and
yellow lights set up around the room.

WHOOOHOOOOOO!

Dance, dance, dance.

She lets herself go, not giving a damn about how she looks or what she's doing, she couldn't care less what the others here think about her.

She's never cared.

But even less now, and when she arrived at the party she couldn't help thinking that the whole lot of them looked like yokels.

But they were happy to see her.

And there's drink.

Two whole bottles of vodka, and she raises her glass as she spins around, puts it to her lips and it's strong but good, whoooahhhhhh.

She feels the rhythm.

Viktor, Hannes, Markus.

They'll all here. What are they doing these days?

Tove spins around, around, around, dancing, and the room turns into a torrent of light, where nothing matters at all.

Malin is lying awake in bed.

Thinking about Peter.

Wants to talk to him, turns on the bedside lamp, calls his number, can't wait any longer for him to call, and he answers on the second ring.

'Hi,' he says. Not 'Hello, darling'.

'Hello, darling. How are you getting on?'

She sits up on the edge of the bed, watches the early rain sliding down the window, the sky outside nothing but black now.

'We had a stroke patient. I'm about to get a bit of sleep, I hope.'

She can see him in her mind's eye. In jeans and a top

in some passageway, then in his white doctor's coat, and she can hear his wooden-soled sandals echoing down the phone.

'Bad?'

'Very. An old boy.'

'Tove's arrived.'

Nothing about losing track of time, completely forgetting when her daughter was due to arrive.

'She'd like to see you.'

'I've got to work tomorrow as well. I'll have to see if I've got time.'

Coolness in his voice.

And she's so fond of you.

'She'll be disappointed.'

'Please, don't go on about it. I have to work. It can't be helped.'

You don't sound disappointed, Malin thinks. Why not?

'OK,' she says.

She makes an effort to soften her voice, lies back on the bed, presses her buttocks into the sheet.

'I wish you were here. I'm feeling lonely,' and she hopes he'll tell her to come to the duty-doctor's room.

'We can see each other during the day tomorrow. OK?'

She takes a deep breath.

Steels herself.

Has to get this said.

'Peter, you know I want a child as much as you.'

Silence.

She can hear him breathing, deeply, slowly, and she waits for him to respond.

'You do know that, don't you?'

The silence continues.

'Don't you?'

And when his answer comes, it's out of nowhere.

'But can you even have a child?'

His words like a slap over the phone. Of course I can have a child, she thinks, even if the doctor said that it might be difficult, he said it was possible. Didn't he?

And Peter is talking now, and she realises that she's unlocked something inside him.

'I looked at your medical notes, Malin, and whatever he said to you, he must have been ridiculously optimistic because he didn't want to disappoint you. Your womb is in a terrible state, it would take a miracle for you ever to bear my child.'

Hard. Resigned.

Impatient.

Malin holds the phone away from her, can't bear to hear this. Then she whispers, in a hissing snake-voice: 'It's not true, it's not true. You're lying. Have you read my medical notes? What fucking right—'

'Every right, Malin. I'm starting to get old. I had to know if it's possible.'

Who are you, Peter Hamse? Malin finds herself wondering.

What you're saying isn't true, but she's starting to have doubts again now, what did the doctor actually say after the operation, she thought he said there was a good chance, but did he really say no chance? Did my brain turn it into what I wanted to hear?

Is that it?

Am I going mad?

'I need you to understand me,' Peter says.

His voice pleading.

She knows she ought to be furious with him, with his harshness, for reading her medical notes, for sounding so resigned, but she can't feel angry.

Instead she looks at the window, the rain forming broad,

heavy rivers on the glass, and sees her face faintly reflected in the rivers, sees her features, her blonde hair draining away, down into an unknown darkness, an even greater river.

'Are you angry?'

He's no longer walking along the passageway.

He's stopped, standing still. She can hear it. No more footsteps. He's breathing slowly and steadily.

'It's so fucking difficult,' he says. 'What are we going to do?'

'There are other options.'

'A surrogate mother? Test tubes wouldn't work. Adoption? That's not for me, you know that, and it isn't for you either.'

Ella.

Tess.

It is difficult to imagine any more beautiful girls, but even if their love is genuine and strong, it wouldn't work, they're too old, Peter's already forty-two.

'What are we going to do?' Malin asks.

Practically impossible, that's what the doctor said.

No.

He said *impossible*.

He said: 'Be happy with the daughter you've already got.'

He said: 'You're young, you could adopt.'

She remembers the doctor's friendly, sympathetic face when he spoke to her before discharging her, when she asked: 'Can I have children?'

He shook his head.

Malin remembers it all now, her memory for words, gestures, is crackling with electricity now.

The doctor's office.

Furnished the way health service rooms always are.

His white hair, white coat, thin lips when he said: 'I'm

sorry, but I have to say this. It would be extremely difficult, not to say completely impossible, for you to have another child.'

How did that happen? Malin thinks.

I got a taxi home.

Slept for almost twenty-four hours.

I woke up. Remembered him telling me that I could have a child.

I was sure of it.

Tried and tried.

How did that happen?

'I'm sorry, Peter,' she says. 'I'm so sorry,' and tears are streaming down her cheeks now, and her tears become part of the unknown rivers on the window, and she's on her own in the room, hears Peter's voice.

'I don't know what we're going to do, Malin. I don't know what I'm going to do. We'll talk tomorrow, or the day after. OK?'

She breathes.

Wipes the tears from her cheeks with her free hand.

Whispers into the phone: 'OK. No problem. That's fine.'

32

Does anything ever turn out fine?
   Nothing.
   Everything.
   Jellyfish tentacles, a thousand kilometres long, are chasing Malin in her dream, forcing their way into her, making their way into her womb, releasing their burning poison and killing everything in her that they can kill, want to kill.
   She's swimming under the surface in cold, dark water, and warm currents are coming towards her, and she knows that life is seeping out of her, and she sees a shining light, a lost star, and she swims towards its rays, but the tentacles hold her back, drag her towards the bottom, and she struggles to get up to the surface, her lungs are about to explode and she knows she can drown in the dream, and she fights, jerks, tries to fend off the speckled water-snakes and eels, and she's burning inside, what's all that poison doing to me?
   The surface.
   I can see it up there.
   The light.
   I have to get there, and her mouth burns as she bites through the jellyfish tentacles, as she chews the heads off the hungry eels, and the warm water is gone, ice washes over her, and she's dying.
   Part of her dies.

Then the stinging tentacles let go.

And she can swim towards the light.

Kick her way up, thinking that it will be OK, but just before she breaks the surface the light disappears.

Tess is screaming in the dream now, her face contorted in unknown torment.

Ella is screaming.

She doesn't sound human. What are they doing to you?

I catch a glimpse of you.

You're leaning against a damp wall, and then you're gone, pretending that your world no longer exists, that what's happening to you isn't really happening.

Is that a coffin you're sitting in?

Aren't you supposed to lie down in coffins?

Then the girls are gone.

I need to get a move on, Malin Fors thinks in the dream, I've got to save you.

I've got to save myself.

But how?

And then the ice and water disappear and Malin hears a familiar voice, and she knows that the voice comes from the waking world, from the other side of dream and sleep, and she takes the chance, escapes from the dream, opens her eyes and puts her hands beneath her, feels that the sheets are wet with sweat, as if she'd drained away, as if something had wanted to drown her in her sleep.

She opens her eyes.

Tove in the gloom. Her face close, and she says in a slurred voice: 'Mum, I feel sick, I've got to . . .'

And Malin smells the alcohol on Tove's breath before she suddenly throws up on her, and she tries to block it, but most of the vomit still hits her left cheek.

The remains of the pizza.

Malin sits up.

'For fuck's sake, Tove!'

And Tove slumps to the bedroom floor, throws up again on Malin's bed, and Malin switches the bedside light on and sees her daughter on the floor, her filthy, wet clothes, hears her mutter something about being 'so fucking hammered'.

'Yes, you're drunk.'

'Deduced by an expert.'

Drunk.

But still smarter than me.

Malin leans over, takes her daughter under the arm and helps her up, then leads her off to the bathroom, where she puts her on the floor of the shower without taking her clothes off. Then she turns the shower on. Tove hisses and swears and protests when the ice-cold water hits her body, but slowly, slowly, Malin sees her daughter come to her senses again.

Malin washes Tove's vomit from her face.

Turns the shower off.

Leans over.

Helps Tove take her clothes off, then gets her to her feet and almost has to carry her to her bedroom. Tove's heavy, so heavy, and Malin can feel her back creak, and in the dim light of the hall she sees her daughter's naked body, a woman's body, a woman in the prime of life.

Tove in bed.

Tove under the covers.

Tove with a green bucket next to her.

Tove looking up at her with clouded eyes, full of love.

'Thanks, Mum.'

And Malin shakes her head, knows better than to reproach her, and she doesn't want to admit it, but somewhere deep inside she's envious of her daughter, would have loved the opportunity to drink herself senseless tonight.

But she can't.

Impossible.

'I'll make some coffee,' she says, and Tove nods in the darkness. Malin can just make out the beautiful features of her face as her daughter closes her eyes, the whole world must be spinning, and then she opens them again.

It takes five minutes for Malin to make coffee.

When she comes back, Tove's fast asleep.

Lying on her back.

Snoring loudly.

Malin crouches down beside the bed and rolls her daughter onto her side, gently, so she doesn't wake up.

Change the sheets.

Put them in the wash.

Wash hands.

Switch on the computer in the bedroom, surf the net, can't sleep now, doesn't want to think about anything.

Tove.

You must be stressed. I'm too hard with you. And then you drink too much when you get a chance to relax.

I'm not going to tell you off. But take care.

The computer.

Google.

Malin types in the words *adoption* and *Vietnam*.

Fourteen million results.

adoption Vietnam mother did not know

Six million results.

She skims through the list.

Downward.

Onward.

Vietnam. Lost children. Adoption.

New words fly out of her head onto the keyboard, and above the hum of the computer she can hear Tove breathing in her sleep.

One result links to a newspaper article.

And she clicks through to the *Vietnam Post*, an English-language paper, and finds herself looking at an article profiling one of the people in the Foreign Ministry who is alleged to have facilitated the fake adoptions.

Then another article, a case resembling the one Johan found, about a woman who was persuaded by the local authorities to leave her son in a children's home, where he would be fed and given an education.

Then the boy was adopted, without her knowledge or permission.

To Holland.

In this instance.

The title of the article is 'Lost Children', and the picture of the woman holding a photograph of her son towards the camera, the despair in her eyes, leaves Malin short of breath.

The woman is said to have been given money to hand her child over to the children's home 'for a while', but nothing was ever said about adoption, just schooling and food.

Her son's adoption has been formally processed in Holland.

Conclusion: No way back.

Say goodbye to your son.

Accept it.

You're never going to see him again.

Then another article about the number of children who are believed to have disappeared that way. Possibly up to five thousand. Ten thousand.

'The mother knew what was going on,' an anonymous source says.

'After all, she even got paid.'

The woman's eyes.

An impossible shade of black.

If grief has a colour, that's it.

How many others were paid, Malin wonders, before the children reached their adoptive parents? And how much did those parents pay?

She carries on browsing.

Types in English: *adoptions Vietnam foul*

A PDF.

An official document from the United States Department of State, with the title: 'A child for a pig'.

The file, sent from the US embassy in Hanoi to the State Department in March 2008, summarises the results of an investigation into accusations of illegal adoptions in Vietnam.

A child for a pig was the anticipated title of an article that was about to be published in the Vietnamese press about how Americans had bought Vietnamese children, and for what price.

The expression had become established in common parlance as the answer to the question: How much does a child cost 'at source'?

The names in the document have been redacted.

A child for a pig.

Malin thinks.

A child for a pig.

Johan Jakobsson is also sitting at his computer, at home in Linghem.

He's sitting at the small workspace on the ground floor, next to the hall, in the cubbyhole before you get to the kitchen. His family is asleep upstairs, and his face looks red in the light of the screen.

His cheeks are flushed with excitement.

During the evening he managed to dig out documents about exactly which projects Patrick Andergren worked on in Vietnam, and what his division and department were called.

He hacked into a computer at Ericsson. Serves them right, when they've refused to cooperate.

And now Johan is looking through the media archive, searching for *Ericsson, bribes, Vietnam,* and he finally finds a lengthy article on the subject in *Dagens Industri.*

He downloads it.

Reads.

The report doesn't identify any individuals or specific projects, but one place is mentioned as the alleged centre for one of the largest bribes that Ericsson is said to have paid for deals in Vietnam.

Da Lat.

Telephone exchanges, mobile networks.

The sum of twenty million Swedish kronor is mentioned.

And Da Lat is precisely where Patrick Andergren is supposed to have been responsible for sales, among them the very project to which the article appears to refer.

Johan looks for other articles.

But the whole subject appears to have faded away, lost in denials and a lack of evidence.

Just like the Swedish police investigations.

What else can I find? Johan thinks. What else?

Plenty of people would consider committing murder for twenty million. Even if we'd prefer not to believe it of ourselves.

33

Tove is more dead than alive on the other side of the kitchen table.

Her face is grey-green, and her dark blonde hair is hanging lankly from her head.

A glass of Coca-Cola in front of her.

It's ten o'clock.

Malin has allowed herself a late start, wanted to see Tove get up, and is trying to concentrate on that instead of last night's conversation with Peter.

What did we actually say?

What did he say?

She doesn't quite trust herself.

But the doctor's words.

She remembers them now, and is Peter going to leave me? I didn't know I was lying, I thought everything was OK.

'How are you feeling?' she asks Tove.

'How does it look like I feel?'

'Great!'

'I suppose you know all about hangovers.'

'That's a bit below the belt.'

Tove takes a gulp of the Coca-Cola, her eyes are bloodshot and Malin watches as she forces down the drink, and can't help laughing.

'It'll get better,' she says.

'You think?'

'I know. As long as you don't start again, because then you risk getting stuck in a never-ending hangover.'

'And we don't want that.'

Malin takes a sip of her coffee.

A wall of rain outside the window.

Maybe this Saturday will bring something good?

'Any more tips?'

'About what?'

'How to get through it?'

'Try two raw eggs in milk, with a dash of Tabasco,' Malin says, and when Tove hears the ingredients she leaps up from her chair and lurches into the bathroom.

Malin, Zeke, and Johan are sitting in the conference room.

Elin Sand has got the day off again, because of her injured backside.

Waldemar and Börje are standing by at home, ready to come in at short notice if anything dramatic happens.

Saturday.

No children in the preschool playground, and the blinds have been pulled down, as if to hide some secret out-of-hours activity.

Malin's just told them about the articles she found, the same or very similar to those Johan had already discovered.

There have clearly been serious problems with adoptions from Vietnam. Not just isolated cases, but systemic abuse. A sick mix of abducted children, money both above board and under the table, poverty, longing, and despair.

'I haven't found anything on their computers that suggests that their adoption was suspect,' Johan says.

'What about the locked folders?'

'We haven't cracked those yet.'

'We'll have to get the adoption agency to send us the

documentation about Ella's case,' Zeke says. 'We need to try to get hold of someone there, even if it is Saturday.'

'Sven's already asked them,' Johan says.

Then Johan tells them what he's found out about the bribes, and the fact that Patrick Andergren worked in the same city, and on one of the same projects in which bribery was suspected.

Da Lat.

When Malin hears the name of the city, she feels an intense longing to get away, to travel around the planet and see more of the world than this godforsaken dump.

'I'm convinced there's something important in those folders,' Johan says. 'I've spoken to the Economic Crime Unit, to see if they can dig out any international information about the Andergrens' finances. I haven't been able to make any progress on that.'

He goes on: 'Those calls from Patrick Andergren's mobile to Vietnam were registered on servers in Ho Chi Minh City – Saigon, in other words. So it looks like that's where whoever he was talking to was when he called. All the ones made in the past year, anyway. That's as far as I've been able to get with the Swedish network operator. Any more precise information would require the cooperation of the Vietnamese telecoms company. I haven't managed to find out anything useful about the email addresses.'

'"Don't fuck with me",' Malin quotes.

'Nothing about that email either,' Johan says. 'I can't get beyond the server.'

'Is it possible to get hold of personal details from whoever owns the server?'

Johan shakes his head.

'They probably have no idea. It's a free server, used by loads of email providers. Tens of millions of emails every day, plenty of which will be using anonymising software.'

Johan rubs his elbow, and Malin can see how tired he is, knows he's taken a deep personal interest in Ella's disappearance, his own children are almost the same age, so sleep will have to wait a while longer.

'But I have managed to get hold of the name of a guy who's supposed to have worked as a consultant for Ericsson in Vietnam at the same time that Patrick Andergren was there. From Linköping, apparently. He's evidently set up his own IT company, you may even have heard of it. Datasonic, to stream audio files faster. Very successful, from the look of it.'

'What's his name?'

'Magnus Nyblom.'

Malin recognises the name, and after a few seconds she manages to place him.

A seriously wealthy man, who goes around the bars acting like he owns Linköping. The same Magnus Nyblom who let the *Correspondent* do a profile of him, portraying him as the saviour of the city.

'Two thousand jobs, I promise!'

That was three years ago.

So far there have been forty new jobs, if Malin remembers the most recent article correctly. Mind you, that's more than most new businesses manage.

'Let's pay him a visit,' Malin says. 'See if he's got anything to say.'

Zeke scratches his head and sucks his cheeks in, making him look more skull-like than ever.

'He's not likely to say anything, is he?'

Malin shakes her head.

'But it's worth a try. We haven't got anything else to go on, have we? We can call people at Saab and Ericsson in for interviews, but that'll take time, and before we do that we need to try to work out who it would be worth talking to.'

'Yes, what about Saab?' Zeke says. 'Have you managed to find anything there? After all, that's where Patrick Andergren was working when he was killed.'

Johan shakes his head.

'It's not easy when they pull the shutters down. Don't even ask how I found out that Nyblom and Patrick Andergren were working on that project in Da Lat. All I've been able to find out about bribery at Saab are cases that took place years before Patrick Andergren worked there. It's serious stuff, though, weapons systems being sold on to third parties, to opposing sides in ethnic conflicts.'

'Maybe he tried to put a stop to something at Saab?' Zeke suggests. 'Or couldn't keep quiet about what he'd seen at Ericsson? There could be plenty of people with money and vested interests to protect.'

'Maybe,' Johan says. 'But that wouldn't explain why the girl's missing. Or why they murdered Cecilia.'

The three of them fall silent.

'If this is connected to those bribery cases,' Malin says, 'or even to the arms trade, it's possible that the people behind it want to scare other people, make them more amenable.'

She pauses before going on: 'That could apply if there was bribery going on while he was at Ericsson, or later at Saab. Unless Patrick Andergren took bribes at Ericsson, and tried to do the same at Saab, but something went wrong?'

'Do you believe that?' Johan asks.

'I'm just thinking out loud,' Malin says. 'Even if most engineers are gentle as lambs, there are probably people in that profession who'd do anything for money as well.'

'You bet your ass there are,' Zeke whispers.

*

Karin Johannison is sitting on a pink bench in the indoor play centre in Tornby industrial estate, tucked away among the units, about a kilometre from Ikea and the Ikano shopping centre.

Three metres away Tess climbs up a small blue slide, and cautiously shuffles out until she starts to move, then laughs and beams when she reaches the bottom.

The ball pool a short while ago.

Tess swam through the strange coloured sea, becoming all the colours of the balls, becoming an amalgam of every feeling for me, Karin thinks, and is aware that what she's experiencing now, in this noisy, jam-packed, badly ventilated play centre is a sort of perfection. Can the feeling of being exactly where you should be ever be wrong? Can whatever a person has done in order to experience that feeling ever be wrong?

I'm hypothesising, Karin thinks.

But the little girl in front of her is no hypothesis, and what she cries in her limpid, gurgling voice is true: 'Mummy, Mummy. Look!'

Balls. Slides.

And Karin knows she'd give her life for Tess's sake.

She'd kill for Tess's sake.

She'd try to do the right thing, at any cost.

And our love is right, isn't it, Tess?

Her mobile rings.

Watch me on the slide, Mummy,

Mummy, Mummy, Mummy.

34

Malin stops inside the door to the play-park. Tries to acclimatise to the noise and the garish colours. In the distance she can see Tess running towards Karin, who's sitting on a bench with her arms out.

Tove.

You used to run to me like that.

That'll never happen to me again.

No child of mine will ever run towards me like that again.

Grandchildren, Malin thinks. But it could be twenty years before Tove decides to have children.

It's already eleven o'clock, and the play centre is at its Saturday busiest. Kids are running to and fro, shouting, climbing, sliding, throwing balls, licking lollies, and at the tables by the door at least three birthday parties are underway, and the floor between the tables is almost covered in colourful, crumpled wrapping paper.

Zeke's waiting in the car.

'I need to talk to her alone,' and Zeke didn't protest.

Malin called Karin after the meeting at the station.

And Karin asked her to come out here, to this Hades for every illusion that life with small children is enjoyable.

Tess in Karin's arms now.

And beyond a bright-blue area of astroturf covered with climbing frames, Malin sees a hand wave in the air, Karin's hand, then watches as Karin puts Tess down, gets to her feet, and walks towards her colleague.

'Hi, how are you doing?' Malin asks, giving Karin a quick hug.

'Fine,' Karin smiles. She clearly has no idea why Malin is there.

Or does she?

Few people can be quite so inscrutable as Karin.

'But Tess is doing even better,' and Karin points past Malin, who turns around. A few metres away, Tess is now sitting in an enormous sandpit with a spade in her hand, concentrating on filling a bucket with sand. She clearly only needed a few seconds in Karin's arms.

Digging.

Making a sandcastle.

Malin looks at Tess.

She doesn't know if she's going to be able to hold back her tears now, if she's going to have an angry outburst, or what.

Over by one climbing frame a mother is trying to tell her son to be more careful, while the boy's father goads him on, saying to the mother: 'He's got to get braver. That's how he's going to develop.'

'What if he falls?' the mother hisses. 'If he breaks his neck?'

Malin turns back to Karin, sits down on the bench, and Karin sits down next to her.

'I presume you wanted to talk about something in particular, otherwise you wouldn't come out here on a Saturday.'

Malin doesn't answer.

Her mind is teeming with thoughts.

How can I say this without sounding suspicious, without making Karin defensive? What words are there?

'Ella, the missing girl,' Malin begins, just loud enough

for Karin to hear her over the noise. 'She was adopted from Vietnam, like Tess.'

'That's right,' Karin says. 'But there are several hundred adopted children from Vietnam in Sweden.'

'You know there have been problems? With parents who were tricked into giving up their children?'

Karin turns to face Malin, who has never seen her eyes so black.

Karin is breathing slowly.

Doesn't break eye contact with Malin.

For a few short seconds Malin thinks Karin's going to attack her, grab hold of her and try to strangle her, then Karin relaxes and her eyes are normal, friendly again.

'I can see what you're thinking,' she says mildly. 'That there could have been something funny about the adoption, that that could be a possible motive for the murders.'

Malin nods.

Thinks: Good, let the conversation go that way, then steer it back to Karin herself.

'I don't think that could be the reason,' Karin says. 'I haven't heard of a single case where the Vietnamese parents have actually tried to get their children back. It's always been about money, for the parents themselves, and the lawyers and officials who act on their behalf.'

Do you believe what you're saying, Karin?

You have to.

I can understand that.

'So you don't know anything you think I should be aware of? Come on, Karin. You wouldn't have adopted Tess without looking into everything very carefully.'

Tess.

Her face is slightly darker than the other children in the sandpit, her hair more black, her laugh louder, with a melody all its own.

The spade in her hand.

Digging's fun.

Water and sand make mud.

'I checked. Believe me.'

'I'm not trying to interrogate you, you do know that, don't you? I just want to know if you're aware of anything that could be useful to us.'

And Karin looks at Malin. For a long time, without saying anything, as if she were trying to read Malin's thoughts.

Then she sighs and says: 'You're paranoid, you know that?'

'I know. Goes with the territory.'

Karin takes a deep breath.

'I adopted Tess via Denmark. I've got dual citizenship, my mum was Danish. Because Sweden blocked adoptions from Vietnam, I went through Denmark, where they haven't suffered the same moral panic as the Swedish authorities. It's even worse in the USA.'

'OK,' Malin says. 'I understand.'

'I know you, Malin. I realised you were bound to wonder.'

Then Karin pauses before going on in a low voice, so low that Malin can barely hear what she's saying: 'Christ, do you think I got hold of Tess through some dodgy deal? That's pretty crazy, you know. Several years ago I contacted an adoption consultant here in Linköping who specialised in adoptions from Vietnam, Swedish–Vietnamese Adoptions. They act as a kind of intermediary between people who want to adopt, and the adoption agencies, they're more efficient than authorised adoption organisations, which are often pretty slow. When adoptions from Vietnam were stopped in Sweden, the bureau opened an office in Denmark instead, and that's when my Danish citizenship came in useful. I wanted a Vietnamese child. I went there with my ex-husband several times, I loved the people, I wanted to help give one of the children in their countless children's homes a whole lot of love. Can't you understand that, Malin? Not everything has to be grubby and sordid.'

Malin looks down at the grey carpet tiles on the floor.

'Aren't you ashamed?' Karin asks. 'Ashamed of coming here and calling my parenthood into question, my right to Tess, our right to love?'

Tess is running towards them now.

She's spotted Malin and smiles at her in recognition, but just as she's about to run into Malin's arms, Karin leans over and lifts her up onto her lap.

Stay cool now, Malin.

Don't look at the children.

See, feel, none of this.

'Did you ever meet the Andergrens?' Malin asks. 'In connection with the adoption? Or at some meeting?'

'What sort of meeting? I've never been to any meetings.'

Karin can no longer conceal her anger.

She gets up and goes over to the climbing frame with Tess, and Malin can see the look of confusion on the child's face, not used to grown-ups arguing.

Malin follows her, and almost trips over two little boys who run past.

'I never met them,' Karin says. 'Never. What do you think of me?'

'I'm just doing my job, and you know that.'

'You're a hyena, Malin, a fucking hyena,' and Karin walks off with Tess to go and stand in the endless queue for the cafeteria.

Malin stays where she is.

Looks around at the children, and gradually the shouting and yelling and laughter turns into a torrent of longing, a longing that can never be fulfilled, but which can be numbed.

Sorry, Karin, she thinks. But I can't help it.

And you're not telling me everything, are you?

Ice cream, Karin thinks.

Clutching Tess more tightly to her.

She looks over at Malin, who's still standing by the climbing frame, she seems completely lost, as if she were looking for her own child among the ladders and steps and platforms.

But there's no child there, Malin.

'What sort of ice cream would you like, darling? They've got soft ice cream, that's lovely, would you like one of those? Mummy will get one for you.'

Malin.

She came in on her own, but Zeke's probably waiting for her out in the car.

Too cowardly to come in.

Unless he just doesn't want to get involved, even though it's his job, maybe he thinks it's too close to home?

Come in, she thinks. But he's made his choice and no it's too late. Isn't it?

Zeke Martinsson.

Could he put up with a three-year-old?

Maybe.

'It's our turn next. Is that what you'd like, a cone? Then I'll get you one, Mummy will get you anything you want.'

Tess's body is soft, and her weight is comforting, her scent a perfume fashioned from everything magical in life.

You're magic, Tess.

As simple as that.

Malin walks towards the car, and in the morning light she looks worn out. Lack of sleep has left dark rings under her eyes, and she stops to rub her eyes, shakes her head like a wet dog, and Zeke hopes she manages to shake everything out of her, but doubts it.

She's ticking now, Malin.

But is she going to explode?

I hope not, but what can I do?

Talk to her? That would only make her angry, the last time I asked how she was, she snapped at me to mind my own business.

Zeke can see Karin in his mind's eye, had to steel himself not to go into the play centre.

He'd have loved to have coffee with Karin and Tess. He's caught glimpses of the little girl a few times, at the station and out in the city.

He'd like to get to know her, the way he's got to know his son and grandchildren. Afresh every day, because children aren't constant, there's always something new, and he sometimes misses that in himself and other adults, the way they're all more or less fixed.

And he longs for Karin, her breath in his ear, her sweat against his, but he knows it's impossible, too late.

And then the physical longing disappears and he simply longs to be in the same room as her, and that's a fairly new feeling for him, and it alarms him, even if he quite likes it, because it gives him courage, energy.

Malin.

A black cloud as she approaches the car.

What does she feel?

She wears everything on her sleeve, shame and anger and frustration and grief. She opens the passenger door with a forced smile and says: 'Let's go and talk to that millionaire consultant. Or was he a billionaire?'

35

'Well, I'm hardly the modest Ingvar Kamprad type,' Magnus Nyblom says, grabbing a large pack of bloody, well-hung fillet steak from the meat counter at the ICA supermarket in Ekholmen.

They phoned him a short while ago.

'I'm on my way to Ekholmen shopping centre. We can meet there.'

Magnus Nyblom had worked out that they'd probably want to talk to him in connection with the murders of Patrick and Cecilia Andergren.

'Happy to talk to you.'

No pulled-down shutters there.

ICA.

Packed with young families doing their Saturday shopping with their trolleys full of unsustainable food, pensioners studying prices, staff loading fresh trays of cheap mince into the meat counter.

Magnus Nyblom's ample frame looks like a statue in front of them. In his tweed suit, he resembles the sales manager at Saab. In the chill air of the shop his pear-shaped face looks red, and his short, stubby nose looks like a fire-alarm button.

'They have good steak here.'

Magnus Nyblom tosses the pack into his basket.

'I'm proud of what I've achieved with Datasonic,' he

says. 'I got over a hundred million when I sold it to the Yanks. Not bad, eh?'

Magnus Nyblom carries on towards the dairy counter.

'I usually come here in the Ferrari.'

'To the dairy cabinet?' Malin asks.

Magnus Nyblom ignores her.

'It's got more space for bags than you think,' he says instead.

Ingvar Kamprad, Malin thinks as she watches Magnus Nyblom put a half-litre carton of cream in his basket. That's who you measure yourself against, isn't it? With one of the world's most successful entrepreneurs? And what are you? Some jumped-up wide boy? A small-time millionaire in fucking Linköping? Could anything be more inappropriate than a Ferrari in Linköping?

Magnus Nyblom puts his basket down on the flecked stone floor.

'Shoot,' he says with a smile, every inch the decent bloke, but your eyes give you away, Malin thinks, as she sees him glaring angrily at an old lady trying to get past.

You're hot-tempered, aren't you?

'You worked with Patrick Andergren in Vietnam,' Zeke says.

'That's right,' Magnus Nyblom says, his voice neutral now. 'I was working as a consultant in Vietnam, and was brought in to help on some of the projects Patrick Andergren was working on. We used to meet up. I acted as a sort of intermediary, you could say. I'm good at the cultural differences between us and the Asians, especially in business, where things can be a bit tricky, which is why people like me get brought in.'

'And what do people like you do?'

'Smooth things over, help people to understand each other.'

'So you were the one who negotiated bribes that would keep everyone happy, on both sides of the table?' Malin asks, and Magnus Nyblom turns towards her, his green eyes flashing black for a fraction of a second. You think I didn't notice, don't you?

He laughs.

Heartily, for a long time, and the other customers start looking at them: surely no one should have that much fun in ICA?

'HA, HA, HA,' Magnus Nyblom rumbles. 'You detectives certainly have vivid imaginations. I helped negotiate deals. Made sure buyers and sellers understood each other. Helped with the numbers, sometimes acted as an interpreter.'

'Patrick and Cecilia Andergren were murdered,' Malin says. 'Their little girl is missing, and there are suggestions that you and Patrick were involved in irregular business practices. If you have any idea where she might be, you need to tell us now.'

She makes it sound as if they know more than they do. Trying to scare him.

But nothing has any effect on Magnus Nyblom.

He adjusts his tweed jacket.

'I'm supposed to know where the girl is? Ridiculous. And there were no bribes. I never saw a single bribe in all my twenty years in Asia.'

'Not in Da Lat?' Malin asks. 'On the project Patrick Andergren was involved in there? A new mobile network and telephone exchanges for an entire province?'

'Obviously I remember the project. I was the person who brought Ericsson and the national telecoms company together. Difficult, but successful.'

And lucrative, Malin thinks.

'So you don't think Patrick Andergren could have been

involved in any instances of bribery during his time in Vietnam or India?' Zeke asks.

Magnus Nyblom laughs again, and Malin feels like strangling him, forcing him down among the fish in the counter next to him.

'You think someone over there might have wanted to silence him?'

More laughter.

'You think this is funny?' Zeke says. 'Well, do you? Two people have been murdered, and a little girl is missing.'

Nyblom laughs again.

Demonstratively this time.

The king of Linköping, the king of fools.

'That's an absurd idea. There were no bribes. Not in Da Lat, not in Vietnam, and not in the rest of Asia. That's just something the media have dreamed up. Got that?'

Magnus Nyblom wanders over towards the drinks and picks up two six-packs of Pripps Blå beer, offering them to Malin: 'Would you like one?'

Magnus Nyblom looks at Malin and smiles, and she smiles back, her cynical smile, it feels right here, and says: 'So you don't know anything about Patrick Andergren that could be of use to us?'

'He was a pushy bastard,' Magnus Nyblom says. 'Seriously. They don't like that in Asia, where you have to be pleasant and smile the whole time, and definitely not try to rush things.'

'You're saying he did have problems there, then?'

'No, no. I was helping them, after all, so there were never any problems.'

'There's one thing I can't help wondering,' Zeke says. 'Datasonic. You came home from Asia and set the company up. It took several years before you earned anything, and

as far as I know there were no other investors. Where did
the money come from?'

'I was a successful consultant. I was involved in multi-
billion-kronor deals. You don't think that makes you rich?'

Idiot, Malin thinks. You're nothing but a smug idiot.

'Did you ever do any work for Saab?'

Magnus Nyblom shakes his head.

'The arms industry wasn't for me. Too dirty. Far too
dirty.'

But definitely lucrative enough, Malin thinks.

Sven Sjöman goes out into his garden.

The grass has grown tall.

It's been far too long since he last felt like getting the
lawnmower out of the garage, the cylinder mower his family
gave him for his sixtieth birthday so he could keep both
the grass and his bulging stomach in check.

He hasn't got much of a gut now. He lost a lot of weight
after the prostate diagnosis.

The contraption sits tucked away in a corner of the
garage, red and smelling of grass, hidden away from his
conscience.

He thinks about the investigation.

At least they've been able to discount the relatives. He
can't help hoping it stays that way, because nothing makes
him more depressed than family feuds that get out of
control and end in tragedy.

He hauls the lawnmower out.

He's soon dripping with sweat as he laboriously pushes
it up and down the grass in the autumn sunshine. It was
raining earlier, but the weather's changed completely. The
wet grass is difficult to cut. He hopes this is the last time
he'll have to mow it this year.

They've been thinking about selling the house and getting

a flat in the city, but the new-builds cost a fortune to buy, and it's impossible to get hold of a decent place to rent.

In practically any other culture a senior police chief like him would be able to sort out a flat within a week.

A day.

But not in Sweden. Such a rigid, law-abiding country. Still, he'd rather have it that way.

There may be a bit of fiddling here and there, nepotism and favouritism, important people may get all sorts of inducements, but it doesn't really amount to much.

The lawnmower jolts.

Stop.

Something must have caught in the blades, and he tips it up, and what he finds makes him feel sick.

A mouse.

Cut in two, and Sven feels like throwing up, but manages to suppress the urge.

The blood makes him think of the bodies in the jacuzzi, the red water, and the little girl, Ella, who must be out there somewhere.

I'm almost sixty-five years old.

I had been heading towards the exit, but now I don't want to stop working.

Because what could be better than making sure that a child is safe?

Malin, Zeke, Johan.

Busy working on the case today. Waldemar, Börje, and the new girl, Elin Sand, won't have stopped thinking about it just because I've given them the day off, I know that.

He walks over to the garage.

To fetch a knife.

Something to remove the poor creature with, then he'll make sure that his little corner of the world looks perfect.

36

A single raincloud is hanging lower in the sky than the others, somewhere out above Sturefors.

Malin can see it from where she stands in the car park of the ICA supermarket in Ekholmen, surrounded by bags, trolleys, and unfamiliar faces.

The cloud is big, mushroom-shaped, dragging great veils of rain beneath it.

They get into the car and head back towards the station. As Zeke turns off by the University Hospital, Malin's mobile rings.

She looks at the time before taking the call.

Half past one, Tove.

'How are you feeling?'

Zeke grins.

Malin's already told him about her daughter's spectacular performance last night.

'Not great. Can't you come home?'

'And do what?'

'Look after me, of course.'

And Malin can't help thinking: So now I'm good enough, now you want me.

Then she realises that this is an opportunity that may never come again.

The case.

Ella.

Johan, Zeke.

An hour or two couldn't hurt that much, surely? I have to choose Tove.

'I'll be there in fifteen minutes,' she says. 'I'll pick up some hangover food. A flat-bread roll, would that work?'

'Thanks, Mum. I should probably try to eat something.'

Malin ends the call. Without her noticing it, Zeke has already stopped next to the Horticultural Society Park to let her out.

Malin can't help feeling that she's going in the wrong direction as she walks away from the fast-food kiosk in Trädgårdstorget with a bag of food in her hand, on her way home to her daughter instead of the other way, towards the station and their investigation.

Tove takes two bites of the flat-bread roll with extra prawn salad before putting it down on the plate and pushing it away.

She looks indecently lively, and the grey-green colour has vanished from her face.

But she keeps saying she feels terrible.

And Malin gets up and clears the food away, doesn't want Tove to have to stare at it.

'Drink some Coke,' she says. 'That'll make you feel better.'

Tove takes a sip.

Puts the glass back on the table and smiles her most attractive smile.

'You're right. I do feel better. God, I felt awful a little while ago.'

Malin remembers what it was like when she first started to get a real taste for alcohol.

The way she used to be able to drink. Almost without ever getting a hangover, but if she ever did get one, the nausea and misery would be gone by lunchtime.

But after that. As the years passed.

It got worse.

And life became a constant grind of getting drunk, feeling hungover, boundless self-loathing.

But also wonderful moments when her body and the alcohol were in perfect harmony, and she's never felt better than she did on those occasions.

As Malin looks at her daughter in the kitchen, she wants to relive that feeling, and feels ashamed that she isn't content with this moment.

'Can't we go and visit Stefan soon?' Tove asks.

'It can't be more than a week or so since you were last there?'

'Sit down, Mum,' Tove says. 'You're making me feel stressed, standing there like that.'

Malin sits down on one of the uncomfortable ladder-backed chairs. Peter's suggested getting her some new ones, but she won't let him, and doesn't feel like wasting her hard-earned wages on kitchen chairs.

'I think Stefan would like to see you.'

Malin takes a deep breath.

'He doesn't even recognise me.'

'You don't know that. I get the feeling he recognises me. So why wouldn't he recognise you?'

'I'm in the middle of—'

Tove interrupts her.

'And even if he doesn't recognise you, it doesn't make any difference. We're still his people, we're the only family he's got, and we have to look after him.'

Malin buries her face in her hands.

Shit.

Tove's right. And all the heartless elitism she's been exhibiting recently is gone, and now wise, friendly Tove is sitting opposite Malin again. Empathy personified, and

Malin wonders if she's been imagining all the cold things Tove has said about other people in their recent conversations.

If her soul, her brain, have been playing more tricks on her.

No. Because Tove abruptly changes the subject.

'Mum,' she says. 'You ought to marry Peter. He's got money, and if I'm going to fit in at Lundsberg, I have to be able to buy stuff.'

Bloody hell.

'You're kidding,' Malin says. 'Tell me you're kidding, Tove.'

And Tove smiles at her.

'I'm kidding, but only a bit.'

'It doesn't work like that, and you know it.'

'If you can't beat them, join them,' Tove says, and Malin can't help thinking that it sounds like she's already started at the Stockholm School of Economics.

'Anyway, Peter,' she goes on. 'Am I going to see him?'

'He's on call.'

'So you said. Do you miss him?'

Tove's smiling properly now, evidently pleased at being able to land a blow precisely where she knows it's going to hurt most.

'Yes, I do,' Malin says. 'This is the fourth night in a row he's been on call. Or is it only the third?'

And she really does miss him now. They can't just leave each other hanging after a phone call like their last one. Malin feels a pressure in her chest, as her whole being contracts towards the healed yet still open wound in her womb.

Tove.

Sitting there in front of me.

So why do I feel so alone?

'You're trying to get pregnant, aren't you?'

I can't do this.

Can't do this.

'No,' Malin says. 'We're both too old, so you'll have to manage without any siblings.'

'You're not too old,' but Malin can see the relief in Tove's eyes.

'Don't worry, Tove. There won't be any children.'

And then Malin smiles the smile she hates so much, the smile that mocks all naïve faith in goodness.

'You should go to the hospital,' Tove says. 'Surprise Peter.'

'I don't think he'd like that.'

'Of course he would. Tom always loves it when I surprise him.'

'So how do you surprise Tom?'

Tove doesn't answer, just grins at her.

'I surprise him,' she repeats.

'He's probably in the operating theatre.'

'He can't be operating all the time. Go and see him, Mum. To be honest, you look like you could do with a hug.'

Tove gets up, and Malin feels how warm she is, and Tove's whole body is vibrating with an energy that seems to have the ability to eradicate all loneliness.

You need rest, Malin.

More than anything else, your soul needs peace.

So allow yourself to sit next to your daughter, allow yourself to watch the film she's just put in the DVD player.

Sit down, sit back, relax.

No.

Don't do that.

Get going. Do what you have to.

Don't just sit there on the sofa next to your daughter, thinking everything's fine.

We need you, we need your help, and we can't scare you into obedience, we know that, so we'll try pleading instead.

Help us, Malin.

Help us find Ella.

Help her. She's so frightened.

And we think you can hear us, but you choose to give in to sleep, and doze off on the sofa, and Tove leans against you, trying to follow the film, but she keeps glancing out of the window, at the rain that's lashing the black church roof clean.

Two black crows in this latest rain.

Pulsing clouds are moving over Linköping, and where will this Saturday take the inhabitants?

Don't they know that everything except pain, fear, and evil are transitory?

Don't the citizens know that they have to nurture love, enjoy it while they can?

Where are you, Ella?
We need your help, Malin Fors, so don't sleep, wake up, go to Peter, and then move on.

37

Malin tries to make her thoughts fit the rhythm of the rain, get the rain to help her think clearly.

She can feel the drops through the hood of her black oilskin, and beyond the sound of them she can hear words.

Desperate, pleading, *Help us, help us.*

The words like whispers through the bushes of the Horticultural Society Park.

The trees look frozen in the rain, and in the light of the streetlamps yellow leaves sail gently down to the drenched lawns.

She's alone in the park.

Darkness is lurking around her, and the moisture in the air swirls beneath the intermittent patches of light.

She remembers the morning they found a naked girl who'd been raped wandering through the park.

But I'm not going to think about that.

I'm going to try to make sense of what's going on now.

She sits down on a park bench beneath an old oak, and the sound of the rain stops, and the voices are mute now, as if they understand that they must leave her in peace.

A child for a pig.

Of course.

A child can cost less than a pig in countries like Vietnam. But the child can also cost millions at the other end of the food chain.

What if someone has taken Ella back? Malin thinks. Kidnapped her, to sell her again, and again and again.

Getting her adopted again, to parents who aren't too fastidious.

Unless her biological parents want her back. And have somehow managed to get hold of money.

A child as young as Ella can be made to forget.

Can be made to lose her memory, suppress a language, become another person, become less than human.

The worst of the worst.

The harems of Saudi princes.

Global paedophile networks, like the one in Australia, like the other one that was cracked recently in the USA, where members had to submit their own films of children being sexually abused in order to be accepted into the group. There are rumours of isolated houses full or small girls and boys, abducted, bought from every corner of the world.

Children held in dark cellars, only allowed out to be abused, filmed, exploited and used for pleasure.

'Am I a human being?'

The deserted park.

That evil could reach Linköping, Malin thinks, it could, but at the same time, why would anyone kill the parents? There must be children who would be easier to abduct than Ella.

The bench is cold.

Chill raindrops make their way through the crown of the oak and fall on Malin's hands, and she turns her palms up, tries to catch the drops.

Cold.

They change form and seep away.

Bribery.

All the rumours, all the smug, insecure men, the insinuations, and the slippery, almost scornful denials of everyone involved, stubborn silence and a refusal to cooperate.

Between the lines.

Don't disrupt these sacred companies.

Don't disrupt them. Let them do their business.

Just look at what happened to Ikea in Russia, where they thought they were bigger than the game itself, thought they could dictate the terms and not pay any bribes.

A whole new meaning to the word naïve.

Us Swedes think we can stay clean in a filthy world.

Yeah, right.

So what have we got so far?

A family conflict that we've discounted.

Rumours of bribery.

An adoption from a country where some adoptions have been cauldrons of pus.

A missing girl.

Who can't be found. At least not in the forest, not on the riverbed.

Malin stands up, wipes her hands on her jeans, then walks up the hill to the old observatory pavilion.

The pine trees are taller here, not much light filters through, and she stands still in the darkness, not sure that they're going to be able to get anywhere with this case.

They really don't know much, and she hopes that Johan's going to be able to find something in the locked folders from the hard-drive, that they can make something of the cryptic emails and mobile phone calls, that someone somewhere has seen the girl, knows something about her.

They've talked about contacting airlines that fly to Vietnam.

Even though they have the girl's passport.

Someone could have used a fake passport with her picture. But they've decided to hold back.

The investigation may end without them having made any progress at all.

With the girl remaining missing, the murders unsolved, the city left in fear.

Malin carries on towards the hospital, keen for something to happen, and she finds herself thinking of Peter's naked body, and wants to give herself to him unconditionally, without any thought that it has to mean something more than closeness and pleasure.

She hasn't called.

Is going to surprise him.

Hopes he isn't going to be busy.

She's pleased she and Tove got some time together, pleased she got past the 'new' Tove and reached the real Tove.

Don't go to the School of Economics.

Malin wants to say that, but knows she's in no position to dictate or influence now, because Tove knows best, and anyway, Malin thinks, how could I give anyone advice on how to live their lives, least of all my own daughter?

Trädgårdsgatan.

Across the road, and she's in the hospital precinct. Past the three-storey, yellow-brick building housing the psychiatric unit, then she looks down towards the loading bay over by the workshops and generators.

She reaches the main entrance, where several patients are sitting in wheelchairs under the protruding green and yellow roof, smoking, sucking poison into their lungs and dreaming themselves away.

The neurosurgery duty-doctor's room is down in the basement.

A bit more luxurious than the other departments', with its own shower.

Malin heads down the stairs beside the visitors' lifts, two floors.

Emerges into a corridor that leads off a hundred metres in both directions. Pipes and cables and rectangular zinc ventilation shafts rattle above her head, and dirty water drips from the ceiling.

Peter.

I'm coming.

You have to be there, and she quickens her pace.

She can feel that her body doesn't want to wait any longer, and I want you to take me hard and fast and slowly and quickly, I want to feel your skin in every possible way.

She says hello to a nurse she recognises from the neuro-surgery department, and the nurse gives Malin a pointed smile, seems to want to stop and say something, but changes her mind and carries on.

Malin opens the door leading to the side-corridor containing the duty-doctor's room.

So many days on call.

Longer than ever before.

But I can't manage without you, Peter.

With or without a child.

Because my body isn't crying out for a child now.

It's calling out for you.

And she stops outside the duty-doctor's room in the gloomy corridor, looks at the grey laminate door and wonders if she should knock.

But why would I do that?

Why would I knock?

If you're in there, you'll be pleased to see me, and Malin imagines she can hear sounds behind the door, but what sort of sounds?

No knock.

And she pushes the handle down, shuts off the world, and in her mind she sees Peter lying naked in the bed, and she gets in next to him, and they vibrate against each other, and everything is open and close, just as it was at the start.

Into the small lobby now.

Another door in front of her.

Sounds.

Clearer now.

And she walks through the short hall to the room containing the bed, and opens the other door now, pretending she can't hear groaning, pretending that there's no sound of bodies slapping together, pretending that this moment isn't happening.

But they're there, right in front of her.

Dimly illuminated, naked bodies.

Peter.

Like one dog behind another, he's standing at the end of the bed with his groin pressed against an unknown woman's buttocks.

Unfamiliar blonde hair.

Groaning, in English:

'Don't stop. Don't stop!'

Then shouting: 'FUCK ME! FUCK ME!'

Stop, stop, stop.

Peter's head turns and he looks at Malin, and at first he seems surprised, then he gives her a look that suggests he feels sorry for her, but that he can't stop, and when the woman cries out 'DON'T STOP!' he carries on, without taking his eyes off Malin, and who the fuck is that cunt?

I'm going to kill her.

I'm going to kill you, Peter.

'FUCK ME, FUCK ME!'

If you think I'm going to let you finish fucking that cunt before I kill you, you're very much mistaken, and Malin throws herself at the bed, forces Peter up against the wall, and the woman falls to one side and Peter yells: 'For God's sake, Malin, calm down,' and the naked young woman rolls onto the floor, where she lies on the orange and red rag-rug and tries to cover herself as she cries: 'What's happening? Who is she, Peter?'

And Malin pushes Peter down onto the bed, reaches for

a pillow, and presses it against his face, hard, hard, and he's clawing at her arms, but the wretched oilskin he gave her so she'd look nice and smart protects her from his nails.

He kicks out.

Tries to scream under the pillow, but I'm going to asphyxiate you, you bastard, and the woman has curled up on the floor and seems unable to move, and Malin can see that she's at least ten years younger than her, and beautiful, and where the hell did you find her?

'Stop, stop,' the woman whispers, looking at me as if I were a monster.

I am a monster.

How long have I been holding this pillow down now? You may think you're strong, Peter, but I'm stronger.

Slap.

Slap.

How does her cunt feel?

Warmer than mine?

'Stop,' the woman sobs. 'You're killing him.'

A monster.

Me?

Kill him.

He grabs at the oilskin, and what am I doing?

Am I killing him?

No, not me, no, not now.

And Malin lets go of the pillow and slowly gets to her feet, then stumbles backwards out of the room, and she sees Peter push the pillow aside and as she runs through first one, then the second corridor, she imagines she can hear him calling after her: 'Malin. Malin! For fuck's sake, Malin, wait! Wait!'

I'm not going to wait, Malin thinks.

Don't you ever, ever fuck with me again.

38

Saturday, 14 and Sunday, 15 September

'Malin!'

The bartender at the Hamlet seems pleased to see her, and Malin is pleased to see the illuminated bottles behind the bar, feel the shabby dark wooden panelling close itself around her, as the sour beer and spirits invade her nostrils.

'A Coke?'

He smiles at her. No fucking Coke, not now, and she says: 'A lager, and a double of that cask-matured tequila, if you've still got any.'

'You're sure?'

She meets his gaze, and the bartender seems to realise that he shouldn't moralise, not to her, not now, not on this rainy night in Linköping.

'I've still got the tequila,' the bartender says. 'No one else asks for it since you stopped coming. So it's good for me that you're back.'

He gives her a wry grin, and she wonders if she should still walk away, not do this, stick it out, do the oh-so-fucking-sensible thing, but then the beer is there in front of her on the polished bar, and the glass mists up and the amber liquid's bubbles rise up the glass and the head slips over the edge and she picks it up, holds it in her hand, then looks at the men and women around her.

Older.

Exhausted.

Alcoholics who have managed to get through life without losing their jobs.

Just their families.

Their dignity.

Their reputation and pride.

And she hesitates again, but then the tequila is there too, in a short, polished whisky glass, and she thinks: I'm no better than them.

Why should I be?

What makes me think that? Imagine that?

And she puts the beer down again and stands up from the bar.

'Are you leaving?'

Feet on the floor.

Then she picks up the glass of tequila, raises it to the people at the bar, turns around, raises it towards the even shabbier figures at the tables, and then she says, far too loudly: 'Fuck it, then, cheers!'

And she opens her throat and feels the warmth of the drink, first on her lips, then in her mouth, and it warms her throat and stomach, and she drains the glass and explodes inside, burning, and the taste of oak and agave and fructose and forgetfulness and friendliness and pleasure and a world free of pain and panic fills her, slowly, wonderfully slowly.

She slams the glass down on the bar.

'Another one,' and while she's waiting for the next tequila she downs her beer in one.

She keeps alternating drinks, and it's exactly the way she's dreamed of it, and she drinks until the world around her consists of lights and sounds, indescribable, utterly devoid of content, a cotton-wool dream in which it doesn't matter that someone leads her out into a cold, rainy street and says: 'Don't ever come here again!'

And as Malin weaves down Hamngatan she has a feeling that something went wrong back at the Hamlet, and she tries to focus on a wall opposite her, but can't remember what could have gone wrong.

What happened at the bar?

She was in a bar just now, wasn't she?

What happened with Peter?

Was I at the hospital?

FUCK ME. FUCK ME.

'I'm going to kill you, you bastard. Kill you!'

And she turns the corner down towards the main square, and tries to walk straight, but still can't help stumbling into the massive fountain surrounding the statue of Folke Filbyter on horseback.

More drink.

More.

People are looking at me, but they can fuck off. Do you hear? On Ågatan she walks up to the rope outside Honest Harry's, and someone yells: 'Get in the queue!' and she hunts through the pockets of her coat, cold drops, it must still be raining, and that's why my hair's so wet, and I've got to have more drink.

'Shut up!'

Red lights, orange lights, turning blue, yellow. Where am I?

In the duty-doctor's room.

FUCK ME.

A child.

A child for a fucking pig.

'Do you hear?'

And she's pulled out her wallet and is holding up her police ID to the two bouncers, snarling: 'You fucking wannabes, let me in. Otherwise I'll get this place shut down. Understood?'

But the bouncers don't reply, and they go away, and I can see them from below now, and how is that possible?

Wet jeans.

But it's nice lying here. The rain is downy, the tarmac like a luxurious mattress.

'Let me in!'

And laughter echoes around her.

'I'm going to kill you, do you get that?' she yells, and then she feels strong hands grabbing hold of her under her arms, lifting her to her feet, then voices saying something like: 'You can see who it is, can't you?'

'Yes.'

'We've got to get her out of here.'

'She must have fallen off the wagon again. I thought she was sorted out.'

'No one ever is.'

The back seat of the car, covered with black vinyl.

Malin knows what sort of car it is.

Recognises the hooks for handcuffs in the side panels.

For a brief second her brain clears, and she knows who she is, how she got there, knows what's happened and what could happen.

'Boys,' she pleads. 'Can't you just drive me home? My daughter's there, she can look after me . . .'

'Where do you . . .'

But before Malin can answer she's back in her own little world of flashing, spinning lights, sounds fading in and out, locked in a world she knows so well, where you have to cling on to the tiniest of handholds to stop yourself falling off the planet.

Tove's lying on the sofa.

Watching some stupid programme where so-called much-loved singers interpret each other's songs.

At the same time she's reading a novel she was given by Klara, her houseparent at Lundsberg, a book called *Freedom*, about some dysfunctional Americans.

The characters seem fairly bewildered.

Just like me.

The catastrophe at the party last night.

Once a chav, always a chav.

They don't see me as a chav at Lundsberg, they don't, and she finds herself longing for the strict demands of Lundsberg, the others' vanity, but most of all the feeling that something is expected of you there, of her, of everyone, and that you actually have a chance to try to become the person you are, within invisible but fairly broad parameters.

You just have to put up with all the nonsense.

Mum never really seems to have understood that you have to take responsibility for your own life, that she can't blame everything, even unconsciously, on Grandma and Granddad and their shortcomings.

She's got to realise that she has moved on because she wants to, not because she's being chased by a load of old stuff.

How is she going to realise that?

She's got to realise it.

If hangovers are no worse than I've felt today, Tove thinks, then drink can't really be that dangerous.

But it is dangerous.

I've seen what it's done to Mum. And to me, as a result. God, I've been so ashamed of her. She's done so many ridiculous fucking things.

But that's all over now.

She's probably having a nice time with Peter up at the hospital. I'm glad she went up there to surprise him.

The doorbell rings.

Who could that be?

Mum's got a key, so it must be someone else.

Tove gets up and goes out into the hall, looks through the peephole.

A policeman, in uniform. Another one behind him, trying to hold a third person upright.

Mum.

Are you hurt?

What have you done now?

And Tove wishes she'd kept her mum at home, or, even better, had stayed up at Lundsberg.

She feels her stomach clench.

She opens the door.

'Are you Tove Fors?' one of the policemen asks, and Tove thinks he looks like a gorilla, but his voice is friendly.

Tove nods.

The policeman steps aside, and she sees the other one struggling to keep her mum upright, and she's all wet, filthy, doesn't seem to be able to lift her head, and she stinks of drink, she's swaying, God, she must be completely hammered.

Much worse than I was last night.

'Can we bring her in?' the policeman asks, and Tove realises how difficult he's finding the situation, how he's embarrassed on her mother's behalf, and together with the other policeman he helps her mum into the bedroom and onto the bed, where she seems to disappear without a sound into an utterly vacant sleep.

The second policeman goes out into the stairwell at once, while the friendly gorilla lingers in the hall but clearly wants to leave.

'We found her further down Ågatan. She wasn't exactly presentable, if I can put it like that.'

Tove nods.

'How old are you?' the policeman asks.

'Eighteen.'

The policeman nods.

'We should really have taken her in. Put her in one of the drunk cells. But no one will find out about this, you can be sure of that. The bouncers at Harry's won't say anything. But you need to keep an eye on her now. Make sure she doesn't choke on her own vomit. Get her on her side and she'll be fine.'

'OK.'

On television in the other room a sell-out who was convicted of drugs offences is singing a hideous Euro-pop song, Mum's crashed out on her bed, and there's a policeman standing in front of me.

What happened? Tove thinks.

What happened?

'Take care of your mum now. Can I rely on you?'

'I'll take care of her,' Tove says. 'I've done it before.'

Everything is black apart from the screen.

How many evenings, how many nights have I sat here like this, Johan Jakobsson thinks, alone in front of his computer while the rest of his family is asleep.

He had some wine with dinner this evening.

Has a glass of wine beside him now.

He was thinking of trying to emulate Allen Ginsberg and Burroughs. Open the doors of perception with drugs, maybe that would help him crack the codes to the folders from Patrick Andergren's hard-drive.

They have no idea where the girl could be.

Not a fucking clue.

He types.

Tries to find ways through the coding.

Drinks more wine.

Tries to see patterns in the structure of the patterns of the code that conceals the actual password.

How does this all fit together?

He taps, reads, knows he's no expert at this, that there are companies in the Czech Republic and India that could probably solve this for him in an instant. Forensics have failed to crack it.

But it costs a fortune to use those private companies. And there's no scope for that in their budget. And those companies would never contemplate doing the work for free, not even if a little girl's life was at stake.

Or would they?

Johan's tired.

Way beyond tired.

He longs for bed, for his wife, feels how the wine seems to be shutting him inside his head rather than opening him up.

Maybe I could email that Czech company tomorrow? Maybe they'd be willing to help anyway?

I could attach a picture of Ella. That would do the trick, surely? They'd realise that we're not just dealing with her life, but the decency of all humanity.

He logs out of the security system's programme code.

Is about to close the folders, the textbox where he's asked to type his 'personal security code'.

Ella.

Bullet-riddled bodies.

You have to be nice to children. Otherwise . . .

And he feels anger rising inside him, hammers at the keyboard, types in: DON'T FUCK WITH ME.

OK.

OK.

His elbow protests at the last mouse-click of the evening.

OK.

And then the miracle that he and everyone else has been waiting for happens.

The locked folders from Patrick Andergren's hard-drive open up.

One by one, they reveal their contents to the darkness of night.

PART 3
On a River Across the World

[Voices, words across the water]

*Come out, Ella! We're looking for you, the game's over now.
Come out.*
    It's a long time since we finished counting.
    Nineteen.
    Twenty.
    Ninety-nine.
    One hundred!
    Off we go.
    We're the ones calling.
    It's Mummy, Ella.
    Mummy. I'm here.
    *And I can hear you too, Daddy can hear you, can you hear
us, Ella? That is you, isn't it, hiding in the dark?*
    I can hear you.
    But you're not here.
    Come here. Come here. I want to go home. What are
they doing, I don't want to, Mummy. Mummy?
    And by the river the woman dips her hair in the slow-flowing
water, makes strange signs to the spirits in the sky, to the faces
of the dead in the clouds. She wields her brush of black hair
carefully, and the colour seeps out, becoming a dark rain that
falls on the wild, green plain, on the mountains.
    The water of the river flows towards its own darkness.
    And all the faces of lonely mothers are mirror-images of

each other, their feelings one and the same, and between their bodies arc crescents of unfamiliar electricity, and they mutter beside all the rivers of the world, every expanse of water:

A child for a pig.

A pig for a child.

A child, a child, my child.

My child.

Me.

You can't leave me like this, because then I won't exist. If my child doesn't exist, who am I then?

Mummy.

MUMMY.

They've tied me down. TIED ME DOWN. I don't want to. It hurts.

No. Where am I?

Am I dead now?

They're filming, Mummy.

They think they're filming me, but they're not.

It happened a few nights ago, and it happened like this, and it was the same night that Patrick and Cecilia Andergren were murdered and their daughter Ella Andergren disappeared.

What happened?

Where?

A man in a house, not far from Linköping, was hit by a shot to the chest, fired from close range.

Violent death came to Linköping a third time that night.

And the man is still sitting there, leaning forward over a table in his house, and the remains of his soul stink and rot and dry out, and he looks down on himself, sees the bullet in the wall, how it turned his death as dark as his life has in many ways been, how everything was filled with black waves of even blacker foam.

39

Fuck, fuck, fuck.

What have I done? What happened?

Malin is lying on her side in bed, staring over the edge into a green plastic bucket, its base covered with vomit.

A hammer.

Smashing at her head. The light from the gaps in the blinds cuts through her eyes into her brain. The rays strafe her to tears, and inside her head ten dwarfs are chiselling away at her brain, grinning scornfully at her.

At her weakness.

And she feels a volcanic wave of nausea rising through her gullet, and seconds later a torrent of bitter lava is gushing out of her into the bucket.

Everything's fine.

She's awake now.

Not dead.

Peter, you bastard, and she feels like having another drink, but there's no drink in the flat, she knows that.

Unless there's actually a bottle of tequila in the kitchen?

Her body aches. She'd like to take her skin off, switch bodies, but she's stuck with who she is.

Stuck.

In bed, and she fends off all the images of yesterday evening, but sees herself smashing an empty tequila glass on the floor of the Hamlet, hears herself yelling FUCK

ME, FUCK ME! at full volume, remembers the derisive way the jaded, broken drinkers looked at her.

Handle your drink.

Or fuck off out of here.

That's where I am now.

Tove. You looked after me last night, I remember that. Are you at home?

Malin hauls herself up into a sitting position, her vision turns black and someone is beating on her skull with a rock now.

Narrowed eyes.

Close them, stand up.

'Tove? Tove!' she calls out.

No answer.

She stumbles to the kitchen, tripping over her shoes in the hall, and is almost floored by the light, even though it's raining and the sky above the church is dark grey.

A note on the kitchen table.

I took an earlier train. Hugs, Tove

Malin sinks onto one of the kitchen chairs.

How am I going to get out of this?

According to the clock on the wall, it's eleven o'clock, and Malin thinks about work but can't really focus, and she has to dash to throw up in the sink, then she drinks yesterday's coffee straight from the pot, and throws up again.

She's still wearing her jeans.

Filthy.

Her white blouse too, and beneath the cotton she feels her skin crawl with shame and anger, and wants to cry but can't.

Can't.

Inside her: the image of Peter, his face a blank, the girl on the bed, on all fours in front of him.

FUCK ME, FUCK ME.

Malin goes into the bathroom, can't bear to look at herself in the mirror, because she doesn't exist, doesn't exist, but there I am, no, not me, and the woman in the mirror looks terrible, grey and red and her face is a shapeless, swollen blob, and her hair is matted, sticky with stinking vomit.

Tove.

You looked after me, made sure I didn't choke. Then you left.

Malin slumps to the floor, crawls to her bed and hunts through the pockets of the oilskin for her phone.

Five missed calls. From Zeke, from Johan.

A text from Johan.

'Cracked the folders. Come to the station.'

Sent at half past eight that morning.

Great, Malin thinks. Fuck.

She crawls back to the bathroom and into the shower, then without taking her clothes off she reaches up and turns the water on, reduces the hot water to a minimum, and soon icy rain is falling on an icy soul.

Who am I? Malin thinks as she sucks up her coffee, black as the abyss.

Can you smell the alcohol?

She's standing behind Johan Jakobsson in the open-plan office, staring at his screen. Zeke's standing next to her, he gave her a suspicious look when she came in, and she could tell that he'd seen through her, and he opened his mouth to say something, then thought better of it.

She took two ibuprofen and three paracetamol at home,

and managed to keep them down. Spent five minutes gargling with peppermint mouthwash.

She's breathing over Johan's shoulder.

He doesn't seem to have noticed anything.

He called her over to him straightaway. Zeke joined them, and Johan said: 'You've got to see this. I found it in one of the locked folders.'

Now she's trying to focus on the QuickTime player on Johan's screen, on Patrick Andergren's animated face as he sits in front of an anonymous white wall and addresses the camera directly.

Ella, it's me, Patrick, your dad. Well, not your biological dad, but your real, best dad.

You'll be older when you see this, if you ever see it. You need to be older to understand.

Listen.

Obviously I heard the rumours when I worked in Vietnam.

About adoptions that weren't conducted properly, where parents were tricked into giving up their children.

That's why I took extra care when we decided to adopt, I checked everything a dozen times, I met the staff at the children's home, I checked all the papers myself, I got my contacts to check them as well, and everything seemed to be correct, your parents really were dead, they died when an unexploded bomb leftover from a Vietcong offensive in 1971 went off in a ditch.

You were six months old at the time, and after that your grandmother looked after you, but then she died as well.

The adoption was quite legitimate. Everyone assured me that it was, and I had made sure myself.

But when the big American report was published in 2009, I felt a chill run through me.

It was far worse than I had ever imagined.

How many children could have been involved?

Five thousand? Ten?

Several thousand were adopted by Americans alone, some of them to adoptive parents who had become infertile by the second-generation effects of Agent Orange.

Not that those individual fates were relevant.

How many of those children had been adopted from biological parents who had been tricked?

There could be so many parents and children who were kept apart because of lies.

Greed.

It's worse to be separated from the living than the dead, Ella.

So I started my investigations again.

I was like a man obsessed.

I would watch you play in the garden by the river as I sat at my computer and waited for fresh confirmation of who you were.

But what would I have done if I had found out new information about you? If you had been stolen because of the lies?

Would I have given you back? Abandoned you?

What would I have done?

Isn't our love the biggest, the most genuine? Could it actually be the case that there is too much love in the world, and that we don't know what to do with it?

Whatever has happened by the time you see this, I want you to know that I love you, Ella. I love you above everything else.

The film ends, and Malin feels sick.

Not because of what she's just seen, but the after-effects of the drink.

And it strikes her that Patrick Andergren must have known that he was in danger. The film is only a few months old.

'I thought this was quite a good start,' Johan says. 'There's plenty more to go on.'

'Why did he record this video?' Malin wonders.

'Presumably he felt he had something to confess,' Zeke says. 'Get it all out in the open.'

'Is there another part to it?'

'No. If he was planning to record any more, he didn't have time to do it,' Johan says.

What do people leave behind?

Why do they do what they do?

Perhaps you'd like to see that video when you get bigger, Ella, and know that I did what I could to find out the truth.

Is this the truth?

That mystery is for the living to uncover, if they dare.

I can hear you, Ella.

You're crying in a dark, damp room, and you're not alone.

You're alive.

I want you here with me, but you're alive, still alive, and that's the most important thing, you have to go on living, because soon Malin Fors will find you, that's what keeps her going.

That's good, isn't it?

She's sitting in the police station.

Going through the contents of my password-protected folders.

Did he take bribes?

Money, Ella.

Money means power.

Power? That's when you can make decisions about another person's life.

No more, no less.

Abuse of power. That's when you steal someone's love.

But what if you don't know you're stealing?

What do you do then?

Malin Fors is wondering: Did Patrick Andergren find out

the truth about your adoption? She suspects something, then thinks about her friend Karin and shakes off those suspicions, they're far too difficult.

She thinks: What's Karin going to do?

What's the right thing here?

When I hugged you, Ella, that was right, wasn't it? Or was it just my feeble attempts to cure my own loneliness?

40

Forget your hangover, Malin thinks, forget all your own worries, suppress them, concentrate on what lies ahead.

Fortunately she can't see her own reflection in the screen of Johan Jakobsson's computer, and she can't read the words, but Johan tells her all she needs to know, and even though the media player is closed now, Patrick Andergren's face and voice are still hanging in the air like some sort of spirit.

'It was a total fucking coincidence that I managed to crack the password,' Johan says.

Johan's swearing, Malin thinks as she bites off the last remnant of the scab inside her lip.

He doesn't often swear, only when he's tired or pleased with himself, and right now both of those apply.

'So, Patrick Andergren had done a whole load of research into their own adoption, questioning the story he was given by the children's home they adopted Ella from in Vietnam.'

Johan goes on: 'In the end he came to the conclusion that Ella's adoption was legitimate. She was an orphan. Her parents really did die when an unexploded bomb went off.'

Johan clicks to open some colour photographs.

A dried-out paddy field fringed with palm trees.

A pit in the ground, several metres in diameter.

'He documented everything. Wrote his own reports about his work, like he was some sort of self-appointed official investigator. Looks like he actually went to see the ditch where they died, to document it and see it with his own eyes.'

'But if the adoption was legitimate, then what's the problem?' Zeke asks.

'He didn't stop with their case. I've found seven other names in the folders, children who've been adopted from Vietnam by Swedish families since 2000. He was looking into their cases as well, and while he was in Vietnam he seems to have spoken to the biological parents where they were still alive, and tried to gain access to official documents, even attempted to make local officials and staff at the children's homes admit what they'd done. It's all documented here.'

'Bloody hell,' Malin whispers, but even the whisper makes her feel faint, her brain seems to swell up even more from the effort of having to move her facial muscles.

'Sounds like a dangerous thing to do,' Zeke says. 'Anyone involved out in Vietnam presumably wanted him to keep his nose out. And the seven families could hardly have been that keen either.'

A self-appointed apostle of truth, Malin thinks. Why? Why not?

For the sake of the children.

So they could know the truth.

'You've got the names of the Swedish families in there, then?' Zeke asks, gesturing towards the screen.

'Yes.'

'Did he speak to them? Does it say? Did they know what he was up to?' Malin asks, her words coming more easily now, as if her skull is getting used to the idea, and the words seem to be suppressing her hangover.

'He spoke to some, but probably not all of them. But it's hard to say how much they would have known about his research.'

'Are there any names of people in Vietnam?'

Johan nods.

'Some of the people involved in Vietnam are named, depending on which province the cases occurred in.'

'Addresses?' Malin asks.

'Yes, for the children's homes and authorities in Vietnam, and in some case for what I think could be the biological parents. And the Swedish families, and the organisations and agencies involved here.'

'Phone numbers? Are there any that match the pay-as-you-go mobile numbers we found before?'

'Yes, they're in a separate document. But just the numbers. It's a scan of a handwritten list, with the initials IN at the top.'

'International numbers?' Zeke suggests.

Malin and Johan murmur their agreement.

'What about the email addresses he was writing to in Vietnam? Are they there?' Malin asks.

'No,' Johan says. 'I haven't found any email addresses at all.'

Johan.

You're a rock.

How much can you have slept last night?

'We can start to make some progress now,' Zeke says. 'We need to check those seven Swedish families. And see what we can find out about those Vietnamese names.'

'If it was one of the Swedish families who wanted to put a stop to his investigations, that still doesn't explain where Ella is,' Malin says.

'It might,' Zeke says. 'Perhaps something went wrong and they were forced to kill the girl? And got rid of the body. People don't always act logically in extreme situations.'

Johan nods.

Malin absorbs Zeke's words.

He could be right.

'If Patrick Andergren was conducting inquiries that left the families thinking they might lose their children, then he was certainly living dangerously,' Johan says.

'I'd kill for less,' Malin says.

'One more thing,' Johan says. 'It looks like all the adoptions he was checking up on were organised by the same adoption consultancy firm. Swedish–Vietnamese Adoptions Ltd. They used to have an office here in Linköping, but that closed when adoptions from Vietnam were banned. According to Patrick Andergren's files, they opened up in Denmark instead. If I've understood correctly, Andergren suspected that the founder of Swedish–Vietnamese Adoptions, a Sonny Levin, was somehow involved in, or at least was aware of, the fact that not all the adoptions were entirely above board.'

Malin feels a chill in her chest.

She's having trouble breathing.

Feels sick again.

Swedish–Vietnamese Adoptions.

That was the agency Karin mentioned.

The consultants she used.

Tess.

I don't want to know, don't want to know.

Sonny Levin.

Karin didn't mention him, but she definitely mentioned the firm, which acts as an intermediary between adoptive parents and adoption organisations.

'Which adoption organisations are involved?' Malin asks.

'The Adoption Centre, Adoption World, and a few others.'

'Could this Sonny Levin have anything to do with the murders?' Zeke says. 'If he was mixed up in something illegal and Patrick Andergren was getting too close?'

'Maybe,' Malin says. 'We'll have to track him down.'

Tess.

In the sandpit at the play centre, on Karin's lap.

'Is Karin Johannison one of the parents he was investigating?' Malin asks. 'Her adoption?'

She notices how both Zeke and Johan hold their breath, swallow, and then their brains start working again.

'Well, is she?' Malin repeats after a few moments of silence.

'No,' Johan says. 'Why?'

Should I say anything about her adoption consultants? Yes, no?

But Malin decides to wait, talk to Karin first.

'I just wondered. She adopted Tess from Vietnam, after all.'

None of her colleagues has previously made the connection that Karin's adoption went through after the ban and wondered how that happened. Unless one of them had worked it out, but like her didn't want to cause any problems for a fellow officer, not until it became unavoidable.

And Zeke. How is he going to keep his head clear in all this?

'OK,' Malin says. 'We need to check out the other families. Look up the consultancy firm and get hold of Sonny Levin. See if the names in Vietnam can give us anything. Have you got an address for him?'

Johan yawns, then says: 'We've got information about the business, but nothing about him personally. Not yet. I was thinking of going to have a quick nap in the rest-room.'

'What about bribery?' Zeke asks.

'Nothing about that at all. I'm waiting for the Economic Crime Unit to get back to me about whether Patrick

Andergren had any foreign accounts, and, if so, what sort of transactions he used them for.'

Johan stands up.

Puts his hand in his pocket, then holds out a pack of chewing gum to Malin.

'Take one,' he says. 'Before Sven and the others get here.'

Malin holds out her hand, takes a piece of gum, puts it in her mouth, and the mixture of peppermint and coffee makes her tongue stick to the roof of her mouth, and her saliva glands start working as if someone had turned a tap on.

Zeke beside her.

She can feel that he wants to say something, knows he's going to confront her as soon as Johan has gone.

The gym.

Vomit-green walls.

The stench of sweat.

Zeke's usual imperturbable expression replaced by anxiety and concern, and Malin can see the fear in his eyes.

'You've got to hold on, Malin. You've got to.'

He's holding her by the shoulders, looking her in the eye, trying to impart something to her, but what?

'Ella needs you, Malin, for God's sake, we've got to find her, and if you start drinking again then everything'll go to hell. Think about Tove, she needs you. Stefan too.'

Neither of them needs me, Malin thinks.

Why should I care?

'I couldn't,' she says. 'I just couldn't resist any longer. I couldn't, and I didn't bloody want to either.'

Malin hears how her voice shifts from almost a scream to a whimper, and she sinks onto the bench press and lets her shoulders drop.

FUCK ME.

The Hamlet, Ågatan, the uniformed officers who took her home, who didn't report her.

Tove, having to look after her.

And now she's fled back to Lundsberg.

Everything she just told Zeke.

But she hasn't told him about the child.

The one she can't have.

About the life that can never, ever be.

She didn't ask what she wanted to: 'What the hell am I going to do? What do people do, Zeke? How can I get through this? How the hell do any of us actually bear this?'

'I'll talk to the guys in uniform. Make sure it definitely doesn't go any further,' Zeke says. 'I'm not going to say anything to anyone, and neither will Johan.'

Malin nods, looks up at him, his skull-like face, the small cuts in his usually so carefully shaven head.

He sits down beside her.

Puts his arm around her and he's warm and Malin feels like sinking into that warmth.

'Pull yourself together now. I'm giving you one chance, no more, because otherwise it could be dangerous for me and all the rest of us to have you here at work. You do realise that? You can't start drinking again, Malin. Because it's not at all certain that you'd survive. You could lose your job, and that would kill you, you know that.'

This job's killing me, Malin thinks.

But at the same time it's the only thing keeping me alive.

Peter.

Stefan alone, so alone in his care home in Sjöplogen.

Tove leaving, no other option.

Ella. Save me.

Who else is going to?

And her whole body is clenched with thirst, and she starts to shake uncontrollably as great big tears roll down her cheeks, and she can feel how small and rigid she is in Zeke's arms, and she stammers: 'What am I going to do, Zeke? What am I going to do? How the hell am I going to deal with this?'

Zeke is breathing deeply.

She can feel his ribs slowly rise and fall.

Then he says: 'Go home now. Get some sleep, and get rid of any visible signs of your hangover. Then come back in a couple of hours, and we'll get going with this. OK?'

Malin feels her body shaking.

She manages to whisper a yes.

41

Malin crumples up Tove's note.

Doesn't want to look at it.

But she understands her daughter, understands why she fled.

Back to what could become her life. A life far from grim rented flats and a desperate alcoholic mother.

Who could blame you, Tove?

The Ikea clock goes on ticking, and Malin feels like drawing the blinds, hiding in the dark, but knows what she has to do.

Exorcism.

It's time for exorcism.

She goes into Tove's room and pulls two big ice-hockey bags that have been in the wardrobe for years, so long that Malin's forgotten where they came from.

But they'll come in useful now.

Exorcism.

Her headache has eased slightly now.

But not the shame, and she avoids looking at herself in the hall mirror as she drags one of the hockey bags to the kitchen.

Then she yanks the fancy stainless-steel microwave oven down from the shelf above the draining board. She drops it in the bag, and hears the glass in the door break.

The Rörstrand crockery.

A satisfying smashing sound as it hits the bottom of the bag.

A birthday present from Peter. She remembers how she pretended to be pleased.

Cupboard by cupboard, drawer by drawer, she clears Peter and all his paraphernalia from the kitchen.

Fills half a bag.

She does the same in the living room.

His iPad.

Stupid, flashy thing.

His bloody awful films. The Complete Sylvester Stallone Collection.

In the bedroom she pulls his clothes out of the wardrobe, fills the second bag with them.

His gym shoes, winter boots, the absurdly expensive green padded coat from Moncler.

Away with all of it.

Out with all of it.

And Malin can feel her panic sweating its way out of her body, the drops trickling down her neck, under her T-shirt, and it feels good. She thinks about calling Tove, to see how she is, to thank her for her help, to apologise, but the last thing Tove needs now is to hear me apologise. At least I know my daughter that well.

Two ugly artistic photographs.

Away with them.

His gloves, winter hat, bathing trunks. Away with them.

Aftershave.

Deodorant.

Shaving cream.

She empties out the washing basket.

Underpants.

A T-shirt.

Burn the lot of it.

Drive him out, and Malin catches sight of herself in the bathroom mirror, smells the lingering stench of vomit in the cramped, yellow-tiled room, and realises that the swelling and redness is now mostly internal.

Eye drops.

She's still got some from when she last needed them.

She fills her eyes.

Blinks.

Fuzzy.

But there I am, there's Malin Fors.

And she clenches her teeth, sees her thin and somehow leathery skin stretch across her cheekbones. The fine lines around her eyes are deeper than ever.

Shit.

What have I done?

She tears herself away from the mirror, spits in the toilet, then drags the two bags, overstuffed with his possessions and clothes, into the hall. You're on your way out, do you hear?

You fucking charlatan.

Don't fuck with me, do you hear?

Then she goes into the kitchen, and her head is thumping as she gets down on all fours by the cupboard under the sink.

She opens the door, digs about with her fingers, and behind the rubbish bin she finds the little hatch in the floor, sticks her hand in and feels the bottle, the glass, against her fingers, and she starts shaking again.

She dislodges it.

Tugs.

The bottle. A firm grip on the bottle.

Now it's there in front of her, the unopened bottle of tequila she bought in a moment of weakness a year ago.

Yep, there's drink in the flat.

The liquid is amber brown but clear, shimmering, beautiful, beautiful, beautiful.

And she gets to her feet.

Opens the bottle.

The smell makes her giddy with desire, the nausea vanishes.

Impossible.

She's about to tip the contents into the sink but changes her mind, puts the bottle to her lips instead, then changes her mind again.

In the hall she tucks the bottle in the inside pocket of the black oilskin coat, the coat's going as well. I have absolutely no fucking intention of trying to fit into someone else's life, she thinks. She puts the coat on, one last time.

She tosses the black high-heeled Louboutin shoes he gave her, the ones she hardly ever wears, into her bag.

She drags the bags down the stairs and out into the grey afternoon, then heaves them into the boot of the car, not remotely bothered about the fact that she'd probably fail a breath-test.

Is he at home?

Malin's stopped outside the yellow-plastered brick building on Linnégatan where he has his swanky bachelor pad.

She was planning to dump his stuff outside his door, but if he's at home he might hear her, and the last thing she wants right now is to see him.

Never wants to see him again.

Christ, she feels like killing him.

She waits in the car with the engine idling.

Exorcism.

It's much worse than this.

I hate you, do you get that? How the hell could you do

this to me? And she can feel tears rising once more and swallows them down, pushing her tongue back to keep the lump safely in her stomach.

Then she drives off.

Heads out towards Sturefors, where she grew up. Linköping passes by outside the windows. Folkungavallen football stadium, the flashy directors' villas up on the heights of Ramshäll, the blocks of flats in Johannelund, the playing fields next to the Stångå River, where some sort of girls' football tournament seems to be going on.

Ella.

Are you still in the river?

She drives past Ekholmen, Hjulsbro. The two districts are within shouting distance of each other, but they couldn't be more different. Hjulsbro, that's where the money lives. Ekholmen is home to the poor, to immigrants, people no one cares about.

Halfway to Sturefors she turns off onto a forest track, heading straight into the dark pine and fir forest, she's been here before, in connection with a case, when Zeke stuck his pistol in a suspect's mouth to make him talk.

She's never seen Zeke so single-minded.

Or angry. Not before, and not since.

She carries on, deep into the forest. Pleased there are no cars parked at the side of the track, she'd rather not bump into any inquisitive mushroom-pickers.

She reaches a clearing.

The world is dark here.

The dense forest forms impenetrable walls, and the clouds, almost black now, are a lid on an unfamiliar room where true loneliness seems to be the only option.

Here.

This is perfect, Malin thinks, and gets out of the car,

and in the spaces between the tree trunks she imagines she can see the faces of the dead, trying to shout at her, yet remaining soundless.

You're there, she thinks.

Everything is always there.

She opens the boot and pulls the bags out, then empties Peter's clothes and belongings onto the track in front of the car.

The things he's given her.

She tears off the oilskin.

Throws it on top of the other rubbish, but only after removing the bottle of tequila and putting it on the bonnet of the car.

The microwave oven.

The high-heeled shoes.

The broken crockery.

His Björn Borg underwear.

The expensive T-shirts, all different colours.

The aftershave.

Everything to do with the bastard.

Maybe Tove would like the shoes? No, we aren't the same size.

Am I completely mad? Malin wonders. Is this actually happening? Or is it something else entirely?

Am I really standing here on this forest track?

The doctor's words ringing inside her: 'Everything's fine. I can't see any reason why . . .'

'I'm afraid I have to tell you . . .'

What's going on?

Fuck with me.

Don't fuck with me.

Malin goes back around to the boot again and takes out the spare petrol can.

She empties it onto the heap of belongings. The acrid

smell rises up towards the clouds and merges with them, and she wonders if it's going to start raining petrol now.

Frenetically she shakes the last drops out of the can.

Puts it back in the boot, then gets a box of matches from the glove compartment.

You're going to burn, you bastard.

The whole world is going to burn.

And Malin lights a match and tosses it at the pile of things, but it refuses to catch.

She lights four matches at the same time and throws them towards the vapour, the things, him, and whoosh!

He's burning.

Tall, clear, icy-blue flames reach for the sky, and she can see him burn, can see him and all his wickedness burning out of her life, and she ought to feel sad but is instead ecstatic, and can't help wondering if that's really what she's feeling, or is it something else?

The plastic on the microwave melts, the clothes burn, and the bottle of aftershave explodes in a puff of flame.

She turns her face up to the rain, the drops are too small to have any effect on her fire.

She screams and screams and screams.

Howls out her rage in a single, long ARGHHHHHHHHH!

Then she falls silent.

Takes the bottle from the bonnet.

And drinks until something inside her says: You won't survive any more, Malin.

42

Malin is walking along Drottninggatan in the rain.

She stuck her fingers down her throat out in the forest, now wasn't the time to get drunk.

It's never the time.

But I want to.

Cars drive past, but the puddles by the side of the road aren't big enough to splash her.

She had her old yellow mac in the boot of the car.

Just as good as the Barbour for keeping the rain off.

The city centre deserted on a Sunday.

Karin's probably at home with Tess.

I've got to talk to you, Karin. The drive back from the forest passed without incident, she stopped at the petrol station at the Berga roundabout and bought three packs of chewing gum, and she's fairly confident she doesn't reek of tequila. She couldn't bring herself to pour away what was left in the bottle in the forest, just held it like a comforting hand as she watched Peter's possessions burn to ashes.

No cars had come along and interrupted her.

The forest had been her space alone, her oxygen. Black, silent rain.

Swedish–Vietnamese Adoptions Ltd.

Sonny Levin.

Zeke has texted Malin a copy of his passport photograph, a typical boxer's face.

Thick neck.

A bullish face, with wide nostrils, as if made to be pierced by a ring.

But oddly friendly eyes, in spite of his harsh features.

Zeke thinks she's at home, getting some rest.

Like hell.

Not now.

Not now it feels like they're finally starting to make some progress.

She taps in the code to Karin's door. Tess's pushchair, a ridiculously expensive model from Urban Jungle, is parked in the stairwell, unlocked.

Malin rings the bell.

Hears a child's footsteps on the other side of the door, a little girl's wavering voice: '. . . ummy . . . door . . . ring . . .'

'God, you look rough. Did you get hit by a bus?'

'Slept badly,' Malin says, taking a large bite of the ham pie Karin has offered her.

Late afternoon now, their last argument tucked away at the back of a dark cupboard.

And rain pouring down outside the living-room window.

Tess on the floor in front of the television.

A film in the DVD player, something about Barbie, all bright colours and shockingly poor animation, but Tess is sitting there enchanted, and that's really all that matters, isn't it?

What children think.

The thought makes Malin smile that crooked smile again.

'What's so funny?' Karin asks.

'She looks like she loves that film.'

Karin sighs.

'You can't control what they like. She hates all the old Disney classics.'

Snow White.

Cinderella.

But reality isn't as pretty as that.

Children born from cinders, in an unexpected fire.

Is that the sort of child you are, Tess?

Malin and Karin eat, and the tea Karin's made has a refined smoky taste, and Malin considers how much to tell Karin, then realises that she may as well tell her everything, because Karin's smart, and is part of the investigation, and is more than capable of putting two and two together and working everything out anyway.

If she isn't too closely involved, Malin thinks. Perhaps she's already lost her impartiality, because of the connections between her, Sonny Levin, and Swedish–Vietnamese Adoptions.

If this is too personal for her.

Malin puts her knife and fork down on Karin's dining table, and sees the chrome cutlery glint in the light of the lamp from PH, it looks almost as if they're floating above the white laminate table top.

Then she tells Karin everything they've found out about Patrick Andergren's research.

That Karin's adoption consultancy has cropped up in the investigation. That Patrick Andergren suspected its own founder and owner, Sonny Levin, of irregularities.

Once she's finished, the two of them sit in silence at the table.

Malin can see that Karin's brain is working at top speed, and the corners of her mouth keep twitching as she tries to keep her cool and not get emotional.

From the television a female choir is singing a gentle song about handsome princes, Tess's breathing barely audible over the music.

'I had dealings with Levin in Denmark,' Karin says. 'He

thinks the Swedish authorities are being far too critical. That it's perfectly possible to adopt children from Vietnam without it leading to tragedy, as long as you know what you're doing.'

Malin listens.

Keen to let Karin find her own words.

'I checked. I was there. He seems to have good relationships with people over there. There was nothing odd about him at all. I had no reason to suspect anything.'

'You're sure?'

Malin rubs one eye.

Then looks at Karin, intently but cautiously.

'I'm sure.'

'Were there any other reasons for the move to Copenhagen, apart from the Swedish ban?'

'Not that I know of.'

'Have you heard any rumours that his business might be less than squeaky clean?'

Karin looks down at the table, waits a few seconds, and then looks up at Malin again.

'What do you want me to say? That I know Sonny Levin plays dirty? That I think he killed the Andergrens to protect himself? That he's taken their daughter back to Vietnam so he can sell her again?'

Tears in Karin's eyes.

'Sell,' Malin says. 'You said sell. Is that what Sonny Levin does, sell children?'

Karin shakes her head.

'That was a mistake, Malin. I said the wrong thing.'

'But you did pay?'

'Everyone pays to adopt.'

'But you paid unofficially, under the counter?'

Karin shakes her head, slowly.

The little girl is still watching the film, entranced.

Doesn't seem to have noticed that her mum's upset.

'I checked as much as I could.'

And what am I supposed to say to that? Malin wonders. What am I supposed to say to you, Karin? I know how much you longed for Tess. I know how much you love the little person sitting on the floor in front of the television. I know how much love you've got to give.

'Do you know where we can get hold of Levin?'

'No. I haven't had anything to do with him since Tess arrived. I've dealt with all the formalities myself, sending pictures of Tess and reports on her development to the authorities and the children's home in Vietnam.'

'Have you got a phone number for him?'

'Only the one on his Danish website.'

'An email address?'

'Same thing there.'

'OK,' Malin says. 'So you don't know anything about Levin or Patrick Andergren's investigations that we don't already know? You have to tell me, Karin. Do you know anything about the other families Andergren was looking into, other people who'd arranged adoptions via Levin? Do you know anything that could help us?'

Karin wipes her eyes with an natural linen napkin.

'I don't know anything, Malin.'

A hint of anger in Karin's voice.

'Nothing at all.'

And Karin stands up.

Stares hard at Malin before saying in a harsh whisper: 'Now go. You and your fucking nosey questions have no business here. Just go.'

Malin gets to her feet.

'Did you pay, Karin?'

'What?'

'Did you pay more than the official standard fee? Did

you give Levin money unofficially? To anyone in Vietnam? Staff at the children's home, local officials? Well, did you?'

And Malin sees something snap inside Karin.

Tess notices, and gets up and runs over to her mum, pulling at her legs, and Karin picks Tess up and buries her nose in her hair.

'What do you think? Do you think I paid? What do you think a child costs? Do you think you can get a child like Tess without paying a fucking high price? Is that what you think?'

'I think—'

'Get out,' Karin says calmly. 'Get out of here. You've got no business being here.'

43

Careful, careful, Börje Svärd thinks as he rings the doorbell.

Careful.

Proceed with caution.

Can Waldemar manage that?

Waldemar Ekenberg is standing next to Börje, on the front steps of a yellow-painted wooden house in Ljungsbro. The little house is in a glade facing a huge field that seems to plunge into Lake Roxen.

The rain has stopped, the wind is shaking the drenched foliage of a pair of linden trees, and yellow leaves are swirling around the neat garden.

A pedal car is parked under the steps. It's made of red-painted tin, an old-fashioned, expensive toy.

What are the people inside thinking? Börje wonders, and in his mind he sees a fleeting image of the fat red-head, Marianne, sees her pink nipple against her white skin, and he'd like to see her again even though he doesn't really go for fat women.

Unless he does, after all.

And he liked her cheery sense of humour, her loud laughter. He likes anything feminine really, the way they toy with him, leaving him powerless to resist doing what they want.

I like being seduced, it's as simple as that, he thinks.

Then he forces such thoughts aside.

Inappropriate.

He hears the doorbell ring.

Voices, saying things he can't make out.

Do they think it's a friend? A salesman? They're unlikely to be expecting us, the police, that much is certain.

The door opens.

A little boy, perhaps six years old, of Asian appearance, pokes his head out. His black hair is sticking up in spikes.

The boy looks surprised.

'Hello,' Waldemar says. 'We'd like to talk to your mum and dad.'

The boy turns around and calls into the house: 'Mum, Dad, there are some men here.'

A man comes out into the hall.

Tall, thin, a questioning look on a face with wide cheekbones, and he asks them in a pronounced southern Swedish accent: 'And who might you be?'

Börje holds up his ID.

'We'd like to ask a few questions.'

'Wow! Are you the police?' the boy exclaims.

They step inside. and Börje keeps a close eye on the man, but he looks neither anxious nor guilty, just curious.

He shows them into the kitchen, and soon his wife joins them, a dark-skinned woman, Börje guesses she's from some sort of Middle Eastern background. She's what he would call a classical beauty, even if the lines around her mouth make her look slightly bitter.

Introductions.

Sam, the boy's name.

Sunnita. Lars.

Kardgren.

But they already knew that.

'Would you like coffee?'

They say yes, and soon the five of them are sitting at

the round, pine kitchen table, surrounded by green-painted wooden panels and blue floral tiles, and there's a smell of cinnamon from the microwave as a bag of homemade buns warms up.

Waldemar gives a brief outline of why they're there.

What they know.

And Börje is surprised by how calm his colleague is, the way he manages to sound confidential and friendly, not aggressive and harsh, the way he can when the mood strikes him.

As it often does.

Börje knows that Waldemar approves of adoption. But perhaps this case is going to change his attitude?

Börje looks at Lars and Sunnita Kardgren. Do they seem shaken? Are they squirming? Do they look troubled?

When Waldemar stops talking, the woman takes charge.

'Lars, can you take Sam into the living room?'

The man stands up. Gestures towards the boy.

Börje thinks the boy is going to protest, he was so excited a few minutes ago that the police were there, but he seems to appreciate the seriousness of the occasion and goes off with his father.

His hair is a carpet of spikes, ten-centimetres long, that sway as he walks.

'He's six years old,' Sunnita Kardgren says. 'And he already knows what punk is. Wanted to try a punk hairstyle. So I did it with sugar water.'

Waldemar smiles.

'They start early.'

'Yes, Lars has been showing him clips of the Sex Pistols on YouTube. He used to be a punk, back in the day.'

Sunnita Kardgren gets up and pours coffee, then puts the plate of cinnamon buns on the table.

'We knew that Andergren was looking into things,'

she says as she sits down again. 'And you don't have to be Einstein to realise that we didn't like him snooping about.'

'I can understand that,' Börje says. 'But we have to look into every line of inquiry in a case like this.'

The Kardgrens are the second family they've visited.

The first family lived in the countryside beyond Rimforsa, and didn't know who Patrick Andergren was, and had no idea that Sonny Levin and Swedish–Vietnamese Adoptions Ltd were involved in anything improper.

'That's nothing to do with us,' the man of the family had said. 'Nothing at all. Everything was above board.'

As they stood there in the hall, Börje and Waldemar had heard the child, an eight-year-old girl, playing in her room. Singing karaoke to old songs by Gyllene Tider and Abba. Outside, nature seemed to be watching over the scene, an overgrown old meadow in front of ancient woodland.

They never saw the girl.

They were shown to the door by the father, who failed to conceal his irritation.

And they had a watertight alibi for the night of the murders.

'Help yourselves.'

Börje takes a bite of a bun, and it tastes wonderful, the way they did when he was a lad, when everything seemed to promise a better life.

'When the investigations appeared, particularly the one conducted by the American State Department, naturally we got worried. Couldn't help wondering if there was anything wrong about Sam's adoption. I even visited the children's home in Vietnam again, and they showed me the same papers we'd been given by Sonny Levin. Everything was in order, they assured me. Sam's parents had been killed in a tuk-tuk accident when he was five months old.'

We're not here to question the adoption, Börje thinks, and asks: 'Did you ever meet Patrick Andergren? At some meeting, or anywhere else?'

Sunnita Kardgren looks away briefly, then turns towards Börje and looks hard into his eyes for a few moments.

'We never go to meetings for adopted children and their parents. We don't have any contact with anyone like that on the Internet either. It's all just nonsense, this idea that Sam would feel less different if he met other children from Vietnam. What makes him feel less different is having more ordinary friends.'

'Did you ever meet Patrick Andergren?'

Sunnita Kardgren takes a deep breath.

'He came here one evening. Told us his suspicions about Levin. That things had sometimes been less than entirely proper, and that he was worried about our case. He asked if we'd seen Sam's parents' death certificates. Can you imagine? That struck me as incredibly impertinent.'

Sunnita Kardgren falls silent. She takes a few breaths before going on: 'I wanted to show him the door. We both did, to be honest, but I listened to what he had to say. What was he expecting? That we'd say, sure, Sam's parents are alive somewhere in Vietnam, and want him back. Let's go and give him back! Yeah, that's what we'll do!

'Sam's been with us since he was eight months old. He's our child, and he's going to grow up here, anything else would be tantamount to abuse. He thinks of us as his parents, he can't remember anything different.

'And that's all I care about.'

Sunnita Kardgren takes a sip of coffee.

Pushes her untouched bun away.

'Do you know what it's like, not to be able to have children of your own?' she asks.

'I do,' Waldemar says. 'My wife and I—'

Sunnita Kardgren interrupts him, and Börje looks at Waldemar and realises how little he knows about his colleague. He's always assumed that Waldemar had never even entertained the idea of having children.

'It's like living with never-ending grief, and everyone else's happiness feels like a slap in the face,' Sunnita Kardgren says. 'It makes you feel deficient, worthless.'

A gust of wind hits the kitchen window.

'You can talk to Lars if you like. He'll say the same as me. We've got nothing but good to say about Levin, and we had no unfinished business with Patrick Andergren. We barely knew him. And we've got alibis for the night they were murdered. My parents were here from Stockholm. I'll give you their number. I presume you want it?'

Her tone is sarcastic now, and Börje can see Waldemar's anger bubbling up until it suddenly bursts out.

'Ella,' he says in a sharp voice, clutching his coffee cup. 'She came from Vietnam, just like Sam, and she's missing. So I'm really fucking sorry that we've had to come and disturb your artificial, non-biological, middle-class life. Just tell us! Do you know anything that could help us find Ella? Like where we could get hold of Sonny Levin, for instance?'

Shit, Börje thinks, as he sees Sunnita Kardgren's eyes darken.

'You can go to hell with that other kid,' she says. 'I can't take responsibility for anyone but Sam. I don't give a damn about any other kids. And no one, least of all a couple of fucking cops playing at being detectives, is going to come here and try to take him away from me.'

And the agitated echoes spread across Linköping, across the Östergötland Plain and the thousand-year-old forests that Sunday evening:

'Get out, how dare you come here and even suggest something like that! GET OUT!'

'Do you really think we'd do something like that? What sort of people are you?'

'We don't know anything. Everything was above board.'

'We had to wait ages to get Arvid. And when Patrick showed up with his insinuations, we thought he'd gone mad. We'd met him through friends of friends, and he seemed OK. But to suggest that there was something wrong with Arvid's adoption? Come off it. Patrick Andergren must have lost it, must have gone a bit mental.'

'We've got an alibi.'

Alibis, alibis, alibis.

Börje and Waldemar, Malin and Zeke.

Met with alibis, wherever they turn.

What love can be built on a lie?

The way I felt when I began to suspect that Ella had come to us in an unjust way shook me to the core.

And I couldn't just investigate our case, Ella.

I couldn't abandon the other children.

Money.

Every question costs money.

Don't blame the parents you meet, Malin.

Don't blame them.

Don't blame Karin.

We would have been capable of murder to keep hold of Ella, no matter what had happened. But we had to know the truth, because without the truth our love was false, even if ultimately we would have chosen false love over no love at all.

That's the way love for your own child works, Malin.

You know that.

You've felt that yourself.

And you've felt what it's like to be denied that love, you know what that does to a person.

Don't judge too harshly, Malin.

Not yourself.

Not Peter.

Not the parents you've met today, or their forge-tempered defence of their lives.

You'd do the same, and you know it. You did it when Tove's life was threatened.

Ella.

You've got to find Ella. That's so much more important than everything else.

Who really cares who murdered me and Cecilia?

We only care about Ella.

It still isn't too late.

44

No messages.

No missed calls.

Nothing to indicate that anyone cares about me at all.

The flat on Ågatan closes around Malin Fors.

She sits down on the chair beside the bureau in the hall.

Hasn't switched any lights on, just lets darkness watch over her, feel the warmth of the unknown come towards her.

Tove.

Peter.

Dad.

Stefan.

My brother doesn't even know what a telephone is. He doesn't know who I am. Is he even capable of love? Is it possible to feel attached to a shadow of a shadow?

She got home late. They've managed to get hold of all the families Patrick Andergren was investigating, all but one, and so far they've all got alibis. All that remains is to get hold of the last family, and put together a list of other adoptions that Swedish–Vietnamese Adoptions was involved in.

They also have to get hold of Sonny Levin. He's registered at an address in Copenhagen, which is also the address of his new company there, Danish–Vietnamese Adoptions Ltd.

When they found the address, Sven called Malin and

said he wanted her and Zeke to catch the first plane to Copenhagen tomorrow morning.

Malin didn't object. She's actually surprised that the police's stretched budget can cover a trip of that sort.

Ebba in reception has booked their tickets, a direct flight, 06.15 from Linköping Airport.

Peter.

Malin shuts her eyes, and in her mind she sees him thrusting deep into the blonde woman.

Two dogs.

What a fucking awful year, only fit for dogs.

Then she sees the flames consuming his clothes and possessions.

And realises that the fire has cleansed her.

She no longer feels so sad.

Or so angry.

She sees his face in her mind's eye, and it's like looking at a black-and-white photograph of some distant relative, long since dead. There's some connection to the person in the picture, but it doesn't mean anything.

Burn, you bastard, and he burned.

Enough, now.

Malin Fors gets up from the chair.

Goes and lies on her bed, tries not to think about alcohol, and succeeds.

She manages not to think about anything, and soon she sinks into a dreamless sleep, into shimmering shallow water, in which both night and day are reflected.

Sleep on the plane, drink coffee just before landing so you wake up.

Zeke as tired as she is, and in the roar of the plane Malin looks out of the window and sees the bright blue sky, the clouds like the softest carpet below them.

They don't speak during the flight, nor during the taxi ride to Vesterbro, past the bland new hotels with their glass façades, past the white-brick industrial units that seem to be slowly disintegrating in the damp Öresund wind.

Copenhagen city centre outside the windows now.

Low-grown parks and blue-green water.

The entire city seems to be built of brick and dirt.

Of exhaust fumes, cigarette smoke, and bacon rind.

Cycles everywhere, even on a cold autumn morning like this. Definitely more muscular than Stockholm. Not to mention Linköping.

The junkies are hanging about outside the Central Station, across the road from the shimmering white façade of the newly renovated Nimb Palace hotel facing the Tivoli Gardens.

The taxi turns left towards Vesterbro, at the junction where the elegant Jacobsen-designed SAS Radisson tower shoots up towards the clouds.

Sonny Levin.

The nose and nostrils of a bull.

Are you here?

Have you got the girl here somewhere? Was it you who killed the Andergrens?

Johan hasn't managed to find out much about Sonny Levin's private life, and the parents they spoke to yesterday had nothing but good to say about him.

'He was reliable.'

'Admittedly, he looks like a thug, but you soon learn to trust him.'

'He really did care about those children.'

How much do you really care, Sonny? Do you care about anything but money? In its last year of operation, his Swedish company made a profit of one and a half million kronor, and that's not counting any undeclared income.

'Did you pay, Karin?'

'Do you think I paid?'

A Danish flag in a restaurant window.

This neo-racist nation has grown fat on pork chops, crackling, beer, and fear, Malin thinks, as the taxi stops outside a rundown, three-storey, art nouveau building.

Malin could see it on Zeke in the plane.

How relieved he was to get away for a bit.

If only to the country of Pia Kjærsgaard and her far-right Danish People's Party.

'So how are we going to get inside?' Zeke asks, as a police car glides past behind them.

No entryphone, no coded lock.

But the door is locked.

Malin can't be bothered to wait. She pulls her key ring from her jacket pocket and finds the lock-pick. But before she can set to work, a man with long greasy hair and brown clothes shuffles up to them.

He stops.

'Do you want to get in?' he asks in Swedish, and when Malin nods he pulls out a key ring and opens the door, before lumbering off without another word.

In.

The stairwell stinks of old rubbish. The dark green paint is peeling from the walls, and a bare bulb hangs from the ceiling. But there's a list of the occupants on one wall, which tells them that the office of Danish–Vietnamese Adoptions Ltd is on the third floor, stairwell B, on the far side of the courtyard.

They cross the yard, which is littered with rubbish, and Malin and Zeke can feel eyes on them from the windows.

Intruders.

What are you doing here?

Who are you? Get lost.

The door to the other building is unlocked, and Malin hears Zeke panting behind her as they climb the three flights of worn stairs, on each step she feels that she's slipping and falling backwards.

They reach the third floor.

A handwritten note on one door, daylight through a narrow window.

DV Ltd.

Enough for a postman.

The name 'Levin' scribbled below.

Malin and Zeke stand there for a moment, catching their breath and listening for any sounds.

They're alone, and there's no noise from behind either the door in front of them or the neighbouring door, where another handwritten note says someone called Pedersen lives.

Malin leans over.

Peers in through the letterbox, but it's angled in such a way that she can only see just inside the door, down at a pile of post.

Weeks of deliveries.

She straightens up.

'There's no one here,' she says. 'No Levin.'

'Let's go in,' Zeke says, and this time Malin gets to use the lock-pick, and the worn old lock gives way after just a few seconds.

The door opens.

They go into the flat.

Into the hall.

In her mind's eye Malin can see an image of Sonny Levin, bullet holes in his chest, or is the image actually here in the flat in Vesterbro?

She raises her hand.

Motions to Zeke to keep quiet.

They've had to leave their pistols at home, impossible to take them on the plane at short notice, even for police officers.

Would they need them now? But a man with a bullet in his heart can't do them any harm. And everything is silent, even if Malin can sense the smell of powder, of a fired pistol.

A few steps and she's in the flat's only room, three metres by four, with one bare window facing a brown brick wall.

'Clear,' Zeke calls from the kitchen. 'Completely empty.'

'Clear,' Malin calls. 'Same here.'

And that's when she sees it, the door, at the far end of the room, and presumes it must lead to a large cupboard, and then she hears noises from inside, whimpering, movement, and she thinks: Ella, is that you? Have we found you?

Johan Jakobsson has found something he thinks might be interesting.

An unprocessed estate from someone who's died.

An Agda Levin, eighty-eight years old, died ten months ago, leaving a house in Vreta Kloster to her son.

The house is on Åstigen, a street Johan knows. Smart houses there, out of reach of him and his family, but beautiful old buildings, lots of ornate woodwork.

They haven't managed to find an address in Sweden for Sonny Levin.

But what if he lives there? In his mum's house? They might be able to find him there, if Malin and Zeke fail to get hold of him in Copenhagen. He hasn't heard anything from them, so maybe they've drawn a blank.

But on the other hand, it's only half past eight, so they probably haven't got far yet.

He's started looking into the various names in Vietnam, parents, local officials, but there's no information on the

Internet. So they'll have to use the formal channels, and that takes time, a lot of time. Time that Ella hasn't got, if she's still alive.

Then the phone rings.

He picks up the receiver.

Ebba in reception.

'A Katarina Karlsson wants to talk to a detective. Preferably Elin Sand, but I said she wasn't available. She hasn't come in yet, has she?'

'What's she calling about?'

'The Andergrens, and their little girl.'

Johan looks around. Börje and Waldemar haven't arrived, but Elin Sand is actually at her desk, drinking coffee and reading the paper.

She was in yesterday too.

Helped him go through the last of the Andergrens' private papers. Hundreds of documents, and she read carefully for nine hours without a word of complaint, even though her injured backside must have hurt like hell from having to sit still for so long.

'Put the call through to Sand,' he says. 'She's here, and I'm busy.'

Johan turns back to his screen again.

Agda Levin.

Thinks: We need to take a look at that house. Who knows what could be in there?

Elin Sand hears Katarina Karlsson's voice on the other end of the line.

She sounds like she's got a cold, and Elin remembers her disfiguring birthmark, her sharp features, as she speaks.

'I didn't tell you everything,' she says. 'But last night I had a dream. I dreamed that I saw Ella in a dark, damp room.'

She's gone mad, Elin thinks.

But she lets Katarina Karlsson go on.

'Ella asked for my help in the dream. Said her mum and dad couldn't help her, that perhaps no one could.'

'So what was it you wanted to tell me?'

Calm.

Matter-of-fact.

A jolt of pain from Elin's backside as she leans too far back on her chair.

Damn.

'Patrick once told me he left Ericsson to get away from the culture of bribery. He said, "I don't give a damn about the corruption. That doesn't bother me any more. But it's a different matter with the children." That's what he said. And I know he meant it.'

Elin Sand makes herself more comfortable, resting her weight on her right buttock.

'You should have mentioned this before.'

'I know.'

'Are you saying we should be looking at the adoptions? That that's the line of inquiry we should be focusing on?'

'Yes.'

'We're already doing that.'

'Look harder. You might find Ella.'

Click.

Katarina Karlsson has hung up, and Elin Sand looks out across the office, at the other weary police officers, and wonders what the phone call meant.

What did Katarina Karlsson actually say? And why did she say it?

No children herself.

Could she have taken Ella? Was that possible? Does she want to mislead us, get us to focus on something else?

Then Elin Sand remembers the outhouses by the forest. Could a child be hidden away there?

Desperate women.

Their bodies crying out for children.

Could she have taken Ella?

Is that what she was trying to say?

Or am I imagining things? Why would she do something like that? I must be imagining things.

I hope my body only whispers when I get to that point.

45

Come out, Ella.

The game's over.

Malin cautiously takes hold of the door handle and wonders if Ella is in there, afraid to come out.

She pushes the handle down.

Pulls the door towards her, and light seeps into the cupboard, and the scratching and whimpering get louder.

Shit.

A grey-brown rat scampers between her legs, into the hall and out into the stairwell.

Malin breathes out.

Then they check through the pile of post, mostly adverts, apart from two old bills from an electricity company.

Nothing else.

'This place has never been used as an office,' Zeke declares before they leave the flat, and Malin nods. On the stairs they bump into the postman and stop him, and in the flickering light of the bare bulb the sinewy Dane with a thin moustache and a pointed nose looks at them sceptically, then says in Swedish with an odd Danish accent: 'There was a Swede here a few times. I saw him. But that's a long time ago now. His business probably didn't do too well here, and that's just as well.'

'Do you know where he might be?' Zeke says, ignoring the insinuation in the man's words.

Racists, Malin thinks. They're all racists, the whole lot of them.

'What do you mean, just as well?'

'What business would those rice-eaters have here?'

'Where could he be?' Zeke repeats.

'In Sweden, maybe. Where he belongs. Just like you.'

Then the postman walks around them and adjusts his uniform, as if he were a soldier manning an invisible national border that had to be guarded constantly to ward off all manner of intruders.

They're sitting in a taxi when Johan calls.

He tells them about the address in Vreta Kloster. Agda Levin's house.

Malin says that they haven't found anything and are on their way back to the airport. There's a plane to Norrköping in an hour.

'Sven thinks we should head out there at once, he wants to send Waldemar and Börje.'

Malin doesn't know why, but she wants to go to the house herself, she can be there in two and a half hours, and it can wait that long.

'I want to do it.'

'OK. Why?'

'I just do.'

'I'll have a word with Sven,' Johan says. 'I'm sure he'll hold off.'

'Thanks. What about Elin, what's she doing? Is she in today?'

'She was here just now, but I can't see her at the moment. She got a phone call, and I haven't seen her since.'

The taxi turns off towards Kastrup. The glass buildings of the airport look expensive, and Malin can't help thinking

Mons Kallentoft

that there's money in this country, so surely they've got space to take plenty of people from all corners of the world.

But Danish society has made up its mind.

We're closed.

No more.

We're fine as we are.

'How did the morning meeting go?' Malin asks.

'We put it off. You two aren't here, and everyone else is up to date.'

'OK. Text me the address, and Zeke and I will head straight there. Send a patrol car to pick us up at the airport.'

'Aye, aye, captain,' Johan says, and hangs up.

Katarina Karlsson wasn't at school, she's off sick for a few more days.

So now Elin Sand is standing outside the door of her cottage, listening to the gradually diminishing rain fall on the surrounding forest.

Everything is quiet by the outhouses at the end of the garden. Are you in there, Ella? Elin Sand wonders, then she thinks about Katarina Karlsson, her face, the lips that seemed redder than they were thanks to her birthmark.

A noise in the forest.

An elk? A deer?

It's easy for someone to be alone out here.

Too alone?

No sound from the outhouses.

Elin recalls the last time she was out here, and how resigned Katarina Karlsson had seemed.

My hand on her shoulder, the bare skin at the back of her neck.

Elin wonders if she ought to approach with caution, what if Katarina Karlsson really does have the girl?

A single woman shouldn't live like this.

This is a place for a couple who love nature.

Who want a lot of animals around them.

The door opens.

Katarina Karlsson.

She's coughing and sniffing.

Dressed in a shabby green dressing gown, so loosely tied at the waist that Elin can see her red underwear.

Katarina Karlsson doesn't seem surprised, doesn't pull her dressing gown more tightly around her, just says: 'You are the one I spoke to a little while ago, aren't you?'

Elin Sand nods.

'Can I come in?'

'Sure. But I might be contagious.'

Elin Sand listens out for sounds inside the house as she goes in. Nothing, and she follows Katarina Karlsson into the living room, watches her walk, can see that she's naked under the dressing gown apart from her pants, and her skin is white, shimmering, with thin veins hidden beneath the skin.

'Have a seat. I'll get coffee.'

Elin Sand sits down on the sofa. The living room is just as homely as she remembers, crocheted tablecloths, family photographs, smart vases, and any sense of loneliness vanishes.

A few minutes later Katarina Karlsson comes back in.

She sits down on the sofa, and the two women sit silently next to one another for a minute or so.

'Have you told us everything you know?' Elin Sand finally asks.

'No. I think Patrick was investigating other adoptions.'

'We know about those. What do you know?'

'Nothing really. Cilla happened to mention it in passing, but I should have told you the last time you were here.'

'Yes, you should. Why didn't you?'

'I like secrets. You must know that yourself?'

The birthmark on her forehead is almost glowing now, and Elin Sand stifles an impulse to put her hand out to touch it.

'You haven't got the girl here with you?' Elin goes on. 'You didn't try to get her, and it all went wrong?'

Katarina Karlsson laughs.

'That's a bit naïve of you. I love Ella, but she isn't my child.'

'I—'

'You think I might have her hidden away in the outhouse? You're welcome to take a look, but all you'll find there is firewood and some old tools.'

'I'm sorry,' Elin Sand says, and realises she can't take her eyes off the gap at the front of Katarina Karlsson's dressing gown, and the glimpse of her almost weightless breasts.

'No problem,' Katarina Karlsson says, leaning back and revealing more of one breast.

Stop staring, Elin Sand tells herself.

She stands up and says: 'I'd better go.'

Katarina Karlsson laughs again, gently rather than scornfully.

'That's probably safest.'

Not far away, at Norrköping Airport, Malin and Zeke get off the plane from Copenhagen, walking down the steps in sunlight that almost seems to have been fired from a vibrating sky.

46

It's just gone half past two when Malin and Zeke get out of the patrol car outside the house they believe Sonny Levin has inherited from his mother.

They can make out a white, two-storey wooden house behind a tall, yellowing hedge, and when Malin turns around she finds herself looking at Lake Roxen, basking in sunlight.

Sunlight, at last.

An almost clear sky, at last.

A bit of clarity in their case at last? If they manage to find Sonny Levin here, what could he give them?

Anything at all could help us move on, Malin thinks as she opens the gate leading to the garden.

The grass is high, and it doesn't look like anyone's done any weeding in the flowerbeds all summer.

Impossible to see any tracks in the gravel path.

The house must be a hundred years old, and all the carved woodwork could do with a coat of paint.

They climb the steps to the porch.

No doorbell, but a lion's head.

They knock.

Faded lace curtains in the windows, an old person's curtains.

Malin has just spoken to Johan.

Nothing new has cropped up on the bribery angle, the check into Magnus Nyblom's finances hasn't produced anything. They're still trying to get hold of the last family Patrick Andergren was investigating, but they're away on holiday.

Elin Sand still hasn't reappeared, she had another doctor's appointment.

Levin.

What if you aren't here, what if we don't find you?

What chance would we have then of making any progress with this case? Things have been going slowly, then quickly, but we really haven't got anywhere at all.

We're swimming against the current, hoping that something's going to come our way, and Malin can feel the sun on the back of her neck, little drops of sweat forming and then evaporating.

'He's not here,' Zeke says, and knocks again.

Malin looks at him, sees that he's thinking the same as her.

'Let's go in.'

Three minutes later they're standing inside the hall, with its peculiar old-person smell, slightly sweet, with a hint of mould and dead skin cells. A smell of time passed, never to come again.

A tap dripping somewhere.

The kitchen? Bathroom?

'Hello?' Zeke calls. 'Hello!' No answer.

'Is anyone home?'

Malin gets no answer either, but on the floor in front of them is a pair of brown leather men's shoes.

They head further into the house, to a living room with two worn Chesterfield armchairs on a blue patterned Wilton carpet, with red-tinted aerial photographs of farms on the walls.

This house will probably be sold, Malin thinks. To a family with children. A rich family, because houses like this cost.

It's the kitchen tap dripping.

Drip, drip.

That noise would drive me mad.

Zeke is walking in front of her through a library, and he pushes to open a white-painted sliding door, but stops halfway and exclaims: 'What the hell's going on here?'

Malin goes up to him.

They shove the door open fully to get a better look.

The stench of dead body hits them with full force and they cough, want to flee the smell, but the sight that greets them forces them to focus.

There, at a dining table, sits the body of a man who's been shot. He's sitting on a chair, and his upper body is hanging across the table, his head askew, and Malin can see a stain of blood that's spread out from his chest.

Bull-neck.

Wide nostrils.

A solid body.

'Sonny Levin,' Malin says.

'You bet,' Zeke says.

Flies are buzzing around the wound. Settling, vomiting, flying off, returning to eat. Enjoying the rapid decomposition.

The corpse stinks. Rays of light filtering through the room's curtains seem to trickle towards the body, motes of dust dancing in its aura.

'Do you think the girl's here?' Zeke says.

Malin shakes her head.

'I think she's still alive, but she isn't here.'

Ella.

For a while we thought you were with Sonny Levin, but look at him, he's lying there in his own filth, so you must be somewhere else.

We can hear you.

You're crying, but almost silently.

Don't be frightened. Mummy and Daddy can hear you.

Our white realm is full of Malin's thoughts.

She's thinking that they need a different forensics expert, not Karin Johannison, this is too close to her, we'll have to bring in Pilblad from Norrköping, that's what she's thinking.

Could Levin have been caught up in bribery?

Could someone have come from Vietnam to shut him up, shut us up?

Don't think that of us.

Try to hear us instead.

We're here. We're here.

So much money, she's thinking. So much love. So much fear and so much protective instinct.

So much instinct for self-preservation?

She walks slowly out of the house, away from the corpse, out into the sun, which receives her with open arms on the front steps.

Ella.

She's going to find you.

We promise.

Don't be frightened.

You're still going to be a human being, no matter what they do to you.

You're a human being, no matter what anyone does to you.

47

Peter Hamse gathers up his things in the dark duty-doctor's room at Linköping University Hospital.

He hasn't called Malin.

She hasn't called him.

Anyway, what would he say? What could they say to each other?

He wonders about his things, his clothes.

He'll have to go and pick them up from hers.

It had to end like this.

How could she lie to me, say the doctor had told her she could get pregnant, when he couldn't possibly have said that?

She's only got herself to blame. And he knows how egotistical the thought, the wish is, and he's only thinking about himself, but he can't help it.

He needs to have an heir.

A child.

A son. Daughter.

With anyone, anyone at all. Perhaps with Vanessa. Perhaps with someone else.

It was a shame Malin had to see what she saw. It could all have happened better, but the end result would have been the same.

Without really wanting to admit it to himself, he has felt their love, his love for Malin, fading over the past few months, and when he surreptitiously read her medical notes, he realised why.

Their love was based on a lie.

An impossibility.

I'll apologise to her, Peter thinks. She won't listen, and he sits down on the hard bed, breathing slowly, tired after the six-hour operation earlier today.

He was so in love with her, proud that she wanted to be his, that strong, beautiful, intelligent creature.

But so difficult.

As if her smile had frozen forever into a cynical grimace.

He couldn't bear that smile.

What it might mean.

What it said about her soul.

So his love was gradually rinsed away, draining into a sea of memories and images entirely divorced from feelings, without any real meaning.

The door to the duty-doctor's room opens.

A moment later Vanessa is standing in front of him.

There's no cynicism in her smile.

You're just happy to see me, Peter thinks. Aren't you?

48

Forensic medical officer Jonas Pilblad is slowly circling Sonny Levin's body.

The stench doesn't seem to bother him.

Malin tries to breathe through her mouth as she watches the doctor.

His stocky, fifty-five-year-old frame exudes experience, and Malin knows he keeps himself up to date with the latest possibilities offered by new technology.

He's wearing a white coat over a baby-blue shirt. The colour of the shirt collar softens the harsh lines of his face, and his aquamarine tie lends a certain dignity to his appearance.

Pilblad is probably trying to look like a character from CSI, Malin thinks. She knows he runs a marathon in a different city each year.

New York.

Or was it Sydney last year?

He looks up at Malin and Zeke as they stand with Sven Sjöman and Johan Jakobsson in the doorway of the dining room.

'As we can all see, he was shot in the chest, just like your other victims. He was hit once in the arm, presumably as he tried to defend himself, and the second shot hit his heart and killed him. He was shot from directly in front, the murderer could have been standing more or less where you're standing now, and I'd say he's been dead for five or six days, so he could well have been killed the same evening as Cecilia and Patrick Andergren.'

Malin looks at her colleagues. They're all thinking the same thing, and she can see from the expressions on their faces that they're all thinking hard.

What is this?

What do we know?

'How long is it likely to be until you can give us more precise details?'

'Give me this evening and tonight.'

Pilblad hasn't asked about Karin Johannison and why they called him in instead.

He probably does care, Malin thinks, then hears a young woman's voice behind her, recognises the voice, and to her surprise feels pleased to hear it.

'I'm here now,' Elin Sand says, and Malin turns around.

'Good,' Sven says. 'We need everyone.'

Elin Sand stops behind Johan Jakobsson, and looks over his head at Pilblad.

'Any idea what you might be able to find? DNA? Prints?' Zeke asks. 'Cartridges?'

'I don't know yet,' Pilblad says. 'But no cartridges. If you let me get on without interruption, it's bound to go quicker.'

'Could he have known his killer?'

'Impossible to say, in my opinion. Now, let me get on.'

The detectives realise that he's right, and head out into the garden just as Waldemar and Börje arrive.

The pair of them look focused as they get out of the red Volvo and walk over to the others. No pleasantries, just an expectant look on their faces.

Waldemar lights a real cigarette and blows the smoke up into the sky with a sigh of contentment.

'We managed to get hold of the last set of parents on

the phone,' Börje says. 'Not a damn thing there either.'

'They've got an alibi,' Waldemar says.

Malin sees Sven nod, then he says: 'Well, let's get going,' and, standing in the sunlight around the patrol car that brought Malin and Zeke from the airport, they hold an informal investigative meeting.

They let Sven talk.

He summarises the current state of the investigation, and no one interrupts him unnecessarily, they know he's got a lot of experience and a sharp mind, as well as the energy and determination required to solve these murders; a determination to see that Ella Andergren is found, in good health.

One of Malin's hands is shaking uncontrollably again. She's relieved she didn't have to put up with that while they were in Copenhagen, but now her body's back, showing its dissatisfaction at the lack of a top-up of alcohol.

Drops of sweat at the back of her neck.

She feels it run slowly down her spine beneath her shirt, like a finger, and sees Peter in her mind, then the flames out on the forest track.

What happened? she wonders.

Let the whole world become a sea of cask-matured tequila.

Drown me in that sea.

Stop shaking, for God's sake.

Sven.

The way he looked at me when he arrived. Does he know about my relapse? She uses that word, she's admitted to herself that she's an alcoholic. She has that level of insight into her affliction.

Sven carries on.

But she's having trouble staying focused.

Is he really saying what he's saying?

Yes, he is.

'We can assume that the murder victim in there is Sonny Levin, even if he hasn't been formally identified yet. And that it's extremely likely that the murders are linked somehow. There are plenty of connections.'

No sign of any curious neighbours.

'So, who killed Levin? Was it the same person who shot the Andergrens? The person behind Ella Andergren's disappearance? We don't know the answer to any of those questions. But I'd say we're dealing with the same killer, seeing as the MOs are similar and they may well have occurred on the same evening. We don't yet know who was killed first, but that may be significant. So, what's this all about?'

Sven pauses before going on: 'Is this anything to do with industrial bribery? Was Sonny Levin involved in that as well? Or is it, which I'd say is far more likely, linked to the adoptions? Who would have had a motive to kill these people? Someone who wanted to put a stop to Patrick Andergren's investigations? Someone from Sweden, or Vietnam? Someone who wanted to silence Sonny Levin as well because he knew too much, or maybe because he was cooperating with Andergren? Because it was him who shot the Andergrens, then had to be silenced once he'd done the job? Someone who's got the girl and wanted to cover their tracks? But who?'

Energy, Malin thinks as she hears Sven speak. Since his recovery from cancer he's had fresh energy, as if that made him even more aware that life is finite. Plenty of detectives working on murder cases deny their own mortality, even though they work with death every day.

They do that to help them bear it, she thinks. I've done the same in my time. Because who can live with the thought that it could be them slumped over a table with a bullet in the heart, or shot in a jacuzzi whose water is red with their own blood?

'We need to keep pushing,' Sven says. 'We've got to find the girl.'

Then he allocates work.

Waldemar and Börje will be going door-to-door, along with Elin Sand and the two uniforms who were in the patrol car.

Johan, Malin, and Zeke will search the parts of the house that Pilblad grants them access to, see what they can find that can give them more information about Sonny Levin's activities and contacts.

'We might be able to find a list of names of his contacts,' Sven says. 'Phone numbers. A computer. Anything.'

'Do you think Pilblad will let us look before he's finished?'

'Not on the ground floor, but maybe you can start in the basement?'

Malin looks up at the house. She and Zeke had a quick look at the rooms in the basement before the others arrived.

Going from room to room.

Calling Ella's name.

And Malin could hear the girl calling back. But her cries weren't coming from any of the rooms in Agda Levin's basement. Ella's voice came from another, unfamiliar room.

What was she calling?

Help me, find me.

Fingers of sweat running down her spine.

Where's the shade? Malin wonders. I need to get in the shade, and she feels herself start to shake even more, her whole body starts to shake.

Shit.

Not now.

Not fucking delirium tremens now.

She sweating more as well. She breaks away from the others and walks off into the garden, where she crouches down under an apple tree, bright red autumn apples hanging like bloated drops of blood from the branches.

Stop shaking, Malin. Take control of your own body.

Sven mustn't see this, but he's coming over.

Don't come, Sven, don't come.

He crouches down beside me.

I can feel his hand running down my spine.

'Malin,' he says, and I'm shaking slightly less now. 'I know what happened. I know how terrible it can be. But this little girl needs you. You know that. Stick it out.'

A wind sweeps in from the dark, ancient forest to the east, shaking the crown of the apple tree. Ripe fruit rains down to the ground around Sven and Malin, without hitting them.

The green grass looks like it's been spattered with blood.

The whirr of a camera.

The journalists have found their way out here, Malin thinks, and feels the shaking get worse again, as if a flooded river were coursing through her body, trying to drown her.

49

The corpse, carried out on a stretcher.

In a yellow body bag.

The ice-blue waters of Lake Roxen were shimmering in the background, dazzling Malin, the water apparently ready to receive both the dead body and death itself. A few wild roses spread their tiny thorns, encouraging the bearers on towards the lake.

Come and drown in my depths.

They spent a few hours searching the house, without result, then waiting for Pilblad to conclude his own examinations, before Pilblad himself found a hard-drive hidden in the basement, in a sealed black plastic bag, behind a freezer stuffed full of berries and mushrooms.

A decade's worth of harvests.

They're assuming that Sonny Levin himself hid it there, but there were no signs that the murderer made any attempt to search the house for files of any sort.

Two hidden hard-drives.

Two secret lives?

The secret lives we all have, Malin thought, as Pilblad handed her the hard-drive in the hall.

'He died on his chair in the dining room,' Pilblad said.

'Was he sitting down when the killer came in?'

'Impossible to say. Maybe he opened the door and let the killer in? But the front door could just as well have been unlocked when the killer arrived, and then locked when they left the house. It's the sort that doesn't need a key to lock it from the outside.'

'Anything else?'

'I can't find any signs of a struggle or a break-in.'

'Was he alone?'

'He or she. Impossible to say, there are plenty of different sets of prints in the house, and footprints in the hall. I'll run the fingerprints through the database, and compare them with the ones Johannison found on Stentorpsvägen.'

No matches in the database from there.

A clear reminder that not everything can be found in the digital world.

That all of reality can't yet be fitted onto a hard-drive.

Malin, Johan, Elin Sand, and Zeke are now sitting around Johan's screen back at the station. Outside the windows dusk is falling, and thin veils of cloud have drifted in from the east, ten thousand metres up in the atmosphere, foreshadowing the rain that has been forecast to drown the Östergötland Plain tomorrow.

Johan's hooked the hard-drive up to his computer, and is manoeuvring to get around the password. He gets in.

Folders.

Lots and lots of folders, numbered from one to infinity. Johan clicks on folder after folder.

Empty, empty.

Malin finds herself thinking about Stefan. Is this how he sees the world? As a series of folders without any content, without any connection to each other? An endless torrent of nothing?

But you do recognise me, don't you, Stefan?

You recognise Tove, don't you? As soon as this is over I'm going to visit you.

'Empty,' Zeke says from where he's sitting, just to the left of Johan. 'Fucking empty.'

'Keep going,' Malin says.

Johan opens the hundredth folder.

Another folder inside it.

Johan clicks on it.

Another folder inside that one.

Click,

click,

click.

A hundred folders within the directory, but no passwords. Johan clicks on yet another folder, and Malin is
tired, thirsty, wants to go home to her flat and just relax.
Or do I, really?

A folder inside that folder.

With a name.

Transactions, Vietnam.

Password-protected.

Johan opens another programme.

'You can take a break,' he says. 'This is going to take a
while.'

Malin and Zeke get to their feet, but Elin Sand stays
where she is.

'I won't be disturbing you, will I?'

Johan shakes his head.

Malin and Zeke go off to the kitchen and pour themselves cups of badly stewed coffee. They head towards the
front door of the police station, but turn back when they
see the dozen reporters and photographers clustered
around the entrance.

'They never give up,' Malin says as they return to the
open-plan office.

'They're just doing their job,' Zeke says, and Malin has
to admit he's right.

She thinks of Daniel Högfeldt, and can understand why
he got fed up with endlessly chasing stories. He's now

working as a press officer for a successful IT company in the city.

Helping drive up its stock market valuation.

Considerably calmer and much better paid than revelations and truths, Malin thinks as she looks over at Johan, who's typing furiously, as if the time for revealing the truth was running out.

What's the password?

Johan's cracked similar passwords thousands of times, there isn't really anything remarkable about it.

But it takes time.

You have to try out codes and other variables, which in turn give codes that can lead to letters, which give numbers, and eventually a whole password.

Give me a number.

A name.

A letter.

He's got a copy of Ella Andergren's passport photograph on his desk. He printed it out the other day, wanted to have it visible to remind himself why he's sitting here at his computer instead of at home with his family.

Tap, tap, tap.

His fingers like machine-gun fire on the keys.

Give me an N.

That's it.

Give me an a.

p.

a.

Give me what?

An A instead.

Give me an L.

What else?

Tap, tap, tap.

Give me an M.
And what do you get?
Nap.
What do you get?
NapALM.
Thank you.

The folder contains information about all the adoptions
Sonny Levin administered via Swedish–Vietnamese
Adoptions Ltd and its Danish successor.

It also contains further locked folders.

Malin, Zeke, Elin Sand, and Johan are skimming through
the documents.

The bureau's own files. Drier than Patrick Andergren's
reports. Nothing but hard, formal facts.

Dates.

Names.

Adoptive parents in Sweden.

The people involved at Adoption World.

Addresses and names of children's homes, people in
Vietnam.

Names of people Malin assumes to be the children's
biological parents.

All the families that Patrick Andergren was looking into
are here, along with plenty more.

One unprotected folder, labelled Denmark.

Only four adoptions in there.

Glistrup.

Lund.

Sörenssen.

And Johannison.

The same basic information as before, seemingly irre-
proachable, correct, Da Nang province, Hội An, but who
knows? Malin thinks as she sees Johan rub his elbow. Who

knows what stories are hidden behind those bald administrative details.

Another folder within the Danish folder.

Two more adoptions.

At the top of the document, in heavy blue lettering: Abandoned 11/11-11.

Tess must have been one of his last adoptions. Why? Malin wonders.

What do you know, Karin, what aren't you telling us? What do all you parents know? One of you ought to know something.

But why would you say anything?

You must be scared you'd be forced to give up your own children in order to save another child.

To save Ella.

But the adoptions have been processed.

Nothing, no one can take your children from you.

But you could still be judged in other people's eyes. Greedy child-snatchers.

You're poor.

We'll take your child.

And give it to someone rich.

Who basically thinks they have the right to take your child. No questions asked.

Eyes closed to reality.

Stefan. My brother. No one wanted you.

We'll take your child, sell it to someone rich.

What you get?

Money for a pig.

Malin rubs her tired eyes.

When it comes down to it, it's no more complicated than that.

Everything can be bought. You just have to be shameless enough to do it.

What happens to the children? Do they all find love? No.

But a lot do. And the vast majority of adoptions must be perfectly legitimate.

That blue lettering: Abandoned.

Why did Sonny Levin stop organising adoptions so abruptly?

Then Malin feels her mobile vibrate in her pocket, a moment before it starts to ring angrily.

Sven Sjöman at the other end.

Tired now, his age audible in the gaps between the words, in his deep, heavy breathing, he's calling from his office on the floor above instead of just coming down.

'Malin. Andersson from Forensics just called. They've done a quick check of Levin's mobile, the calls he made and received. The only numbers he called in Vietnam are pay-as-you-go mobiles, and several of those are the same numbers Patrick Andergren called. The numbers that were on his IN list.'

'Can we find out anything about the numbers, their GPS locations?'

'Of the Vietnamese numbers?' Sven asks. 'We won't get anywhere with those. The operators over there haven't even responded to our initial request yet. How are you getting on?'

'Johan's cracked some of the codes. So we're going through a load of files about the adoptions Levin was involved in.'

'Anything useful?'

'Not really, not yet, anyway. Just a mass of factual information.'

'Keep digging.'

'Those calls,' Malin says. 'When were they made?'

'Levin and Andergren were still calling some of those numbers in Vietnam until just a few days before the murders. There was one call Levin made to which he got no answer.'

'OK, good to know,' Malin says, thinking that whatever was going on, it was still going on right up to the end, and still is.

But what?

'Speak soon,' Sven says, then hangs up.

Yep, Malin thinks, then looks at Johan and Zeke, who have been waiting to show her something.

'According to these documents,' Johan says, 'in eighteen of the twenty-five cases, the same woman at Adoption World in Norrköping was responsible for the Swedish adoptions that Sonny Levin was involved in. A Siv Lennartsson.'

'We should talk to her,' Zeke says.

Malin nods.

Feels her brain shaking inside her skull, and hears a little girl whispering something she can't make out.

50

My name is Ella.

I am Ella.

Aren't I?

It hurts. Stop it. No, I don't want to.

They've stopped now.

Mummy.

Daddy.

I don't know any more. I don't want to, Mummy. Come here.

It's hot. Water. I'm thirsty, come, come now. I keep calling, but you don't come.

It's nasty here. I don't want to be alone. I don't want to. But I'm not alone. Where am I?

I flew in an aeroplane, Mummy, high up, and you weren't there.

There are other children with me here.

Really, really scared. I don't understand what they're saying. Yesterday one boy disappeared. He was a little boy, and where did he go, Mummy?

If I'm nice and quiet you'll come soon, Mummy and Daddy, you'll come soon, because that's what they promised.

I play.

Hide-and-seek with myself.

Like I'm not me any more. Not Ella. And then Ella can't be scared or sad.

Then they don't know what to film with their camera. Mummy. Come. You too, Daddy. The whole family.

'You fucking bastard,' Malin screams into the stairwell, and Peter Hamse feels himself almost pushed backwards by the words, by the force of her anger.

'Get out! Go to hell!'

He's come after work.

It's as well to get it out of the way.

Pick up his things.

Move on.

No looking back.

He knew she'd be difficult to handle. Sad, angry, but crazy?

No, she should have calmed down by now, but there she is, standing in the doorway screaming at me.

Peter climbs a step closer to the third floor landing, holds his hands up, says: 'Calm down, Malin. Just calm down. You're scaring the life out of everyone in the building.'

'I don't give a shit who I'm scaring. You're a fucking bastard!'

And suddenly she looks even more bitter, even more angry, as if she's just realised something.

'I could have been in Stockholm now,' she yells. 'Head of crime up there, if you hadn't said you wanted to stay here. I could have got away from all this crap.'

'I'm just here to get my things. I can understand that you don't want to . . .'

Her face contorts into a tortured grimace, but what was she expecting? That I'd beg for forgiveness?

She seems to be fighting back tears.

He takes a couple of steps towards the door, towards her, and all the times they've been close to each other flicker past his eyes as fleeting images.

Dad's seventy-second birthday down in Skåne.

Their room in the Hotel Angleterre in Copenhagen.

And the nights they've lain pressed together in bed at home in the flat.

The whispers, the words. When did they disappear?

What happened?

Malin.

And he feels like giving her a hug, going inside, saying everything will be all right. And then she says in a calm voice: 'How could you read my medical notes? How could you fuck that cunt, whoever she is? Don't you understand that you should have looked after me now that you know how badly hurt I was? That that's the way it's supposed to work?'

He takes another step forward.

Close to her now.

Who is she, Malin Fors? The person standing in front of him isn't the person he thought he knew. Who am I?

A baby producer.

Nurturer of a dynasty.

As if my wish destroyed our love when it became clear that love couldn't serve its purpose.

'Malin, I . . .'

But what can I say?

'Not a step closer, or I'll kill you.'

'I can just pick my things up, can't I?'

'No apology? No explanation?'

'You know why, Malin.'

That crooked, cynical smile.

'Yes, because you're a bastard. We could have adopted.'

Peter shakes his head.

They only ever discussed that in passing.

And the last thing he's ever wanted is a kid that is someone else's, and pretending it's his own child, a child that doesn't even carry his genes.

'I can have my things, can't I?'

Then she laughs.

A crazy, loud, almost witch-like laugh.

'Ash,' she says.

'Ash?'

'Yes, go for a drive in the forests around Sturefors, somewhere out there you'll find a pile of ash in the middle of a forest track. That's where your fucking things are.'

'You've burned my things? Is that what you're saying?'

'You should be fucking glad I didn't burn you.'

Crazy.

She's crazy, Peter thinks. What sort of world is she living in?

But then he sees himself in the duty-doctor's room, pumping Vanessa from behind, sees Malin come into the room, see them, know that she's been abandoned because her womb can't bear a child.

That's the world she lives in.

That's the world we all live in.

'Goodbye, Malin,' he says, turning around. 'Look after yourself.'

He walks down the stairs, smelling the stale odour of disinfectant mixed with lingering damp.

'Idiot,' she yells. 'You fucking idiot. I never want to see you again.'

We'll probably bump into each other in the city, that's all, Peter thinks. You won't see any more of me than that, Malin Fors.

Tequila.

The bottle.

She's brought it up from the car.

In her hand now.

Stockholm.

Fuck it all.

She's standing at the window looking out at the church, as the clouds sink lower over the evening-black roof.

It felt good, yelling at him like that.

She imagined she could see a hint of something sinking into his thick head just before he left.

She's had more than enough things sink in for one lifetime.

Way more than enough.

Some crows land on the church roof.

They look in her direction for a few moments before flying on.

Three murders.

And a little girl no one can find.

People thirsting for love, and me standing at this window with my wrecked body.

I could open the window.

Slam into the pavement. Put a stop to all this.

But I'm too cowardly.

And if I'm going to die, I might as well drink myself to death.

Have a bit of fun on the way.

Peter.

I'm fucking well not going to let you win. I'm not going to let that gunshot win.

She tips the tequila down the sink.

Looks forward to tomorrow.

To more moments on the planet.

Malin's dream that night: How much does a child cost?

Who earns most from a child? Who pays most?

The person who wants to love it?

Or the person who wants to sell it, over and over again?

51

Pull yourself together, Malin thinks, as she listens to the sound of the car engine.

Move on.

Never look back, because the past will kill you.

I need to keep hunting, moving forward.

Hunting out evil.

They've had a short meeting.

Pilblad hasn't managed to find any matches in the fingerprint database. But the rest of his report isn't finished yet.

They've confirmed that the adoption angle is their main line of inquiry, that they can't get any further with the corruption angle, and that there really isn't any evidence to suggest that it might help them solve this case.

'Keep digging, keep reading, leave no stone unturned.'

Sven's concluding words after the short meeting, and Malin and Elin Sand have set off for Adoption World in Norrköping to meet case manager Siv Lennartsson. Zeke's got an appointment with his dentist, he was going to cancel, then realised that there was no need for all three of them to go to Norrköping, and now Malin can feel the car's vibrations in her body, like a faint current coursing through her muscles, her cells, and she can feel herself almost being steered by an invisible force that's whispering in her ear: 'Find the girl. Find Ella. Find her, find her.'

Mons Kallentoft

Ella.

Your body isn't lying in one of the fields of rape we're driving past, is it? You're not in one of those red-painted cottages, one of those scrubby forest clearings? Not in one of those crooked old haylofts? You're not under this mono-chrome sky.

No, you're somewhere else.

And we're going to find you, Malin thinks, as the car forces its way along the E4. She can feel that something's close to breaking now, that all emotions are finally coalescing into one single feeling, but which one?

Which emotion are we looking for?

Love?

Hate?

Something else?

Fear.

An ill-suppressed fear seems to be practically oozing out of Siv Lennartsson's eyes as she receives them in her office in the turn-of-the-century building on Avenyn in Norrköping, where Adoption World is based. She's in her fifties, with permed hair, dyed red, and thin wrinkles spreading out from her green eyes. Thin lips, and her voice is firm yet oddly uncertain as she asks them to sit down on the sofa at one end of the room.

Elin Sand tries to make herself comfortable on the sofa, which is far too low for her long, denim-clad legs.

One picture of Vietnam on the wall: the verdant limestone karsts of Ha Long Bay. A tourism poster from Nigeria, a picture of Cape Town, and Siv Lennartsson's slim frame moves lightly around the room, seems almost liquid in her batik dress, and Malin is prepared to bet the woman facing her and Elin does yoga and jogs regularly.

She sits down on the other side of the desk.

You're scared, Malin thinks. Why?

And of whom?

Siv Lennartsson nods in Elin's direction, prompting her to explain why they're there. Elin says they'd like to question her about Sonny Levin and Patrick Andergren. Perhaps she knows something that might be connected to their case, seeing as she handled so many of Sonny Levin's adoptions?

Siv Lennartsson nods again, more forcefully now, and Malin can see that her brain is working hard behind those green eyes.

What can I say?

What dare I say?

'Did you ever have any suspicions that there was anything wrong with the adoptions Sonny Levin came to you with? With the children he arranged?' Malin asks.

She wants to confront Siv Lennartsson with facts, as if they already know everything.

'As far as I'm aware,' she replies, 'there was nothing wrong with any of the adoptions he negotiated. They were all correctly researched, from what we could judge.'

'Do you do your own investigations on location?' Malin asks.

'Not in these cases. But it does happen.'

'But you have local contacts in Vietnam?'

'Naturally we checked everything with the authorities there. All the paperwork was in order.'

'You never suspected any impropriety?'

'How do you mean?'

'You know what I mean,' Malin says.

Siv Lennartsson doesn't answer, and she avoids looking Malin and Elin in the eye, staring instead at the picture of Ha Long Bay.

At the jungle-clad islands in the distance.

'There's so much demand,' Siv Lennartsson says. 'And our resources are limited. That means that energetic consultants like Sonny have to do a lot of the work. We become more like the necessary third party required by the authorities.'

'So there could be shortcomings in your checks?'

'No, never. But every child has the right to a family.'

'So you don't know anything about Sonny Levin that might be helpful to us?' Elin Sand asks. 'Like we said, he was found shot yesterday, and his murder could be connected to his work.'

'If you do know anything, you have to tell us,' Malin says.

Siv Lennartsson shakes her head, seems to be pretending they aren't there, that this meeting isn't actually happening at all.

'Do you know why he stopped arranging adoptions so abruptly?'

'Well, obviously adoptions from Vietnam have been banned in Sweden until further notice.'

Don't play stupid, Malin thinks, and Elin Sand says: 'But not in Denmark, where his business was based recently. Why—'

Siv Lennartsson interrupts her.

'I don't know. No, I don't know. What do you actually want?'

'We want you to tell us all you know,' Malin says. 'About Patrick Andergren as well. Did you know about his investigations?'

'I'd heard about them. Nothing more.'

'How? Did he call you?'

'He asked for information, which we gave him. He called me a few times. That's all.'

'What were your conversations about?' Elin Sand asks.

'I told him the truth. That we at Adoption World had

never suspected or found any irregularities in the adoptions we facilitated from Vietnam. And not with the ones in which Sonny Levin acted as a consultant.'

'How many times did you talk to him?'

'Three, maybe.'

'Did Patrick Andergren mention any names to you?'

Siv Lennartsson shakes her head.

'What sort of names?'

'People he thought were involved in dodgy adoptions.'

'No. There weren't any of those.'

'You took care of Ella's adoption,' Elin Sand says. 'So you must have met Patrick Andergren then?'

'Yes, that's how it usually works.'

'Did he use Levin?'

'No.'

'And then Patrick got in touch and asked a lot of annoying questions?'

'Stop it,' Siv Lennartsson says. 'I've told you what you came for.'

'You helped bring Ella over here.'

Elin's voice as rough as sand now.

'Stop it.'

'You're responsible for her, in a way, aren't you?'

'Stop.'

And Malin can't help thinking that Elin Sand is brilliant, quite brilliant.

'So tell us,' Elin Sand says. 'You might not know anything specific. But you're an intelligent person, and I can see there's something troubling you.'

Siv Lennartsson shuts her eyes.

And when she opens them again, that repressed fear has vanished.

'I'll give you a name,' Siv Lennartsson says. 'But you must never, ever reveal that you heard it from me.'

Malin waits, as does Elin Sand, better to let Siv Lennartsson talk now rather than ask more questions.

'I think you should try to get hold of Liv Negrell.'

'Liv Negrell? Who's she?' Elin Sand asks.

'She's Swedish, maybe ten years younger than me, about the same age as you,' Siv Lennartsson says, nodding towards Malin. 'I met her once in Saigon a few years ago, she was working for H&M as a factory inspector, and was involved in adoptions as a sideline. She told me she was thinking of giving up the inspections and concentrating full-time on helping people like Sonny Levin and us find children for adoption. I don't know if that's what she did, but it's possible, she could very well have been working in Vietnam behind the scenes without our knowledge. It's possible she was working with Sonny Levin. I got the impression that she had a very good grasp of the culture and people over there, and she knew the language. She had the contacts and the knowledge to do it, basically.'

Contacts.

Language, knowledge.

You must have suspected that some of the adoptions from Vietnam were dodgy, Malin thinks. But you didn't want to see it.

'Why should we talk to her specifically?'

But Siv Lennartsson doesn't answer Elin's question.

'Liv Negrell called me when adoptions from Vietnam were banned. Asked what I thought of the situation.'

'So you did know, then?'

'What?'

'That she was working as an adoption consultant in Vietnam.'

'That was my understanding, yes. Definitely. She was involved in finding children, anyway.'

'Go on,' Malin says.

'Sonny Levin mentioned her name in passing a few times. Maybe she was still working for Sonny when he moved to Denmark?'

'OK,' Malin says.

She's wondering what it is that Siv Lennartsson is actually telling them.

She can feel thoughts buzzing around her head, but she can't make them go in the direction she wants them to.

'What are you trying to tell us?' Elin Sand asks.

'I don't know,' Siv Lennartsson says. 'I'm not sure I want to know. But something about Liv Negrell used to make me feel cold inside. I got the feeling she'd be prepared to do anything at all to get hold of children. But, like I said, all the paperwork was always in order.'

'Did you ever meet her again?' Malin asks.

'No, just that once in Saigon. But sometimes you just know, don't you?'

Malin nods.

'You know.'

Thinking: But you still did nothing? You let these dirty adoptions happen, even though you knew, deep down.

'Did Patrick Andergren mention her? Liv Negrell?'

'No, he didn't. You have to understand,' Siv Lennartsson says, 'that when I started this job, I wanted to help people who can't have children of their own. It took me years of trying, and it was hell. I want to help the people I meet. Sometimes I think that adoptive parents love the children more than their biological parents are capable of. It's strange, but I've never seen greater love. And the children have better lives here. Much better.'

She pauses, before adding: 'And sure, I do feel a degree of responsibility for Ella. But you're the ones who have to find her.'

52

Words are firing through Malin's head as the windscreen-wipers sweep aside the rain, sending little torrents of water down towards the bonnet.

Adoption organisations relying on consultants.

Adoptions abruptly abandoned.

Children.

Missing children.

Ella.

And Liv Negrell.

An unknown woman, surfacing from the dark depths of the investigation.

A woman with an alleged appetite for children.

Our woman?

But why should she be?

Malin hadn't wanted to ask Siv Lennartsson about Karin's adoption. Anyway, what would she know? It had been processed in Denmark, after all.

She shuts her eyes. Tries to rest.

Zeke.

Presumably back from the dentist now.

Does he want Karin back?

Of course he does.

Such are Malin's thoughts as they turn into the car park in front of the police station just after one o'clock.

Soon Malin and Elin are standing beside a swollen-cheeked Zeke, behind Johan Jakobsson's chair, staring down at his screen. Börje Svärd and Waldemar Ekenberg are right behind them, and Malin can feel Börje's sweet, garlicky breath on her neck. Unless it's Waldemar's stale air? But that never smells of anything but sour nicotine, sometimes smoke as well.

While she and Elin were in Norrköping, Johan managed to get into one of the last locked folders on Sonny Levin's hard-drive.

This one also turned out to contain further folders, but those weren't password-protected, and dealt with some of the adoptions Sonny Levin arranged through his business.

'Supplementary material,' Johan says, opening one of the folders, titled Sii Moon Kyi / Nina Warg.

Not one of the children Patrick Andergren was investigating.

Johan opens the only document in the folder.

'I want you to see this for yourselves,' Johan says.

And they read in total silence.

Malin finds herself breathing deeper and deeper, and hears Waldemar Ekenberg mutter: 'Fucking awful, just fucking awful.'

Sii Moon Kyi.

Daughter of an illiterate hotel cleaner and a farm labourer in a village close to Hue. Father fell ill and died quickly of Agent Orange-related cancer, mother seven months pregnant when he died. Gave birth to a healthy daughter. Wanted to keep the child. The local authorities wanted to take the child into care in a children's home for a few years, in exchange for the mother being given a sum equivalent to 250 USD. The mother agreed after the shack she lived in was broken into twice in a short space of time, and after she was threatened by a man with a knife who tried to take her daughter.

When the mother went to fetch her daughter home a year or so later, the authorities told her that wouldn't be possible. Because she had accepted the money and signed the accompanying papers, she had agreed to have the child adopted, and been paid for it. The girl, Sii Moon Kyi was already living in Sweden with new parents, and is now two years old.

Case closed.

Malin shuts her eyes.

She swallows hard before opening them again and carrying on reading.

In Hue, Children's Home number 57. With the help of members of the provincial administration, the staff are paid to produce documents stating that Sii Moon Kyi is an orphan. They tell me the real situation, confirming what LNG has already said.

I feel my usual doubts. But LNG insists: no girl, no deal. Her new parents in Sweden need the girl, I think. And she'll have a better life there than with her biological mother.

A child for a pig.

You knew you were stealing children, Malin thinks. Why on earth am I trying to find your killer? You got what you deserved. Who gave you the right to make decisions about love, to decide whose love was worth most?

LNG, Malin thinks.

Must be Liv Negrell.

We have to find this Liv Negrell.

She thinks about Patrick Andergren's list, the initials at the top, IN They've been assuming they stood for International Numbers, but they could easily mean Liv Negrell, with the first initial written sloppily so that it looks like a capital I.

Patrick Andergren could have been on to her.

Whatever it is she's doing.

And both he and Cecilia paid for that with their lives.

Ella.

You're the reason I need to find Sonny Levin's killer. Because maybe then I'll be able to find you too?

'Who's LNG?' Waldemar asks, and Elin Sand looks at Malin. Malin nods, so Elin Sand tells the others what Siv Lennartsson said when they questioned her, and then Malin explains her theory about the initials.

Johan scrolls through to another part of the document.

Received 200,000 SEK today from XX, on top of the usual fee. 125,000 of that went to LN.

A thousand pigs for a child.

XX must be Sii Moon Kyi / Nina Warg's adoptive parents in Sweden.

Then another short note, dated several months later.

Sii Moon Kyi was delivered today to Mona and Kristian Warg. After a short ceremony at Children's Home 57 we all took the plane back to Saigon and checked into the Park Hyatt.

Malin reads those words again.

'How many files have you had time to check?' Malin asks. 'How many cases like this are there?'

'There are eight folders here,' Johan replies. 'I've checked five so far. Same story in each one. A couple of the names match the ones on Patrick Andergren's list. He was trying to uncover the truth. Some of those parents must have been lying when you spoke to them, or at least weren't telling the whole truth about their adoptions. That's if they actually

Mons Kallentoft

knew what was going on, of course. Perhaps they made a conscious choice not to notice.'

'They must have had doubts,' Börje says. 'Even if none of the parents we saw so much as hinted at any suspicions.'

'We'll have to talk to them again,' Waldemar says. 'And we need to consider whether or not they've committed any offences.'

Johan opens another folder on the hard-drive.

'I don't even want to look at what's in this one.'

Yin Sao Dao / Tess Johannison.

No, Malin thinks.

'Don't open it,' she whispers, and Zeke says: 'That's enough now, how would this help us? Is there likely to be anything we don't already know?'

Malin finds herself nodding.

'I'll take Karin's folder myself, if no one objects?'

General murmurs of assent.

A sign of respect for their colleague.

An awareness that they have to stick together as a group as far as they can, otherwise their struggle against evil would be impossible.

'OK,' Elin Sand says, in a brittle voice that doesn't match her size.

Malin and Zeke are in a rarely used, windowless conference room on the first floor of the police station.

The room has dark grey walls and the ventilation works badly.

They've brought a laptop in with them, and have opened the folder about Karin and Tess.

Don't want to believe what they're reading.

Don't want to.

For Karin's sake, for Tess's sake, for her biological mother's sake.

'I'll have to talk to her,' Malin says. 'Ask her about this.'

And Zeke sits in silence beside her, as if he's lost a little more of his faith in humanity.

'Do it. Go and talk to her,' Zeke says.

'You don't want to?'

'There's a lot I want to talk to her about, but not this.'

The words are glowing on the screen, but Malin knows she has to try to let go of the details and try to see the bigger picture here. She changes position and shuts the laptop.

'What does this mean? Really?' she asks.

Zeke focuses.

'To start with, it means that there were a number of people who might have wanted to see Sonny Levin silenced for good. He knew too much. The parents in the eight cases documented in those extra files, the people involved in Vietnam, maybe even that Siv Lennartsson you saw at Adoption World. They could have wanted to see Sonny Levin dead. We'll have to check them all again.'

'But top of the list might well be Liv Negrell,' Malin says. 'She's cropping up all over the place. Siv Lennartsson mentioned her, she's in Sonny Levin's notes, and Patrick Andergren wrote her initials next to those Vietnamese phone numbers. And we've got unambiguous statements saying that she received money, in both Karin's and that other case. That she'd got hold of children in pretty sick ways.'

'Somehow this is connected to Patrick Andergren,' Zeke says.

'Maybe he was just getting too close with his investigation into the adoptions,' Malin says. 'That must be it, mustn't it?'

'But what? Who?'

'Think about it.'

Malin wants Zeke to say the name this time.

'Liv Negrell,' he says. 'If the abbreviation is right.'

'And she could even have a use for Ella.'

'How?' Zeke asks. 'Any of the people we just mentioned could have killed her as well, to get rid of a witness.'

'She'd find Ella useful as a commodity,' Malin says, giving voice to a thought she'd rather not think.

'We've got to find her,' she goes on, then stands up and uses the internal phone to call Johan. Thirty seconds later he's sitting on the other side of the table.

'Liv Negrell,' he says. 'I'll see what I can find out. Should I read what it says in Karin's file first?'

'No, don't,' Malin says. 'Let me talk to her.'

'Is it bad?'

'Just go, Johan,' Zeke says. 'Don't read it.'

'You're doing a brilliant job,' Malin says. 'But trust us. Don't read the file about Karin. Keep your head clear.'

Johan nods before leaving them alone, and Malin knows he won't look at the folder.

'Fucking, fucking shit,' Zeke says, slumping in his chair.

What can I say? Malin wonders.

'Ella,' she says. 'It's not too late for you yet,' she adds, as an idea begins to take shape.

53

Sweat on her brow. The Stångå River beside her. Feet drumming on the ground. Running gear stretched over her straining muscles.

And the mantra inside her: Turn back, turn back.

But Malin doesn't want to turn back.

Even so, she slows down and stops by a hedge, and looks out across the river as heavy, irregular raindrops make its surface look pockmarked.

She turns back.

Runs towards the flat, speeds up, feels her heart pounding in her chest, feels her thoughts clear as the world around her is transformed into a flood of lights, bleeping sounds, and the vague outline of an abandoned tarmac road beside dark water.

Where is Ella?

Why are you missing?

Sonny Levin. Why did he put such a sudden stop to his Danish adoptions? Was he sick of the filthy business he was caught up in? Did he want to get out? Confess and make amends, or just put things in motion? Was that why he kept such scrupulous notes on some of his adoptions?

Breathe, Malin.

Breathe. Run faster.

Don't hold back.

Somewhere far ahead you'll find what you're looking for.

It's now clear that Sonny Levin was earning money from what was essentially the abduction of children from their Vietnamese parents, so that he could hand them over to desperate Swedish adoptive parents whose emotions had got the better of them.

It's clear that large amounts of money were being exchanged, and that Liv Negrell had benefited from this.

Presumably money had also been distributed to officials in Vietnam as well, to people working at the children's homes.

But why did he stop the adoptions?

Conscience?

No.

Well, possibly.

Malin's feet are bouncing on the ground in her light running shoes, her head full of oxygen and endorphins.

Maybe he stopped because he and Liv Negrell could make more money elsewhere? In another country?

But there was nothing to suggest contacts in any other country.

Eventually her body slows down.

She stops again, sits down on a bench, sweat streaming down her flushed cheeks.

How could you make more money from children than through dodgy adoptions?

Her heart seems to want to stop beating.

Doesn't want to help her brain think this thought.

Don't fuck with me.

I'm gonna fuck you.

You sell them as sex slaves.

As sex slaves.

To men and women who can only access those circles by submitting new recordings of the sexual abuse of children.

They sell children to people like that.

They can't be people.

They can't be the same as me.

They mustn't be the same as me.

And Malin stands up, wants to throw up, puts her fingers down her throat, but there's nothing there.

Did Sonny Levin have links to that sort of network? Does Liv Negrell?

Was that what Patrick Andergren was beginning to suspect? If so, he would have been challenging some powerful forces: Money, lust, shame.

Dark, darker, darkest.

Way down at the bottom of the lowest circle. Paedophiles. Frozen traitors against humanity.

Was Sonny Levin unable to cope with the business? This new, more lucrative business, if that's what it was? Dodgy adoptions is one thing, but selling children to paedophiles? Did he want to pull out, and got himself murdered? Did he find out about something, someone? After all, he seems to have wanted to do the right thing for the Swedish parents, and in his notes he appeared to have genuinely believed he was giving the children a better life.

With what right? And why, really?

Money. In the end everything is always about money.

Or lust.

Those are the preconditions of life.

Malin feels like throwing up again.

Shouting, crying, disappearing.

A child for a pig.

A child is a pig.

Malin wants to vomit up her pounding heart,

because that heart

isn't needed in this world.

DON'T FUCK WITH ME, DON'T FUCK ME,

DON'T, don't, please sir, don't do this

Don't
I'm a human being.

The hot jets of the shower on her skin.

She's called Sven at home. Asked him to check with Interpol, to see if there's anything in their investigations of paedophile networks that could possibly be connected to this case.

She tries turning the tap, wants more force, hotter water.

Impossible.

She's reached the maximum allowed by the fittings of the rented flat. But she wants more, and wonders about getting a hammer from the bedroom cupboard and knocking some sense into the mixer unit.

Karin.

What were you thinking?

I want.

Want a child.

There's nothing wrong, as long as I get the child.

The doctor. He said there wouldn't be any problems. It would be fine. We should try a bit longer. Or did he say something else?

He said something else.

Karin.

Your truth is also something different. One you can bear to live with.

Adoption.

I want the child.

I'll buy it.

Someone's selling a child.

But to whom?

Love, or lust?

The one paying most. For some people, it's good business.

Hotter, hotter, hotter water.

Do we have to give up what we love most in order for it to live?

Are we capable of making that sacrifice?

Some people are forced into it.

What could I sacrifice?

Tove? Stefan? My love?

Reasoning vanishes first.

The doctor said: You will never be able to have a child.

He said it, straight out.

You will never be able to have a child. And I denied it.

The hammer.

I'm freezing.

When did it get so cold?

I want to beat this world into submission. I don't want to have to submit.

I want, I want, I want.

I only want love. I have to have love.

Can anyone live without someone to love, to be loved by?

Karin.

Malin steps out of the shower.

Ready now.

Ready to go and see Karin.

Where's the boundary?

Hotter, hotter, hotter.

How hot can it get? How dark? I, Sonny Levin, knew my killer, and maybe I got what I deserved, and maybe there's a special place for people like me, murder victims who deserved it.

But I never disturbed the balance.

I never, ever disturbed the balance.

I just moved love from one place to another. I never killed anyone. Unless lost love is a sort of death, unless something disappears along the way before it is revived.

Don't try to tell me those children aren't better off with us in the West. In the families I arranged for them.

DON'T TRY TO TELL ME THAT.

What could those impoverished mothers give their children? No education, often not even enough food for the day, isolation, desperation, humiliation, dirt, dengue fever, parasites, anguish, insecurity, violence, rape, all the cruel faces of poverty.

Does the mother have the right to decide her child's fate in those circumstances? Isn't it our duty to take care of those children, to give them love, in all its forms?

Security can be a close neighbour of love. Knowledge, peace in which to grow to be a good soul.

Love can be classified.

Ranked.

That much is obvious.

And why should biological maternal love, or paternal love, for that matter, always come first?

For fuck's sake, don't bring children into the world if you can't look after them.

Don't blame ignorance.

Poverty.

Don't blame anything.

Love your children, make sure they get all the opportunities they deserve.

Otherwise I'll take them from you.

Took.

That's how it was.

But now, now something else is going on, and I'm held down in boiling water by an eternally burning net.

I know my killer, as the very worst of myself.

54

The lamp in the stairwell is broken, and as Malin climbs the two flights of steps up to Karin Johannison's flat, it feels like she's in a coffin.

The doorbell's probably charged with electricity in this damp, Malin thinks, shaking her yellow raincoat, and seeing the black coat burn in the forest.

It was half past nine when she left home.

Something like twenty to ten now, and her finger is quivering, her whole hand is shaking, but she has to make herself press the bell.

Has to.

She puts her ear to the door.

What's behind it? What's happening? How is love affected by a guilty conscience? You do have a conscience, don't you, Karin?

No sound of a child inside the flat. But the television's on.

She's home.

Are you expecting me? You must have suspected that this would come out, and Malin suddenly realises that she's going to have to be careful now, even if the woman on the other side of the door is one of her few friends.

Tess is your child.

Don't take my child.

Don't fuck with me.

Her finger on the doorbell.

The sound of it ringing, close but so far away.

Here I am. Ella.

I'm not playing hide-and-seek now.

Mummy once told me I used to be a little fish, a dolphin in her tummy, and it sounded silly.

But I'm playing at being a dolphin now.

I'm a dolphin now.

I haven't got any legs. No arms either.

I'm trying to get the others to play dolphins with me, because it's so wet here that it feels like swimming underwater with your eyes shut, because it's so dark here as well.

Mummy!

Daddy!

I want to call out to you, but fish can't do that, so I only pretend to. I'm just pretending to call out.

I'm pretending everyone here is nice.

No.

I don't want to, don't want to, don't want to.

I'm a dolphin, I'm a fish.

Look at me, Mummy.

You mustn't look.

Fish don't play like that.

Not like in the film.

I'm not a little girl any more.

So there.

Zeke Martinsson looks at his wife Gunilla as she stands at the kitchen sink. Methodically washing the pots and pans from the evening meal, the things that can't go in the ancient Cylinda dishwasher.

Mons Kallentoft

She's talking about the garden. What flowers she's going to plant next year.

She's talking about Martin. About which school their grandchildren should go to when they get bigger, now that it looks as if they'll be staying in Linköping.

She talks and talks, and in spite of all the thousands of words, nothing is ever actually said, and he feels like going over and strangling her, get rid of her for good, yell that he dreams of making love to Karin Johannison, whatever she may have done, hard and soft and slow until she cries up to the stars in pleasure.

He feels like strangling Gunilla.

Make her shut up.

Make her listen.

And it occurs to Zeke that it feels perfectly natural to think of Gunilla as dead.

So he gets up.

Goes out into the hall, puts his jacket on and opens the front door.

'Where are you going?' Gunilla calls from the kitchen.

'Out for a walk.'

'Will you be back?' he thinks he hears her call.

'No,' he shouts. Then he's standing out on the porch. He closes the door and walks along the paved path towards the gate in the hedge. He stops. Looks up at the house, sees Gunilla washing up.

He walks away from the house, towards the city, feels the cold evening air fill his lungs as the raindrops break up as they hit his head.

Malin and Karin are standing facing each other in the dimly lit living room.

The incense burner, no smoke.

The illuminated red lanterns from the market.

The propaganda poster. The tank ready to drive out intruders.

The television is muttering and flickering, some documentary about the sea, and outside the window a bus glides past along Drottninggatan.

Tess is asleep in her bed in Karin's bedroom.

When Karin realised why Malin was there she asked her to leave, and now Malin asks calmly, in spite of her agitation: 'Is it true that Tess's real mother didn't want to have her adopted? That she was tricked into it?'

The look in Karin's eyes gets sharper, and they flash dark in the gloom as she says: 'I'm her real mother. I always have been.'

'So you didn't know? Is that what you're saying? So what Sonny Levin wrote in his notes was all lies?'

'It's all lies. What do you think?'

'I think you're lying to me.'

Karin takes a step towards Malin.

'I'm her real mother.'

And before Malin can stop herself, she hears the words coming out of her mouth: 'You've never been her real mother.'

Karin raises her arm.

'You're going to hit me now?'

She lowers the arm.

'I'm her real mother now. And you know that.'

Malin wonders who this person in front of her in the semi-darkness is, who this creature is.

'How could you?'

'How could I what?'

'Don't play dumb. What he wrote is the truth, isn't it? You knew. And you paid, you bought someone else's child because you wanted one of your own.'

Karin turns towards the window, and Malin can see a

Mons Kallentoft

vague outline of her face reflected in the wet glass. Her features fade away, contort, dissolve in the reflected lights on the other side of the street.

'You think you know everything, Malin. That you can do anything. You're such a bloody know-all, you make me sick.'

Whispers.

That are really shouts.

Love me.

Let me love.

'She's better off here. With me. You should see the children's home. No child should have to live like that. And there was nothing wrong with the adoption, he said everything was in order, and I didn't know anything.'

'According to his files, you knew everything and agreed to everything. You didn't care.'

'NO,' Karin shouts. 'NO!'

And she moves back, away from Malin, shaking her head and whispering: 'No, no, no. It wasn't like that, it wasn't like that at all, Tess is mine, she's an orphan, her parents are dead, her biological mother's dead, she is. You have to believe me.'

You'll never be able to have a child.

Am I a human being?

No, I'm no human being.

'Are you sure, Karin? Really sure?'

Karin stares at her, then off towards the bedroom, Tess must be fast asleep, then she stares back at Malin again.

'What were you told in Vietnam?' Malin says.

'Shut up, shut up, shut up!'

'What if you were her biological mother, what if that was you? What if it was you trying to get to sleep every single fucking night, knowing that someone had stolen your child, that your child was on the other side of the planet with the people who'd stolen her from you?'

'Shut up.'

'You were so desperate.'

Karin shakes her head.

'Everything was in order. Tess's father and mother are dead. They are.'

'No, Karin.'

And Malin watches as Karin's face seems to split open and shed its skin before she yells: 'Who the hell are you to judge me? At least I look after my child. I take responsibility for Tess, and that's a hell of a lot more than anyone can say you did for Tove. You've always let her down, you've never understood what an incredible gift it is to have a child to love.'

And Malin shouts back: 'Don't drag me into this. Or Tove. We're nothing to do with this at all.'

'Of course you are, and you know it. You're a bad mother, Malin, and I'm a good one, and that's what this is all about, don't try to tell me any different. You want to salve your own guilty conscience by trying to take Tess away from me. You can go to hell. Just go to hell!'

And Malin can't help herself, she feels her arm swing, and her open palm slaps Karin's cheek hard, and hears the loud slapping sound as skin strikes skin, and she screams: 'You bitch!'

Karin staggers back from the force of the blow, then she hunches up and throws herself at Malin.

'I'm going to kill you, do you hear?'

And they tear and pull at each other, and Karin's stronger than Malin thought, and she feels Karin's foot on her knee and collapses backwards, onto the wool rug covering the parquet floor, and then Karin's on top of her again.

Biting.

Hissing.

Screaming: 'Go to hell! Just go to hell!'

Mons Kallentoft

Malin tries to hold Karin away from her, is she trying to bite my throat? Then she pulls her towards her instead, holds her hard, hugging her instead of hitting, muffling the blows with her warmth, and saying: 'There, there. It's OK.'

Karin struggles in Malin's arms.

But Malin hugs her tighter.

Whispers: 'What he wrote is true, isn't it? You remember now, you remember.'

And Karin's body goes limp, and soon Malin sees tears streaming down her cheeks, feels those tears become her own, and realises that she's staring at a mirror-image of herself.

Karin rolls to one side.

They lie there on the rug, side by side.

Crying and panting, then they hear a voice: 'Why are you on the floor?'

What are you going to do, Malin?

What are you going to do, you and Karin?

I who was Sonny Levin watch you leave her.

Do you believe her when she says she's never heard of Liv Negrell?

What are you going to do?

Are you going to condemn her, Malin? How can you put everything right?

I had a boundary.

I refused to cross it.

And I was shot in the chest.

There are people without boundaries, Malin. You know that already.

Ella.

Is she with people like that? With someone like that?

I'm in the very dampest of worlds. Steam jets from black holes, tearing the skin from my flesh, but I feel no pain.

I see myself vanish, reappear, and it never ends.

I am a world of steam.

I am who I am and who I became.

I wanted love.

I thought I knew something about it.

I thought I was doing good.

Was I wrong?

55

Malin is walking along Drottninggatan in the dark, watching her shadow bulge as the cars pass by from behind.

She wishes she could creep along by the walls, to stay out of the rain. Disappear from the world, be alone until loneliness no longer exists.

She left Karin once Tess had gone back to sleep.

What could she say? Obviously she wasn't particularly happy with Karin. She should have said something sooner, given the state of the investigation, but it isn't a crime to withhold information if no one specifically asks for it. If Tess were my child, I'd keep my mouth shut too.

I can't ask Karin to expose herself. To reveal the truth about how she got Tess.

Was any crime committed in connection with the adoptions? Has Karin committed a crime? A crime under Swedish law?

She hasn't got the energy to think about that now.

Everything will get sorted out in the fullness of time, the lives of everyone caught up in this mess will be good, fulfilled. It's just going to take time.

Should I hand the children back?

Should I tear them from their Swedish parents' arms, ignore their cries?

Will the parents in Vietnam spend a lifetime grieving for the living?

The adoptions were processed.

Who cares how it happened? No one can actually prove what did happen. One person's word against another's, one love against another, time gained against time lost. What are a few documents on a murdered man's hard-drive?

The mothers in Vietnam will have to go down to the river and the monsters at night and weep. They'll have to sit by their gas stoves and hearths and try to breathe, try to live with the fact that their children were stolen from them.

No one cares about the rights of the poor.

Malin doesn't feel up to thinking that thought to its conclusion. Because she knows the answer.

No one cares about the rights of people without money. No one ever has.

Inside her she sees the picture of the Vietnamese mother, the one she found on the Internet.

Karin.

What right?

Another car behind Malin.

She walks through the late evening in a yellow raincoat, her shadow chasing itself, but also something unknown further ahead, beyond all shadows.

Zeke Martinsson saw Malin leave the door of the building where Karin Johannison lives, and crouched down behind a parked car on Klostergatan so she wouldn't see him.

Now he watches her disappear along Drottninggatan, her shadow forming anew each time a set of car headlights went past.

He jogged the four kilometres into the city.

Inside his jacket he's wet with sweat.

He knows what to do, remembers the code to Karin's building, and feels no hesitancy as he makes his way up the stairs and knocks on her door.

Doesn't want to phone.

Doesn't want to wake Tess.

Wants to see Karin in person.

He realises she and Malin must have had a fairly anguished conversation, and hopes Malin managed to stop herself from apportioning blame.

No answer.

He knocks again.

There's no peephole in the door. Maybe she thinks Malin's come back, and doesn't want to open up.

'It's me, Zeke.'

The lock rattles.

And she's standing there in front of him. Wearing a long red nightdress, and the initial anxiety in her face vanishes as her eyes meet his.

She backs away.

He steps into the hall and shuts the door behind him.

'Malin was here,' she says.

'I know.'

'No one can take Tess from me. No one but me.'

Zeke nods.

'Are you judging me?'

'No.'

'Tess is sleeping. She soon went back to sleep.'

'It's complicated,' Zeke says. 'But I'm here. No matter what happens.'

'I don't know what's going to happen. What to do.'

'I've left her,' he says. 'I've left her for good.'

Karin nods.

'You're here now.'

'It was a big mista—'

Karin puts her finger to her lips and hushes him.

Then she holds out her hand to him and he shrugs off his jacket, takes her hand and kicks off his shoes, then follows her into the bedroom, where he sees Tess lying in the small bed by the window looking out onto the courtyard.

'We'll have to be quiet,' Karin whispers. 'She got a bit of a fright earlier, but I think she's sleeping soundly now. She usually does.'

'I can be quiet,' Zeke says.

'I know,' Karin says.

A drink this evening.

Malin is standing outside the Pull & Bear pub. The bar is full of customers, as she listens to the rain streaming off the roof of St Lars Church.

Tequila.

Just one.

I can manage to stick to just the one.

And now – how did that happen? – she's sitting on the only free stool at the bar, looking at the tartan wallpaper, the bright red cheeks of the man beside her, and turning a glass of tequila in her hand. She raises it to her lips, hesitates, then sees Tess and Ella standing on the floor of the bar next to her, lonely children in the midst of the grown-ups' noise and commotion, and she closes her eyes, feels the sharp, hot drink in her mouth, and swallows, letting the wonderful liquid run slowly down into her stomach, where it burns so fiercely it warms up her whole body.

Water.

I want to drink this rather than water.

For the rest of my fucking life.

She lowers the empty glass and puts it down on the bar.

Tess is gone now.

Ella too.

Malin raises a finger to the bartender. She knows he recognises her, knows who she is, what she wants.

He fills her glass.

Once.

Twice, three times, four, five, and now the world has no edges, her heart is calm, and she drinks, chasing down the tequila with cold, bitter lager, and the damp chill of the beer glass feels good in her hand, as if nothing is burning any longer, as if all the eternal fires of hell have stopped burning.

Cheeks.

Blood vessels beneath unfamiliar skin.

Looks, voices.

We know who you are.

You're drinking again? Is that what you're saying? Give it a rest.

The noise.

The voices.

The voices beyond the voices.

I know my killer, as the very worst of myself.

Tess.

Ella.

You have to find her, Malin.

Ella.

Give me the envelope.

Give me a television set, a refrigerator, a dishwasher, give me all the things you take for granted.

Give me air conditioning.

Give me your child.

How much?

How much is a pig?

How much is a child?

Same price, my friend.

The living and the dead exist alongside each other in this case, the boundaries have been erased. Malin knows that now, and she drinks another tequila, and the warmth inside her is the chill of unknown women, and she feels like screaming, throwing the glass at the mirror in front of her.

She hasn't dared look at her own face.

Because who would she see?

Peter.

Give me a child. Let it take root inside me, I'll be a better mother this time: 'I promise, I promise, I promise,' and the bartender leans towards her, says: 'Whoever it is you're talking to, Malin, I promise not to serve you another drop this evening.'

And just as she's about to protest, her mobile rings.

A name.

Johan.

She presses the wrong button twice, then gets it right on the third attempt and hears his voice.

She's drunk, Johan thinks. Drinking again.

What can I do?

She's eating herself up from the inside, and one day it won't work any more.

No one can live like that.

'Listen, Malin,' he says. 'I got hold of a Swedish guy in one of the telecom companies in Vietnam, the network for one of Liv Negrell's numbers, or what might be her numbers. Apparently he used to work with Patrick Andergren at Ericsson, and liked him, and he'd read about the murders online. So he's got hold of the GPS coordinates of the Vietnamese number when the phone was switched on.'

'What?'

'Are you listening, Malin?'

'Run that by me again.'

Johan repeats what he just said.

'So you got a response about the Vietnamese numbers?'

'Not through official channels. We sent a formal request, but haven't heard anything.'

'What?'

'Go home and get some rest.' And without really knowing why, Johan goes on: 'She's mostly been in Saigon. But she's also been in Linköping. At Stentorpsvägen, and at Sonny Levin's house. The dates match, Malin. Can you hear me?'

Johan can make out the noise of happy, drunk people. Hears Malin Fors say: 'I promise. It's OK. I promise.'

56

How to cure a hangover?

Malin wakes up, drags herself to the shower, throws up, goes into the kitchen and takes out the last hidden bottle of tequila from the cupboard above the fridge.

And she drinks.

Deep swigs.

And before she even reaches the bathroom she feels better, feels her hangover leaving her body, and she rinses her mouth, brushes her teeth for ten minutes before getting dressed, then walks through the city to the police station beneath a jagged grey sky that seems to want to press her into the tarmac.

Just after eight o'clock the investigative team gathers. Sven, Börje, Waldemar, Johan, Karim, Zeke, Elin Sand, and Malin.

Johan at the whiteboard.

An overhead projector switched on beside him, Liv Negrell's grainy, black-and-white passport photograph on the whiteboard.

Eyes wide apart. Hair that looks dark in the picture. Sharp features, but grainy.

A spectre as much as a person. Rumour rather than detail. Siv Lennartsson has confirmed that the photograph really is of Liv Negrell.

Sven Sjöman lowers the blinds.

Shuts out the children playing in the garden of the preschool.

Mons Kallentoft

Johan goes through what he's found out. Malin hasn't managed to make any sense of what he tried to tell her the previous evening, so all the detectives in the room listen intently to Johan, as they always do when a case opens up and focuses clearly in one direction, a moment when the truth seems to be within reach.

'According to the GPS coordinates we've managed to get hold of for the mobile number that in all likelihood belongs to Liv Negrell, she was at the scenes of our two murders at the times the crimes were committed.'

Can anyone smell on my breath that I was drinking last night?

But none of the others has looked at me oddly. And that tequila has put a stop to the shakes.

No one.

Not even Zeke or Johan have looked concerned.

'She seems to have arrived in Sweden the day before the murders,' Sven says. 'Then she left the country the morning of the day after the murders. She arrived from Ho Chi Minh City via Helsinki, if we can believe those GPS positions.'

'We can,' Karim says, then goes on: 'Which means that it's entirely possible that Liv Negrell arrived in Sweden, travelled to Linköping and murdered three people. But why such a brutal crime? A few adoptions can hardly be enough of a motive for murder?'

'They could be,' Johan says. 'We're talking about large sums of money.'

Johan gives them some figures he's found in American documents released by the FBI.

'Patrick Andergren could have been getting too close to Liv Negrell in his investigations,' Malin says. 'So she decided to silence him and Cecilia. And then she silenced Sonny Levin. Maybe he knew too much.'

'Could be,' Sven says.

'Shouldn't she have taken the computer, then? Their mobiles?' Börje asks. 'Try to clean up after her?'

'Maybe she didn't leave any tracks. We haven't really found anything. Or perhaps she just realised there was no point,' Malin says. 'There are so many different ways people can store information these days, not just on their own computers. There are loads of online file-stores, for instance.'

Börje nods.

'But why did the adoptions stop so abruptly?' Malin goes on. She has her own theory, but wants to lead the others' thoughts in that direction.

'Because those involved could get money elsewhere,' Zeke says, but no one wants to grasp that idea, they have their own suspicions, but are reluctant to examine them.

'I know what you're getting at,' Sven says. 'At Malin's request, I checked with Interpol to see if there were any connections between our case and any of their investigations into child trafficking by paedophile networks. They were quicker than usual. Just before this meeting started I heard that one of the phone numbers we're assuming belongs to Liv Negrell has appeared on their radar too. They haven't looked any further into that particular number yet. But the investigation in question involves a network that trades in children for sexual exploitation.'

So now we know, Malin thinks.

'That means that the girl could still be alive,' Elin Sand says.

'Liv Negrell could have taken her back to Vietnam to sell her a second time,' Malin says.

'Was she sold the first time?' Sven asks.

'We don't know. It looks as if that particular adoption was legitimate.'

'We need to know more,' Karim says. 'If this woman really is behind the murders, we need to find out where she is, and try to get more evidence that she really does have the girl.'

'We haven't got any GPS coordinates since she presumably landed in Saigon. The phone must be switched off,' Johan says. 'But she should be there.'

Malin turns to him.

'What do we know about her?'

'Not much,' Johan says. 'Born 16 April 1971 in Bålsta. She went to high school in Eskilstuna, then spent a year studying economics in Stockholm. After that she left Sweden. She's supposed to have worked for H&M as a factory inspector in Asia, but they haven't been able to confirm that. I haven't found any living relatives.'

A person as a grainy black-and-white photograph, the sort you'd find in a flea market. A person as a shadow made of damp leaves and dark blood.

Maybe it has to be that way, that someone like that exists yet somehow doesn't. That there's no point trying to understand someone like that. Better just to capture her. Kill her.

Pull yourself together, Malin thinks. She can feel the effect of the tequila leaching from her body.

'Have we managed to get any definite DNA from the perpetrator from either of the crime scenes?' Waldemar asks.

Sven shakes his head.

'As you know, Karin didn't find anything. We're still waiting for Pilblad's report, but I don't think we should be holding our breath.'

'And no matches from the fingerprints?'

'Not from what Pilblad has said so far. The first check drew a blank. She must have been wearing gloves.'

'She's probably not in our databases anyway,' Zeke says.

'What airlines fly Saigon to Helsinki?' Karim asks.

'Finnair?' Malin says. 'That's most likely, isn't it?'

'We need to check their passenger manifests for the days in question.'

We should have done that already, Malin thinks.

'Do you think she was flying under her own name?' Johan asks. 'On a trip like this? And if she's got Ella with her?'

Elin Sand bites her bottom lip before saying: 'We'll have to send pictures to Finnair. Of Ella and Liv Negrell. Get them to show them to their cabin crews at once. Someone ought to remember them, if they were there. They must have stood out. A frightened little girl, a woman who had a hunted look about her, unless she was ice-cold. Maybe . . .'

'I'll get on to it straightaway,' Johan says.

He stands up to leave, but stops.

'I've also had a call from Economic Crime. They haven't managed to find anything to suggest that Patrick Andergren had any international bank accounts. But they did say that doesn't necessarily mean he didn't, particularly not in Asia. Banks aren't terribly forthcoming in countries like Singapore, the Philippines, Vietnam, and Indonesia.'

'Desk jockeys,' Waldemar snorts, but none of the others reacts, and Johan leaves them.

'My thinking is that we need to talk to the other parents who appear in Levin's files. Check their alibis, and ask about Liv Negrell,' Sven says. 'Börje and Waldemar, can you take that?'

Waldemar nods.

Pulls a face.

'Tread carefully. They're likely to be the subject of future investigations. So take it easy, don't start up anything silly.'

Sven stands up.

Pulls in his stomach under his white nylon shirt.

'These murders are somehow connected to Liv Negrell,

Vietnam, with the adoptions, with children who, one way or another, are being treated as commodities,' he says. 'The girl's disappearance as well. We keep going. I want to know more about Liv Negrell. I want us to get her. We haven't got time to go through official channels.'

'Are we starting an investigation into the adoptions already?' Elin Sand asks. 'We're fairly certain that things haven't been done properly in at least a number of cases.'

Sven sighs.

'Once our case is solved I'll be handing that part over to the National Prosecutors' Office, and they can take over. That isn't our case. Understood?'

Not a word about Karin.

Not a word about the childless mothers and fathers in Vietnam.

Just handing it over, a desire to be freed from responsibility for something impossible.

You're choosing not to see, Sven. And I can understand that.

Then Malin sees Sven adopt his end-of-meeting expression. He looks so tired again, like he did before his operation, as if his recent energy has been a mask, a last flaring-up of a tortured life as a detective.

'Does everyone know what they're doing?' he asks.

The detectives mutter, and Malin thinks: Does anyone ever know what they're doing?

Her left hand starts to tremble.

Her mouth feels dry and she looks around the room, even though she knows there's nothing there that can fend off her rising nausea.

When the meeting is over Malin takes Zeke aside, leading him off to a corner of the corridor where a window looks out on the car park.

'Can you make any sense of this?' she asks him.

'I know what you mean,' he says, and Malin thinks that Zeke's going to get angry, but instead he sighs and smiles.

'I'm making about as much sense of everything right now as you are. Not much, in other words. But we're doing what we have to do.'

Malin looks down at the corridor's blue linoleum floor. Looks up at Zeke.

'And Karin?' Malin asks.

'What about her?'

'Tess. Your feelings.'

'I'll do the right thing. Just like you. You can rely on me.'

'What's the right thing, though?'

'I thought you knew,' Zeke says, then leaves her alone with the view of the cars and old barracks buildings where the country's warriors spent a whole century waiting in vain to be called into action.

It only takes two hours.

Then the call from Finnair comes through.

Sven Sjöman is standing by his desk, looking down at the blue canopy above the entrance to the University Hospital, when the airline's head of security calls, and tells him in a melodic Finnish-Swedish accent what they've managed to find out at short notice.

Three people in the cabin crew of flight FI 947 to Ho Chi Minh City on 11 September have identified Liv Negrell and Ella Andergren, who were travelling together on the flight. They all remember the woman with the child, the way the woman seemed very focused, the girl scared and anxious, then she curled up and fell asleep, 'as if she'd been given a tranquilliser to deal with a fear of flying. It's not unusual for children to be afraid of flying.'

The head of security pauses before going on: 'So there was no real reason for the staff to feel concerned.'

Liv Negrell had flown under the alias Tara Stevenson, with a British passport, and Ella had a Swedish passport, the stewardess who checked their passports at the gate remembered that. She must have been the passenger called Ellen Stjärnberg.

Fake passports.

That's why we found her passport in the house on Stentorpsvägen, Sven thinks. Liv Negrell had got hold of forged passports.

'That's all, I'm afraid,' the head of security says.

'That's a lot, thank you. And thank you for being so prompt, we really appreciate it.'

'Don't hesitate to contact us if there's anything else we can do.'

And one and a half hours later, after checking with Karim Akbar, Sven calls the head of security back to ask if there's any way he could arrange two complimentary tickets to Saigon, for two Swedish detectives, Malin Fors and Zacharias Martinsson.

Ten minutes later the head of security phones him.

'There's a plane leaving at midnight. Two seats booked. Open return.'

'I want to take Elin,' Malin says when Sven tells her about the trip.

Sven smiles at her.

'You can't all go,' he says. 'And she's too inexperienced.'

57

Wednesday, 18 and Thursday, 19 September

'We're leaving tonight,' Malin says as she stands by the cooker.

Karin Johannison is sitting on an Arne Jacobsen chair in her kitchen, watching Tess on the other side of the table, who is eating soured milk from a chipped, blue and yellow striped bowl.

'More.'

'You've still got lots left, darling.'

'More.'

Karin reaches across the table and pours some more into the half-full bowl.

The child eats.

Malin and Karin look at Tess, then at each other, and Malin repeats: 'We're leaving tonight.'

Karin stares out of the window for a long time, at the yellowing crowns of the trees out in the yard, their leaves tired and drab in the early evening light, even the lingering drops of rain fail to brighten them up.

'I've checked,' Malin says. 'The flight isn't fully booked.'

'You mean . . .'

'You know what I mean.'

'It's impossible.'

'Nothing's impossible, Karin, you have to—'

'I don't have to do anything.'

'No. But you're one of the wisest people I know.'

Tess bangs her spoon on the table.

Her bronze-toned face is flecked with soured milk, her eyes are bright, and she seems full of energy as she squirms down from the chair and disappears into the living room.

'Zeke called,' Karin says.

Malin sits down next to the chair Tess has just vacated.

'So I already knew you were going.'

'There are seats,' Malin says, and Karin gets up and walks towards the bedroom, and Malin follows her.

On the white bedspread is a case, half-full of light clothes for the pair of them. Beside it, a bag full of toys and children's books.

'I've already booked tickets,' Karin says. 'We'll just have to see what happens.'

'OK,' Malin says. 'That makes sense.'

'We have to make sure it's at least possible.'

Malin nods.

Wonders what she's set in motion, realises that she isn't the driving force behind any of this, just a small body caught in a current that's stronger than the world itself.

'Tove?'

'Mum? Hi.'

Malin holds the phone in one hand as she packs her yellow plastic case with the other.

'I just wanted to let you know I'm going away.'

'Where to?'

'I've got to go to Vietnam for work. The plane leaves later this evening.'

Tove falls silent. Malin wants her to ask why her mum has to travel to the other side of the globe, but Tove doesn't seem interested.

She had to look after me. Help me to bed, get a bucket out. See me at my very worst.

'I went to see Stefan yesterday,' she says.

Malin reaches into the wardrobe and pulls out a white cotton dress.

'Did you hear what I said?'

'I heard.'

And Malin feels like throwing the phone at the wall and going into the kitchen to drink some of the tequila that's waiting on the worktop.

The bottle's almost empty.

'Mum, are you there? He seemed well.'

Tove.

Your voice.

I want to hang up now.

'How are things with Peter?'

She knows nothing. I'd forgotten she doesn't know. Could she have heard from him?

'Fine. He's coming over tonight.'

'But you just said you're going to Vietnam tonight. How can he be on his way over?'

'I meant he just left. I said the wrong thing.'

Tove's turn to be silent now.

'I need to pack,' Malin says. 'I just wanted to call before I go to say that I love you.'

'So say it.'

'What?'

'That you love me.'

'Your mum loves you, Tove. OK? You know that.'

'Say I.'

'What do you mean, I?'

'Say I love you. Not your mum loves you.'

'Is there a difference?'

'There's a world of difference, Mum, you can see that, surely? And I love you too.'

★

They're back together.

Malin saw how Zeke's arm lingered on Karin's shoulder as she lifted the sleeping Tess out of the car in the multi-storey at Arlanda, how he held her as they checked in for the flight to Helsinki, how the tense silence in the car on the way there was still full of a strange warmth.

We have to do this.

And we're doing it together.

Malin hadn't felt part of that warmth.

She'd felt alone in the car. Now she's looking out at the twinkling lights of Vantaa Airport on the outskirts of Helsinki as the plane that's going to take them to Saigon taxis out to the runway.

Malin has the address of Tess's biological mother, it was listed in Sonny Levin's files.

She can't help thinking that there's something naïve about this, the notion that things could somehow be put right, that it might be possible to mend something that's broken.

But how?

How could that work, and what would the after-effects be?

Her head rubs against the cold plane window.

Night beyond the glass.

Whatever happens with Karin and Tess in Vietnam, things are already screwed up. Pain is already a fact.

What's going to happen? Are Tess and her biological mother going to hug? Carry on as before? Is Karin going to go home and leave Tess there? Could that happen? Would it be good if that happened?

Who knows, but the trip is happening.

Everything must be made possible, even if the whole enterprise is hopeless.

Because a child should never be stolen from its mother.

Should it?

What do I know?

I'm just trying to find some sort of reality to cling onto. One I can live with.

'You'll never be able to have a child.'

'You knew, Karin, you knew.'

How can you live with a truth like that?

You tell yourself over and over again that there's a different reality, and you end up believing it.

And that belief enables you to survive.

But someone else may not.

And now?

One mother is going to lose her child, whatever happens.

A child her mother. The child may lose its whole existence.

And two people will be ruined. Maybe sometimes it's too late to put things right. Sometimes you have to accept things as they are.

But which Western person is capable of that degree of insight?

Tess is sleeping on the seats in the middle row, the plane is barely half-full, so there's plenty of room for the four of them.

Zeke and Karin.

Sitting on either side of Tess, but Malin can see they want to be close to each other.

Who am I going to be close to?

Who would ever want to be close to me? Spoiled goods, a damaged package that always has to be returned to its sender.

I'm not needed here.

The plane shoots across the heavens. The drinks trolley goes past and Malin asks for three small bottles of bourbon and a glass with no ice.

The sound as the alcohol hits the plastic.

She takes deep gulps, doesn't notice Zeke looking at her, wanting to stop her, but he lets it go, pretends to be asleep, lets Malin drink herself to sleep as the plane makes its way around the planet.

He wants to hold out his hand to Karin.

But he puts it on Tess's head instead, buries his fingers in the girl's hair, and where is this going to end?

Maybe the way I feel now is the way you feel before an operation, one you know is going to save your life but leave you disabled?

It's going to happen.

You know that.

But you can't understand or comprehend what's happening, or what its consequences are going to be.

58

How do you find anyone in the chaos that is Saigon?

The balcony of the Hotel Majestic faces the sluggish, brown-grey Saigon River, and twenty metres below Malin hundreds of angry motorbikes splutter past, a steady stream of mechanical worker-ants carrying the city's inhabitants on their padded shoulders.

On the other side of the boulevard, restaurant boats, three storeys high, lie at anchor. Their twinkling lanterns sway to and fro in the dusk light, and behind them the cargo ships slowly make their way down towards the harbour, where steel cranes stand out against the sky like burned-out dinosaur skeletons.

Beyond the jungle on the other side of the river there's a row of white warehouses, and Malin can make out some shabby wooden buildings and abandoned stores a kilometre or so away.

The warehouses are full of eyes, staring at her with their gaping black windows.

There could be anything in those buildings, Malin thinks.

Her room is furnished in an old-fashioned colonial style, but the heavy green curtains and solid lacquered furniture don't suit the heat, which mounts gentle, steaming attacks on the senses, sticking her thin white cotton dress to her body, almost massaging her toes in her sandals.

It's a quarter to six.

They landed two hours ago, and headed straight to the hotel.

Karin and Tess are down by the little pool in the inner courtyard.

Swimming.

She and Zeke managed to bring their dismantled pistols into the country without any problem. Their bags weren't checked at customs. A rare exception was made at Arlanda, Sven must have worked a miracle with the security staff there.

Malin looks over at the lofty span of the shimmering bridge further down the river, and has a sense that Saigon is a city with its best days ahead of it, a city that has survived and can survive everything; the people below her are fodder for the great dreams of politicians.

Johan has sent her an email.

He's worked his way through Liv Negrell's previous GPS coordinates in Saigon. She's spent a lot of time in what seems to be an industrial area in the west of the city, as well as the Park Hyatt Hotel, and a residential complex just behind the former parliament building.

The signal still hasn't reappeared.

Are you here, Liv? Malin wonders, looking down at the stream of motorbikes.

Hears the roar of their engines, feels the exhaust fumes tickling her nose.

Is the shadow that is you actually here?

She goes back inside the room, picks up the phone on the bedside table, and dials the number of Zeke's room.

Answer, Mummy.

It's Ella.

I'm here.

They haven't done anything. It wasn't me they filmed, and it didn't hurt. It didn't hurt.

Nothing happened here, Mummy.

And the nasty lady, I can hear her, who's she talking to? What are they saying?

It's too hot.

I want to get out now, Mummy. I want to get out.

No.

I don't want to get out.

Yes, I do. Because if they do it one more time, maybe they'll stop and leave me alone. If I go to them and am nice, they'll leave me alone later on.

That's right, isn't it, Mummy?

We're going to get out.

We're going to, Mummy, Daddy, is that you coming now?

'Do you feel up to it? Or shall we wait till tomorrow?'

'I'm up to it.'

Malin and Zeke take a taxi out to the industrial area where they believe Liv Negrell has been.

The sky has grown dark above them, as the car carries them through a city where everything is strange. Incomprehensible signs in black and red squashed next to Latin script on garishly lit signs, bundles of electricity cables dangling at head-height, children playing on the pavements, so close to the road that the trucks and motorbikes seem to devour their half-naked bodies.

Smiling faces, serious faces, twinkling eyes behind thin fringes, dark glances into their taxi.

Who are you?

What do you want here?

Everywhere banners with red stars on a gold background, incomprehensible slogans.

Salesmen.

Hissing woks above ice-blue gas flames.

Boiling cauldrons.

A smell of chilli and ginger through the taxi's open windows. But also dirt, decay, outstretched beggars' hands.

Malformed bodies.

After three sharp corners they emerge onto the main road that leads to the airport, driving past ancient, swaying, two-storey wooden houses packed tightly between shiny new glass constructions.

A few kilometres beyond the airport the taxi turns off.

The streets get progressively narrower the further they go, then the driver takes a right turn and they drive on alongside a tall wall with peeling white paint, shadowless, nothing to block the taxi's headlamps.

When they reach a gate in the wall the driver stops.

'It is here,' he says in stilted English.

'Can you wait?'

He nods.

Malin gives him ten dollars, five too many, and says: 'More if you wait.'

She can feel the cold, hastily assembled pistol against the side of her body, her thin jacket pressing the metal gently against her ribs.

The gate of the deserted factory complex is open.

And in the starlight they see a cluttered yard lined with three industrial buildings with corrugated roofs, each about seventy-five metres long.

Quiet in here, and it seems to Malin as if the noise of the city can't reach beyond the wall and the gate, and she hears a dog bark.

Be prepared.

A second later a black shadow comes rushing towards them and Malin draws her pistol and aims it towards the barking and snarling, then lifts it into the air and fires, and what must be a dog whimpers and turns back, aware that it's met its match.

All hope of secrecy gone?

The sound of the shot rings out.

But no other noises.

Malin and Zeke move on, into the darkness.

Into the first building.

Malin puts her pistol back in its holster and they switch on the torches on their mobiles. In front of them is a large empty room with a concrete floor and iron beams rising five metres towards the concertina roof. The floor is pitted with large holes where there must once have been machines.

'There's nothing here,' Zeke says.

The same thing in the second building.

They enter the third and last factory building, and Malin can hear the dog whining behind them, but it keeps its distance.

This room is different.

Smaller, and ahead of them a black corridor leads off towards what must be an even smaller room.

The light from their mobiles leads them on.

Into the corridor.

Past empty, litter-strewn cells that must once have been the factory's administrative offices.

Can we hear anything?

Can I hear anything?

A rat?

A pig?

A child whimpering?

'Did you hear that, Zeke?'

'What?'

'Wasn't that a girl crying?'

'I didn't hear anything.'

Zeke moves on, and soon they are surrounded by darkness, kicking open door after door, but even the sealed rooms are empty.

Then Malin hears the crying girl again.

'Did you hear that?'

Zeke shakes his head.

They enter the last room, and there's a rusty iron hatch in the floor, locked with a shiny and clearly relatively new padlock.

A broken camera tripod beside the hatch.

Zeke draws his pistol and they take cover behind the doorpost as he fires three shots and breaks the lock open.

The shots make their ears ring.

Malin grabs the handle of the hatch, but Zeke yells: 'Wait!' and Malin stops and looks at him.

'What if it's booby-trapped?'

What if Ella's down there?

Other children?

But surely we would have heard them by now?

I heard them, you, Ella.

Malin grabs the handle again.

Zeke takes cover behind the door, but I don't care if I get blown up now.

I pull.

Malin manages to swing the hatch open and shines her mobile down into the darkness.

An empty hole, about two metres deep.

Malin jumps down into it, illuminates the walls, and she can see rings fastened to the cement, chains on the floor.

A prison pit.

Someone's been here.

You, Ella.

Other children.

But you're not here any more.

So where are you?

It's getting more and more urgent.

I curl up.

If I hold my knees and tuck my head down towards my stomach, maybe I'll be invisible when she comes.

Now the door opens and they come in, but not her, the lady. It's two others.

I put my hands over my ears, don't want to hear the other children scream, don't want to, don't want to, and it's light now.

Aaaaaaaah. I scream.

I wish I had four hands.

So I could cover my eyes too.

And the children wriggle like fish, they are fish, aren't they, Mummy?

Dark again.

Silent again.

I curl up. I'm a girl with four arms.

You can have as many arms as you like, darling.

We're with you.

Can you hear us?

Feel us?

Daddy couldn't bear to look at first, but if he can't bear to, who could?

No one can hurt you if you don't want them to.

You have to believe that.

But you're not where Malin Fors is looking.

She needs to look in a different place, and we see the children who were with you just now, they're having injections in their arms and fall asleep, then they're put in bags and carried out to a white van that takes them out into the swirling chaos of Saigon.

Next time it will be your turn. So she needs to hurry.

Ella.

Don't be frightened.

We're with you.

We're the warmth you can feel.

You're a human being, Ella.

Never let yourself forget that.

59

Malin has climbed out of the hole in the factory floor, and is shining her mobile down to light up the rings on the walls and the chains on the ground.

'Those are for holding people,' she says, and the dog, definitely a dog, is growling behind them but still daren't come forward.

'Small children,' Zeke says.

'What do we do?'

'We do what we came for,' Zeke says. 'See what we can find out before contacting the Vietnamese police.'

'Could be more places here?'

'You mean holes to keep children in?'

'Yes,' Malin says.

'We checked carefully. I'm sure we didn't miss anything,' and then Malin hears the children who were once chained up in the pit crying again. In a present within the present within the present, they're trying to understand what's happening to them, in a never-ending present that's full of pain and fear.

The camera tripod.

I want to kill someone, Malin thinks.

Where are the children now?

In a padded Australian basement?

In a soundproofed garage in Dortmund? Nancy? Falsered? Norrköping? Vagnhärad?

'Where are they?' she whispers.

'I don't know where the children are, Malin,' Zeke says. 'Only that they aren't here.'

'OK, let's go,' and she slams the hatch shut, closing in the children's crying and screams, hoping she's sending them to a different world where children's screams are always transformed into joyous, unrestrained laughter.

The taxi is waiting for them.

The driver is singing, tapping out the beat on the steering wheel in the illuminated cab, and the dog is just a few metres behind them as they cross the factory yard towards the gate and the car.

It growls.

Barks.

Stands on guard beneath a crystal-clear, pulsating black sky.

'The driver can't have heard the shots,' Malin says.

'Doesn't look like it,' Zeke says. 'Right, let's head to that hotel now.'

The Park Hyatt Hotel is located on a busy square just a kilometre or so towards the city from the river. It's an overblown building in the French colonial style, and its white stucco is floodlit against the darkness. Saigon's new aristocracy emerge from limousines at the entrance, wealthy Vietnamese businessmen who have made a fortune since the country opened up to foreign investment.

The showy splendour makes Malin nervous.

Has the dirt from the factory left visible stains on my white dress?

No, not in this light, and a doorman in a white uniform and a tall black hat holds the door open for her and Zeke.

Large Chinese silk paintings of beautiful women in

traditional dress hang from the ceiling in the lobby. A magical glow lights up the metre-tall orchids sticking out of shiny green ceramic pots.

'So she comes here regularly,' Malin says as they move further into the hotel.

'Yes, according to the GPS,' Zeke says.

'But where? The lobby?'

'The bar?'

'Let's try the bar,' Malin says, and neither of them is willing to admit to the other what a ridiculous idea it is to look for Liv Negrell here, if she's even in Saigon.

But it's all they've got to go on, and they're both feeling alert in spite of the long journey.

Almost eight o'clock now.

The bar.

Its décor more futuristic than any Malin has been in before.

Subdued lighting above a glass bar counter, black velvet sofas positioned around walls clad in black leather, the whole place reeks of a degree of wealth that's invisible out in the streets.

Liv Negrell.

You've sat here, Malin thinks. Drinking champagne with the money you've earned from stealing children from their parents and selling them to the highest bidders.

They sit down at the bar, and a young woman with her hair slicked back puts a menu in front of them without a word, then leaves them.

'Coke,' Malin says. 'I'll have a Coke.'

Zeke smiles.

'I'll have a beer.'

The subtle smell of alcohol in the bar makes one of Malin's hands start to tremble, and she feels like ordering

Mons Kallentoft

all the strong spirits in the whole damn bar, but she can't let herself lose her focus here, has to keep her wits about her for Ella's sake, for all the children's sakes.

'Good that you're drinking Coke,' Zeke says.

'What do you mean?'

'You know what I mean.'

'No, I don't.'

'Just be careful, Malin. For God's sake.'

'I am careful,' and Zeke bursts out laughing, then the young waitress takes their order.

Malin pulls out the picture of Liv Negrell.

Shows it to the waitress, who shakes her head and says: 'No, I have never seen this woman.'

She shows the picture to all the staff.

Negative responses.

Are they lying?

Their narrow eyes don't give anything away.

What is true here, what is false?

Who knows?

Utter discretion.

I'm a stranger.

Malin folds a twenty-dollar note inside a piece of paper with her phone number on and gives it to the waitress, saying: 'If she comes around, call me.'

The woman's smile is impossible to read as she takes the money.

'So many guests.'

Then Malin and Zeke sit in the bar.

And wait.

Watch guests come and go, diamond rings sparkle, prostitutes arrive with clients, Western businessmen in tailored suits drink toasts with dry martinis the size of small umbrellas.

The whole time Malin's hand is shaking so much she has to lift her glass with the other one.

Three Cokes, three beers, and three hours later, they haven't seen any sign of Liv Negrell.

Zeke yawns.

'Let's give up on this for now,' Malin says.

Zeke nods.

'We need sleep.'

Malin pays the bill with her Visa card, then points at a door leading straight out to the street.

'Let's go that way,' she says, unwilling to face the splendour of the lobby again, to feel the silk paintings and ceiling brushed with gold-leaf pressing her down into the polished marble floor.

She pushes the door open.

They walk slowly towards the river.

She receives a text message from Sven.

No results yet from interviews with parents in Levin's files.

They walk on.

The moist heat of the night caresses them, making them sweat.

On the bottom of the Saigon River a water snake wishes that the warmth and star-light would reach down to him, if only for a few seconds.

But the bottom of the river remains dark and cold.

60

Warm, thin skin, not yet coarsened by time, the feeling of having a whole body to embrace, arms reaching around your neck, unable to hug you tightly enough, get close enough.

Breath against breath.

Heartbeat for heartbeat.

Karin Johannison is sitting in the armchair in her hotel room with Tess in her lap.

Her daughter is tired and excited at the same time, and her black hair still carries the smell of chlorine.

The room: the furniture, the smells, the heavy silk fabrics, the worn tiles in the bathroom, it's all very familiar, and wakes plenty of memories.

She stayed at the Majestic when she came to collect Tess.

She watched her sleeping in a bed like the one over by the wall. Sleeping on her own with her mum for the first time.

Watched her take cautious steps, as curiosity got the better of fear, and the feeling that you were mine, mine, mine, no one else's.

I was in such a hurry to get away from here.

And now we're back.

Can't, won't think about it, but we have to, because otherwise everything's just a great big lie.

And you're worth more than that.

The sounds of Saigon outside the window.

The motorbikes never sleep, the boats on the river are blowing their horns, and the constant noise of the people forms a backdrop to all the mechanical commotion.

The room smells of hidden mould. The television is on, but Karin has turned the volume down as she watches a Communist dance troupe in green uniforms wave red flags with yellow stars.

Tess.

I'm never going to abandon you.

Karin hugs her again, harder, holding her even closer, and beyond the chlorine she can smell calm and meaning and sweetness, as the blood pulses through her body, and Tess looks up at her.

In the semi-darkness of the room her eyes seem to be made of some precious, unfamiliar black stone.

Somewhere she's crying, your biological mother.

She is.

Did I do the wrong thing?

I did the wrong thing.

I did what I had to, then I told myself a convenient truth, and it became true.

Like the politics of this country.

The truth of yellow stars against red blood.

Like our need to find a way of looking at the world in a way that helps us cope.

Karin relaxes, and Tess curls up on her lap.

'What are we going to do?' she asks. 'Where are we, Mummy?'

'We're in Vietnam.'

'That's where I come from.'

'That's where you come from.'

Karin clutches Tess tightly to her once again, because if she can just hold her hard enough she'll find courage and strength, and maybe she and Tess will become one and the same, impossible to separate, like water from water, somehow, some time, their union as unending as the river and the rain.

When she and Zeke have got as far as the Sheraton, something makes Malin look around and say: 'Let's go back.'

And something makes Zeke say, even though he's tired of risking his life in the city's crazy traffic: 'Yeah, let's go back.'

They turn around and walk back to the Park Hyatt, and Malin pushes the door to the bar open and looks into the shimmering gloom, and there she is, Liv Negrell.

Her brown hair is lit up in a pillar of light, and the sequins around the low-cut top of her black dress are sparkling. Malin can see diamond rings on her fingers.

Black eyes.

Lips painted red, high cheekbones. Liv Negrell, the woman in the passport photograph, but really it could be any smartly dressed Western woman.

Malin stops.

Backs away through the door, out of sight of the woman they've been looking for. Zeke gives her a questioning look and, in the lights of the cars and motorbikes and the restaurants on the other side of the street, he says: 'What is it?'

'She's in there. What do we do?'

'Maybe she knows we were asking about her.'

'Unlikely. If she did she wouldn't be sitting there.'

'No, that makes sense. But if we go back in, the bar staff might get it into their heads to say something. They might think we're old friends. We'll have to wait outside, keep an eye on her. See where she might lead us.'

'OK. You wait out here, I'll go inside,' Malin says. 'I'll

watch the lobby, and we'll be in touch when she leaves. Have your mobile ready.'

'OK.'

They split up.

Zeke paces up and down the pavement. The night is warm, and people stream past him, many of the women wearing shimmering, full-length silk dresses with a floral pattern.

Malin quickly checks out the lobby and takes up position on a padded bench close to the toilets, hidden, but with a perfect view of the entrance to the bar.

Twenty minutes later Liv Negrell emerges from the bar. She glides past Malin in the semi-darkness of the lobby, and Malin feels like jumping her, forcing her up against the wall and asking: Where's Ella? What the fuck have you done with her?

Murderer.

But she knows they must wait.

Knows they have to see where she might lead them.

She sends a pre-written text message to Zeke.

Now, in the lobby.

Then she stands up, calling him on her mobile as she follows Liv Negrell towards reception and the doors where the doormen are still smiling and bidding new guests welcome.

'Come around to the front,' she tells Zeke. 'Get hold of a taxi.'

Liv Negrell walks out and stands by the waiting cars.

Malin stops ten metres away from her, beneath the arched, golden ceiling of the entrance hall. She sees the staff nod to Liv, hears them say something in Vietnamese, then a taxi pulls in a little further along the approach to the hotel with Zeke in the front passenger seat, and he beckons her over with a discreet gesture.

Malin walks over to the taxi and jumps in the back seat.

'I've told him to wait,' Zeke says. 'And said we want to follow her. I've told him we'll pay well.'

The Vietnamese taxi-driver waits, his face expressionless, as if this were something he did every night.

A silver BMW is driven up and stops in front of Liv Negrell.

She gets into the driver's seat.

Drives off.

And the taxi-driver puts the car in gear and follows Liv Negrell into the Saigon night.

They don't go far.

After five minutes in slow-moving traffic, they pass the former parliament building.

Soldiers armed with semi-automatic rifles lined up in front of the white, 1950s box.

Palm leaves sway against the polished black sky.

They turn three times.

Right, left, right, then Liv Negrell steers her BMW into the drive of a newly built, glass and concrete tower. Malin reads on a sign by the entrance: Dream Luxury Condominiums.

There's an email address to write to if you're interested in buying or renting an apartment in the building: lc-dream@nlc.viet.

The Vietnamese email address they never managed to trace: nlc@nlc.viet.

Must be this building, nlc. Negrell Luxury Condominiums? Malin thinks.

Could the building's residents be given an address containing the initial of their surname?

She says nothing to Zeke.

They need to focus on the pursuit.

The taxi-driver hesitates, then pulls up by the pavement outside. The BMW has stopped at the entrance.

'Very good,' Zeke says.

But Liv Negrell doesn't get out. Instead she starts the car again and drives off, and then the car is gone, must have disappeared into an underground garage.

'Shit,' Malin whispers.

'Calm down, we know she's here.'

'Shall we go in?'

'Yes,' Zeke says, and they get out of the car.

Malin hands the driver a twenty-dollar note.

'You'll get another one if you wait.'

The driver nods, and Malin sets off after Zeke. He's standing at the entrance to the building, talking to a security guard, then the guard holds the door open.

A white marble floor in the lobby.

Bulging leather sofas and thick green carpets with stylised orange water-dragons.

A glass reception desk in front of them. A young female receptionist is talking into a headset.

'What do we do?'

'We bribe her.'

'OK.'

Malin walks up to the desk, takes a hundred-dollar note from her pocket and puts it down in front of the woman.

'Do you speak English?'

The woman nods.

'A Western woman, with a silver BMW. We need to find her, what is her apartment number?'

What's the plan? Malin wonders. What are we actually going to do? Wait for her, get her into her apartment and force her to talk?

'I know her,' the young woman says, taking the money from the desk. 'Apartment 16b, penthouse.'

'OK.'

'You can go up.'

'Her name?'

'Miss Catherine. Catherine Duvall.'

They hear a lift ping, and a few seconds later they see the woman who calls herself Liv Negrell / Catherine Duvall / Tara Stevenson appear around a corner and walk straight towards them in the lobby, but she walks past without looking at them, without paying them any attention at all.

Malin and Zeke turn around.

Liv Negrell is still wearing her black dress.

The security guard at the entrance suddenly stands to attention and salutes her.

'It was her,' the receptionist says behind them. 'You are international police, right? Has she done something terrible?'

'No,' Malin says. 'Worse than terrible.'

A white van with tinted windows pulls up in front of Liv Negrell.

The door opens.

She gets in.

The van drives off.

Malin and Zeke run for the door, and as they look to their left they see their taxi already in the drive, their driver with a blank expression on his face.

'I thought you might be in a hurry,' he grins as they throw themselves into the back seat, hoping that they haven't lost the white van before the pursuit has even begun.

61

Tess is asleep.

She's lying on the bed, arms stretched out across the white sheet.

Karin goes out onto the balcony.

Where's Malin?

Zeke?

The city roars like a torrential waterfall all around the clock. Ready to swallow up anyone who dives too deep into its currents.

The whole city is untamed water.

Millions of desires, people, spinning motorised wheels, and down on the river the last party boat turns its lights off, vanishing from sight as if it had never existed.

Tess.

If I close my eyes, are you still there? I daren't even blink, even if I know I must.

She wishes Zeke were there, she feels like pulling her dress up to her hips, tugging her pants down and having him with her, in her, and she is ashamed at her body's contradictory feelings, the way everything can exist in the same moment: shame and lust, love and desire, responsibility and flight.

Police sirens.

A blaring ambulance.

A group of Indians in colourful saris walks past on the pavement of the boulevard below. Their stocky bodies are hidden by metres of orange fabric. Beggars try to follow them, but are fended off by the group's servants.

A starry sky above the city.

They have to find you, Ella, Karin thinks. You can have a good life. That's all I really want. That you girls have good lives, can experience all the love this world has to offer you.

She looks out across the streets and river and warehouses in the distance.

What's happening tonight?

Malin, Zeke?

Across the river, in among the trees.

Seen from the bridge stretching across the river, Saigon becomes a confusion of winking and fading lights, and inside the taxi Malin can hear nothing but the sound of the engine and her own breathing.

The river is black beneath them now.

The lanterns on the boats have been extinguished, and dark hulls disappear under the bridge.

The white van ahead of them. Two cars in between.

Where are we going?

On the other side of the bridge the van turns off and the taxi-driver follows at a distance, and they drive through a district consisting of nothing but tin shacks, then enter what looks like a patch of jungle, where the taxi-driver turns the headlights off so as not to give them away.

A gap in the vegetation.

On the far side of the river Malin catches a quick glimpse of the Hotel Majestic, and finds herself wishing that Karin was standing on her balcony trying to find them, wishing that Tess was asleep and that Karin could somehow think of a way out of this.

My path leads onward, she thinks, looking ahead at the van's brake lights.

Then the tall palm trees and undergrowth come to an end and they reach the warehouses Malin saw earlier that day from her balcony. The buildings are lit up by a few weak street lamps, and the van has vanished.

'Where is it?' Zeke says.

The taxi drives forward slowly, and at close quarters the buildings are enormous, four storeys high and hundreds of metres long, surrounded by overgrown grass and pitted tarmac.

The buildings seems to be empty, abandoned to disintegrate slowly in the tropical heat and damp, but Malin can't help thinking that they look strangely beautiful in the starlight, and inside her she can hear a girl calling out.

'Help me! Rescue me!'

And it's you, Ella, and we're coming, I'm coming now.

But she recognises the voice.

It isn't Ella's voice.

That's my own voice I can hear, Malin thinks. My own voice, at different ages, and then she hears a boy cry out, and she knows who the boy is too, and knows she'll never be able to comfort him, and wants to hear herself again, respond, soothe all the desire, the longing, the sorrow contained within the voice's plea.

'Rescue me. Help me.'

They catch sight of the van again. It's parked next to the furthest block, in front of a large black doorway.

The taxi-driver stops.

Switches the engine off, and says: 'I will wait.'

Zeke and Malin get out, draw their pistols and start walking towards the van and the doors.

*

Mons Kallentoft

They creep along in the darkness by the wall of the warehouse, towards the white van.

A thickset Vietnamese man with his hair in a plait is standing with his back to them, wearing jeans and a pink T-shirt, with a pistol tucked into the waist of his trousers.

We can take him, Malin thinks, and she sneaks up behind the man while Zeke aims his pistol at him.

Treading lightly.

Even so, she manages to step on a twig, which snaps.

She's three metres away from the man, and he turns around, fumbles for his pistol, stumbles, and Malin throws herself at him, bringing the butt of her gun down on his left temple.

The man falls silently to the ground.

Malin catches her breath, and beside her the light of the street lamps reflects weakly off the side of the van.

Zeke creeps up behind her.

'Let's go inside,' Malin says.

The black doors are slightly ajar, and close up Malin can see the pattern on the doors, beautiful, dark-blue fish carved into the wood, huge catfish surrounded by hundreds of tiny eels. The broad jaws of the catfish look as if they're about to snap shut, like the doors themselves.

Darkness is pouring out of the gap, streaming towards them.

They move towards it and step into the warehouse, ready to be swallowed up by whatever it is that awaits them in there.

62

In spite of the darkness, Malin and Zeke can sense how big the room is, and can just make out a wall thirty metres to the left of them.

No sound.

A thin streak of light is filtering in under a door in the distance, and they creep towards it, and Malin hopes the man she's just knocked unconscious isn't going to come around.

The door.

They stand on either side of it so as not to block the light.

Malin puts her ear to the door. The metal is cold against her cheek.

Silence.

No voices, but this must be where Liv Negrell went, alone, or with whoever else was in the van.

Malin feels for a handle with one hand, finds it towards the bottom of the door, opens it and peers into a smaller room, where a bare light bulb is hanging from the ceiling.

Dirty grey walls.

An unpainted concrete floor that seems to be stained with patches of what looks like dried blood.

Was this a slaughterhouse?

Can I smell iron and death in the air?

Another door in the wall opposite.

Mons Kallentoft

They move towards it, put their ears to it, is there anyone on the other side?

And now they hear voices.

A woman, some men, children sobbing quietly.

They're talking Vietnamese. English. Some swearing in Swedish.

Malin gestures to Zeke.

Then she kicks the door in.

Karin Johannison has fallen asleep next to Tess, and a mosquito has settled on her neck, has found a shallow vein.

She pulls her daughter's body closer to her in her sleep.

The country comes to her in her dream.

Bombs. A burning night sky sinking to the ground, and glowing petroleum jelly eating away children's skin, mines exploding in paddy fields, mutilating their parents.

People with their mouths sealed up by deformities.

People sacrificed, valued at no more than a few dollars, for the simple reason that other people simply don't believe that a life has any real value.

Green uniforms.

Fluttering flags with stars on them form a sky in the dream, and Karin is running with Tess in her arms, they're both naked and there's nowhere for them to run except into their love for each other.

The water around them is full of snakes, sharks, electric eels, ready to sting them to death.

There's no life outside the dream.

But there must be.

A life for me, for Tess, for us, for her, them.

For Ella.

And I'm going to wake up tomorrow, and maybe I'll be

forced to give you up, I hope I know what the right thing to do is when that moment comes.

Two Vietnamese men dressed in jeans and white vests are standing in the middle of a room lit up with floodlights. One is short and squat, the other taller and thinner.

There's a video camera set up in front of a white cloth. An iPad on a small table.

A massage table next to the cloth, black leather straps hanging from its padded top.

The camera is playing back a film, and the crying children's voices are coming from the camera's small speaker.

On the adjustable screen Malin can make out images she never wants to see.

Liv Negrell is standing with her back to Malin and Zeke, and she turns around, looks at Malin, and her face registers first recognition, then fear, anger, and Malin raises her pistol and shouts: 'Stand still, or I'll shoot!'

The skinny man jerks, and with almost inhuman agility throws himself at Zeke, clutching for his throat.

But Zeke jumps aside and fires a shot that misses, and a moment later the man is on him again.

From the corner of her eye Malin sees the shorter man rushing at her, only a metre away from her now, and she sees something flash in his hand and spins towards him, aims, squeezes the trigger, and there's an ear-splitting blast. A bloody rosette appears on the man's thigh and he starts to bellow before hitting the ground.

He screams.

Clutching his leg, and then he falls silent again, and Zeke is fighting the tall man now, trying to hold him at arm's length.

The short man is lying on the floor.

Malin hopes she didn't hit an artery, but hasn't got time

to worry about that now, because she sees Liv Negrell rooting about beneath the massage table and grabbing hold of a pistol.

Shit.

Zeke.

He's rolling around on the floor with the other Vietnamese man.

Is he winning or losing?

We have to win.

And Malin points her pistol at Liv Negrell.

'Drop the gun!' Malin yells.

'And who the fuck are you?'

The two women take aim at each other, and from the corner of her eye Malin can see that Zeke is now beneath his opponent, trying to break the grip of the hands around his throat, and he has to succeed.

'Drop the gun. I'm a police officer. We know what you've done,' and Malin waits for the shot, for her body to be torn open by hot metal.

But no shot comes.

Zeke has managed to get the skinny Vietnamese man's hands off his throat, and takes hold of his neck instead, and Malin can hear the man gurgling as he gasps for breath.

'I'll shoot,' Liv Negrell screams, but it's Malin who shoots, squeezing the trigger, and the bullet slams into the wall past Liv Negrell, who throws herself backwards and vanishes into the wall as if she were a spirit.

'Shit!' Malin shouts. 'She's running!'

There must be a hidden door, and Zeke has got the Vietnamese man on his back now, is still holding his thumbs over his throat.

Where's his gun?

There.

On the floor.

And Malin can feel that Zeke doesn't want to stop himself, that he wants to go on pressing until the heart in this stranger's chest stops pumping the minuscule amount of oxygen that it's still receiving.

Bodies.

Sounds: sobbing, groaning from the screen.

Movements.

Don't want to hear, don't want to see.

They're filming samples of the goods.

Strangle him.

'No, no,' someone whimpers in Swedish on the screen, Ella's voice, Malin recognises it from the video Katarina Karlsson showed them in her cottage.

The voice has a darker tone now, full of sorrow.

You're a human being.

'Zeke,' she yells. 'I'm going after Negrell.'

He shouts back: 'OK,' and she sees him let go of the unconscious man's neck and bang his head against the concrete floor.

The short Vietnamese man's face is white with shock, and he mutters something almost inaudible in English.

Is he saying: 'Don't fuck with me'?

No, something else, and Malin rushes towards the wall where Liv Negrell disappeared.

She feels between the bricks, presses against them, and the wall gives way, and suddenly she's running through a long passageway lit up by weak strip lights hanging from the ceiling on black cables.

Ahead of her.

A figure.

A woman fleeing.

I'm going to get you.

And Malin hears a door open and close, and just seconds later she's at the door, throws it open, and finds herself in the tropical night. The heat envelops her, and for a moment she feels like stopping, but she sees Liv Negrell kick off her high heels and disappear among the palm trees on the other side of a gravel yard.

Swallowed up by the jungle.

She's running towards the river, Malin thinks.

The stars are shining even brighter now.

Malin runs after Liv Negrell.

Into the dense vegetation, along a narrow path, and everything smells of life here, not of decay like at home, and Liv Negrell stops on the path ahead of Malin, raises her pistol and the flash from the barrel is like the flare of a volcano, and Liv Negrell's tense face is lit up in the sudden sharp light.

The bullet whines past Malin's ear.

She shoots back, but her hand is shaking and she misses, and Liv Negrell continues into the darkness, down towards the river.

Malin can feel her heart pounding in her chest.

Bursting forward.

Closing in on Liv Negrell, metre by metre.

She's chased people like this plenty of times before.

Chasing herself each time, and the dream-like figure in front of her will always escape her, even if she manages to catch up here and now, in this city, at this particular point on the planet's surface.

The jungle comes to an abrupt end, and Liv Negrell vanishes from her field of vision, seems to disappear into the underworld.

Malin runs forward, towards the place where Liv Negrell has just been swallowed up by crackling darkness.

She runs.

Sees the buildings on the other side of the river.

They look like spaceships, fallen from a merciless heaven, and the clatter of motorbikes can be heard across the water.

She reaches the point where Liv Negrell disappeared.

A steep slope of packed earth drops twenty metres to the silent river where the boats have all gone, and Liv Negrell is slowly sliding down, and she raises her pistol towards Malin, fires, misses again, then the gun clicks and she tosses it away.

Malin throws herself down the slope, sliding quickly after Liv Negrell, and soon they're rolling together towards the river, and then the world changes, the hard earth becomes a soft, yielding surface, and the mild air becomes tepid water, and Malin feels her feet touch a muddy riverbed, imagines eels and catfish nibbling at her calves.

Shallow here.

She yells out in anger and pain: 'Where are you?'

There you are.

Malin sees Liv Negrell swimming out into the river, trying to become one with the water and the darkness, but Malin swims after her and grabs her by the leg, her dress, and pulls her closer and closer to the riverbank.

Liv Negrell kicks, snarls, gurgles, roars into the night, then she calms down, lies back exhausted on the bank with her arms above her head.

Malin's soaking wet dress is clinging to her body.

Where's my pistol?

In its holster.

When did I put it back there?

Will it work?

She squeezes the trigger and a shot rings out.

A splat of mud flies up next to Liv Negrell.

Malin sits astride her, pushes the pistol into her mouth, and sees the woman chuckling silently.

Why is she laughing?

Why?

Is dying funny?

Malin pulls the gun from her mouth, stares at the unknown yet still oddly familiar woman's face, and wonders what it is she's looking at.

'Don't shoot me,' the woman says. 'If you kill me, you'll never find the girl.'

Malin.

Hear my confession now as I beg you to save my daughter. As I beg you not to kill the woman in front of you on the riverbank.

I, Patrick Andergren, took bribes when I worked for Ericsson in India and Vietnam.

If your colleagues in the Economic Crime Unit were better at digging, they'd have found my accounts in Singapore, from which payments were made to children's homes in Nepal, Vietnam, India, and Cambodia.

I took bribes.

Arranged deals.

Then I distributed the money to the people who needed it most.

If that's a crime, then I'm guilty.

I used the bribes to try to put something right. Now I know how naïve I was.

How could I imagine that I knew what was right?

Love, genuine, pure love for a child can never be wrong, can it?

Or can it be so right that it becomes wrong?

And what was I going to do with everything I found out?

Don't you dare reopen old wounds.

Don't you dare spoil things, making threats and destroying everything.

Give me my child back! They stole my child.

*THEY STOLE MY CHILD! THEY STOLE MY
CHILD!*

Wouldn't you have listened, Malin?

What are we supposed to do?

How are we to know what's right and what's wrong?

But I do know one thing: you need to rescue Ella now.

That will be enough.

*I shall drift on in my nothingness, slowly absorbed by a
whiteness that's warm and cold at the same time, a whiteness
that is our world.*

My world of lonely question marks.

63

Liv Negrell is walking ahead of Malin with her arms raised, along the path through the dense, damp jungle darkness.

The sounds and smells of the city are behind them, the traffic fumes, the thousands of voices transformed into a single murmuring force.

'Don't shoot me,' Liv Negrell says.

She turns around, and in the darkness her face becomes a mask, a human mask that doesn't give away any emotion.

'Shut up,' Malin says. 'Keep walking.'

'I'll take you to her. I'll show you where I've got the girl.'

Have you got her in the warehouse?

Where?

Has Zeke found her? Can I shoot you now?

I'm going to kill you.

And palms and creepers seem to close in around Malin, forming a darkness more dense than any she's ever experienced, her filthy clothes are clinging to her body, and Liv Negrell says: 'We can do this together. You've got no idea how much money there is to be made from this.'

'From what?' Malin asks as they get closer to the warehouse.

Something in her voice seems to encourage Liv Negrell, make her think Malin's wavering.

'I sell the children,' she says. 'I sell them to Australians and Indians, Indonesians and Japanese. They make films with them, sell them on as slaves.'

'Slaves?'

'Sex slaves. Paedophiles love fucking. They'll pay anything to fuck children, and once they've wrecked them, they kill them and bury them somewhere in their own countries. They film them being killed. There are people who get turned on by that as well.'

Her finger on the trigger.

Malin squeezes it.

Close to losing control now.

But she can see the warehouse up ahead. Lit up like a cathedral in the darkness.

'They pick the children up here. A hundred and fifty thousand American dollars per kid. Two hundred thousand.'

Am I a human being?

I'm going to pull the trigger.

I have to.

But she knows things. She can lead us onward.

To Ella, and Malin looks over at the warehouse, some hundred metres away from them now as they emerge from the jungle, out into the open gravelled yard.

Zeke.

What are you doing? Is everything OK?

Zeke is crouching beside one of the Vietnamese men.

He found some discarded rope in a corner. He's bound both men tightly, they're not going anywhere, and he's used a strip of his T-shirt as a tourniquet around the wounded man's thigh to stem the bleeding.

The men are silent.

Know they've been beaten.

The video camera is switched off.

Zeke has checked carefully, but has found no trace of

any other door, any hatch in the floor. He's listened hard, hasn't heard any sounds, any whimpering, but he's still convinced. The children, and Ella, are here somewhere.

It isn't too late.

The man Malin knocked unconscious out by the van hasn't come around yet, and he too is tied up now.

Zeke wonders where Malin has got to.

Has she caught Liv Negrell?

He feels his stomach clench.

What if Malin's lying dead out in the jungle?

What if Liv Negrell is on her way back here?

He grips his pistol more tightly, stands up and goes over to the iPad that's connected to the video camera. He closes an open window on the screen, and the iPad's desktop is covered with small icons representing QuickTime videos, he starts up ten of them at the same time and what he sees makes him feel sick.

Zeke stops the films.

Staggers backwards, into one corner of the warehouse, and throws up, but knows that his feelings are no use to anyone right now.

He goes back to the iPad. He opens the email programme and it's all there: Liv Negrell's contacts, buyers, name after name, and he thinks, We've got you now, you bastards, and then the warehouse door opens and Liv Negrell walks in, closely followed by Malin.

They're both filthy with river mud.

Like the dead returning to the land of the living.

I'm here.

It's me, I'm here.

We're here.

You have to hear us.

We're close. We're not hiding.

Come to us.

So what happens now?

Malin looks at Liv Negrell in front of her, at Zeke over by the iPad.

'We know everything,' Zeke says. 'You killed the Andergrens, and you killed Sonny Levin.'

Liv Negrell seems to hesitate for a moment, then she says: 'They got too close. And Sonny got too weak.'

We're listening to a mask speak, Malin thinks, a mask created to conceal the very worst within us.

The pistol.

She raises it again.

Towards Liv Negrell.

And she wants to fire, but Zeke holds up his hand at her: hang on, it isn't too late yet.

'If you let me go,' Liv Negrell says, 'I'll show you where the girl is. She's close. That's why you came, isn't it? For the girl's sake?'

Let you go?

Are you mad?

'Where is she?' Zeke roars.

'I'll shoot you if you don't tell us where she is,' Malin says.

Liv Negrell smiles at them.

'So how does that work, then? Who do you think you are?'

'OK. We'll let you go,' Malin says. 'But only if you give us the girl first. Prove that she's still alive.'

'You're lying. Why would you let me go?'

'Because we've got no choice if we want to find her,' Malin says.

'We don't give a damn about you,' Zeke says. 'We just want Ella.'

Liv Negrell seems to weigh up her options, then walks to one end of the room and leans over, presses the wall close to the floor, and a small hatch swings open.

Zeke swears under his breath.

And Liv Negrell says something into the opening in Vietnamese, in a soft, friendly voice, as if she were talking to pet dogs, and Malin stares at the black hole as she hears Liv Negrell say in Swedish:

'Ella, you can come out now. There's no danger.'

The light.

I, we, can see it now.

But of course there's danger.

Mummy, Daddy.

Is that you? But you can't be here, I saw, in the basement, I woke up, crept downstairs, and I saw her and you in the basement.

I remember.

I don't want to remember.

It's her voice, and she's calling me in Swedish now, come out, come out, there's no danger, and I don't want to be here any more, even if it's her out there.

I want to get out, Mummy.

I want to be free, Daddy.

And I creep out into the light.

Towards the nasty voice.

She can't be the only one out there?

And the others follow me out into the light.

As if I knew something they don't.

As if they thought I was the kind one. The nice fish, the dolphin. The one who's going to be kind to us.

Malin sees a little girl come out of the hole, naked, dirty, silent.

The girl crawls across the floor, and it's Ella.

Ella, and Malin calls to her: 'Come to me!'

Liv Negrell waits.

Stares at the children as they crawl, one by one, out of the hole and into the light of the room, and Malin doesn't take her eyes off her, keeps her pistol trained on the shadowy figure.

Four, five, six naked children.

Three boys, three girls.

Somewhere Zeke has managed to find some thin, colourful sarongs, and the children sit down in a circle, close to one another, and Zeke crouches down beside them, speaks gently in a language that must be totally alien to them, reassures them that everything's going to be all right now, as he wraps them in the soft fabric.

Ella.

She's right next to me now, and Malin bends down and hugs her with her free arm, and whispers: 'There now, there now. Everything's all right now,' and she imagines she can hear Patrick and Cecilia Andergren's voices.

Hear them soothing their little girl: *She's rescued you, Ella, nothing else bad can happen to you now*, and Malin moves towards Zeke and the other children, and whispers in Ella's ear: 'Sit down with the others, this man's name is Zeke and he's the kindest man in the world, he's going to give you a sarong so you don't get cold.'

Ella reluctantly lets go of Malin and goes over to sit next to Zeke, huddling up under a length of fabric.

Malin waves her pistol at Liv Negrell, indicating that she should walk towards the door of the warehouse.

She obeys, and soon they're standing outside the building.

'You kept your promise, now I'm going to keep mine. Run down to the river and disappear. I'll say you got away.'

And the mask face in front of Malin smiles, and at first Liv Negrell stands still, then she turns and starts to run towards the darkness.

Ten metres.

Fifteen.

Then she stops.

Turns her head and screams at Malin: 'I'm going to kill you. Do you hear? If I ever see you again. DON'T FUCK WITH ME!'

Then she runs on.

Runs into the darkness.

Malin raises her pistol, wants to fire, was thinking of firing, that was the plan, to kill the woman in front of her, to make her death part of herself, eternal, complete, and Malin squeezes the trigger, pulls, then at the last minute tilts the gun up so that the bullet misses.

The shot echoes in the darkness.

There's no point in killing you, Malin thinks.

The shadow ahead of her stops again.

And Malin doesn't hesitate, she rushes after the indistinct figure, runs faster than she's ever done, and Liv Negrell takes flight now, runs, but far too slowly.

Malin catches up with her.

Throws herself at her.

She feels Liv Negrell's body against hers as she knocks her to the ground, and they roll around until Malin sticks her pistol into the woman's chest and whispers: 'Give up. I've got you now.'

And Liv Negrell stops, and out of her mouth come the words: 'You'll never get me.'

Above them the cloudless sky forms an endless vault, where every star is a forgotten child's longing for love.

64

That night everything that needed to happen happened.

The Vietnamese police arrived on the scene.

People from the Swedish Consulate.

Malin stood in the glare of the blue lights outside the warehouse with Ella in her arms, watching the Vietnamese police work, thinking: Don't fuck this up with corruption in your ranks.

Don't you dare.

But the looks on their faces are serious, no one could be indifferent when confronted with this.

Malin and Zeke's explanations are riddled with holes: We had to come straight from Sweden, follow our leads without involving anyone else. There wasn't time, if we were going to save the girl, the other children.

'And the result speaks for itself, right?'

Ella has been taken to hospital by a young female diplomat.

She clung to Malin, and Malin didn't want to let go of her, but in the end they parted, and she watched as Ella curled up in the diplomat's arms in the back seat of a black car, holding on tightly.

'We'll take you home to Grandma. We'll come and get you in a few days,' Malin mimed as the car pulled away.

The other children were taken to a different hospital by the Vietnamese police.

Liv Negrell and the men were arrested and taken away. Liv Negrell said nothing more.

She waited beside her accomplices in the warehouse with her eyes closed until they were all driven away.

Evidence was secured.

Interpol was contacted.

International arrest warrants issued.

Networks within networks within networks.

How many children could we save? Malin wondered as she stood in the blue light outside the warehouse. How many have been lost? How many more will be lost?

What's the price of blindness?

She thought: A modest amount in an envelope and pretty much any authority figure in this country could be made to accept fake pictures of a happy child with a family in Denmark.

But the child would never have reached Denmark.

It would find itself in an underground pit in Melbourne. In Hong Kong. Tokyo.

London.

Paris.

Berlin.

Linköping.

Cities, she thought. Adults without any boundaries are the darkness in the black sky.

The children are the dots of light. It's our job to save them.

They got back to the Hotel Majestic late that night.

Zeke disappeared into Karin's room, couldn't be bothered to keep up the pretence any longer, and Malin was left alone in the damp hotel corridor.

The city was rumbling outside.

Clattering, spluttering.

Refusing to sleep.

Not needing any rest.

Malin took a deep breath, and felt the ingrained dirt weighing her dress down.

She knew that what might be the worst task of all still lay ahead of her.

They all got up early the next morning.

Climbed into a rented car and drove towards the outskirts of the city.

They drove to the children's home where Karin had collected Tess.

It had been turned into a Western-style supermarket.

They drove out of the city.

North, then east.

Zeke at the wheel, Malin beside him, Karin and Tess in the back seat. In the low-lying landscape the palm trees stuck up like grenades frozen mid-explosion above paddy fields where women in dark ochre-coloured trousers and tunics stood with their heads bent away from the rising sun.

The fields were gradually replaced by jungle, the number of motorbikes decreased, while the bicycles increased, and they encountered lorries laden with coconuts, timber, and barrels of rubber, signs of this unfamiliar country's march towards development.

Single children by the side of the road.

Groups of children.

Playing as if the traffic couldn't touch them, as if there were some invisible barrier between them and the massive vehicles that threatened to crush them.

They drove on in silence.

Even Tess seemed to measure her words.

They stopped at a garage to get more petrol.

Bought curry from an old woman in a small village that consisted of simple single-storey concrete shacks with rusting tin roofs.

Around noon the road grew dusty, and the closer they came to the coast the flatter the landscape became, and the grass grew over a metre tall, and behind the thick clumps they could see cone-shaped hats, burdens being carried, and muscles flexed out in the fields.

Malin tried to imagine what Karin was thinking.

Her feelings about what might be about to happen.

But she drew a complete blank.

Just a sense that love must have its way, that right can be wrong and vice versa, and that all we human beings really have in common is the impossibility of avoiding that fact.

A wave.

Impossible to withstand.

The only option is to go with the flow and try to keep your head above water for as long as possible.

They passed the outskirts of Da Nang and the salty, agitated smell of the sea found its way into the car, and Tess slept on her mother's arm. The little girl hadn't shown any sign of anxiety when she was awake.

They followed the coast south towards Hội An. Saw buses full of Chinese tourists stop to unload their passengers at the new high-rise casinos that lined the shore, and beyond the buildings the sea was angry, strange undercurrents singing seductive songs.

It was early evening when they drove into Hội An, red lanterns were glowing in the darkness above the river, making the shabby plaster of the merchants' houses shine like the varnished patina of old paintings.

Mons Kallentoft

Malin unfolded a piece of paper and read the name and address.

A woman's name.

They discussed what to do.

Should they look for a hotel, or try to find the address?

'Let's do it now,' Karin said. And Tess had woken up: 'Do what, Mummy?'

Karin didn't answer her daughter, and in the rear-view mirror Malin saw her stroke Tess's back and heard the sound of rough skin against soft cotton.

They asked a man selling hats which way to go.

He pointed out of the town, and it was dark by the time they reached what they thought was the right place. The cicadas were chirruping the last of their song as Malin got out and crossed the gravel in front of the little gathering of tin shacks, glancing towards the palms that lined the river, silhouetted against the first hint of starlight in the sky.

Zeke followed her.

Some wiry men in shorts and vests were sitting in front of one of the houses, smoking and passing a bottle of Mekong whisky between them.

Malin asked for the address, asked about the woman, awkwardly sounding out the name, and the oldest of the men shook his head and said: 'I've never heard of that address, and I've never heard of that woman, I don't know who she is. Are you sure you're in the right place? Are you sure you're meant to be in Hội An?'

Malin held out a twenty-dollar note to the man.

He took it.

Looked her in the eye, and Malin tried to discern something in his black pupils, but could see nothing.

He gave the note back.

'I know why you're here. But I can't help you.'

One of the others passed him the bottle.

He took a swig, then looked away.

'Ask the spirits down by the river,' he whispered to them.

They got back in the car.

Drove away.

'Wrong place,' Malin said, and they found an unassuming little hotel by the river. In the morning she watched the sun rise above its rippling water, and knew that this river had appeared in her dreams, as a portent, a desire for possibilities, a flowing dream within a dream, a longing to be able to put everything right.

They drove to the place where the children's home that Tess was supposed to have come from originally was meant to be.

But there was no children's home. Just a paddy field, with unfamiliar birds of prey circling in a flame-blue sky.

They drove to the town hall in Hội An.

Tripped on the steps of the run-down colonial building.

Tried to find the men who had signed the forms.

But those men didn't exist.

They drove to Da Nang. Tried to find the names behind the documents there.

But there was no one there either.

A man in Da Nang town hall helped them to call Saigon, but they were told that no one could help them, that all the files from the month in question had been destroyed in a flood after last year's monsoon, and that all paper records and computer disks had been ruined.

They returned to Hội An.

For three days they searched for the woman who might be Tess's biological mother.

A sea of faces.

Stern faces.

Smiling faces.

Wary but well-meaning faces.

Not masks, but faces.

Looks in their eyes that seemed to wonder: Who are you? What do you want here? What can you do for me?

Malin went for a walk on her own beside the river.

She felt her feet sink into the muddy bank, crouched as she ducked under swaying palm leaves, and the sun's rays were welders' torches on her body. Sometimes she thought she could hear a woman weeping, but the woman remained invisible, and Malin lingered by the river until evening, maybe then she would be able to hear the woman's tears falling on the water?

But all she found in the darkness by the river were mosquitoes and silence and loneliness, and a strange murmuring that she no longer wanted to hear: *A child for a pig, a child for a pig.*

The spirits are murmuring, Malin thought. Lost spirits that have nowhere else to go.

On the fourth day they gave up.

Malin and Zeke returned to the hotel late that afternoon.

'We've done all we can now,' Karin said when they found her sitting with Tess on a sun lounger by the hotel pool.

Bottles glistening in the bar alongside.

But Malin felt no urge.

'We've done all we can,' she agreed, and Zeke nodded his consent.

Tess wanted to play in the pool, so Malin told Zeke and Karin they could go for a walk through the city together if they wanted some time alone.

'I'll watch Tess.'

She saw them walk off through the hotel garden, then watched and listened as a delighted Tess turned herself into a dolphin in the fading light, and Malin leaned back on the sun lounger and stared up at the sky, and before her eyes the stars rearranged themselves, their individual lights forming a single pattern, fluid but eternal, a perfect image that she hoped signified love, and a few kilometres away from where she was sitting a woman stepped out of her tin shack, wandered down to the river, let out her long hair and then let her tears fall slowly into the black water.

She knew that they had been looking for her.

Why they had come.

Who they had brought with them.

But she let it pass.

For the child's sake.

For the child who had reached her hand out into the world and found something better in the damp veil of the future, a life that could be hers.

Epilogue

Malin in a bed.

It could be any bed.

Anywhere, any time. The room where she is sleeping is moist and warm, the air dry and cool.

And in Malin's dream Tove picks up a dandelion clock and blows the seeds out into the light of the dream.

They're free now, Mum, she whispers.

They're free now.

Not like you, Mum, but like me.

They're free, just like me.

Don't miss the other titles in the *Malin Fors* series

MIDWINTER SACRIFICE, SUMMERTIME DEATH, AUTUMN KILLING, SAVAGE SPRING and THE FIFTH SEASON

Out now in paperback

Also available as eBooks and as Digital Audio Downloads

THRILLINGLY GOOD BOOKS
FROM CRIMINALLY
GOOD WRITERS

CRIME FILES BRINGS YOU THE LATEST RELEASES FROM TOP CRIME AND THRILLER AUTHORS.

SIGN UP ONLINE FOR OUR MONTHLY NEWSLETTER AND BE THE FIRST TO KNOW ABOUT OUR COMPETITIONS, NEW BOOKS AND MORE.